W9-AKD-997

J

THE
HEADMASTER'S
WIFE

THE GREGOR DEMARKIAN BOOKS BY JANE HADDAM

The Headmaster's Wife

JANE HADDAM

ST. MARTIN'S MINOTAUR
NEW YORK

www.minotaurbooks.com

Library of Congress Cataloging-in-Publication Data

Haddam, Jane, 1951–
    The headmaster's wife / by Jane Haddam.—1st St. Martin's Minotaur ed.
      p. cm.
    ISBN 0-312-31314-4
    EAN 978-0312-31314-2
    1. Demarkian, Gregor (Fictitious character)—Fiction. 2. Private investigators—New England—Fiction. 3. Preparatory school students—Fiction. 4. Children of celebrities—Fiction. 5. Preparatory schools—Ficion. 6. Teenage boys—Fiction. 7. New England—Fiction. I. Title.

PS3566.A613H33 2005
813'.54—dc22

                                            2004057824

First Edition: April 2005

10 9 8 7 6 5 4 3 2 1

For Matt
—with my fingers crossed

People are never so sincere as when they assume their own moral superiority.

—THOMAS SOWELL

Every individual human being ... carries within him ... an ideal man ... and it is his life's task to be ... in harmony with the unchanging unity of this ideal.

—FRIEDRICH SCHILLER

Totus mundus facit histrionem.

—ANONYMOUS, SAID TO HAVE BEEN WRITTEN ON THE WALL OF THE GLOBE THEATRE IN THE TIME OF SHAKESPEARE

THE
HEADMASTER'S
WIFE

PROLOGUE

1

later, **Mark DeAvecca would** say that he could see the body from the moment he first looked out the narrow arched Gothic window at the north end of the Ridenour Library's narrow catwalk—he could see it lying there, on the snow, under the stand of evergreens near the pond. It wasn't true. The body wasn't a body. It was alive. If Mark had been able to stand next to it, he could have heard it breathing, in and out, in and out, in a ragged contrapuntal staccato that sounded a little like broken bells. He could have felt the fear, too—or maybe not, since his own fear was as all-encompassing as anything he had ever felt in his life. His head was full of fuzz. The muscles in his hands were twitching spasmodically. He was so tired, it was as if all the blood had been drained from his body. He kept closing his eyes and trying to think of the word. What came into his head were scenes from *Buffy the Vampire Slayer*. Bats with human heads and fangs seemed to be hovering around his head. They darted away to hide in the stone arches in the ceiling whenever he turned to look for them. He closed his eyes and counted to ten. He flexed his hands and felt the pain in his joints like needles under his skin. *Exsanguinated,* he thought. *That's the word I want.*

It was nine o'clock on the night of Friday, February 7, 2003, and as cold as Mark could ever remember it being. It was so cold there was ice on the inside of the window he was sitting next to and ice on the stone frame around it. The glass was leaded and heavy. That was supposed to mean something. He couldn't remember what. Usually he came up here when he couldn't face one more person wanting to look into the deepest reaches of his soul. Today he only wanted to read two short pages in *The Complete Guide to Family Health,* a book he had been carrying around with him for five days. It was big, and heavy, and awkward, and there was always the danger that somebody would notice it and ask what it was about.

It wouldn't be so bad if they ever came up with anything except clichés, he thought. *What does it mean that they look into the deepest reaches of my soul and come up with clichés?*

The book was lying on the floor. He was sitting on the floor. The floor was made of stone and was as icy as the stone frame around the window. He flipped the book open to the double-page spread on Huntington's chorea and rubbed the side of his face until the skin under the stubble started to burn.

Depression, he thought. *Yes. Mood swings. Twitching. Inability to concentrate. Memory loss. Clumsiness. Forgetfulness. Nervousness. Mental deterioration. Yes and yes and yes and yes and yes.* The problem was, there was a single *no,* and it was the answer to the most important question.

"Huntington's chorea is caused by a single dominant gene."

Dominant, Mark thought. *Dominant means it always exhibits. If you have it, it exhibits. And you had to have had a parent who'd had it, and parent would have exhibited.*

Mark put his head down between his knees and tried to breathe. He had no idea why he wanted to believe he had Huntington's chorea instead of a simple mental illness, schizophrenia, something. He was very sure he was going crazy. He had been away at school now for five months, and in that time he seemed to have managed a 180-degree personality turn. He no longer recognized himself in the mirror. He no longer recognized himself as a human being. If he'd been allowed to have a cell phone, he'd have called his mother five times a day just to hear her voice. After about a week of that, she'd probably have driven up here to Massachusetts to get him.

Maybe I should go home, he thought. *Maybe they're right and I just don't belong here.*

Out in the quad somewhere, the carillon was ringing. It did something or other every quarter hour and tolled the hours when they came. It went on all night, so that if you lived in Hayes House or Martinson, in one of the rooms facing the chapel, it could wake you up from a sound sleep. Mark's hands were twitching. Sometimes his shoulders twitched, too, and sometimes the joints in his hands just felt so thick and out of sync that he found it hard to move them.

It would be giving up to go home, and that much about him had not changed. He did not give up, not ever. The one time he had wanted to—in that first year after his father had died, when life had seemed like a tunnel without end—he had known, with the kind of absolute clarity most adults couldn't manage to save their lives, that to do it would be to die himself. He'd been less than ten years old.

There has to be something wrong with me, he thought. *It can't just all be in my head.*

But that wasn't true, and he knew it; and so he unwound his body and began to get up. There was nothing to do but go to work and salvage what he could, even if it wasn't much. He didn't understand a word of what he read anymore. He'd finish a page and couldn't remember if he'd been reading John Donne or his biology textbook. He drilled himself for hour after hour in German, or got Fraulein Lieden to do it with him, and half an hour after he was finished it was is if none of it had ever happened. It was cold, but he was sweating like a pig. The sweat was pouring down his back as if he'd just run the Boston Marathon. He was tired, but he knew that if he lay down he would not be able to go to sleep for hours. He had had at least six cups of coffee since lunch; but if coffee was supposed to wake you up, it didn't work on him. He was the walking dead.

He looked out the window again and for the first time thought it was odd. There was a . . . person . . . lying there in the snow, alone, under the trees. It was a person dressed in black, but there was nothing unusual about that. Half the school liked to dress in black and to pretend to be alienated from all things material and capitalistic. Maybe whoever it was had passed out. It was Friday, and the school was supposed to be drug and alcohol free, but Mark knew what that was worth. There was enough marijuana in Hayes House alone to supply a hospital full of terminal cancer patients. If you got caught at it they sent you to intervention, and after a few months they asked you to write up the story of how you beat addiction for the *Windsor Chronicle.* Mark knew people who had beaten addiction three or four times, although they'd only been allowed to write about it once, at the beginning. It was like the pictures the *Chronicle* ran about the memorial service for 9/11. The real pictures had been ruined some-how, and so the school had had them all go back into the quad and pretend to be doing it again, so there would be photographs for the story about how sen-sitively the school was handling terrorism issues.

Everything about this place is fake, Mark thought—and he was almost him-self again for that split second. Then the feeling faded, and the insight along with it, and he pressed his face to the glass and tried to get a better look at the person in black lying under the tree, not moving.

If he lies there long enough, he could freeze to death, Mark thought, but there was something wrong with that, something he couldn't quite put his finger on. There was something wrong with the body lying under the trees. Mark was sure that it wasn't a student, although he wasn't sure why he was sure. The person was big, but a lot of the seniors were bigger. He tried to imagine a Windsor Academyteacher getting smashed on vodka and grass and passing out on the ice twenty feet from Maverick Pond, but it didn't compute. The faculty drank mineral water they bought from a small local company run as a cooperative and talked about how important it was not to allow the liquor companies to invade the rain forest. They didn't wear black either. They preferred earth tones and Polo shirts and books most people found too boring to read.

Something is wrong, he thought, but he was drifting in and out of consciousness again, in and out of coherency. If he didn't get moving, he'd find himself trapped up here after lights out. He'd already done that once this term and been handed sixteen hours of work jobs because of it. They had been absolutely convinced that he'd done it on purpose because they'd rung the bell three times and sent a librarian through the stacks calling out for anybody who might not be paying attention. He hadn't done it on purpose though. He'd just zoned out. He'd just stopped existing in this body and been somewhere else, except not, because he couldn't remember anything else. If he'd believed in ghosts, he would have thought he was one.

He took another look out at the black figure under the trees then bent over and picked up his book.

If he went the long way around back to Hayes House, he could stop to see if whoever it was needed any help.

2

Marta Coelho had been grading papers for four hours, and she still wasn't close to done. Her eyes hurt. Her arms hurt, too. Mostly she found herself thinking obsessively about the fact that she had never spent a Friday night not working, at least not during term time, in this entire academic year. It was the kind of thing that, phrased in the right way, she would have thought of as a good thing about Windsor Academy before she had come to it, but like most of those things—and there had been a lot of them—it now felt egregiously wrong. She found it hard to believe that she had defended her dissertation only eighteen months ago, and that her dissertation committee—at *Yale*—had been absolutely certain that she'd find a faculty place within the year. If you couldn't find a university job with a degree from Yale, what did you need to do to find one? It was hard to remember, now, that this particular job had seemed like a godsend when it was offered to her because she was up to her eyeballs in debt from college and grad school and close to being evicted from her apartment. It was hard to remember the things she had told herself when she'd written the acceptance letter and walked down Chapel Street to mail it. Bright, committed prep school students had to be better to teach than bored, not-so-bright college students stuck at a fourth-rate state college and wanting only to get through their core courses as quickly and painlessly as possible. A school committed to equality, diversity, and truly innovative ideas in education had to be better than the routinely brutal mediocrity of the high school she had escaped for Wellesley and then the Ivy League. Had to be, had to be, she thought now. There was nothing that anything had to be. Life sucked, as the kids liked to say, and you couldn't even make yourself feel better about it by thinking about sex.

The office was a high-ceilinged room on the first floor of the Ridenour Library, the one building on campus that looked like it belonged on a campus. The lights above her head hung down on long, dark poles and ended in wide globes that gave out too much light. She could see her reflection in the leaded-glass windows in front of her desk, and her head looked as if it were encased in a helmet of light. *I should dye it a different color one of these days,* she thought absently. Then she tapped the stack of papers in front of her, the ungraded ones, ten to twelve pages each, researched and footnoted. It was impossible to explain to anybody who hadn't had to put up with it just how bone-numbingly boring it all really was, day after day with these kids whose lives had been so perfect they might as well have been produced by Disney. She'd heard all the stories about alcoholic mothers and absent fathers, but she didn't believe any of it. It was the kind of thing rich people liked to say about themselves in order to appear to be Suffering, and therefore all that much more Virtuous. She knew something about alcoholism and absence. Alcoholism was her father getting fired from his fourth job in two years. Absence was the ritual placement in foster care, three months here, five months there, over and over again—never the same family; never the same school bus; but always the same school—so that everybody knew, all the other students, all the teachers, and she would walk the halls very careful never to let her body touch another person or another thing. If she hadn't been a *truly extraordinary person*—far and away better than those boarding school girls she'd met when she first went to Wellesley—if she hadn't been unlike everybody and everything around her, she would never have ended up where she had. She'd have been waiting tables back in Providence the way her sister still did. Marta couldn't remember how long she had gone on thinking of herself as a *truly extraordinary person*. She did remember when she had stopped. It was on that day she had walked down Chapel Street to mail the letter telling Windsor Academy that she would be happy to teach American History and serve as a dorm parent in Barrett House for the next full school year.

She swiveled her chair around so that she could look through the open door onto the hallway. She always kept the door of her office open. When she closed it, she felt as if she were suffocating. She heard the sound of heavy footsteps in the hall and then saw, suddenly, the hulking figure of one of the students she liked least and respected not at all—Mark DeAvecca, looking as usual as if he had fallen off a garbage truck and was still wearing the odd banana skin. He said, "Hi," without looking at her. He was staring at the floor, something else that was usual. He either stared at the floor or over your left shoulder. He never looked directly at you, and his body was never completely still. She mumbled something in reply that could have been anything except encouragement. He kept moving until he was out of sight. There he was, that bright, eager prep school student she had heard all about, a monumental mess who never did the reading, never handed his homework in on time, and never studied for tests. He might as well have been playing football at some farm belt regional high school where all the kids wanted was to take over the family farm, except that he was no good at sports either. He just had a famous mother and a rich father, and that was all he needed to get into a school that was supposed to be more selective than most American colleges. Marta knew, too well, what "selectivity" meant when it came to schools. It meant that they were places that were very careful about who they let in of those people who could not be said to already belong.

For a second she felt energy surge through her as if somebody had turned on her switch. She was suddenly purposeful and angry. She bolted out of her chair and across the office to the door. She stepped into the hall and looked both ways for Mark. She had no idea what she intended to say to him or why she wanted to say anything. She only knew that she wanted to grab hold of him and do *something*. When she saw that the hallway was already empty, she felt angrier still—and then the door at the other end opened, and Alice Makepeace came in from outside, wearing that black, hooded cape that fell to the floor and always reminded Marta of *The French Lieutenant's Woman*.

"Marta?" Alice said.

Marta did her best not to cringe. Alice was the headmaster's wife, and no matter how progressive and egalitarian Windsor Academy was supposed to be, junior faculty did not piss off the headmaster's wife without expecting some repercussions from it. Marta bit her lip and looked in the other direction, the direction she had seen Mark go. Alice was . . . one of those people. She had an accent like William F. Buckley's. She was too tall, and she actually looked good in leather jeans.

Marta had never looked good in much of anything. She was not fat, but her thinness did not make her attractive or fashionable. If she had tried to wear black leather jeans, she would have looked like a sausage in a natural casing.

"Mark DeAvecca just went by," she said. "I was trying to catch him."

"Ah, Mark," Alice said, shaking out her hair. She had long, wavy, thick hair. Marta didn't believe for a moment that the bright red of it was Alice's natural color, although she knew it had been once. Still, nobody cared about that, natural or unnatural. Nobody cared about anything except the special effects.

"He's going to fail history," Marta said. "Or he's going to come damned close. I've talked to him and talked to him. Nothing seems to help."

"He doesn't seem to be adjusting well, no," Alice said. She pushed the cape back over her shoulders. Black cape, black leather jeans, black cashmere turtleneck sweater, black boots—Marta couldn't look at her; she was too ridiculous. Except that she wasn't. She was perfect. It was hard to bear.

"I don't think it has anything to do with adjusting," Marta said. "I think he's irresponsible, that's all. He doesn't do anything. He has reading assigned in every class. He's supposed to take notes. He never does it. I know. I've asked to see the notes. I don't think he's ever bothered to study for history, even before he came here."

"He had excellent grades in history," Alice said. "He had excellent grades in everything."

"There are ways to get excellent grades without doing any work," Marta said. "You can have your mother do it, for instance. I don't suppose his stepfather would be any help, but his mother—well, there's always that. You could go to a school where it matters more who your parents are than what work you're doing. There's that, too. Everybody's so hyped on how rigorous this place is. If it's rigorous, he doesn't belong here."

"Doesn't he?"

Marta flushed. She had been ranting—again. She was getting a reputation for ranting. She knew what Alice Makepeace said about her behind her back.

She's terribly earnest, that was the line she used to everybody, and now everybody used it, too. Marta *was* terribly earnest, and very dedicated, and of course a complete bore and an utter frump. It was, Marta thought, all true, and she didn't care.

She turned away, back toward the inside of her office, where the papers still sat stacked and waiting for her. It was Friday night, and she wanted to be in Boston with friends, out to dinner, at a silly movie about superheroes, in a dark club listening to a band no one had ever heard of. She didn't want to correct Mark DeAvecca's research paper, which would be a mess, badly argued, inadequately sourced, physically disintegrating. She didn't want to be at Windsor Academy at all, except that she had no place else to be where they would pay her enough money so that she didn't have worry about it.

"Well," she said.

"You're not adjusting too well either," Alice said. "It's not uncommon, really, for people who are used to more structured and traditional schools. It's hard to get past the dominant paradigm and learn to experience something new."

"I'm fine," Marta said. She was still looking into her office. She didn't want Alice to see the expression on her face, which was not the expression of a teacher dedicated to progressive ideas and the encouragement of diversity in every aspect of campus life. She could, she thought, recite the entire text of the viewbook they had sent her when she'd first applied for this job. It had been written by a good PR firm in New York that specialized in "development" materials for academia.

"I'm fine," Marta said again, turning back to look at Alice's bright red hair. "You're all wet. You've got snow on you."

"I should have. It's snowing again. We're supposed to get eight inches by tomorrow morning. Maybe you should knock off and get a little rest before you finish whatever you're trying to finish."

"Research papers. I've got a lot of them."

"Yes, I know you do." Alice shrugged. "I've got to knock off though, or I'll miss the library. One of these days I'm going to get organized well enough to remember to pick up my books in the afternoon. Are you sure you'll be all right by yourself?"

"Of course I will."

"Well, you only have to go back to Barrett House. There's that. Have a good time with your papers."

"I will," Marta said.

Alice shrugged a little and walked away, in the same direction Mark had gone, and Marta stood in the hall and watched her leave. The doors at both ends of this corridor were fire doors. They had air closures. They made a hissing sound when they fell back into place, if you listened for it.

Marta went back to her desk and sat down again. The first paper on the stack belonged to Sue Wyman. It would be serviceable and unimaginative, but it wouldn't require much correcting. She took the paper clip off and spread the sheets across her desk. She picked up her red pen and adjusted the glasses on her nose. She thought that she really should do something about getting contact lenses.

It was minutes later, when she had gotten to the point where Sue was arguing doggedly in favor of an "expanded understanding of the role of women in the American Revolution," when it suddenly occurred to her: it made no sense at all for Alice Makepeace to come in the door she'd come in and go out the door she'd gone out if what she was doing was coming in from the outside to go to the library. You could get in from the outside from that end of the hall. Just beyond the fire door, there was a breezeway that connected the office wing of the library to the main part, but the main part *was* over there in that direction. If you went out the door on the other end, the only way to get into the library was to go around the pathways to the front. It was like going from Boston to New York by way of Philadelphia. It made no sense.

Marta took off her glasses and put them down on Sue Wyman's paper. She rubbed the bridge of her nose and then her forehead, as if rubbing would wake up some faculty of discernment she'd never yet possessed. Did Alice Makepeace ever make sense? Was she supposed to? The answer was "probably not," to both, and it was all beyond anything Marta was capable of understanding anyway. If there were different kinds of intelligence, then she lacked the kind that fit well in a place like this.

3

Philip Candor did not work on Friday nights, or on Saturday nights either, not even to the extent of correcting papers or hosting dorm students in his apartment. He didn't go to Boston or go to clubs. He didn't drink, and he didn't feel comfortable sitting in cramped little rooms where the music was loud enough to drown out thought when he wouldn't even be allowed to smoke. That had been a big issue, a few years ago—the fact that he smoked and wouldn't give it up. They couldn't very well fire him for smoking when they'd known he was a smoker when they hired him, but they had hired him over a decade ago. Times change, ideas change, people do not change. Sometimes Philip understood his father almost well enough to accept that the man had been, legitimately, who and what he was. It wasn't always paranoia when you felt civilization closing in on you like one of those trick rooms in an old *Outer Limits* episode where what you thought was your hotel room was really an alien device for crushing you to death. There was the fact that so many people needed nothing more or less than control, control of themselves, control of their property, control of you. There were times when he missed what he had grown up with. He surely missed the openness and emptiness. There was nowhere in the entire state of Massachusetts where you could go to be completely and irrevocably away from people. Here, even in the national parks, you were never more than half an hour away from truth, justice, and the American Way.

He adjusted his thin, gold wire-rim glasses on the bridge of his nose and moved slightly to get a better look at Maverick Pond. This was not a good window from which to see the water. He was on the side of it with the stand of evergreen trees blocking off the view, and he was in Martinson House besides, which meant that he was at the wrong angle to see it without making an effort. He didn't usually bother to watch what went on out there because it was usually the same old same old. Sex, drugs, and rock 'n' roll were everywhere, it seemed, even in fancy New England prep schools where the tuition ran to thirty thousand dollars a year. He wondered if their parents had any idea at all what their kids got up to when they were left on their own on a campus like this. He wondered if their parents cared—but that was an issue for another night with a different theme song. He shifted a little on the edge of his big leather club chair and tried to see more clearly across the pond to the library. All the security lights that were supposed to be on were on. The paths that ran along the library and through the quad were well lit. Everything was empty. He could swear he'd seen Alice Makepeace's bright red hair, but there was no sign of it anymore.

Shit, he thought, half falling onto the hardwood floor that had been so big a selling point for the dean of faculty when he had first been recruited out of Williams College to come and teach. He straightened up and stretched. This window was not supposed to have a view of the pond. He got to his feet and tried pressing his body against the glass. There was nothing out there, no matter what he had thought at first. The campus was dark and quiet. The carillon had rung nine just a few minutes ago. In another hour it would be weekday curfew, and everybody would be expected to be back in their dorms and ready to pretend that Windsor was a school just as strict, with students just as unsophisticated, as the one in *The Trouble with Angels*.

He stood back away from the window and ran his hand through his hair. Seen but not heard, he was every human being's picture of the Complete New England Preppie. He had the fine features, the tall and slight body, the slightly too-long hair, the wire rims, the wool crewneck sweaters. He was as perfect as a model in a J. Crew catalogue, until he opened his mouth. He had been able to learn to dress at Williams, but he had not learned to talk. He thought he would die still issuing forth with that nasal western twang.

I sound like a hillbilly, he thought yet again, and for a split second he could see Alice Makepeace's face the first time they had ever talked, that look of shock and the hasty attempt to suppress it. "You're from the South," she had said, after too long a pause.

"I'm from the West," he'd corrected her, and then, "Wyoming," knowing that he had nothing to fear from the lie. She wouldn't know the difference between his accent and a Wyoming one any more than she would have known the difference between Kmart and Target. He didn't think she had ever been to either, and he didn't think she had ever spent time in the American West except on ski resorts and in luxury hotels, where somebody might be holding a conference. That was before he knew about her politics, of course, and for a while the revelation of her seeming passion for the Revolution had worried him a little. He'd known too many people who'd had a passion for the Revolution and meant it—although it had been a different revolution than hers. He soon realized he had nothing to fear, at least directly. She was no more interested in real poor people than she was interested in real revolutionaries. She lived in a bubble of self-regard that required nothing to feed it but the reflection of herself that she saw in the eyes of male students and male junior faculty, who took her to be the goddess Athena come to life—or something. Philip thought he ought to do something to prick that bubble one of these days when he was feeling as if he had nothing to lose.

There was movement on the path. Philip held his breath, and then let it out only seconds later. It was nobody, really, only Mark DeAvecca, weaving a little as usual, looking disoriented. If Philip had had to guess about Mark, he would have said a combination of speed and downers, something to rev him up in the morning and keep him up during the day, followed by something to bring him down again when the rev got too painful or too out of control or had just gone on too long. He had brought it up at a faculty meeting a month ago, and the usual things had been done. One of Mark's dorm parents had searched his room while he was out at class. The school had a handy little rule requiring the dorms to be locked and off-limits to boarders during the school day. Nothing had turned up, even though it had been a very thorough search, with the head of Security present. They had looked between the slats, under the bed, and under the carpet, and tapped along the walls of the closet to find a hollow space. Philip wouldn't have believed it if it hadn't happened, but it turned out that Mark did have his act together in at least one respect. He hid his stuff with the ingenuity of a master criminal. He didn't hide it in his backpack either because that was always lying on the floor of the breezeway with a hundred other backpacks, often overnight; and one night, after everybody else was in bed, Philip himself had gone through it. Nothing.

Mark stopped again, turned again, and shook his head. His entire body seemed to be trembling, but that could be the cold. Philip grabbed his coat off the back of his chair and went out into the hall and then onto the back porch. It was cold as hell. Philip could feel the pain of it in his hands, even though he had them stuffed into his pockets. Mark wasn't moving.

"Mark?" Philip said.

Mark turned around, looking confused. "Mr. Candor?" he said. Then he blinked, shook his head slightly, and shrugged. "Philip," he said. "Sorry."

A lot of the kids who came from more traditional schools had trouble with this business of calling their teachers by their first names. Philip had trouble with it himself. Still, it had been over five months. Mark should be used to it by now.

"Are you all right?" Philip asked. "You look—" *You look drugged to the gills,* Philip thought, but he didn't say it. He understood the concern about lawsuits, too.

"I'm all right," Mark said. Then he turned back to look in the direction of the pond again. "I'm fine, really. I just thought I saw—"

"Saw what?"

"You're going to think this is stupid."

I think you're stupid, Philip thought, but he didn't say that either. Besides, it wasn't true. Mark DeAvecca wasn't stupid. He was just a mess.

"What do you think you saw?" Philip asked again.

Mark shrugged. "I thought I saw a body."

"A what?"

"I told you you were going to think it was stupid."

"A *dead* body?"

Mark shrugged. "I don't know. I guess. I guess not. I mean, I hadn't thought about dead. It was just lying there, and I could see it from the catwalk window. You know that window up over the main reading room?"

"Of course I know it."

"I was sitting up there by myself, just sort of reading and things, and I was looking out the window and there it was."

"The body?"

"Under the trees. I didn't really think of it in terms of dead. I mean, it wasn't moving, but I thought it was somebody who'd gotten drunk. You know. I watched it for a long time."

"How long?"

"I don't know. I lost my watch. I was sitting up there for a long time though. And I kept watching it. And it never moved. So I thought—"

"Male or female?"

"What?"

"This body. Male or female?"

"I couldn't really see, but I think it must have been male. It was—big. I don't know. And it was odd big. I remember thinking that it wasn't a student. Couldn't be. Because it was big. Except some students are big. I don't know. It was dark, you know, in the catwalk, and it was dark outside. There isn't a light on that side of the pond."

Philip hesitated. This was not a con. Mark DeAvecca was perfectly serious. It wasn't even impossible to imagine. Students did get drunk on Friday nights. They usually hid in their dorm rooms to do it, but one of them could have wandered onto campus and passed out. The campus was open to the town. Somebody could have wandered in from one of the little restaurants on Main Street.

"Is the body still there?" Philip asked.

Mark shook his head. "I went to check, you know, because I thought it was dangerous. Whoever it was could freeze. It's cold as hell tonight. So I thought I'd go down and see who it was and either get him to move or get some help to move him, but when I got there he was gone."

"Just gone?"

"Yeah."

Mark was looking at his shoes. Philip felt the impatience rising in him like bile. "Was there any sign that he'd been there?" he asked. "Were there footprints in the snow? An impression of a body under the tree? Anything?"

Mark blinked. "It's not snow. It's hard as slate, for God's sake. Everything's iced over."

"All right," Philip said. "You ought to go back to your dorm. Nobody's there now at any rate. You don't have to worry about somebody freezing to death."

"No," Mark said.

"Go directly back to your dorm," Philip said. "Don't wander around. It is cold tonight. You're going to freeze without gloves in this weather."

"I lost my gloves," Mark said.

That figures, Philip thought, but it was one more thing he didn't say. He stood and watched while Mark walked away from him up the path to Hayes House. The kid was completely zonked. He wasn't even functioning. He had probably imagined the whole thing. It was a miracle he wasn't seeing pink elephants and snakes in the shower as it was.

Still, there was always the chance. When Philip was sure Mark was on his way up the Hayes House back porch steps, he turned in the other direction and went down the path toward the library and the pond. The pond was actually quite a distance away. The school said it didn't build closer because of worries about wetlands regulation and the environment, but the real reason was worries about what water damage could do to the foundations of buildings. He went down along the office wing of the library—there was Marta Coelho's office light, still on—and then past the big Gothic hulk and onto the open campus. Mark was right. It wasn't really snow anymore. It was all iced over and hard, like a shell on the land.

Philip skirted the edge of the pond, moving slowly, looking for any sign of a "body" or anything like a body; but he could see, long before he got to the stand of evergreens, that there wasn't a body there. Philip went up close. There were no footprints, but he was leaving none himself. There was no impression of a body under the trees, but there probably wouldn't have been, even if the body had been real.

Philip Candor did not, for a moment, think that the body had been real. He thought Mark DeAvecca had been hallucinating, which was only to be expected. Mark should have been hallucinating for months, considering just how messed up he was most of the time.

Philip looked around. He could see the catwalk window, still glowing from the light coming up from the main reading room. He could see the first corner that led to the office wing. He could not see the dorms. This was the most isolated edge of the pond, the place farthest away from people and buildings and cars. There was something about it he definitely didn't like.

Stupid kid, he thought.

He dug his hands ever deeper into his pockets and started back to Martinson House and his apartment.

4

Peter Makepeace had been counting drops of water falling from the icicle on the porch, but if he was completely honest about it he would have to admit that he had started and stopped counting several times and had no idea how many drops of water had fallen. *I'm going to have to do something about the leak in the porch roof,* he thought, but it wasn't his job to do anything about the leak in the porch roof, just as it wasn't his job to be sitting in his own study on a Friday night thinking about his wife having an affair with a student. The words "having an affair" popped into his head unasked for. It wasn't the way he put it to himself when he thought about it deliberately. She's *fucking* a student, that's what he meant to say. More specifically, she was fucking a particular student, this year's entry in Windsor Academy's annual socioeconomic diversity sweepstakes. It was incredible just how cynical he had become in the few short years since he had taken this job. It was even more incredible to remember that Alice hadn't wanted to come here or to any school. She had wanted to take a job in a factory or run away to Fiji or become an artist in Greenwich Village. It was either the wonderful, or the terrible, thing about Alice that her imagination had never progressed beyond the kind of thing most people gave up as silly when they graduated from college.

Up on the wall next to the big multipaned window that looked out onto the quad were the plaques and pictures and framed credentials that had always defined Peter Makepeace's life—his diploma from Andover, his bachelor's degree from Harvard, his Ph.D. from Princeton. There was a black and white of him in his uniform for the Knickerbocker Greys. There was another black and white of him as a six-year-old in the blazer and tie that had been required for his private day school in Manhattan. These were the memories of a life lived in absolute harmony with itself. At no point, at no time, had Peter Makepeace ever for a moment strayed out of the orbit into which he had been born and out of which he knew he would never be comfortable. Other people might have played with the idea of throwing it all over and becoming revolutionaries or shoe salesmen in Kansas, but Peter knew himself better than that. He knew *them* better than that. He did not have the gift of social mobility. He was uncomfortable trying to make conversation, not only with students on scholarships, but with the ones whose families, however well financed, had not been well financed for long. He had the kind of voice—the kind of accent, let's be honest about that, too—that people from the outside routinely made fun of, convinced he had to be putting it on. He did not look right in clothes that were truly casual. Somehow his jeans always looked pressed, and his T-shirts always looked as if somebody had starched them. It was not his fault. He was who he was. It was just easier to be that than it was to try to pretend to be something else for the sake of—what?

The other picture on the wall that mattered, the one that always caught him first, was the one of Alice in her coming-out dress. It wasn't a formal coming-out portrait, or one of those staged tableaux of flocks of girls meant to bow together at a mass presentation ball. Alice had thrown out the formal one years ago, and she'd been presented at half the mass presentation balls in the Northeast. She would have thrown this one out as well, except that it belonged to him. He had taken it himself at her private party, and it had come out so beautifully— that incredible cascade of bright red hair—that he had had it enlarged and framed to keep long before he was ever "going out" with her and certainly long before she had ever agreed to marry him. Those were in the days when she was declaring, along with half her class at Smith, that she would never marry at all. She had threatened to cut off her hair. She had wandered around her campus and the streets of New York in Birkenstocks and peasant blouses made by women's cooperatives in Guatemala. It didn't matter. Alice was Alice. She never had cut her hair. She never could have because image mattered to her far too much. She had given up the Birkenstocks and peasant blouses, too, and not because she had married him or because he had come here to Windsor Academy to be headmaster and make her the headmaster's wife.

The icicle was still dripping. It was bitterly cold out on the quad. He could see the temperature on the round L.L. Bean thermometer he had mounted on the outside wall. Minus nine degrees Fahrenheit. Cold enough for anybody. The porch must be warm somehow. Maybe there was a crack in the sealant around the window letting out heat. This was one of the great things about being headmaster and not an ordinary teacher anymore. He didn't have to live in a dorm. He didn't have to share his space with students who would be only too happy to find a way to embarrass him. He knew he shouldn't think that way about students. Most of them meant well enough, and most of them were not that happy to be away from their families at this young an age. He hadn't been happy with it either back at Andover. It was odd what you went on doing that you didn't intend to do at all.

16

He was in his study at the front of the house. He went to the door and locked it, although he couldn't imagine who would bother to come in without knocking. Not only were there no students here, there were no children of any kind. Alice didn't want to contribute to the world's problems with overpopulation. Peter thought it was more the fact that she didn't want to cramp her style. Alice had never had much interest in turning herself into an earth mother. He tried the door and it felt secure. He went to his desk and sat down behind it. He should turn the desk around so that he would be facing the window when he worked. He liked to face a window when he worked. It made him feel less constricted and blocked in. The desk was turned this way because he knew, instinctively, that that was what the trustees expected, and his motto was always to give the trustees what they wanted in little things. That way it was a lot easier to get what he wanted in the big ones.

He reached into the pocket of his trousers and came out with a small key ring, sterling silver on a fob made to look like two tennis rackets and a ball. He found the smallest key on the ring and used it to open the long center drawer of his desk. The drawer was empty except for a single manila envelope. He took the envelope out and put it down on the green felt blotter in the middle of his desk. The sweat had come out on his forehead. It was incredible, really and truly incredible, how carefully he had made his life all of a piece.

The manila envelope seemed to pulse. He turned around to make sure nobody was looking through the window at him. That was silly because of course nobody could. There was a tight growth of hedge bushes hugging the walls of the house. Anybody who wanted to get close enough to see what he was doing through the window would get torn apart by evergreen needles.

He opened the envelope and took out the photographs inside. They were bad photographs, really, and black-and-white, but there was nothing he could do about that except spend so much money he would make himself conspicuous; and that would really and truly defeat the point. The sweat was not just on his forehead now. It was on the back of his neck and running down the sides of his arms. It was in the small of his back. His lungs felt as if they were encased in iron bands, razor thin and pressing against the softness of his flesh whenever he took a breath. He remembered the day he had installed the first of the cameras in their bedroom, the day Alice had gone to New York with her best friend from Smith to attend some kind of rally against George W. Bush. There were times when Peter Makepeace blessed George W. Bush.

The first of the photographs was of Alice with a student who had left the school last year, graduated, and gone on to the University of Denver or one of the other places where rich boys who don't want to work very hard liked to get together in fraternities. Alice was sitting astride him as if she were Lady Godiva and he were the horse. She was holding her legs wide open, so that he could clearly see the tuft of her hair in that place. If he'd been able to use color film, it would have looked like a flame. The boy's face was out of sight, hidden by some pillows and a fold of the sheet. It didn't matter to Peter Makepeace, and it probably hadn't mattered to Alice. It said a lot about her that she did not shave herself there and yet she very carefully did shave her underarms and legs.

The next picture looked distorted. The camera was on the ceiling of their bedroom, in a corner, disguised by a hanging plant. He'd had to disguise it with something. From that angle, some . . . positions . . . looked less probable than others. This was a simple thing really. Alice on the bed on her hands and knees and the boy coming at her from behind, not just doing it doggy-style, as they used to say when Peter was at Andover, but ramming it up her behind, half off her and half on, his face contorted, hers pulled into a grimace, her breasts hanging down. Peter could almost see them sway. The pictures all seemed to be alive anyway. They moved like the photographs in the Harry Potter books. Peter's mouth was dry; his brain felt too big for his head.

The third photograph was the one that always made him stop because it proved that this was all deliberate. It wasn't just a few cases of desperate, over-whelming passion. It wasn't that Alice needed sex and he wasn't giving her the sex she needed and so she found herself overcome with desire and just gave into it. In this photograph the boy was tied to the bed, not with twine or rope from the garage, but with black leather straps that had obviously been made for the purpose. Peter had seen them for sale in shops in Boston. The boy had a gag in his mouth and a black leather blindfold over his eyes, and those had also been professionally made. Peter wondered how she had gotten hold of them. She couldn't have just waltzed into a store somewhere and bought them her-self. There was her hair. It made her stand out. Maybe she'd gotten the boy to buy them. Maybe she'd sent away for them on the Internet and just trusted that she would be home when they came and that nobody else would get hold of them. In this photograph she was kneeling between the boy's spread legs and bent over so that her hair half fell in front of her face. Enough of that face was visible so that Peter could see she had the boy's penis in her mouth, so deeply it seemed to be climbing down her throat.

Boys, Peter thought, *they aren't really boys.* That was true. This one, the "boy" from last year, had been eighteen at the time the photographs were taken. He'd been as big as a house and stronger than Peter had ever imagined himself capable of being. The boy this year—yes, of course there was a boy this year, there was a boy every year—was sixteen, and Peter suspected that that was deliberate. Alice would know the law and know what she needed to do to stay inside of it. She served on the boards of organizations dedicated to "fighting child abuse." Of course the child abuse they were fighting was the abuse done to girls. The only time Alice had ever been interested in the abuse done to boys was when it had looked like a policy of the Roman Catholic Church.

Peter shuffled through the photographs and came up with the ones from *this* year, new ones, only a few weeks old. He really couldn't breathe. It was impossible. He knew this boy. It wasn't a boy he would have expected Alice to take up with because Alice—in the end, when she wasn't watching herself, when she wasn't acting a part for the rest of the world—was who she was. She could no more help herself than he could. This boy, though, this boy was all wrong. He was from the wrong background. He had the wrong looks. He had the wrong tastes in sex. The photographs from this year were all predictably vanilla, no odd positions, no leather equipment. The boy's thick, dark hair fell on Alice's breasts as he leaned over her, pumping away in the missionary position.

Peter suddenly wished he had it all on tape, that he could run it back for himself in video the way other men ran porno films to get themselves in the mood.

"There's one thing you have to remember," a good friend of his on the board had said when Peter had first been appointed headmaster, "a headmaster is always a headmaster. No matter what he does. No matter where he is. Once you take on the title, anything you do will be interpreted as being not your own actions but the actions of the headmaster of Windsor Academy. It isn't a comfortable position."

No, Peter thought, *it isn't a comfortable position.* It paralyzed him. He had no idea what he was doing with these photographs. He had no idea what he wanted them for. He couldn't see himself divorcing Alice. Even if she agreed to give him a divorce without a struggle, it would be a disaster. The headmasters of New England prep schools did not get divorced from the women the Board of Trustees expected to act as mothers to the students under their care. What was worse, he didn't want to get divorced from Alice. He didn't want his life disrupted in any way. He only wanted—what?

To find the leather equipment, where she'd put it, what she did with it when she wasn't using it. To see her exposed, not physically, not by the circulation of these pictures, but *exposed,* right down to the bone, so that everybody could see her for what she was. Peter's real problem was that he didn't know what that was. He had a terrible feeling Alice didn't know either. He reached out for the photographs and swept them up. He put the envelope back into the drawer. He shut the drawer and locked it. Once the photographs were out of sight, he could breathe more easily, but he still couldn't think.

Michael Feyre, he thought, and the idea was so absurd he simply stopped thinking of it. Even with the pictures in the drawer, he couldn't imagine Alice panting over the body of that thick, awkward, unimaginative clod.

There was no such thing as a Working-Class Genius, Peter thought. There was only one mediocrity after the other, each given a glow by rich people like Alice who preferred their romances written by Dreiser rather than Barbara Cartland.

5

For the first six months Cherie Wardrop was at Windsor Academy, most of the rest of the faculty had insisted on pronouncing her name as if it were the French endearment: "Che-RIE," people would say, passing her on the walks in the quad or coming up behind her in the line in the cafeteria, proud of their boarding school French, and she would go along with them. Windsor was a miracle, as far as Cherie was concerned. It was hard enough to find a job of any kind these days. To find one just outside Boston was a near impossibility, and to find one in a boarding school that served the children of the very people she had admired so much as a child was—well, impossible, that was all. It was worse than impossible; it was silly. There were days when she woke up, looked at the bedroom around her, and thought she had somehow been transported from the kind of novels she used to write in secret in the eleventh grade. She'd been careful with those novels at the time. She'd known better than to write them so that the characters had the kind of names she was so fascinated with because she'd known that if she did somebody would be sure to find them, and then everything would go completely to hell. She wondered if it would have been different if she'd grown up out here instead of in the Midwest, if her parents had been rich and sophisticated instead of middle-class and midwestern. People here certainly liked to think they were different. They liked to think of themselves as "citizens of the world." It was one of those things Cherie still hadn't managed to understand. On the other hand, Melissa *had* been born and brought up around here. She had even gone to a boarding school like this one called Miss Porter's, where Jacqueline Bouvier Kennedy had actually been a student. Melissa was just as fascinated by all these people as Cherie was and just as determined to stay part of the world they lived in.

The truth was, Cherie's name was not pronounced like the French endearment. It was pronounced "cherry." Her mother had named her after Cherry Ames, the heroine of a series of books for girls that had been popular when her mother was still in grade school. *Cherry Ames, Student Nurse,* the first one was called, and then the series went from there. *Army Nurse,* that was one—Cherry Ames went off to fight the good fight in World War II. *Dude Ranch Nurse. Private Duty Nurse. Jungle Nurse. Boarding School Nurse.* She should have read that last one, except that she couldn't have. She couldn't read any of them because the books were arranged carefully on a built-in bookshelf in the living room protected behind a thin sheet of soft plastic, preserved for all time. The closest Cherie had ever come to reading any of the books was listening to her mother tell her the stories, which happened several times a week from the age when she might have been interested in fairy tales. Other mothers read Dr. Seuss to get their children to sleep. Cherie's told the stories of Cherry Ames.

I wonder what she wanted? Cherie thought now. It was one of the great questions of her life. Maybe her mother had wanted to be a nurse, but, if so, it was hard to understand why she hadn't just become one. One of her mother's sisters was a nurse. It wasn't as if Cherie's grandparents would have put barriers in Cherie's mother's way. It wasn't as if Cherie's mother had the usual excuse either. She hadn't become pregnant out of wedlock, and if she had she would have been able to get an abortion, if that was what she'd wanted, and go ahead with her plans. An abortion is what Cherie's mother said she'd wished she'd had when she found out that Cherie was not only not interested in being a nurse but was actually going to leave home for the Northeast and become a liberal and a member of the Democratic Party on top of it. Even worse than that, Cherie insisted that everybody know she had become a member of the Democratic Party.

"I'm not insisting on their knowing," Cherie had said, trying to be patient, trying to be calm. "It's not like that. I just think people should stand up for what they believe in—"

"How can you believe in a perversion?" her mother had said. "The Democrats are no better than Communists, that's all they are. And they're atheists. You were brought up to believe in God."

That was her junior year at the University of Michigan, and of course her mother thought it was all the university's fault—the entire state thought that

Ann Arbor was nothing but a collection of Commies and perverts. Maybe it *would* have been different to grow up out here. At least people didn't call other people "Commies," and only ignorant people used the word "pervert." Maybe words made a difference in the long run.

There was movement behind her, and Cherie looked back to see Melissa coming through from the kitchen carrying a mug of tea. Melissa was a miracle too, in a way. They had met fifteen years ago at a summer training camp for women activists in Virginia, and everything had fallen into place so quickly that Cherie had distrusted it at first. Melissa had grown up in New York. She was used to taking control of her life and getting the things that mattered to her. This whole plan that they'd come up with—to go from school to school, to be paid for seeing the country—had been Cherie's idea, but it had only happened because Melissa insisted.

"What are you looking at?" Melissa asked now. "Have they decided to stage a festival of spring in the snow or what?"

"You shouldn't say things like that," Cherie said. "That's the kind of thing that drives people like Alice Makepeace nuts. And we want to stay."

"We want to stay, yes," Melissa said. She sat down in the big leather armchair and stretched out her feet. "We want to stay at least because it would be impossible to get as good an apartment anywhere near Boston for less than it would cost to lease a Porsche. But that doesn't mean you need to be on pins and needles all the time."

"I've always been on pins and needles."

"Persecution in the Midwest. I know."

"It wasn't persecution," Cherie said. "It was—" She shrugged and went back to looking out the window onto the quad. "Do you know who I saw a moment ago? Mark DeAvecca."

"Stoned as usual, I take it. It's Friday night."

"You can call it stoned if you want to."

"It's the best way of putting it," Melissa said. "It fits his behavior. I've known dozens of kids like him in my life. There's a soft underbelly of them in every good school."

"He's a brilliant kid," Cherie said. "I know a lot of people around here think he's stupid, but it isn't true. It comes out every once in a while when you talk to him."

"He'd have to be a brilliant kid," Melissa said. She curled her legs up under her. "Look, I know I make fun of this place a lot. It's hard not to make fun of it. They're so damned self-conscious about how progressive they all are, they make political correctness look sane. But even I know that the work here is not easy. If he wasn't a brilliant kid, he couldn't get away with the crap he pulls without flunking out."

"He's not even close to flunking out. I know a dozen kids with grades worse than his."

"Exactly. And that in spite of the fact that he doesn't know where he is half the time. But Cherie, no matter how bright he is, there's nothing you can do for someone like that."

"Everybody thinks he takes drugs," Cherie said again, feeling mulish. "His roommate takes drugs sometimes, what's his name, Michael Feyre. You can smell it on him."

"Well, yes," Melissa said, "Michael Feyre is not a brilliant kid. He doesn't hide it very well."

"With Mark DeAvecca, it's not like drugs. It's like—"

"What?"

Cherie shrugged. "Senile dementia."

"Senile dementia?" Melissa said. "The kid is sixteen, for God's sake, and you think he's got Alzheimer's disease?"

"No, not really." Cherie shook her head. "It's not that I think he has it, it's that that's what it's like. He *does* things. He forgets things—he'll be sitting in class and we'll be working out a problem, and he'll do it. He'll sit right there and do it. Then we'll move on to something else, and maybe ten minutes later I'll ask about the problem, and he won't remember it. He won't remember a thing about it."

"Drugs."

"No," Cherie said. "If it was drugs, he wouldn't have been able to do the problem in the first place. There's something going on with that kid. I wish I knew what it was."

"Don't bother. I mean it, Cherie, there's no point in bothering. The kid's got a famous mother and a rich father. A rich and famous father, come to think of it."

"Stepfather," Cherie said automatically. "His biological father is dead."

"Whatever. It doesn't matter. They won't throw him out of here, and they won't do anything about what's going on because they don't want one of the paying customers to leave, and they don't want a lawsuit or, worse, Mama to hit the Op-Ed pages of all the best newspapers blasting them to hell."

Cherie bit her lip. The carillon was marking a quarter hour. She'd noticed the clock in the kitchen at nine fifteen just a little while ago. It had to be nine thirty. The quad was empty. She'd always hated the cold. Back in Ann Arbor, she'd promised herself that as soon as she had the chance she'd go somewhere warm. She'd do her graduate work in Florida or Hawaii. She'd move to Texas or South Carolina and civilize the Bible Belt. Instead, she'd done her graduate work in Wisconsin and then moved to New Jersey, to the first of the boarding schools. The only way she could have managed to get any colder would have been if she'd gone to Alaska, or if they had boarding schools at the North Pole.

She turned away from the window. Melissa was still sitting in the big leather chair and still sipping her tea, black tea, the strong kind.

"There's one other thing," Cherie said.

"What's that?"

"Alice Makepeace doesn't like him."

"Doesn't like Mark DeAvecca?"

"Exactly."

"That's just because he's Michael's roommate, don't you think?"

"I don't know," Cherie said. "I know he must be in the way, but that hardly seems like enough of a reason. She really doesn't like him. Not at all."

"Then that's one more reason for you to stay away from him," Melissa said.

"He's my student."

"I mean stay away from his problems," Melissa said. "I really hate to be the heavy here, Cherie, but the simple fact is that that woman is dangerous, and you know it. She's dangerous in ways I can't begin to count. She's dangerous to anybody who gets in her way—"

"You'd think somebody would catch on to what she's doing," Cherie said. "This is the third student in three years. One of them is going to file a complaint one of these days. And don't say she'll just talk herself out of it. People don't just talk themselves out of it these days. Think of the priest scandals. She'll go down, and she'll bring the school down with her."

"Maybe. My only concern is that she doesn't bring us down first. She—does things to people, Cherie, you know she does. She can get almost anybody fired if she wants to, and she isn't brutal about it. She's got a lot of finesse. But you're just as fired with finesse. And you don't want to be fired—or in jail."

"No," Cherie said. "That's true enough."

"The only way to survive in these places is to do what we originally planned. It's worked so far and no fuss. Alice Makepeace is one of those women who gets what she wants the way she wants it. She's got the conscience of a Roald Dahl villain. Don't get in her way. If it's true and she really doesn't like Mark DeAvecca, then Mark DeAvecca will get shown the door and you won't have to worry about him anymore."

"But I *will* worry about him," Cherie said. Then she turned back around and looked out the window one more time. Everything looked dead, or worse. She wished that spring would come. Everything always felt better in the spring. That had been true even back in Michigan.

Maybe what was really wrong with her, and with Melissa, was the obvious—that Alice Makepeace was exactly the sort of woman both of them wanted so very much to be. It was terrible to think that people couldn't be happy no matter how much they worked at it. It was terrible to think that people, even women, would choose danger over safety, intensity over security, flash and dash over the solid day-to-day of love. It was terrible to think it, but it was probably true, and it was especially true of both of them. Now she had a whole raft of student accounts to rectify, and the house accounts to do. She should have a stack of student IDs to verify, too, but they were gone, and she hadn't had a chance to get them back again. One of them belonged to Mark DeAvecca. It was the third one he'd lost this year.

6

James Robert Hallwood should have been a professor in an Ivy League English department in the 1950s or even earlier, when erudition and elegance were assumed to be the goals of anyone with half a brain in his head and nobody laughed at Clifton Webb. Well, James admitted, probably everybody laughed at Clifton Webb; they just didn't come out and say what they were thinking because in those days homosexual men were not only supposed to be in the closet but invisible. They were not invisible, of course. James may never have been a professor in an Ivy League English department, but he was old enough to remember the 1950s. He'd had an uncle whom everybody had referred to as a "confirmed bachelor," as if a taste for going into New York and hanging out in Greenwich Village bars was the sign of a man too dedicated to chasing girls to ever settle down. People sniggered—that was the word, too, sniggered, something different from "laughed" or "chuckled" or even "derided," a word with a world of meaning in it, a sense of time and place. James had not sniggered. Even then he had been plotting a path, and although it included confirmed bachelorhood—he'd known that much before he was twelve—it did not include Greenwich Village bars. The real difference between the young and the old was that the young had no sense of the realistic.

What looked to rational people like insurmountable obstacles seemed, to a teenaged boy with a true spirit of invincibility, just a few silly details to be ignored more than to be overcome. Now he wasn't sure if he had been lucky or unlucky. He would not have found it easy to live in a time when being what he was could get him arrested and sent to jail. He wasn't good at dissimulation, and he didn't have the patience for pretense that surely had been required of men like Clifton Webb. The problem was, he had no patience for so much of what had come in the same boat that had brought the need for pretense to an end: victim's studies, feminist criticism, gender-race-and-class. There was something truly obscene about holding the *Pietá* up to the light and seeing only the basis for a diatribe on capitalist retrogressions or the triumph of hegemonic male privilege.

Outside, the carillon was doing one of its minor jiggles. It was a terrible carillon, politically correct, like everything else at Windsor Academy. James checked the clock on the wall behind him and saw that it was ten thirty. Then he turned back to what he was doing at the counter and looked out the window. It was not a good view from this kitchen. There was a good one, out on the quad, in the living room; but faculty apartments being what they were, one view per unit seemed to be the best that could be expected. This window looked out on the long stretch from the library to Maverick Pond. In the winter, with the snow piled high, it looked like a wasteland.

He poured black coffee into large, bone china cups and put the cups on his best serving tray. He put the silver sugar bowl there, too, but not the cream pitcher, because neither of them used cream. It fascinated him a little. They were both "effeminate" men, in a way of being "effeminate" that had gone out of style many years ago; but neither one of them had women's tastes. The coffees were plain black brews, good Colombian, and imported, but without the bells and whistles of the kind of person who found Starbucks a personal affront to aesthetics. There was no cinnamon or French vanilla. There was no sales slip in the utility drawer indicating a buying trip into Boston to the place where a pound of ground coffee beans cost as much as a small car.

Out in the wasteland, there was movement. James stopped what he was doing, his hands full of silver teaspoons, and watched the figure in black walking away from the pond with her head bent into what must have been wind. There were no lights out there, but he knew who it was, knew it as surely as he would have if he had seen her red hair flashing under one of the security lights. He wondered what she was doing out there at this time of night, and alone. Alice

Makepeace was never alone, and when she was it was because she was coming or going to an assignation. He couldn't imagine what kind of assignation she could be having at Maverick Pond in the middle of a cold February night, when even the squirrels weren't interested in making love in the out-of-doors.

He put the teaspoons down on the tray. He watched Alice Makepeace reach the top of the hill near the west door of the library and then begin to move along the path toward the quad. She was wearing that floor-length black wool cape she'd affected since the day he'd first met her. She looked like she was auditioning for a part in an all-female remake of *Zorro*. The way things were these days, somebody probably would make a female *Zorro*, and then all the girls in the English Department would write essays full of torturously complicated language for the *Publication of the Modern Language Association* saying, basically, that it was a Very Good Thing to show women in nontraditional roles, and that the movie would probably result in the death of capitalism and the coming of a utopia built on nurturing, cooperation, and classically female values.

Alice Makepeace had disappeared out of sight in the quad. James picked up the tray and began to carry it into the kitchen, thinking that he ought to put something sensible on the CD player before the night got too quiet for either his comfort or David's. He didn't know when that had started—the uncomfortable feeling they both had when there was too much silence between them—but it *had* started, and James had been through enough of these things to know that it meant the relationship was winding to a close. It was too bad really. He didn't love David. He didn't have much use for all this new talk of love and relationships and permanency that characterized this phase of the "gay" movement. He refused even to call himself "gay." Still, it was too bad. He and David were companionable. They had been together a long time.

David was sitting in the wing chair with his feet up on the ottoman going through the illustrated catalogue for the Turner show at the New York Metropolitan Museum of Art. It was an old show, years in the past. James couldn't believe David was really interested.

James put the tray down on the coffee table and sat in front of it on the couch. You *could* see out the window here to the quad, but there was no sign of Alice Makepeace trudging her way to the headmaster's house. He wondered where she had gone.

David put down the catalogue and reached for his coffee. "Where have you been? You're not usually any more than a couple of minutes in the kitchen."

"I was watching someone out the window, a mystery."

"Oh?"

James shrugged. "Not really. An anomaly, really, that there's probably some stupidly simple explanation for. I saw Alice Makepeace coming up from Maverick Pond."

"Alice Makepeace is who—the headmaster's wife?"

"Exactly."

"And what's at this Maverick Pond?"

"Nothing, really," James said, "that's the mystery. It's just a water hole in the middle of a field. Everybody pretends to admire it because it's part of nature, and there's a demonstration out there every spring when the administration decides it has to spray to get rid of the mosquitoes. But there isn't anything . . . there."

"So what was she doing there?"

"I haven't the slightest idea. She has affairs with students. If the weather was somewhat warmer . . ." James shrugged.

David had picked up his coffee cup. Now he put it down again, interested. He taught at a university in Boston. James knew he looked on Windsor Academy as a kind of exercise in surrealism. He was always asking James why James didn't just move to some place like Emerson, or even Tufts. James had his degree. He even had his publications. David, on the other hand, had tenure, and he had lost the sense of insecurity that was the inevitable accompaniment to being new and unknown in a strange school.

"Isn't it funny?" David said. "Are you sure she's having an affair with a student?"

"Of course I'm sure. It's not the first one she's had either. I think she looks on it like a tradition."

"Do other people know about this? Is it—common talk around the campus?"

James considered that. "Not exactly," he said slowly. "She's not blatant about it really. And I don't think her husband knows."

"Prep school headmasters are like college presidents; they never know anything."

"Possibly. In this case, though, I think she's made a certain amount of effort to keep him from finding out. But people do know. It's hard not to know in a place as small as this."

"And they don't do anything about it?"

"What are they going to do?"

David picked up his coffee cup again. "Think about it. What do you think would have happened if it had been one of us with a student?"

"Ah," James said.

"I know you don't like to be political," David said. "Even so, you do have to face reality some of the time. If it had been one of us with a student, we'd have been out with our luggage before we'd had time to pack. There wouldn't even have been an inquiry. You know that as well as I do."

"I suppose," James said.

"Don't just suppose," David said. "It's ever since the church scandals, and you know it. Especially here, this close to Boston, everybody's walking on eggs. That's a cliché. I know you don't like them, but there it is."

"Yes," James said.

"The rumors don't even have to be true," David went on. "Nobody even bothers to investigate anymore, half the time. All you need is a student with an axe to grind, somebody you're going to give a less-than-stellar grade to, and there it is. I've heard of three cases in the last two weeks. Oh, they didn't happen all at once, or all in the same place, but it amounts to the same thing. You can't be too careful. And you can never be sure."

"I don't have affairs with students," James said stiffly. "What do you take me for?"

"It's not what I take you for," David said. "It's what *they* take you for. All of *them*. Sometimes I understand the black separatists, I really do. Sometimes I wish we could go somewhere without *them*."

"Who's *them?* The entire straight world?"

"Maybe."

"Don't be ridiculous," James said. "Besides, I don't know what you're upset about. Aren't you always telling me that it's so much better at the university level, where they don't have to worry about hysterical parents and homosexual men can be honest about who and what they are? I thought the university was a paradise for diversity, or however it is you phrase that on a day when you're trying to get me to quit my job."

"Nothing is a paradise when it comes to this," David said. "It's a witch hunt, literally. It's the same sort of hysteria there was a few years back with satanic ritual abuse. It doesn't matter what's true. Doesn't it bother you that that woman, what's her name—"

"Alice Makepeace."

"Alice Makepeace can have an open affair with a student, whom I presume is under eighteen—"

"I think he may be under sixteen."

"Under *sixteen*." David shook his head. "Think of that. Under sixteen. When it's one of us with somebody under sixteen, it's child rape, as if we'd set upon a toddler and buggered him brainless. More than half the cases of priest abuse were against girls, but you never hear about them. The head of the largest organization for priest abuse victims is a woman, but you never hear about her either. You only hear about us."

"Yes," James said.

"I wish you'd come to your senses," David said. "I wish you'd think about what you're doing. I know you don't like to get involved in causes, but there's a good reason to get involved in this one: self-preservation. What are you going to do if somebody turns on you in this place? You don't even have a pension."

"Yes," James said again. His coffee cup was empty. He couldn't remember drinking what was in it. There didn't seem to be any reason to argue with David since he didn't really disagree with him. Yes, it was a jungle out there. Yes, he could be betrayed and crucified at any moment. Yes, he could lose all he had, which was—what?

"You know," he said, "it's not just a pension; it's equity."

"Excuse me?"

"Equity. This is a faculty apartment. I don't own it. Some of the other teachers have bought vacation property, you know. It doesn't make sense, if they're living here, to buy an ordinary house that they wouldn't use in the school year, so they buy vacation property. But I haven't even done that. I don't know why. It never really caught my imagination, real estate."

"I'm talking about the apocalypse," David said, "and you're talking about equity."

"Look." James got up. "I went into Boston the week before last and got something to protect myself. It's not as if I'm ignoring the apocalypse altogether."

"Got something to protect yourself?" David said. "What are you talking about? There's no way to protect yourself against false accusations and envy and spite. It's not the Iraqi War you're fighting here."

"We had protests against the Iraqi War," James said. He went over to the high-backed secretary and lowered its hinged writing surface. It was a beautiful piece of furniture, one of the few he owned, and it had taken him nearly two years to find and buy it. "These Regency-era writing desks are really wonderful," he said. "They always have a secret drawer. Do you ever wonder what it must have been like to live in the time of Jane Austen, when people took manners seriously?"

"You don't take manners seriously," David said. "I don't think you take anything seriously."

The secret drawer popped open. James took the gun out and checked it quickly to make sure it was loaded. Then he brought it over to the coffee table and put it down again.

"It's brand-new," he said. "A .45. I don't know what that means, but I do know that it's more powerful than a .22. It's probably not as powerful as a .357 Magnum, but those are hard to get. I thought of a few other possibilities, an antique German Luger, something with style, but in the end it seemed sensible to opt for the utilitarian."

"You're insane," David said. "They could fire you just for having this. And it wouldn't do you any good. It's not the kind of protection you need."

"Maybe not," James said, "but it makes me feel better. I thought about it for a long time believe me. I don't know why it does, but it makes me feel better."

"What if somebody gets hold of it and shoots you with it? What if somebody gets hold of it and shoots somebody else with it? What do you think you're doing?"

"Maybe I'll shoot Alice Makepeace with it," James said calmly. "I've thought about that, too, you know. It's truly remarkable how often I think about it."

"You're insane," David said.

David's voice sounded petulant and childish—another good sign, James thought, that their relationship was about to be over. People are petulant and childish all the time, but it's only at the end of things that we notice.

James got up and put the gun back into the secret drawer, then clicked the drawer back into place, where it looked like nothing but a bit of carved desk front. All of these secretaries had the same secret drawer in the same place. Anybody who had ever seen one before would know right where to go to find the treasure.

"You're insane," David said again, sounding neither petulant nor childish this time.

James went back to the coffee table, picked up the tray with the coffee things on it, and headed back out to the kitchen to wash up.

Edith Braxner had never really believed that men and women had sex. She knew, intellectually, that it must happen—all the children who showed up at the doors of schools every September couldn't be the result of artificial insemination—but the whole thing seemed to be so uncomfortable that she couldn't understand the point to it. For a long time she simply hadn't thought about it. She was old enough to have gone through school and college at a time when women were expected to be virginal until they reached the altar or died trying. She'd had no interest in getting married, and the only thing that bothered her about the era's mania for virginity was its tendency to spill over into what she thought of as sensible things. It annoyed her to discover that men found it erotic, and faintly disreputable, that she had done well in a class on anatomy. It annoyed her even more to discover that many women thought the same way, as if they were convinced that they themselves couldn't have remained intact and pure if they'd paid attention in their biology classes and not left school under the misapprehension that having sex while standing on one's head could not possibly result in pregnancy.

She was in graduate school when the sexual revolution hit, and she found it immediately relaxing. She did not lose her own virginity—how could you lose something that you didn't really have?, was what she wanted to know—but it seemed as if everybody else did, and in the wake of that she found that men began to leave her alone. She had never been a pretty girl or a pretty young woman. Her features were broad and flat. Her hair was dull. Her body was thin enough but of no particular shape. She thought that there were many girls across the country exactly like she had been who did what her own mother had wanted her to do. They "did something" about themselves. They went on exercise programs. They used makeup. To Edith, it had all seemed a colossal waste of time. It wasn't that she knew it wouldn't work anyway, although it wouldn't. It was that she knew she didn't care enough to keep it up. She would put in this enormous effort. She would primp and pump and spend. She would have a curious half hour in front of a mirror somewhere, checking out the changes the dyed hair and Elizabeth Arden lip gloss made. Then it would be over. She would have work to do. She would forget. Everything would go back to being the way it was. She would be out a lot of time and money, and maybe be less of a person than she had been before.

Once she'd started thinking about it, Edith decided that, for many people, sex had to have an ulterior motive. They didn't fall into bed because they wanted to fall into bed but to get something else, not sleep, not ecstasy. At least that was true of women. With men, Edith was never quite sure. She got along well with men. She always had. If they weren't intent on doing something physical, they were straightforward and uncomplicated. They didn't worry overmuch about their emotions or take things personally. She liked boy students better than girl students, too. It was hard to get boy students to do any work at all; but when you did, what they gave you was likely to be risky and original. Girls worked hard, and diligently, but they stayed within the lines. They played by the rules. They would hand you a twelve-page paper that had absolutely nothing new to say.

Like me, Edith thought, because it was true. She had always been a good student and a conscientious one, but she had never had that spark of originality that would have made her a brilliant one. She had never failed to get a grade below an A in any course she had ever taken anywhere, but she had also never failed to do the expected thing. She had gone from a small town in upstate New York to Wellesley. She had seen immediately that there were belles and swots, and that she was a swot. She had looked with some curiosity on the girls who were a third thing nobody was ever willing to label with a word—the ones who were expected to explode into fame or significance once they graduated— and known immediately that she was not what they were and never could be.

It didn't really matter, in the end, because she was what she wanted to be; and now, in her early sixties, she had what she had wanted from the start. She read five languages other than English and spoke three. She had spent sabbatical years in Rome and Paris and Salzburg. She had this lovely, large apartment looking out on the quad and the rising neo-Gothic spires of Ridenour Library, just a few steps from Main Street in Windsor, which was the kind of place she'd only been able to dream of in her childhood. It was a wealthy place, but intellectual, too, full of people who liked to go into Boston to hear Beethoven and walk through the museums, who valued excellent tea and quiet contemplation as much as other people valued trips to Disney World. She had never been to Disney World herself. She had never even seen a Wal-Mart. What she liked best were nights like tonight, when she could sit in her big club chair near the vast multipaned window in her living room drinking Double Bergamot Earl Grey that she'd ordered from the Stash Tea Company, reading Thomas Mann's

33

Buddenbrooks in German for the fifth or sixth time. All her correcting was done. She always got her correcting done early in the day because she hated to clog up her evenings with too much bad news about human nature. She had her accounts done, too. Every single student in her House had had her allowance money and drawing account checked and rechecked until there was no possibility of an error of even a penny. The Lytton House outlays for Letitia Markham's birthday party and the pajama party they'd given for Valentine's had been totted up and reconciled with the bills. She was a lot of things, but she was not one of those women who got a good education and did not put it to use.

She had been thinking about that—all those debutantes at Wellesley in her era, going out with the same Ivy League boys they'd gone out with when they were still at Miss Porter's or Madeira—when Alice Makepeace had come striding out from around the other side of the library and then onto the quad, that ridiculous cape streaming out behind her in the cold February wind. Edith had always found Alice Makepeace oddly comforting. Not only was she just like all those debutantes Edith had once known at Wellesley, but she so obviously indulged in sex for ulterior motives, and ulterior motives that were easy to discover and discern. *Power,* Edith thought, watching Alice make her way back to the headmaster's house, that bright red hair whipping and flashing under each of the security lights in turn. What Alice Makepeace wanted was the sense of power she got from the boys whose lives she made a misery year after year, that and the thrill of the exotic, of the vicarious experience of poverty and want. Of course Alice romanticized it all. Alice romanticized everything. Edith had known that the first time they'd met. Under the romanticism, though, there was a simple need, naked and raw. Edith may not have spent any time in bed with men, but she knew that need as thoroughly as she knew the difference between Single and Double Bergamot Earl Grey tea.

Alice disappeared, going off on a side path somewhere. She was not a straightforward woman. Edith did not find it odd that she would not be able to take a straightforward path home. She was about to go back to her chair and her book when she saw somebody else, and the somebody else gave her pause. Mark DeAvecca. Practically everybody in school thought Mark DeAvecca was taking drugs, handfuls of them. They were trying to ease him out of the school without actually confronting him about it because—Edith had heard this from one of the secretaries in the dean of Student Life's office—they had done a secret search of his room and not been able to find a single thing. Even his roommate hadn't had anything, and that was Michael Feyre, who came from one of the less savory neighborhoods of Boston and had connections. There was obviously something wrong with Mark. He sat through classes and didn't hear a word that was said. He handed in homework that was only half-done, or didn't hand it in at all, or did it and then left it on the study desk he'd been using in the library so that it was lost, never to be found again. She would have thought he was stupid beyond belief except that she remembered him from the first two weeks of classes, when he had been very different.

It probably is drugs, she thought, watching him move unsteadily down the path toward her window. She wondered where he had been. He seemed to be coming from the direction of Maverick Pond, but that made no sense. There was nothing out at Maverick Pond this time of year, and the cold was bad enough to give you frostbite if you decided to go out there and contemplate nature. Mark DeAvecca did not seem to be the kind of person who would want to contemplate nature under any circumstances. She had a lot of sympathy for that.

He had stopped on the path and turned to look behind him. Edith bit her lip and made up her mind. She stepped out of her apartment into the hall. She stepped out of the hall onto the back stoop. She hated being outside on the campus on weekend nights. It was always too deserted.

"Mark?" she called to him.

He looked up. "Ms. Braxner?"

Edith did not correct him. The culture of the school didn't matter to her at all. She preferred to be addressed formally, and all the students addressed her formally. Even Alice Makepeace addressed her formally on occasion, but that was a story with a different moral and not one she wanted to think about now.

"You look frozen," she said. "Worse than frozen, really. Where have you been?"

Mark looked around. "Out to the pond. And around. I was talking to Philip for a while."

"Philip Candor?"

"Yes."

"About what?"

Mark looked around again. "I went back to Hayes and I was going to go to bed, but it was still bothering me, so I sort of turned around and came back out; and then I went down there to see, and it wasn't there. Of course it wasn't there. I imagined it, I guess."

"Imagined what?"

"Nothing," Mark said. "This is where? What house is this?"

"Lytton."

"Oh, right. There was somebody named Bulwer-Lytton, am I right? They didn't name the house after Bulwer-Lytton though, did they?"

"No. He was an English writer from the nineteenth century. Famously bad."

"Okay."

Edith hesitated. She did not usually fraternize with students. She did not like this pretense of equality that Windsor Academy was so desperate to foster. She didn't like to know too much about her students' private lives. Mark DeAvecca's private life positively frightened her. *Still,* she thought. *Still. He looks so cold.* There were traces of ice in his heavy dark eyebrows.

"You could come in if you like," she said. "I've got a pot of tea. I've got hot chocolate if you'd rather have that."

"Thank you," Mark said. He wasn't looking at her. He never looked at anybody directly. He turned in a complete circle and then faced her again. The muscles in his face were twitching. While she watched him, his whole body seemed to convulse, quickly and painlessly. It was over in a moment.

"Come in," she said. "You don't look well. Have you been to the infirmary?"

"The infirmary isn't open."

"I meant anytime in the near past."

"I go every once in a while," Mark said. "There's never anything wrong with me. I don't have a temperature. They send me back to class."

"I didn't say I thought you should miss class."

"I know. I know. I don't know what's wrong with me. Maybe nothing's wrong with me. Except, you know, it was never like this before."

"Like what?"

Mark shook his head. Edith was beginning to feel the cold. She wondered why she hadn't felt it long ago. There was something odd about this scene. It was as if they were both suspended in space, riding in a bubble without weather. There was a wind in the quad, though, the same wind that had blown Alice Makepeace's cape around her legs. Edith thought it was going to take her an hour before she got herself warmed up again once she was back inside.

"Come in," she said. "Warm up. Have something to drink. You look awful, and I'm freezing."

"Thanks anyway," Mark said, "but I've got to get some sleep, I think. Sometimes it feels like I haven't slept all year."

"You look as if you're sleeping now, right on your feet."

"Sleepwalking," Mark said solemnly. Then he turned away from her and looked across the quad, all the way to the other end, where Hayes House was. "I don't remember leaving and coming out again. I don't remember it. I remember deciding to do it, but I don't remember doing it. I don't remember anything until I got down to the pond, that was the second time at the pond, I think. I don't remember. I don't remember. That's what this year has been like. I can't ever remember anything."

Edith almost said something, too sharply, about the fact that he almost never remembered his homework, but she bit it back. Maybe it was drugs. Maybe he was stoned all the time. There was certainly something wrong with him. He was swaying on his feet. She thought he might pass out right in front of her, but it didn't happen.

"If you're not going to come in, go back to Hayes," she said. "Go back right now. Go to your room and lie down. You shouldn't be wandering around in the condition you're in."

"The question is, what condition *am* I in?" Mark said. "That's it, you see. The infirmary says there's nothing wrong with me. For a while I thought I had that thing, Huntington's disease, Huntington's chorea—"

"Does it run in your family? Did one of your parents have it?"

"No."

"Well, then."

"I know," Mark said, "but the thing is—"

"What?"

"Nothing," Mark said. "I must have been hallucinating, and that's a first. I've never hallucinated before."

"Go back to Hayes," Edith said.

Mark nodded slightly. Edith stood back a little, giving herself the partial shelter of the doorway, and watched him head off down the path in the direction of Hayes House. Had he really already been there once tonight and then come out again for a . . . hallucination? What were the drugs that caused hallucinations? She'd never paid much attention to the drug information that floated around campus like confetti in Times Square on New Year's Eve. She wasn't interested in her students' drug lives any more than she was interested in their sex lives. Mark was bobbing and weaving as if his bones had half melted under his skin. Edith stepped all the way back into the hall and closed the door in front of her. Lytton House was very quiet tonight, as quiet as she usually liked it to be. Now it felt oppressive and stale.

She went back into her apartment and closed that door, too. She sat down in her big club chair and looked at her cup of tea. They all just assumed the boy was on drugs. It was the most obvious explanation for the way he was behaving.

It had suddenly occurred to her just how much trouble that boy's parents could make for this school if it turned out they were all wrong and something was really the matter with Mark.

8

Alice Makepeace knew that her husband had a surveillance camera in their bedroom, and she knew what it was he used it for. Every once in a while, when he was safely out of state at a conference of independent school heads—the euphemism drove her crazy; when had they decided to hide the elitism of it all under cover of that bourgeois word "independent"?—she went into his study with her spare key and looked through the photographs in the desk. They were terrible photographs more often than not, grainy and unreal, nothing at all like what she had really experienced in bed. She was not afraid of the photographs any more than she was afraid of Peter. It would hurt him far more than it would hurt her if anybody ever knew what was in them, just as it would hurt him more than it would hurt her if anybody ever found out about the boys. She was no Mary Kay Letourneau. She wasn't conducting a grand passion or working out the demons from a tackily wretched childhood spent feeling guilty and ugly on the streets of some subdivision in flyover country. She had had a wonderful childhood, thank you very much, and an even more wonderful young adulthood. She had been to Paris four times before she was eight. She had spent every one of her winter vacations on the Riviera right up until the year she married Peter, when they had had no winter vacation because he was taking seminars at Harvard and attempting to beef up his résumé. She should have realized, then, that this was what it would be like—the unutterable boredom, the endless sameness of it all, day after day, week after week, year after year, with nothing to look forward to but the malice in the eyes of the old ladies on the board, the ones who hated her for merely existing.

Boredom was the key. In the end everything came down to that. Most of the time Alice lived in a positive fog of boredom, and she knew herself too well to think that she could do what most women in her position did to make the time pass. It was a tradition in "independent" schools that the headmaster's wife had a teaching job at the school or a place on the support staff. Husbands and wives worked together almost always because that meant two paychecks and a more viable household income from jobs that—except on Peter's level—didn't really pay much at all. Alice could not see herself as a counselor. She could not see herself teaching English. She could not see herself at faculty meetings. She could barely see herself making her way across the quad every morning to have dinner in the cafeteria, although she did it, the way she did everything that was required of her.

She was not bored tonight, although she was oddly light-headed. It confused her because she didn't often get dizzy. She'd come into the headmaster's house by the side door. She was standing in the little mudroom with its built-in storage bench and its brass wall hooks and its full-length mirror hanging on the door that led into the kitchen. Some nights she stood in front of that mirror and contemplated the realness of herself. There were times when she did not actually feel entirely real. Tonight she felt more real than she wanted to. She stripped off the black leather gloves and put them down on the bench. She took off the cape and hung it on a hook. The black leather of her jeans almost blended into the black leather of her boots, giving her an uninterrupted visual line. She was a tall woman. This made her look taller still, as did the fact that the boots had three-inch heels. One summer when she was in college, she had taken a trip to Greece with three of her cousins. They had gone to the harbor at Rhodes, and she had stood there on the shore thinking of what the Colossus must have looked like, if it had ever existed, with one foot on one side of the water and the other on the other. Later, Julianne—the "smart one," as the family liked to call her; the uptight idiot with the grades everybody was always marveling about, as if it mattered to them when none of them had cared one way or the other all the time they were in school and wouldn't have liked anyone who did—had said it wasn't true. The Colossus didn't really bestride the harbor. It had just been a statue, off to one side. Alice had thought, immediately, that that was too bad. It was the kind of thing she would have liked for herself, to be tall enough to stand like that, with her legs so far apart ships could go through them.

She was wearing a black silk blouse, her best one, bought in New York on one of the buying trips she took to get away from Peter. Peter was glad to let her take them. He wanted to get away from her. She leaned over and took the gloves off the bench and looked at them. They did not seem to be any different than they had ever been. She supposed they had no reason to be. She wished she could get rid of this jumpy nervousness that was making her feel like running back out the door and down the quad and into the night to nowhere.

She dropped the gloves again and went through the door into the kitchen.

The light was on in the living room. The television was on, too. The sound coming from it was the weird flat hush of public broadcasting documentaries. She wondered why the announcers on PBS always felt they had to whisper when they talked.

She went through the kitchen to the living room. Peter was sitting on the long, floral couch, his shoes off, his feet up on the coffee table. That was as close as he ever came to informality unless he was in bed—and even there he wore tailored pajamas, dark blue with white piping, bought at Brooks Brothers. At the moment he was in sports jacket and tie. His trousers still had perfect center creases.

"Where have you been?" he asked, not turning around.

There was a drinks tray on a small occasional table set just behind the couch. Alice bypassed the gin and the vodka and the Scotch and opened a small bottle of Perrier. Like most of the women she knew, she only drank wine, and only good wine, and only episodically. The last thing she wanted was to start guzzling booze like an advertising executive at lunch. *God,* she thought. They could have put her down in the middle of one of those ethnic restaurants in Boston, the ones that got written up in the weekend section of the *Globe,* and the only way anybody could have told her apart from all the other suburban Boston ladies with their memberships in WGBH and their days at the Gardner Museum would have been by her hair, and that was a good enough reason never to let herself go gray. Even the—things—she did didn't set her apart. She was convinced that half the women she saw with their beaten-silver Native American jewelry and their J. Jill flowing-linen summer skirts did all the same things she did, or worse, and then wrote about them in journals kept meticulously, year after year, on the assumption that they would one day provide the basis for a novel of sensitivity written by a woman who cared. That much, at least, she had to congratulate herself on. She did not keep journals, and she did not expect ever to write a novel.

"Alice?" Peter said.

"I'm here. I'm getting some Perrier."

"Where have you been?"

"Walking."

"Outside?"

"Of course outside."

"It's not the weather for it. It's below freezing."

"Nine below," Alice said. She looked into the little silver cannister, but the ice that had been in there had melted into water, and there were no more slices of lime to be found. She walked around to the front of the couch and took a seat on the chair at its side, the chair that was positioned exactly as it had to be so that the person sitting in it couldn't see the television screen at all.

"I wish we could think of some place else to put the television set," she said. "Sane people don't have television sets in their living rooms."

"Most people have television sets in their living rooms."

"Most people aren't sane. But I think you're wrong anyway. Most people have television sets in their family rooms. They leave their living rooms free for company. We keep it in here the way Catholics keep statues of the Virgin in their gardens. It looks like something we worship."

"Catholics don't worship statues of the Virgin."

"Don't get silly. There ought to be somewhere else to put it. Maybe we could get rid of it altogether. I never watch it."

"I do."

"I know."

"I'm not going to apologize for watching television, Alice. I'm not even going to apologize for watching *The West Wing*."

"I didn't ask you to apologize."

"Oh yes, you did. You always do."

"We're going to have to do something about this marriage. It's gotten to the point where we don't have fights anymore; we simply assume we've had them."

"We're not having a fight. I asked you where you'd been. You're avoiding answering."

The glass of Perrier was half-empty. Alice Makepeace was definitely a half-empty, not a half-full, person. She leaned forward and put it down on the coffee table. She could not remember the first time she'd met Peter Makepeace. He was one of those boys who had just always been around, going to the same dancing classes, going to the same parties. Everybody knew him, and he knew everybody. Alice did remember when she had first decided to marry him and how carefully she had thought it all out: what the marriage would mean, just how much she would be able to put up with. In the end it had turned out far worse than she had hoped. It did matter that she had never expected it to turn out well.

"Are you going to tell me where you've been?" Peter asked. "You've been out for hours."

"I haven't really been anywhere. I've been walking. And yes, in the cold. It's minus nine, if you want to know. Or it was a little while ago. I just wanted . . . to move around."

"All right."

"I stopped in the library for a while. I talked to Marta Coelho. She was working."

"Marta's always working."

"I know."

Peter shifted slightly on the couch. The PBS documentary, whatever it was, was going off. Alice hadn't paid any attention to it so all she knew was that it wasn't one of those awful evenings of swing or Liberace that all the PBS stations had become enamored of in the last decade. Peter had a bald spot on the top of his head. It was only the size of a nickel, but it would grow. She wondered if he would try to compensate with a comb-over.

"It's not a dirty word, you know," Peter said, "work. I don't understand how you can spend so much time working for the causes you do and then look down on somebody like Marta, who takes her work seriously."

"I don't look down on her for taking her work seriously."

"But you do look down on her."

"She's a cipher, Peter. She might as well be a voice program. HAL the computer had more personality. She was worrying about Mark DeAvecca by the way."

"Ah," Peter said. "Well, one of our mistakes."

"She said something along the same lines. That he's irresponsible. Of course you think he's on drugs."

"Don't you?"

Alice looked away. "I've talked to his roommate, Michael Feyre. Michael doesn't think he's on drugs."

"Would he tell you if he did?"

Alice was still looking away. "He's got no reason to lie. I don't think they're friends, particularly."

"Mark isn't really friendly with anybody. It's hard to know what he's doing here. And I remember his application, too. It was one of the best I've ever seen."

"And he's Elizabeth Toliver's son and Jimmy Card's stepson, and that never hurts around here either."

"No," Peter admitted, keeping it pleasant, "it never does. It never hurts anywhere. That's life, Alice. It's been that way since the dawn of time. It's going to be that way tomorrow."

"Yes, well," Alice said. She got up. She couldn't sit in this chair any longer. She wanted a shower. She wanted her nerves to calm down. She wanted not to look at herself in the mass of pictures in their silver frames lined up on top of the television console. "I'm going to go get ready for bed. I want to read. And I think it's odd that you've never considered the obvious."

"What's the obvious, in this case?"

"The obvious is that Mark DeAvecca is mentally ill. That he's, well, schizophrenic or paranoid. That doesn't always show up right away, you know. Many people have perfectly normal childhoods before it sets in. Then it does set in and they become . . . dangerous."

"You think Mark DeAvecca is dangerous?"

"I think he could be," Alice said. "He certainly isn't stable, is he? He wanders around as if he's half-dead most of the time. He can never remember anything. He mumbles to himself. I saw him do that once in chapel. He was just sitting by himself—twitching and mumbling under his breath."

Peter had leaned forward, his arms on his knees. "What is this about, exactly? What are you trying to pull?"

"I'm not trying to 'pull' anything."

"Yes, you are. Mark DeAvecca is no more dangerous than I am. He doesn't have the energy to make his bed in the morning, never mind hurt anybody. What did you do?"

"What did I do about what, Peter?"

"I don't know," Peter said. "I really don't know. I wish I did."

"All I did was point out the obvious, Peter. Which is that that kid is definitely off, somehow, and none of you know for sure that he isn't dangerous. I'd think that was the first possibility you'd want to consider."

"What did you do?" Peter asked again.

Alice turned away and walked out of the living room into the hall. The muscles in her neck felt as tight and hard and sharp as barbed wire. She thought she was getting a migraine or worse. The staircase was long but not steep. This was an old house, older than the United States itself. It was on the tour the Windsor Historical Society did every year to raise funds for architectural preservation. Alice was on the committee. She was on most of the committees that mattered. She raised funds for WBGH during pledge-drive weeks when even the people who were committed to public television didn't want to watch it. She served on the board of the Windsor Food Bank, which did its business in Boston and not in Windsor at all, since nobody who was poor enough to need a food bank could afford to live in Windsor. She had a subscription to the symphony and to the ballet. She contributed to an experimental dance company and a little magazine of women's poetry. She belonged to the National Organization for Women and People for the American Way. She was, she thought, a complete and utter cliché.

Peter had changed the channel on the television set. He would not be coming up after her anytime soon. She started up the stairs and wished she hadn't worn these particular boots tonight. They always made her feel unsteady.

She was a complete and utter cliché . . . except that she wasn't.

9

Once, when he was very small and his father was still alive, Mark DeAvecca had convinced himself that there was a dinosaur in the kitchen. They were still living in England then, in the house on Roslyn Avenue in Barnes, and the kitchen wasn't big enough to contain a small pony, never mind a dinosaur. He was small enough so that he hadn't started school yet, or at least not real school. Trying to fix it in his memory now, he thought he must have been about three, old enough to be beyond the toddler stage, not quite old enough for the nursery school he would later attend five days a week, three hours a day, at a small, brick building only a couple of blocks from home. The important thing was that he was too small to have any realistic concept of size. He became convinced that there was a dinosaur in the kitchen, and nothing his mother or his father said to him could change his mind or make him feel less afraid. He sat in the living room for long hours, reading a book in a chair or watching *Blue Peter* and *Captain Scarlet* on the television, and all the time he could hear the dinosaur moving heavily in among the table and chairs, in and out of the cabinets, in the crack between the refrigerator and the wall where the yardstick had fallen. He had just learned to read, and the books he picked up were very simple, mostly Dr. Seuss books his grandmothers sent him from the States. He liked to plow his way through them. It made him feel as if he'd done something very important when he'd managed to read every word in one of them. He would wait in the narrow entry hall for his father to come home, and then he would report. *This* was in the book today, and *this* and *this*.

After the dinosaurs came, he could never remember what was in the books. He read them and read them, but they didn't make any sense. Part of his mind was always somewhere else, waiting for them to get out, waiting for the swinging door to the kitchen to glide forward and let one of them into the dining room, where they would move in and around the tables and chairs there. He was convinced he was going to die. He was even more convinced that he was not going to die, but that both his parents were, and he would be left on his own in this house with nothing but the dinosaurs for company.

Now he was in the little back hall of Hayes House, which had been a mansion once before it had become a dorm. It really was a large house, unlike the house in Barnes, which had only seemed large because he himself had been so small. He looked at the phone on one wall and the light coming from the crack under the door to Sheldon LeRouve's apartment. Sheldon LeRouve was yet another teacher he didn't get along with, although he had the good luck not to have him for a class. Maybe it didn't matter. He didn't seem to get along with anybody, except a few of the kids, and even then he was odd man out most of the time, an interesting figure on the sidelines, not the kind of person anybody thought of first. He felt a little dizzy. He was definitely very tired. He tried to remember what had finally rid the house in Barnes of its dinosaurs, but he couldn't. They were there, and then one day they were not there. He wasn't afraid of the kitchen anymore. He could read when he wanted to read and watch television when he wanted to watch television, and his mother would let him. He could go into the kitchen by himself and get chocolate biscuits out of the cannister in the cabinet next to the refrigerator. He didn't think he had done anything, or that anybody had done anything, to make them go away.

Biscuits, he thought now. That was a blast from the past. They called them "cookies" here. He'd been back long enough so that he nearly always remembered that. He thought of his first day at Rumsey Hall, where he had gone to school in Connecticut after his father had fallen ill and his parents had moved back to America to get his father's cancer treated. He had been in the second grade, and he had truly loved the look of the place, wide open on green lawns, lots of space, lots of low, white buildings. The problem was that they had spent the first part of the day singing, and he hadn't known any of the songs: "America the Beautiful," "The Star-Spangled Banner," "It's a Grand Old Flag." He had grown more and more frustrated over the course of a long hour. He wasn't used to being out of things. He wasn't used to not knowing all the answers to all the questions either. He was growing desperate to do at least one thing that would prove to everybody that he was just as smart as everybody else, if not more so, and suddenly he had heard a strain of music that was completely familiar. That was when he had stepped forward and started singing, as confident as he had ever been in his life that he was about to get something right. Mrs. Seldenader set the pitch on her harmonica and started in on the piano, and instead of "My Country, 'Tis of Thee," he'd come out with, "God save our gracious Queen. Long live our noble Queen. God save the Queen."

It was, he thought now, a metaphor for something, a prophecy of this year. There were dinosaurs in the kitchen again, and nothing he did was right. Except that it was worse, really. That first day at Rumsey Hall, his teachers had liked him and considered him bright. He just hadn't known enough about how America worked to fit right in. In this place he knew that most of his teachers had no use for him at all. They thought he was stupid. They thought he was a slacker. They thought he was a liar. He sometimes felt as if he'd wandered into a dystopian Wonderland, where the Mad Hatter's tea party took place in the Spanish Inquisition's best dungeon and the White Rabbit had fangs.

He went out into the main hall and across it into the large, high-ceilinged living room. There was a small clutch of Korean students watching something on television, maybe a DVD or a tape. He looked up the long flight of stairs and thought that it was just too much, right this second, to climb it. He didn't understand why he was so tired all the time or why he couldn't eat. He thought he must have lost twenty pounds since he first came to Windsor, but he was getting almost no exercise at all. He didn't like exercise all that much. He wasn't a sports person. He just didn't usually feel right unless he was moving around a little, and this year he moved less and less. It felt more and more difficult to move. He wished, suddenly, that he could be back in Connecticut. He had been chafing at that routine by the time it was over. Now it seemed to him like a haven of sanity, a time when he had been somebody else, when he had been himself.

He started up the stairs—there was nothing for it; he wanted to lie down, and he had to go up to the third floor to do it—and as he did he heard Mr. Le-Rouve's door open and Mr. LeRouve himself step out into the hall.

"Mark? Is that you?"

"That's me."

"Did you sign in?"

Mark had not signed in. He had signed in every other night of his life in this place, but tonight he had not signed in. He had no idea why.

"Sorry," he said. "I forgot."

Mr. LeRouve made a noise—Mark wondered why he always thought of him as Mr. LeRouve, instead of Sheldon; he was supposed to call him Sheldon, but he couldn't ever quite believe that was the case with any of his teachers, and he didn't really like it—and Mark turned away from the stairs to go on to the back and fill in the sign-in sheet. It seemed to be about ten o'clock, but that didn't make much sense. He couldn't remember what he had been doing for the past hour. He couldn't remember where he had been. He tried to fix himself in time, but all he could remember clearly was being in the library with the family medical book reading up on Huntington's chorea. He had come to the conclusion that it was just another excuse. He wanted an explanation for why he was the way he was, but there was no explanation. Maybe he had always been like this; maybe he hadn't. But this was the way he was now, and there was nothing he could do about it. He wondered, sometimes, if his mother would like this person he had become.

Mr. LeRouve was standing next to the sign-in sheet. Mark had to brush against him to get at the pen tied to the wall with a piece of fraying string.

"You don't smell like liquor," Mr. LeRouve said. "There's that."

"I don't drink liquor," Mark said. He picked up the pen and tried to sign his name in cursive. He couldn't make it happen. His hands didn't work right. His hands hadn't worked right for months. He went to printing, which wasn't much better—*I print like I've had a stroke,* he thought—and when he was done it occurred to him that Mr. LeRouve thought he was lying.

He let the pen drop and stepped back. "Sorry," he said. He thought he'd said it before, but he wasn't really sure.

Mr. LeRouve shrugged. Mark turned away and went back into the hall, to the stairs. When this had first started happening, when he had first realized that people did not believe the things he said, he had tried to fight it. He had staged knock-down fights on a couple of occasions, with teachers skeptical of even the smallest things—that he had lost a book, that he had forgotten an appointment, that he wasn't feeling well. Especially that last thing. Nobody here believed him when he said he was ill, no matter how ill he felt, and he'd felt ill often these last few months. He went to the infirmary and they took his temperature and told him he was all right. He felt so weak he could barely stand up straight, and they told him he looked well enough to them. He didn't know what to believe anymore. He thought it might all be psychological. He was homesick. He was somehow getting around to punishing himself for his father's death—although that was ridiculous, considering the fact that he had never felt guilty about his father's death before. Whatever it was, he had learned not to tell people when he felt unwell, not even when he felt sick enough to pass out, which was something he had done at least once, fortunately only nominally in public. He had been sitting in the cafeteria in the off-hours trying to study for his American History class, and the next thing he knew he'd just—not been there.

He got up to the second-floor landing and stopped. He could barely breathe. His mother had had better wind when she was still smoking two packs a day. He came around the landing and started up again. There were so many things he had learned not to do here or not to mention. They didn't like it when he read books on his own that weren't required for study. They were always reminding him that his grades were mediocre and that he wasn't getting his work done. He needed to be concentrating on his assignments and not wasting his time with trashy, pop-cult novels. He supposed there was some point in that. His grades were mediocre. He must not be studying hard enough. What was worse, he really wasn't reading much of anything except those trashy, pop-cult novels. They were, these days, all he could get himself to understand. It would be interesting to know when that had happened, too.

Halfway up to the third floor, he stopped again. He was winded again. He could barely see straight. He took three or four deep breaths. His throat hurt like hell. It often did, these days. His head hurt, too, in that dull throbbing he had come to associate with "not having any air." He counted to twenty. He flexed his fingers. The joints in them hurt. He started back up the stairs again. Why was it that his life reminded him so often of the old, original version of *Invasion of the Body Snatchers,* where all the people who were taken over by pods were so unnaturally, unchangeably calm? He was not calm. He was nervous and stressed all the time. He twitched when he least expected it. He still felt like a pod person.

He reached the third-floor landing. His room was on the far end, but the hallway was dark and he could see that no light was coming from under the door. Michael was either out or asleep. He was most likely out. Michael had a varied and active social life. Mark wondered what it was like to have an affair with a woman like Alice Makepeace, the kind of affair that everybody would know about so that even the teachers looked at you and wondered. It had to be better than having the teachers looking at you and wondering if you were an idiot or a drug addict. Mark was sure of that, in spite of the fact that he didn't much like Alice Makepeace. She was beautiful. He wasn't so out of it that he couldn't recognize that. He didn't trust her. There was something—*wrong*—about the way she was, something off, that made all his defenses go up automatically.

He opened the door to the room he shared with Michael Feyre, and the first thing he noticed was that the window was open. The room was ice cold and there was a wind coming in, blasting in his face, making the hair on his arms go stiff. Michael had to be out. He wouldn't have lasted ten minutes in the cold in this place. Mark snaked his hand around on the wall next to the door until he found the light switch. Always before, when he'd gotten a new room, it had taken him only a week or so to know instinctively where the light switches were on the walls. In this place, he had to learn over and over again, time after time.

He turned on the light. He looked into the cold room for a great long minute without reacting at all. Everything was a mess. The drawers had been pulled out of both the desks and both the dressers. There were books and papers and clothes everywhere. The laundry bags had been ripped apart. There was dirty underwear on the floor. Someone had smashed the big round alarm clock he and Michael called the Alarm Clock of Satan. Its hard, crystal face guard was shattered. Its hour hand had disappeared.

They're going to have a fit about the mess in here, Mark thought, and then, only then, did he acknowledge what he had seen first, the most obvious thing in the room, the elephant in the middle of the floor.

Michael Feyre's body was hanging from a rope thrown over one of the snaking pipes belonging to the sprinkler system. His neck was bent at an odd angle. His muscles were twitching. His eyes were bulging out. There was a bruise on his neck that looked as black as if somebody had tried to color in his skin with permanent marker.

They're supposed to put a hood over your head when they hang you, Mark thought, and then, only then, could he make himself turn and run into the hall to get help.

PART ONE

There's no way of knowing if the tree you plant will also turn out to be the tree you hang yourself from.
 —JOSE SARAMAGO

Those who are kind to the cruel will be cruel to the kind.
 —TALMUD

It's never easy to distinguish between a social visionary and an outright loon.
 —ROBERT FULFORD

ONE

1

It had been years since Gregor Demarkian spent much time thinking about his older brother, Stefan, and then it had only been a glancing thought occasioned by the fact that he was back on Cavanaugh Street and Cavanaugh Street was not what he'd expected. Now, standing at the window of his apartment and looking down at the construction crews beginning to arrive for their day at Holy Trinity Church—or what was left of it—it occurred to him that this was very odd. There had been a time, when he was very small and Stefan had just gone into the army, that he had thought about him every hour of every day, with an intensity of fear and hope that had blocked out every other emotion. Looking back on it, he found he couldn't reason away the conviction that he had known, from the moment Stefan had put on his uniform and walked out the door, that he would never see his brother again. The whole idea of war had been a matter of confusion, and at that point he had never known anyone who had died except the very old people on the street who had never seemed alive to begin with. It wasn't an understanding of life and death that had convinced him, any more than it was an understanding of war that had made him feel, at the time and forever afterward, that he didn't approve of it. Stefan had seemed so tall standing at the door, holding his hat under his arm while their mother draped herself over his chest and wept into the khaki buttons on his government-issue shirt. It was odd to think that he knew, now, that Stefan hadn't been tall at all. He'd barely been five ten, and Gregor himself was now well over six feet.

Maybe, Gregor thought, it would have been easier to remember accurately if Cavanaugh Street had been the same as it was then. Everything was too clean, and too well taken care of. The fire escapes had all been moved around to the back. The brownstones had been scrubbed free of dirt and pollution and age. The stoops had been transformed into entryways, complete with low, white stone pillars and polished slate inlays on the surfaces of the steps. He remembered playing on this street when he was nine or ten years old—long after Stefan was dead—and hitting a ball into a clothesline stretched from a window on one side of the street to a window on the other. Mrs. Bagdinian had stuck her head out and cursed him in Armenian, and he and all the other boys had run away.

Down the hall at the back of the apartment, the bathroom door opened and closed. Bennis said, "Gregor?" but kept on moving, into the bedroom, where she already had her things laid out on the bed. The bedroom door did not close. That was something else that had changed. Gregor's late wife always closed the door when she dressed, even after they'd been married for twenty years, and Gregor was willing to bet that his own mother had done exactly the same. That apartment had been a cramped series of small boxes on the fourth floor of a tenement, where half the apartments had to share a bathroom in the hall. He had felt rich beyond measure because his own family's apartment had had a bathroom to itself, and he had not been kind to the children he had seen tramping back and forth to the little cubicle at the back of the floor. Then he had gone to school and for the first time met people who did not live in places like Cavanaugh Street, and from that day to this he had never felt rich again.

Bennis came into the living room. Gregor did not turn around. The construction crews were unpacking their equipment. Some people had stopped to watch them begin work. One of those people was Fr. Tibor Kasparian.

"Tibor's up and around already," he said. "It's incredible that we never hear him leave in the mornings. He's like a ghost."

"He's on the floor below us. Are you watching the construction? Can you see it from here?"

"Not really. I can see the trucks. They just came in. We must be late."

"It's eight. Granted, we've been going to breakfast at seven for a while now, but there's no real need for it if you're not on a case, and you've turned down four cases in the last three weeks. More, in the last eight months. Do you ever intend to get around to telling me what all that's about? Have you decided to stop working?"

"Would it bother you if I had? Would it be too much as if I'd turned into a gigolo?"

"Christ," Bennis said. "Sometimes you are truly and sincerely one of the most annoying men I've ever met. Nobody even uses words like 'gigolo' anymore."

"No, I suppose they don't."

"And we live in your apartment, not mine. And you won't let me share expenses. And the last I heard, your investments were doing just fine, which beats mine, since you're apparently clairvoyant and know exactly when to pull out of the stock market—"

"The trick with the stock market is to never get into it."

"Whatever. What brought this up, Gregor? 'Gigolo' is a nasty word, especially in this context, especially since it's not even close to true. Or maybe that's my background. It's the principal paranoia of every rich girl's parents that somebody will marry her for her money."

"I don't know what brought it up," Gregor said. "I was looking at the street and thinking about my brother. Did I ever tell you I had a brother?"

"Yes. Older. Died in the army."

"Right. He's buried where my mother is, in the same cemetery where my wife is buried. I haven't been there in ages, and the last time I went I only went for Elizabeth. There ought to be something on the street to remember them by. I don't know what. I keep thinking of the Vietnam Veterans Memorial Wall, but that isn't what I mean at all, really. I don't know. Maybe we could carve something into the sidewalks. 'At this spot stood a five-story walk-up tenement where the apartments were all too small and where Sofia Valdanian Demarkian heard that one of her sons was dead and the other had been admitted to Harvard Business School.'"

"On the same day?"

"No, of course not. Nearly two decades apart. Doesn't it ever bother you? Or are all the places you grew up in still intact so that you can go back and see them exactly the way they were?"

"My childhood home has been inherited by a nonprofit foundation, and I wouldn't want to go back and see it in any case, especially if it were still intact, as you put it. Gregor, *why* aren't you working? I know I used to complain about how much time you spent on it, and I know I used to worry that you'd end up getting shot, but this isn't good for you. It really isn't. And it's not as if nothing interesting has come up. John Jackman—"

"Has he been talking to you behind my back?"

"It's hardly been behind your back. He's a friend of mine. He had that case in December of the woman who was poisoning her husbands, you remember; she'd already gotten away with three of them, and he was afraid she was going to get away with another—"

"She didn't."

"No, she didn't, Gregor, but she'd have been in jail a lot sooner if you'd helped, and you know it. And he asked for your help. I've never known you to turn down John when he asked. I think he was insulted."

"Then I'll have to apologize to him."

"This is impossible," Bennis said.

He heard her fussing with something behind him, but he didn't turn around to look at her. He was still looking down on the construction trucks and the people on the street. They were people he knew, by and large, but for some reason they didn't look familiar, any more than the street did. He wanted to think it was just the time of day. Back before the church had been destroyed, he and Bennis had gone to breakfast every day at seven, instead of eight, and maybe the people on that schedule had been different than the people on this one—but he really knew it was not. They looked wrong, though, all of them. They looked very wrong.

Behind him Bennis had come around the back of the couch and sat down. He could hear her feet going up on the coffee table, even though he knew she wasn't wearing shoes. She never wore shoes in the house. In the summer she didn't even wear socks.

"Listen," she said, "I know you feel responsible for that mess out there. I know you do. But nobody else does. Tibor doesn't. Lida doesn't. Hannah and Sheila and Howard don't. Nobody does, really. And it doesn't make sense for you to think that. And you know it."

"It's not that simple."

"It is that simple, Gregor. He'd have done what he did even if you'd never have existed—"

"He wouldn't have done what he did to this church."

"He'd have done it to some other church. Or to police headquarters. *She'd* have done what she did, too. She was unbalanced as hell. You have to know that."

"Tibor could have died."

"He didn't die. Nobody died. A lot of structural damage was done to the church, and now it's being rebuilt, that's all. And that's not necessarily a bad thing."

"It was a landmark."

"It was a landmark badly in need of updating. It was drafty. It needed a new heating system. It needed new flooring in the sacristy—"

"Well, for God's sake, Bennis, we could have done all that without blowing the damned thing up."

"Yes, I know we could have. My point is that the church was not a child, and it was not a pet, it was a building. And as sad as it is to see a building destroyed when it's been a vital part of the neighborhood for decades—"

"More than a century."

"More than a century. It's still just a building, Gregor, and it's being put back up. It's not being replaced by condominiums. You're not going to find a Wal-Mart staring at you from across the street."

"I don't think Wal-Mart builds in cities."

"I don't care where they build. You're making a huge leap of the imagination to give yourself a reason to feel guilty here. You're in some kind of clinical depression. You barely eat. You're driving Lida and Hannah crazy, and the Melajians think it's all my fault. We don't even talk anymore."

"We're talking now."

"No, we're not," Bennis said. "I'm lecturing you. There's a difference. You need to go back to work. It's not about making money or being a gigolo. It's not about whether I want you around the apartment. It's about your sanity."

The knot of people at the construction site had grown larger. It bothered Gregor to think that he hadn't noticed the new people come in. "The thing is," he said, "none of it interests me anymore. A woman who was poisoning her husbands. Well, yes. Women do that. For the insurance money. Because their husbands cheat on them. You might make a case for self-interest in the theory of women as serial killers. Women serial killers rarely kill for sexual satisfaction, which men almost always do. But you know, Bennis, I've been doing this for thirty years now. Over and over again. What's the point of doing it some more?"

"It interests you," Bennis said, "or at least it does when you get into it. And you help to get people off the street who are a danger to the innocent people on it."

"And there will always be a couple of dozen more out there whom I don't get off the street. Nobody can get them *all* off the street. They're—part of us.

That's what we don't ever accept, I think. We want them to be monsters and aliens, and they're just the kids next door and the women at the PTA meeting."

"So what? So we take the police off the streets and don't even bother to try?"

"I didn't say that," Gregor said. "I was just trying to explain why I'm not interested."

"Bullshit," Bennis said. "You are interested. I've seen you sitting up watching *American Justice* and *City Confidential*. It's not that you're not interested; it's that you don't want to get involved."

Gregor pressed his face against the glass. Father Tibor had been joined by Grace Feinmann. That was two people from the building who were out and about without his having noticed their leaving, and Grace lived above them, so it wasn't that. She was carrying a thick sheaf of papers and waving them around in front of Tibor's face. The papers were probably sheet music, and later today she would probably begin the practicing that would fill the house with harpsichord music until whenever it was her next concert started. *Probably, probably,* Gregor thought. Everything was probably, or probably not.

"I'm going to the Ararat," Bennis said. "I've got nothing against keeping you company under ordinary circumstances, but it ruins my day to spend breakfast with you in a funk. Get your coat and come with me."

"I'll still be in a funk."

"I'll have a lot of other people to take my mind off it."

Grace and Tibor had left the construction site and were on their way up the street. They would be going to the Ararat, too. Directly across from Gregor's apartment, Lida Arkmanian came out the front door of her town house and squinted in the direction of the construction. When Gregor got particularly maudlin, he wondered what would have happened to him if he had married Lida right after they'd both graduated from high school, which is what everybody but his mother had expected him to do. His mother had expected him to take advantage of that scholarship from the University of Pennsylvania, and Lida had married Frank Arkmanian and settled down on Cavanaugh Street.

"You know," he said, "maybe we ought to stop circling the question and just get married."

There was absolute silence from the couch behind him.

"This is good," he said. "I expected a lot of answers to that suggestion, Bennis, but I will admit I never anticipated silence."

"Is it a suggestion?" Bennis asked. "I couldn't tell. It sounded like an . . . observation."

"It was."

"Ah. Maybe you ought to try again if you ever decide to turn it into a suggestion."

"You're making this very hard for me, you know."

Bennis got up off the couch. "Maybe I'd just feel a little better if you'd actually look at me when you said things like that. I'm going to the Ararat, Gregor. Come if you want to."

There was more movement, more rustling, the sound of Bennis's feet slipping into clogs, the sound of clogs on the hardwood floor of the entryway, the sound of the apartment door opening and snicking quietly shut. Gregor stayed where he was until he saw Bennis come out the front door of their building and start up the street, a small, thin, irrepressibly elegant woman with a cloud of black hair that floated around her head like a storm. He tried to decide if he'd just proposed marriage to her or not. He really didn't know.

I don't want to get myself involved in anybody else's criminal conspiracies, he thought, but the sentence sounded pompous to him even as it echoed inside his head, and it wasn't what he had meant anyway. If he could figure out what he did mean, he might be able to do something about Bennis, and about a great many other things.

2

Gregor had been thinking about his brother, Stefan, because Stefan had had a fiancée when he went into the army, a Cavanaugh Street girl with Armenian parents who went to Holy Trinity Church every Sunday and worked part-time at a little bakery that had once existed two doors down from Ohanian's Middle Eastern Food. There was something that had changed for the worst about Cavanaugh Street. Gregor had loved that bakery when he was a child. He could take a quarter into that place and come out with a big piece of *loukoumia,* or those round honey pastries with the pistachio nuts whose name he could never remember anymore. Lida would know what they were called. She would probably even make him some. Once, about three weeks after they'd had the news that Stefan had died, Gregor had come across the girl he'd been engaged to sitting on the stoop in front of the bakery with her apron held up over her face, weeping silently and steadily and without the sobbing convulsions he had come to assume were natural to women in tears. The sight of her had fascinated him. She was crying for Stefan. He was sure of that. She was only crying, though, and not going to pieces, and for some reason that made her grief much deeper and all the more real. He had wanted to cry for Stefan himself, but he hadn't been able to. He had lain in bed night after night, staring into the dark in the direction of the ceiling, thinking about nothing. Stefan had been, and now he was not. He was nothing. There was nothing in the other bed in the room, and there would never be something again. Death had seemed to him then to be literally absence—not the absence of life, but absence in its essence, the *definition* of absence. He had really been very, very small, less than five years old, and he hadn't had the words he needed to describe what he felt. It was as if a great, gaping hole had opened up under his feet. It wasn't the pit of hell, the way the priest sometimes said. There was no fire down there. There was no devil. It was just a hole, going down, never stopping, a hole with nothing in it. That was what the girl seemed to understand, sitting there without sobbing, that nobody else around him did. He'd wanted to go up to her and sit beside her. He didn't think he could comfort her. He didn't think there was any comfort left in the world. He hoped that she could calm him. He was not afraid. You couldn't be afraid of nothing. He was only paralyzed, and for days it had seemed to him that there was no point in breathing.

Right at this split second, he was still standing at the window of his living room in his third-floor apartment on Cavanaugh Street, the new Cavanaugh Street, where the buildings were town houses or condominiums and the women wore fur coats without fear of being set on by animal rights activists. *Where death is only a rumor,* he thought, but that wasn't exactly right. People died here. They just didn't die the way Stefan had, or the way so many of the people had in the cases he had worked on over these last thirty years. Sometimes, when he had a hard time getting to sleep, he could see their faces in the only way he had ever known most of them, dead faces, laid out on gravel drives or carpeted bedroom floors, eyes glazed, mouths slack, flesh gray. He couldn't put names to most of them. You forgot the names after a while unless something truly awful had happened to make you remember. He remembered the names of most of the child victims. He lost the ones of the women raped and murdered by the men who thought killing was a natural part of sex. God, how many of those there had been. That was life in the FBI's Behavioral Sciences Unit, and now they didn't even use the unit anymore, or they'd reorganized it or something. He had never been a profiler. First he had been an investigator. Then he had been an administrator. If there was some explanation for why people did what they did, some reason that fit the greater purposes of the cosmos, why some men could only reach orgasm if the woman they were with was soon to be a corpse, Gregor didn't know what it was. He'd never understood murder on any level. Even the obvious murders—that woman of John Jackman's, who was killing her husbands for their insurance, racking up the cash, playing at killing the way high-stakes gamblers played at casinos—seemed to him overdone, overfelt, overemoted. Maybe the truth of it was that murders were committed by people who took themselves too seriously, by people who could not see into the future and understand that life would end for everybody, even for them, and that the things in it were not as important as that fact.

It's me who's taking myself too seriously, he thought now, although he really didn't entirely mean it. It was hard to look at yourself and know when you were being overwrought, especially when you were upset. Still, he was tired of standing the way he was standing. His back ached. The street below him was almost clear of people now. The sun was too high in the sky, although he could tell from what few people there were, and what people there had been, that, sun or no sun, it was very cold out there. He looked around and found his wallet and his cell phone on top of the television. He put them both in his pocket, although he often didn't carry the cell phone. *That* felt overwrought and ridiculous. There might be a point to it if you had children and worried about emergencies. There might be a point to it if you were the president of the United States and the fate of the world hung on your decisions—now *there* was a thought, the fate of the world hanging on the decisions of George W. Bush—or if you were the vice president and needed to know if the president had been assassinated. There was another thought. It didn't matter. He just thought it was silly, carrying a cell phone the way most people did, as if taking a call from their wives about what they wanted to have for dinner tonight was so important it couldn't wait until they were safely in an office or a phone booth and able to sit down when they talked.

He checked his other pocket for keys. He could always get into his place by asking old George Tekemanian, because old George had copies of all the keys, but old George wasn't always at home these days. Gregor got his long, black coat off the coat stand in the foyer and put it all the way on. He didn't bother looking for a hat. He didn't care how cold it was. He thought men looked ridiculous in hats. He'd thought that decades ago when all men were assumed to be required to wear those felt fedoras that served no other purpose than to make them look like Christmas trees topped by the angel of death.

He went down to the first floor and tapped on the door of old George's apartment just in case. There was no answer, meaning that old George had either gone down to the Ararat to schmooze or off with his grandson Martin and

Martin's wife, Angela, probably to buy a machine that cut cube steaks into paper dolls you could dress up in parsley nurse's uniforms. He went out onto the street and looked around. There was nothing much to look at. The street was as it had been since he had moved back to it soon after his wife, Elizabeth, had died and he had retired from the FBI and the only life he had ever felt completely comfortable in. By then he wasn't comfortable with that life either. He had no idea if he was comfortable with this one.

He stopped at the construction site and spent a moment or two watching the crews hauling a large piece of stone to a well of concrete that seemed to have been constructed as a place for it. If he'd thought about it at the time, he would have said that he expected a new church to rise on the site of the old one in about six months to a year. It had been longer than six months, and the new church had barely been started. There had been a lot of debris to clear away, and too much left standing that could not be left standing if reconstruction was to take place. For months nothing had happened out here but blasting and tearing down and hauling away, as if the contractors were in league with the people who had bombed the place and they only wanted to finish the job.

He made himself stop looking at it and walked on up the street. He considered buying the paper at the newsstand or Ohanian's and decided against both. The news made him mostly depressed these days. He went into the Ararat and looked around. Bennis was not in the restaurant. This was where she had said she was going, but this was not where she was. Tibor was sitting by himself on the long, low padded benches of the window table. Grace was gone, too.

Gregor unbuttoned his coat and wondered what it meant that he hadn't noticed the cold while he was walking outside. He put the coat on the hook next to the window table and slid in opposite Tibor.

"Where's Grace?" he said. "I saw you walking with Grace near the church this morning."

"She went with Bennis to buy a velvet dress," Tibor said. "This is a requirement for the concert Grace is playing at the week after next, I think. Or next week. She needs a velvet dress."

Linda Melajian came over with a cup and a saucer and the Pyrex coffeepot. "Gregor," she said, "I'll order you a breakfast special as soon as I get Hannah Krekorian her cruller."

"I don't want the breakfast special, Linda, thanks. I'm not hungry. I'll just have coffee."

"Oh, for God's sake," Linda said.

"What?" Gregor said. "I'm not hungry. It happens. I can't always eat two pounds of sausage and potatoes in the morning."

"Forget always," Linda said, "you haven't eaten anything for breakfast for two weeks. It's like you're on a hunger strike or something."

"Do I look like I'm on a hunger strike?"

"So, fine, what is it? You've decided you hate the food here? You're too good for us?"

"*Linda.*"

"I'll get you the breakfast special," Linda said, "and you'll eat it."

She whirled around and went marching away across the room to the narrow door at the back that led to the kitchen. Gregor watched her with something like shock.

"That was interesting," he said. "Whatever is wrong with her?"

Tibor cleared his throat. He was younger than Gregor, but he had been more hardly used. He looked older. This morning he also looked tired.

"It is you there's something wrong with, Krekor," he said. "You do not act like yourself."

"I don't see who else I could be acting like. I am myself."

"You are not yourself," Tibor said again. Gregor might have been imagining it, but Tibor's accent sounded thicker than it had for years. Tibor was having the breakfast special. He had a big oval plate in front of him with scrambled eggs, sausage, fried potatoes, and toast spread across it like the debris looters leave after a citywide blackout.

"Listen," Gregor said. "I think I proposed to Bennis this morning."

"You think?"

"It was a little complicated. I didn't exactly put it—in the form of a question. I didn't exactly—"

"Well, Krekor, you must have done something exactly because Bennis was here and she was not in a good mood. She was in a very bad mood. She was, ah, furious—"

"Angry as hell?"

"That, yes. Angry as hell. Snapping at people. Throwing things. I do not think this is the way she would be if you had just proposed to her. I think she would have said yes and gone shopping."

"Bennis doesn't shop much."

"She would shop for a wedding, Krekor, believe me."

"Right," Gregor said.

Linda Melajian came back with the breakfast special in her hands. She slammed the plate down on the table in front of Gregor hard enough to make the sausages jump. "There was one coming up and I diverted it to you. Eat something. Maybe you'll make more sense."

"Why am I not making sense?" Gregor said.

"Men," Linda Melajian said. "God, I don't understand what any of you think you're doing. I really don't. You've all got your heads screwed on backward, and then you blame it all on us when things go wrong."

"Linda," Gregor said, "what are you talking about?"

"Eat your breakfast," Linda said, turning her back on them and marching away again.

Gregor pushed the plate away from him. He couldn't imagine eating all that food. It looked like one of those precautionary photographs in a nutrition textbook: eat a meal like this, dripping with fat, and you'll die of coronary disease before you're thirty.

"Wonderful," he said, "now she's mad at me, and I don't even know why."

"She's mad at you because Bennis is mad at you, Krekor; you don't need to think about it. But you are not yourself. And you should think about that."

"Am I really not myself just because I don't feel like working? Is there something about me that ceases to be a real human being if I don't want to investigate another murder? Other people retire. They go fishing or they join a country club and play golf. They read books. Why is that supposed to be so completely off-limits for me?"

"You have not joined a country club to play golf, Krekor; and more to the point, you're not happy. Tell me about proposing marriage to Bennis."

Gregor took a long sip of coffee. It was too hot. It made his throat scream. "I told you. I didn't do it straight off like that. I didn't ask the question. I just . . . brought it up."

"Brought what up?"

"The fact that we probably ought to be married."

"And you said it like that? That you 'probably ought to be'?"

Gregor thought back about it, but he couldn't remember exactly what he'd said. He did remember the sound of Bennis's voice, and it hadn't been good.

"Something like that," he told Tibor. "I don't really remember how it went. I was thinking of my brother, Stefan."

"The one who died in the army."

"That seems to be all I've ever told anybody about him. But, yes. That one. The only brother I've ever had. I was thinking about what it was like when he died, what I had felt like, and I was looking at the construction on the church.

64

You can't really see it from my window, you know, but you can see the trucks parked out front. So I was looking at that, and then I just sort of brought it up."

"And?"

"And she grabbed her stuff and walked out. I'd say stormed out, but when Bennis storms she's a lot more active than that. I don't seem to be able to do anything right these days."

Tibor reached across the table and took one of Gregor's sausages. It was one of those paradoxes that tended to make Gregor depressed. Gregor was tall, but anything but thin. He looked like an older, out-of-shape Harrison Ford, or what Harrison Ford would have looked like if he'd aged ten years and never had a personal trainer. Tibor was short and wiry and as thin as bone, no matter what he ate.

"It is not the wrong thing," Tibor said, "asking Bennis to marry you. So I assume that you didn't ask. You said something instead."

"Asking is saying something," Gregor pointed out, "but I didn't put it in the form of a question. And then she asked me if I was asking, and I said not exactly, I was observing, or something like that."

"And now she has gone shopping. Yes, Krekor, I do see. You will have to find her and ask her properly. It will be all right."

"I don't think I can ask her properly," Gregor said. "It's—I don't know what it is. It feels wrong on some level."

"It seems wrong to you that you and Bennis should be married?" Tibor was surprised.

"No," Gregor said. "It seems wrong to me that I should ask."

"You think she should ask you?" Tibor was even more surprised.

"No," Gregor said, feeling exasperated. "I don't know, Tibor, I'm sorry. It seemed wrong to ask; and then she was upset with me because I didn't want to help John with his black widow case, and I couldn't get across to her how boring it all sounded. One more black widow. One more serial killer. Over and over again, the same things, the same motives, the same means, the same situations. You'd think human beings would have more creativity than that."

"And that's why you don't want to work? Because murder has become boring?"

"I don't know," Gregor said.

Linda Melajian came back, saw that a single sausage had been eaten, and didn't bother to give another lecture. She just refilled his cup with coffee and went away.

"I think you should go and find Bennis and make things up with her," Tibor said. "Not go now. Wait until she comes back from shopping. She's not in a good mood when she shops. But when she comes back, make it up with her."

"I suppose," Gregor said, but he did more than suppose really. He had every intention of making it up with Bennis, who was the only other person on the planet besides himself that he considered entirely sane. It was like that old joke about the Amish couple in their isolated farmhouse. "Everybody in the world is crazy but me and thee, and I'm not too sure about thee."

He picked up his fork and tried a potato, but it tasted like cardboard and sand.

3

Twenty minutes later, just as a jackhammer went off at the construction site, Gregor Demarkian walked home down Cavanaugh Street. He had come far enough back into his senses so that he did notice the cold this time. It was brutal. The wind was brutal, too. Construction projects sometimes came to a halt because of bad weather, but maybe that was only for snow or rain. This bad weather had not stopped work on this site.

He stopped in front and watched the workers doing things he didn't understand. He hadn't the faintest idea how a building went up or what kept it up. He kept his hands in his pockets and his head down in the collar of his coat. The jackhammer made a wall of noise, blocking out the world.

He didn't hear his cell phone go off—he couldn't have, even if the ringer had been on—he felt it, vibrating against his hand at the bottom of his pocket.

He pulled it out and said, "Yes?" into the air, where a receiver ought to be.

Somebody said something he didn't understand, and he said, "Wait."

The jackhammer was making it impossible for him to hear anything at all. He walked up the street toward his apartment a little ways, and then a little ways more, until he got to the intersection and had to cross.

"Sorry," he said, "there was construction going on. This is Gregor Demarkian. Who is this?"

There was so long a pause on the other end of the line that Gregor thought for a moment that it was a wrong number. Then he heard somebody clearing his throat.

"Mr. Demarkian?" the someone said. Gregor thought the voice was familiar and not at the same time. It was a very young voice, and it sounded as if it had been crying.

"Listen," the voice said, "I'm sorry to bother you, and I don't know if you remember me, but we've met; and I thought you were the only person I could think of who would know what to do. And you stayed with us that time, and you did know what to do. So I'm sorry to be so messed up. I mean, my name is Mark DeAvecca—"

TWO

1

Gregor Demarkian would not have agreed to go up to Massachusetts to see Mark DeAvecca if he had believed that anybody had actually murdered anybody else. His malaise about work was neither feigned nor neurotic. The idea of "investigating" anything made his mind numb. Things did not need to be investigated as much as they needed to be understood. That was the decision he had come to, on one of the long and all-too-silent nights after he and Bennis had had their argument in the living room. It wasn't that Bennis wasn't speaking to him. Bennis was incapable of not speaking to anyone. She was the kind of woman who preferred to have her fights bare-knuckled and in overtime. It was more that they weren't having a fight at all. Bennis was speaking to him and usually polite about it. She went down to the Ararat with him for dinner. She went shopping with Donna Moradanyan Russell and came home with packages. She made coffee and sat at the kitchen table with him while she drank it. It was more what she wasn't doing that was the problem. She wasn't chattering to him about matters on Cavanaugh Street or with her publishers. She wasn't reaching for him in bed at unexpected times of the night. She wasn't lecturing him. What bothered him the most, if he were honest about it, was that she wasn't fighting with him. It was an ominous sign. Bennis had been fighting with him almost from the day they'd met. It was her preferred method of engagement. Gregor didn't like to think what it meant when she was not engaged in it.

He tried to tell her about Mark DeAvecca after he got the call—after all, she'd met him; she knew his mother slightly and his stepfather very well—but although she had listened for a few minutes in what appeared to be interest, she'd drifted off on him in no time at all.

"Do what you want to do," she'd said, while he was caught in one more futile attempt to explain what had so bothered him about that phone call.

He'd looked away and tried again. "He doesn't sound like himself," he'd said. "He sounds drugged."

Maybe it wasn't so strange that a teenaged boy sounded drugged. If it had been any other teenaged boy, Gregor wouldn't have thought so. Maybe Bennis hadn't spent enough time with Mark to realize how out of character it all was. There were other "maybes," but Gregor didn't want to think about them. He made himself think about the fact that "drugged" didn't really describe what he was hearing.

Eventually, he'd made a few phone calls. He didn't know anybody in the Windsor Police. He hadn't even known there was a town called Windsor in Massachusetts until Mark called. He did know many people in the Boston Police, and Boston was close enough, the city of which Windsor was a suburb. Everything was Webs these days, cities most of all. He was old enough to remember when the suburbs were an embarrassment that nobody from the city ever wanted to admit to having come from.

The man he finally found in Boston was named Walter Cray. He'd trained for the Bureau once about twenty years ago—Gregor would have been a very new special agent and no longer at Quantico—and then decided it wasn't for him. He'd come back to Boston and joined the police. He'd kept in touch with two of the members of his training class, and one of those was a good friend of Gregor's from their days on kidnapping detail.

"Definitely a suicide," Walter Cray had said, when he'd had a chance to look into the situation and call back. "I've had an earful of the forsenics all morning. No chance of anything but suicide—"

"There's always a chance, though, isn't there?" Gregor interrupted.

"If you want to think Agatha Christie, yes. If you want to think real life, no. Kid hung himself from one of those sprinkler pipes. In his dorm room at, let's see, Hayes House. He stood on a drafting stool. You know what those are? Like bar stools, and almost as tall, but a little more sturdy."

"Yes, I think I do know what those are. The stool was in the room when they found him?"

"Kicked away to the side and in the room," Walter said. "It was the roommate who found him. My guy in Windsor says the roommate is a mess, drugged to the gills in all likelihood, but of course they can't go barging in there and accusing him of it. Don't ever think that money doesn't matter, even in the drug war. It matters in more ways than you'd think."

"I know," Gregor said. "What about the note?"

There was a pause on the other end of the line. "Okay," Walter said, "that was the peculiar thing. There wasn't any note."

"It's not all that peculiar for there not to be a note, surely," Gregor said. "Lots of suicides don't leave notes."

"True enough," Walter said, "but then you've got to look at the room. It was tossed, no matter what those people say about how messy the boys were."

"Tossed?"

"Ripped to shreds. And the window was left open."

"In below-zero temperatures?" Gregor interrupted.

"Right," Walter said, "and the room was freezing."

Gregor threw it away. As if someone was trying to disguise a time of death, which doesn't make sense with a suicide.

"I know," Walter said, "it's one of the things the guys in Windsor aren't happy about. They're also not happy about the location. You know anything about Windsor Academy?"

"No." Gregor's knowledge of upscale private schools was limited to the things he'd heard in the Bureau and from Bennis, and he couldn't keep them straight in his head for any amount of time longer than necessary to make a polite noise in a conversation that bored him.

"Windsor used to be a girls' school," Walter said. "Then, around 1975, it went co-ed; and when it did it rewrote its mission somewhat. Not that it hadn't always been sort of liberal, you understand."

"What do you mean by 'liberal'? Do you mean the rules were relaxed?"

"Well, that too. No, I mean liberal politically. And not just liberal. You've heard all those stories about private schools where the alumni refused to speak to Franklin Roosevelt because he was a traitor to his class. There are schools that make a habit of being a traitor to their class. Windsor was always one of them: in favor of the New Deal; in favor of the welfare state."

"That's a positive thing, surely," Gregor said. "What would you want instead?"

"Not saying I'd want anything," Walter said. "I'm just trying to put you in the picture. After 1975, Windsor went not just liberal but right out on the limb of limousine radical. Not as radical as some place like Putney, you know, where the kids run a farm and do manual labor because it's good for them—"

"At thirty thousand dollars a year?"

"Yeah, I know. That's what I thought. Anyway, not that radical, but radical anyway. They've got a Socialist Club at Windsor. They've even got a Liberal Club. They don't have a conservative club, and you're not going to find anybody admitting to voting Republican. They're big on 'diversity' in the most obvious modern sense of the word. They go out of their way to attract African American and Hispanic students—"

"But there's nothing wrong with that either," Gregor said. "None of this sounds in the least bit negative—"

"It's because I can't explain it very well," Walter said. "It's, I don't know, very—fake, in a way. It's hard to put a finger on it. Are you intending to go up there?"

"I was thinking of it, yes."

"You'll see in a day or two. It's impossible not to see. It's an attitude. It's like a miasma almost."

"You've been there?"

"We took our daughter up to look at the place," Walter said. "She ended up at Exeter with a nice scholarship. We're very proud of her."

"You must be."

"She hated Windsor on sight," Walter said, "and I don't blame her. It's all so—forced. As if everything's intentional. It's all so self-consciously on the right side. I'm making a hash of this. The thing is, about the kid who died."

"Michael Feyre." Gregor had written it down.

"Right, Michael Feyre," Walter said. "He's the kind of kid Windsor goes looking for, except that he's white, which means they never would have had him if he hadn't had money. I'm making even more of a hash of this. Michael Feyre was born to a single mother in some godforsaken small town in northwest Connecticut, one of those women who get pregnant for the first time at fifteen and work in convenience stores. Windsor likes poor kids, but Windsor prefers their poor kids to be minorities. You know what I mean? It was one of the things my daughter picked up on and didn't like."

"But they accepted this Michael Feyre," Gregor said.

"Not as a poor kid," Walter said, "that's the intriguing thing. Michael Feyre's mother is named Delilah. She goes by 'Dee.' She's famous in New England. She was all over the papers here because she won the lottery. And not just the lottery. She won a nine-figure Powerball jackpot."

"*Nine* figures?"

"Something like three hundred million dollars," Walter said. "I don't remember the exact amount. She worked in this convenience store. One night she got off work and bought six Powerball tickets—and kazam. Trailer park to anything she wants in half an hour. She went on Jay Leno, I think."

"My God," Gregor said.

"Well, people do win the damn things," Walter said. "And she did the kind of thing people do when they win, I guess, including sending the kids to private schools. I don't know why she sent Michael to Windsor, but she did. And now he's dead. And she's not much interested in fading into the sunset."

"She thinks he was murdered?" Gregor said.

"Not exactly, from what I can figure out," Walter said, "but she thinks something is screwy up there and that there are things they aren't telling her, and she's probably right. Those schools have a near mania about lawsuits, and she's in a position to launch a good one and never feel the pain. And that's why the Windsor cops are so nervous. On the one side, they've got the school, with serious old money and serious power behind it. On the other side, they've got Dee Feyre, who's hopping mad and possessed of huge gobs of money, plus pretty damned savvy about how to use the papers to get her story out. The school has managed to keep the lid on it for the past week, but that's not going to last long. I'll bet you anything that by Saturday, the story's going to be all over everywhere, and then the shit is really going to hit the fan. You going to go up there and make it worse?"

"Maybe," Gregor said.

"You want a contact in the Windsor Police?"

"I don't want them to feel that I'm stepping on their toes," Gregor said. "I'm not going up there to interfere with their investigation. I happen to know the family of Michael Feyre's roommate."

"DeAvecca," Walter said, laughing. "I forgot about that. The roommate is Elizabeth Toliver's son and Jimmy Card's stepson. More shit-hits-the-fan material."

"I agree. Mark's distraught."

"I can bet. And high as a kite, if my guy is to be believed. Listen, let me give you Brian Sheehy's number. He's chief of police. He won't mind your coming up. Hell, he just might welcome it. It wouldn't hurt him any to have somebody to take the heat off when the going gets rough, and it most definitely is going to get rough."

"I'm not going up to investigate," Gregor said.

"He won't care. I'll give him a call and tell him you're coming. I mean it, he'll think you're a godsend. They're all holding their breath down there. It's only a matter of time."

"Right," Gregor said. Then he thought to wonder what it was that Walter Cray wasn't telling him.

2

It wasn't only Walter Cray. It was Mark DeAvecca who wasn't telling him things, although he thought that with Mark it might be the result of the confusion that seemed to have taken over his entire personality since the last time Gregor had seen him. He tried to discuss that with Bennis, too, but she never got interested. He would start and she would interrupt him with questions about the kind of trivialities she'd never bothered to think about before. Did they have enough toilet paper on hand or should she pick some up when she and Donna went out to the Costco warehouse store on Saturday? Did he think it made sense to switch the can shelf in the pantry with the jar shelf? Which did he prefer, the blue stoneware plates or the white china ones? It was like living with a lobotomized Martha Stewart before the indictment. Bennis talked about vegetables. She talked about cutlery. She talked about the drapes in the living room. She even managed to deliver a somewhat spirited monologue on the relative merits of paper versus cloth napkins. Other than that, she was oddly disconnected, as if all the things that would ordinarily matter to her—the people on Cavanaugh Street, the news, Gregor himself—had been wiped clean from her mind. It was eerie living with her. It was as if she had become a ghost.

"I thought she'd be glad I'm taking an interest in Mark's problem," he told Fr. Tibor Kasparian at the train station as he was getting ready to board the Amtrak to Boston. "The day before yesterday, she was telling me she wanted me to go back to work. And here I am. Not exactly back to work, but at least doing something of the sort of thing she had in mind. And she still isn't speaking to me."

"I thought you said she was speaking to you, Krekor," Tibor said, "only not in a very good way."

"It's like living with a robot," Gregor said. "I don't know what she expects of me. I don't know what she wants anymore."

"She wants you to say something about that remark about marriage," Tibor said.

Gregor brushed it off. "She didn't exactly leap for joy at it the first time I said it. I'd say that this relationship was just on the way out. It happens. Except that two days ago, it was fine. And I can't see Bennis ending a relationship in less than thirty thousand words."

"Your train is here, Krekor," Tibor said.

His train was there. It had been there all along. He got onto it with his head still mired in confusion. He couldn't remember how long it had been since he'd started a case with this little interest in its outcome. Except that it wasn't a case, he reminded himself. He was only going to Massachusetts because there was no danger it would ever become a case. He stowed his suitcase above his head in first class and thought about just how badly it was packed. Bennis usually packed for him. This time, she had barely glanced at the case lying open on the bed. The clothes had piled up in it without order or organization. Gregor had no idea how women got so many clothes into suitcases. When he packed, the damned things filled up before he had half of what he needed. He thought he might have been trying to look pitiful in the bedroom while he worked, but he wasn't sure. Looking pitiful was not something he was good at. He was too tall, and he had spent too many years cultivating an aura of competence and decisiveness. Bennis, at any rate, did not seem to notice. She went in and out, back and forth, and ten minutes before he was due to leave, she left herself and went down the street to he knew not where. Maybe she had gone to Donna's so that she wouldn't be around to be forced to kiss him good-bye.

Gregor had brought the material he'd amassed on Windsor Academy to look over on his trip, but he couldn't make himself concentrate on it. He had a nice little pile, both printed off the Web site and cadged from a friend of Bennis's in Philadelphia who ran the guidance department of a private elementary school. It was a good thing he'd been introduced to the woman already. Bennis didn't mention her when he mentioned Windsor Academy, and she didn't offer to make a call and grease the wheels when Gregor mentioned her himself. Come to think of it, Gregor thought, Bennis herself probably knew something about Windsor Academy and half its Board of Trustees. She hadn't mentioned that either.

New England went by in a blur of ice and dangerously weighted overhead wires. He had never really liked Connecticut, and he liked Massachusetts even less. They were both far too enraptured by their revolutionary past and far too little interested in being revolutionary. He tried to read through the copies of the *Windsor Academy Chronicles* Bennis's friend had given him. They were copies of the kind of thing colleges sent to alumni to keep their interest up in contributing to their alma mater. The stories were all laudatory and studiously noncontroversial. The back of each issue was taken up by year-by-year class reports that all read as if their writers chirped when they spoke. Gregor got similar magazines from the University of Pennsylvania four times a year. He wondered what it was about class notes that nobody could ever tell the truth in them. They would announce that old Sheldon DeWitt had died suddenly in his home at the much-too-early age of fifty-four. They would not mention that Sheldon had drunk himself to death after being released from federal prison after serving a ten-year term for a stock-fraud scheme that had destroyed the venerable brokerage house where he'd worked for two decades. It was even odder when you realized that Sheldon's story had been all over the news when it happened and the subject of a true-crime book and a made-for-television movie.

Gregor Demarkian didn't recognize any of the names in the class notes section of the *Windsor Academy Chronicles*. He didn't know if that was because he really didn't know them or because he couldn't focus. He found himself wondering if Bennis would have known them. There were times when he thought Bennis knew everybody on the planet, or at least everybody who might at any time have had any reason to be called "prominent." Maybe he was just thinking about Bennis, with an excuse or without one. He had been thinking about Bennis more often than not now for over ten years. He was sure that, although relationships changed, this one would not change like this, this fast, over just one remark he'd made about marriage—or something. He was, he realized, completely unsteady. He wanted to get out his cell phone and call Bennis now, wherever she was, and demand an explanation. He didn't do it because he was afraid she'd give him one.

When he got to Boston, he had two choices. He could take public transportation—first the MTA, then a trolley out to Windsor—or he could take a cab, which would cost an arm and a leg. He decided on the cab. He didn't care about the money, and he was too old to leap nimbly on and off subway cars. He stood in the cab line less than a minute before he found somebody willing to go out to the suburbs; and as soon as he got settled in the backseat, he got out his cell phone and called, not Bennis—although his fingers almost did it all by themselves—but Mark DeAvecca. The first number he called gave him an answering machine. He checked his book again and called the second one, which turned out to be Mark's cell phone. It rang and rang. Gregor checked his watch. Maybe he was in class. It was only two o'clock. He hung up and checked the book again. Mark had a pager number. It was incredible the way these kids were wired up these days. Gregor searched around his pockets until he found his own pager and sent up a silent prayer that Mark would be able to receive actual messages on his. Then he typed in:

HAVE ARRIVED, ON WAY TO WINDSOR INN

and sent the thing.

That is, he thought he sent it. He was never entirely sure. This was something else he needed Bennis for. Bennis understood the machines. Tibor understood the machines. Gregor was awash in a sea of his own ignorance. If the time ever came for a truly paperless society, he would be dead meat, lost and homeless without a clue as to how to work his own pager.

Boston became the Boston suburbs. It barely mattered, at first, since city block blended into city block without change. Then the landscape got greener, and the houses got farther apart, and the architecture became clapboard and Federalist instead of brick and generic. There were signs everywhere marking historic sites. He got out the *Windsor Academy Chronicles* again, but they made no more sense to him now than they had on the train.

What bothered him, deep down, was that his relationship with Bennis *had* changed as the result of that one small comment, and that would mean that it had never been what he thought it was all this time. It was not the kind of thing he was good at thinking about. It was not logical. It was not linear. It was not sane. It was information in a language he didn't think he knew how to speak. It made him feel hollow, as if his rib cage were an echo chamber, and all it was doing was delivering bad news.

3

Mark DeAvecca was waiting for him at the front door of the Windsor Inn when he got there, but in the first few moments getting out of the cab, Gregor didn't recognize him. The cabby put his suitcase on the inn's front step and took his fare and tip without comment. Gregor watched what looked like a homeless man hovering in the background, shifting restlessly from foot to foot as if he were on speed. Then the cabby retreated and the homeless man came forward. Gregor was just about to turn away brusquely and grab his suitcase when he realized it was Mark.

"Good God," he said, "what's happened to you?"

"Excuse me?" Mark looked confused. Gregor saw immediately what Walter Cray had been referring to on the phone. Mark not only looked drugged out, he looked as if he had been drugged out nonstop for months. His hair was matted with sweat. His clothes were not quite clean. There was a stain running down the front of his yellow cotton sweater, and it was so dingy and stretched out of shape it was barely possible to tell that it had once been expensive. He rubbed the palms of his hands together compulsively. "I think I need more coffee," Mark said. "I think I'm falling asleep."

Gregor thought he was on the verge of passing out, but he didn't say so. He motioned toward the front door with his head and started inside. Mark followed him, much too slowly, looking completely disoriented. Gregor stopped at the front desk and got the key from a bored-looking man who took the time to look past Gregor's shoulder at Mark. The look of distaste was palpable.

"Room two seventeen," the man said.

Gregor headed for the elevators with Mark still in tow. They were self-service elevators. That was a good thing because the few other guests in the lobby were looking at Mark very oddly, and Gregor didn't blame them.

"I told you this was a nice place," Mark said, getting into the elevator beside Gregor. He looked dubiously at Gregor's case. "Would you like me to carry that? I always carry my mom's suitcases, or I used to before she married Jimmy. I'm sorry I didn't say anything before."

"That's all right." Gregor kept a grip on his case. Mark did not look capable of carrying anything for very long.

They got to the second floor. The elevator doors opened. They got out and walked down the hall, Gregor watching the numbers of the doors and moving slowly because Mark seemed to be having a hard time moving. They got to room 217 and Gregor unlocked the door.

"Are you sure you're all right?" he asked Mark, even though he knew the answer to that one. Mark was not all right. He wasn't even close to all right.

Mark came in behind him and headed across the room to the chairs near the window. He sat down and shook his head. "I'm fine," he said. "I'm actually having a pretty good day. Sometimes I can't think at all, but it's not like that now. I'm just so tired. And I've got a sore throat. And I've got work jobs."

"Work jobs?"

"Yeah," Mark said. "It's—it's sort of like detention. When you screw up, they give you work jobs to do to make up for the infraction."

Mark didn't look capable of making his bed, never mind doing something called "work jobs." Gregor threw his suitcase on the bed and opened it. "You're a mess," he said. "Have you got any idea what you look like? What's happened to you?"

Mark put his face in his hands. "You know," he said. "I know what everybody thinks, and it isn't true. I'm not taking drugs, unless you count caffeine as a drug, which I guess it is, but you know what I mean. I just can't remember things. I keep losing things. I've lost my student ID twice, and I need that to get my allowance out of my student account. I just forget."

Gregor came to the edge of the bed and sat down. "Mark, if you're not on drugs, there's something seriously and truly wrong with you. You need to be hospitalized or something. You're—"

"I know," Mark said. "I found this thing, we studied it in biology, called Huntington's chorea. It fits perfectly. But it can't be that because there isn't anybody in my family with it. I thought maybe my dad, you know, might have had it, because he died so young maybe it just hadn't shown up yet; but then one of his parents had to have had it, and my dad's mom is still alive and she's fine, and my dad's dad died at sixty something and he never had it. So it can't be that."

"What does your mother say?"

Mark looked up. "I haven't said anything to my mother. Well, I mean, yeah, I have, sort of. But I haven't, you know, made a thing about it. It's hard to explain. She thinks I look pale, so she got me these vitamins." He rooted around in his coat and came up with a prescription bottle. He shook the last capsule onto his hand. "I'd better take this. I don't think it does any good. And maybe they're right, do you know what I mean? Maybe it's just me. Maybe I'm just too stupid to be here."

"You're one of the least stupid people I've ever met in my life."

"I'd have said I was smart enough before I got here, but I don't know anymore. Do you know what I did last week?"

"No."

"I got a zero on a quiz," Mark said. "A *history* quiz. An *American* history quiz. It's usually my best subject. And the other weird thing was that it was on the election of 1800: Thomas Jefferson and John Adams. I read a book about it last summer. And I couldn't remember any of it. I sat there and looked at the paper and none of it made any sense at all. And of course they think I didn't study a damn, except that I did, and it just didn't matter. My mind went completely blank. I got questions wrong on stuff I knew cold before I ever came to Windsor. Maybe it's psychological. Maybe I just don't want to be here."

"Why don't you leave then? I can't believe your mother would insist on your staying if she knew you didn't want to."

Mark looked away. "That would be quitting. I don't like to quit."

"Better quitting than killing yourself," Gregor said. He looked back at the clothes in his suitcase. "Look, we're more or less the same size—I'm heavier than you are and a bit taller, but I've got some things that will work. Sweat-pants."

"You wear sweatpants?"

"Sometimes. It seemed like a good idea to bring some. You could fit into those. And I've got a sweatshirt. And some brand-new boxer shorts still in their store bag. Go take a shower, and I'll order us some room service. When was the last time you had something to eat? You look like you've lost twenty pounds."

"I went to lunch," Mark said. "I think we had pasta. I don't remember. Did I tell you about that on the phone? I can't remember anything."

"You said something about it, yes." Gregor got up and started looking through his things. The sweatpants were black. The sweatshirt was a deep ma-roon. Bennis must have picked it out for him. He put both of those on the bed and went looking for the bag with the boxer shorts in it.

"It's not just that Michael died," Mark said. "I can still see it in my head. It was incredible. And they wanted to put me back in that room. Did I tell you? The police are finished so they wanted me to move back in. They still want me to move back in. The dorms are all full. They don't have any place else to put me."

"Where have you been staying while the police did their work?" Gregor found the shorts. *Socks,* he thought, and went looking for those.

"I've been staying with one of the houseparents. He's not married or any-thing, so he's got some extra space. But that's not a good situation because he hates me. God, I sound stupid. I sound like one of those complete fuckups who are always complaining about how everybody hates them, but the real truth of it is that they're fuckups."

"What is it you've been—screwing up while you've been staying with this houseparent?"

"What? Oh well, I'm sort of a slob. I've always been a slob. That's not new to Windsor. But the thing is, I don't know. I don't know how to explain it. They think I'm not smart enough to be here. And they think—"

"What?"

"I don't know," Mark said. He tried straightening his spine, but it was a halfhearted effort. "I know Michael committed suicide, Mr. Demarkian. I know it's not a murder, okay? But there are things, things I think I saw—"

"You only think?"

"I could have been hallucinating," Mark said. "I think I do that sometimes. I'm not sure. And sometimes I black out. Did I tell you about that, about blacking out?"

"No."

"One day I was crossing the street right out on Main Street here, or I think I was, I think I must have been. The thing is, I can't remember it. I don't know how I got there. It was the middle of the afternoon and there was a lot of traffic and I just sort of . . . came to in the middle of this intersection. And people were honking at me and giving me the finger and screaming at me. I don't know how I got there. I don't know how long I was standing there. I was just standing there, not moving. And I don't know why."

"Mark, listen to me." Gregor sat down on the edge of the bed again. "You really do need to be in the hospital. There's got to be something physically wrong with you."

"I think so, too, but I can't imagine what," Mark said. "I must have looked through that medical book twenty times. More. Huntington's chorea was the only thing I came up with. And I feel like such a jerk, do you know what I mean? I don't fail at things. I really don't. Except now that's all I do. And then Michael—" His hand came up and fluttered in the air. He shrugged. "I don't know how to explain it. But there's something wrong. And there was that thing I saw, and maybe it was a hallucination, but I don't think so. So I thought, you know, you could come up and check into it."

"I did come up."

"Yeah, I know. Thank you. I'm sorry to be such a . . . whatever. To be so out of it. I'm not all the time, you know. Sometimes I'm half-sane for a couple of days, and then it goes back like this."

"Take a shower," Gregor said. He got up and threw the boxer shorts and sweat clothes into Mark's lap. "You'll feel better when you get cleaned up. I'll call for room service. Is there something you'd particularly like to eat?"

"Just coffee," Mark said. "I don't have an appetite much these days."

"Take a shower," Gregor said.

Mark bunched the clothes into his hands and stood up. He swayed when he got to his feet. For one nervous moment, Gregor was afraid he was going to fall over. Then he righted himself and began to walk across the room to the bathroom. He walked, Gregor thought, like an old man. Father Tibor, who was at least middle-aged and who had led a very hard life in the Soviet Union before coming to America, was more steady on his feet.

Mark went into the bathroom and shut the door. Gregor waited to hear the sound of the shower going on. When he did hear it, he went around the side of the bed to where the phone was and took it off the hook. It was a good thing that it was almost impossible to hear human speech over the sound of running water. He got out his address book and flipped through it. He did not want to call room service right off.

The phone was picked up on the other end by a secretary, which he had been expecting. People like Elizabeth Toliver did not answer their own phones, especially in the middle of a working day when they were in their offices.

"This is Gregor Demarkian," Gregor said. "If Liz is available, I'd appreciate it very much if she'd talk to me. Tell her I'm up in Windsor, Massachusetts, and I've got something to tell her about Mark."

The secretary made all the right noises, and Gregor sat back to wait until Liz picked up. He hoped Mark was going to take a very long shower.

THREE

1

Barrett House was a girls' dorm, and under most circumstances Marta Coelho found it unbearable. Today, with classes called off and an edict come down from on high that they were all supposed to spend the afternoon in their offices "making themselves available" to "any student in need," she thought it was a kind of haven. Marta did not like being in her office when she had no papers to grade. She couldn't sit there reading the way some of the other faculty did, and she was no good at inventing activities for herself to do during office hours. Some teachers just forced appointments, calling out one student or the other and insisting that he had to show up and be seen, or scheduling make-up quizzes and exams so that they coincided with the time spent sitting at their desks. Still other teachers had students who actually wanted to visit. Marta didn't know what to think about that. She had always expected to be a good teacher. She was very competent in her field. Even stuck here in the suburbs of Boston in this joke of a job she had written two papers and submitted them to conferences for the summer. She tried to keep out of her mind the fact that institutions mattered. No matter how good her papers were, they would be judged wanting next to papers from faculty at colleges and universities and even more wanting next to those from faculty at *good* colleges and universities. Academia was a hierarchy. It was no wonder that so many academics were obsessed with gender, race, and especially class. They lived in the only caste society in America. The stratification was far worse on campuses and among them than it would ever be in America at large. Marta knew because she had come from the bottom of that particular pyramid in the real world, and yet she had been able to negotiate it. There was no way to negotiate this. Judgment came down from on high. You were "placed," and depending on where you were placed, you knew what you were allowed to expect. The knowledge made her skin crawl, but she could never completely suppress it. *It wasn't fair.* That was the problem. That was the kind of thing that kept going through her head. *It wasn't fair*—as if she were a four-year-old with a problem on the playground instead of a grown-up with a Ph.D. and a job, a life, and a future. She had to keep telling herself that. She had a future, even if it wasn't a future she much wanted to reach.

The problem was this: it was four o'clock in the afternoon, and Ridenour Library was deserted. The campus was not much livelier. Marta was sure that if she went over to the Student Center she would find people in the cafeteria and the computer rooms, but they were not the people she wanted to see. They were students, or the kind of faculty who liked to prowl student hangouts and scold the people they found about wasting their time. Marta often felt the urge to scold herself, but she held back. She didn't like to get into face-to-face conflicts with kids whose parents could buy and sell the endowment. She didn't like face-to-face conflicts with anyone. Today she was particularly worried about face-to-face conflicts, or anything else, with Mark DeAvecca because Mark DeAvecca was making her feel guilty. Of course she never wanted face-to-face anything with Mark. He made her so angry; she had a hard time not spitting at him. Now, though, he could genuinely claim to be distraught. Anybody would have been distraught to find what he'd found in his room. Marta thought she herself would have been completely out of her mind for weeks. Sometimes she even imagined it: Michael with his eyes bulging and his tongue hanging out. That was what people had been saying on campus for days. Of course none of them had been there, except for Mark and a couple of the students on his dorm floor, and the faculty houseparents, and the police, and the administrators. *Christ,* Marta thought, *there must have been a crowd.* It wasn't any of those people who were telling stories about what Michael had looked like though. Mark wasn't telling stories. Mark wasn't talking to anybody at all; and Marta had heard, from more than one other faculty member, that he had even stopped the restless roaming around campus that had driven them all so crazy.

"It's like he's gone into a cocoon," Claire Hadderly had said, leaning against the coffee cart in the faculty lounge at the end of this very corridor. "Maybe when he emerges, he'll be a butterfly that doesn't stink."

He still stinks, Marta thought. She had seen him this morning, walking across the quad by himself and looking for god only knew what. He was so aimless. He was so useless, really. If she had been a different sort of person, with different priorities, she would have wanted to shake him.

Now she walked out of her office into the corridor and listened. It sounded as if half of everybody had gone home. James Hallwood was still in his office. Marta could hear the sound of opera coming out his open door. It wasn't turned up full blast the way it often was when he was in his apartment—all the students in his house complained about it—but it was clear enough so that Marta could even identify the opera underway. It was *Aida,* with Leontyne Price in the lead, singing at the Metropolitan Opera in New York. James would call it a "venerable recording," and then explain why it was so much better than the more modern recordings made in Germany and Spain. That had been among the hardest things she had ever had to learn. It wasn't enough to prefer opera and classical to hip-hop and early sixties movie music, or Italian films to Hollywood blockbusters, or serious literature to bestsellers. You had to be able to distinguish between even the supposedly important. You had to prefer Paganini to Beethoven, Leontyne Price in *Aida* to Beverly Sills in *Aida,* the novels of Paul Auster to the novels of Jonathan Franzen. Taste was an intricate web, and the first rule for surviving inside it was never to admit that you knew you were talking about "taste."

Marta went back into her office. Her books were neatly stacked on her desk. Her correcting was arranged in folders. There was nothing she needed to do about either. The rest of the week stretched in front of her like an abyss. She hated having time to think. She put the correcting folders into her cordovan leather tote bag and got her coat off the back of her chair. If she'd seen herself walking down Main Street in Windsor, she would have dismissed herself as being just another one of those NPR ladies, those women who infested every upscale suburb on the East Coast. High boots with stack heels. Long, wool skirt in the winter that changed to a long, cotton one with a print in every other season. Good cashmere twin set under a good wool coat. In spring and summer, the twin set would be made of heavy cotton, in carefully calibrated colors. This was a uniform, just as the fondness for opera and Paul Auster was a uniform. It was important to have your cotton sweaters in watermelon and teal instead of red and blue.

I'm driving myself crazy, Marta thought. She slung her tote bag over her arm and went out, down the corridor toward the front of the library where the door opened onto the quad. She thought about the night Michael had died and about Alice Makepeace going out the wrong door when she said she was going home. She let herself into the big, open front foyer and waved to the women at the desk. She could never remember their names, although she'd probably talked to both of them dozens of times, in the library and out. She went out the front door into the quad. It looked deserted. The lights were on along the pathways. It was already getting dark.

If she went back to her apartment now, she'd have one of those nights when she just wanted to throw something, hit something, do something. She did not understand people like Michael Feyre, who committed suicide, but she did understand people who committed murder. She could cheerfully have murdered two dozen of the students on this campus and called the world a better place for it.

There were lights on in some of the faculty apartments. She stopped where she was and looked toward Martinson House, the house she herself had always wanted to live in because it was closest to the library's front door and the largest and most elaborate in its design. Not only were the lights in Philip Candor's room on, she could see Philip himself pacing back and forth in his living room, his head bopping from side to side. He wouldn't be listening to opera either. He wouldn't even be listening to the Beatles or Chuck Berry, who had become the standard guilty pleasures for people who taught in places like Windsor Academy. That was the power of the Baby Boom. There were so many of them, they could incorporate their music even into the halls of Intelligent Taste.

Marta did not stop to wonder why, when she had a problem or needed to feel steadied in a storm, she always went to Philip Candor. She didn't stop to wonder why everybody on campus went to Philip in the same circumstances, so that he served as the unofficial anchor of Windsor Academy. It had been going on for so long, it felt natural. Philip Candor was a very steady and straightforward person.

She went up the front steps of Martinson House and into the hall. She went down the back hall and stopped at Philip's door. He was listening, she thought, to Eminem. She only knew it was Eminem because Philip had once told her.

She knocked twice and waited. The music was not turned up very high. She was sure he could hear her. Then again Philip sometimes didn't answer if he didn't want to answer.

The music stopped. The door opened. Philip looked out. He was, Marta thought, the calmest person she had ever known.

He stepped back and held the door all the way open. "Marta," he said, "don't tell me you're worried about Gregor Demarkian, too."

"Who?"

"Never mind." Philip closed the door behind her. "I've had a few visits to-day, that's all. I thought you must have been hanging out in the faculty lounge with practically everybody else. Can I get you some coffee? Or tea. I've got herb tea, if you want it."

"Oh, yes," Marta said. "I would like herb tea. Camomile, if you have it."

"I always have it."

"I don't like the faculty lounge," Marta said, sitting on the edge of the couch. There were two things you learned early in your acquaintance with Philip Candor. You didn't sit in his favorite chair, and you didn't ask him to put out his cigarette in his own apartment. He had a cigarette going now. He always had one going.

"I don't like the faculty lounge much myself," he said. "They don't let me smoke there, but that can't be your problem."

"No, no, of course not. It's just—I don't know. I feel on display, as if I had to put on a performance: dedicated prep school teacher with all the right atti-tudes."

"So what's the problem? Don't you have all the right attitudes?"

"I don't know," Marta said. "Maybe not. Sometimes I just get so angry here I don't know what to do with myself. I mean, here's this beautiful school, with every possible facility, and there are all these kids, with parents with money and with opportunities I couldn't have dreamed of when I was their age, and, I don't know. So many of them don't deserve it. I would have killed for a place like this when I was their age. I didn't even know places like this existed."

Philip came back with a teacup and a small plate to put it on instead of a saucer. Marta didn't bother to be surprised. Philip always had hot water ready and cookies from the bakery on Main Street. If he'd had a house of his own in-stead of a faculty apartment, he'd have had a fire in the fireplace, too. They weren't allowed to light fires in the fireplaces of the faculty apartments, al-though some people did it. It caused too much havoc with the fire insurance.

Marta put her teacup down on the coffee table. It took at least five minutes before it tasted like anything. "The thing is," she said, "I was wondering. They really are sure that Michael Feyre committed suicide, aren't they?"

"From what I've heard, yes," Philip said. "In fact, definitely yes, and I got that from one of the women in the dispatcher's office, not from Peter Make-peace. It wasn't the kind of thing somebody else would have found it easy to stage."

"That's what I thought. Somebody said something about the tongue and the eyes, you know, but I didn't understand it. And no, don't explain it. I don't even like thinking about it. It's not about that anyway. It's not about what makes them sure Michael didn't commit suicide."

"What is it about?"

Marta looked down at her hands. "It's about Alice Makepeace."

"Ah."

"Oh, don't say 'ah,' Philip. Everybody on campus knew she was sleeping with that boy, and from what I've heard there have been other boys. And she's, I don't know, she's such a compelling person, isn't she? She's somebody you have to pay attention to."

"She's very beautiful, even at forty-five," Philip said, "and she's the headmaster's wife. Of course you have to pay attention to her."

"You know what I mean. She commands attention. She does. She's just one of those people, charismatic people, something."

"And that's what you were thinking about, Alice Makepeace?"

"What? Oh no. It was about the night Michael Feyre died. I saw her the night Michael Feyre died."

"Where?"

"In the library," Marta said. "Not in the library proper but in the office and classroom wing. I was correcting papers, and she came in to talk to me."

"What about?"

Marta shrugged. "Not anything, really. I'd just seen Mark, you see, and I was in a bad mood, so I was talking about Mark. And she was making excuses for him or something. I don't know. That kid ought to be expelled."

"Maybe. What about Alice? It doesn't sound like she was doing much of anything."

"Oh, she wasn't," Marta said. "It wasn't that. It was after she left. She left by the wrong door."

"What do you mean, the wrong door?"

"She said she was going home. But to get home, it makes the most sense to go into the library proper and through the library foyer and out the front door. I mean, President's House is right across the quad. But she went out the other door, out the back."

"Out the back or out the side?"

"Out the back," Marta said. "To get to the side door, she'd have had to go down the corridor the same way from my office as she would to get out the front, she'd just have had to stop earlier. But she went the other way. There isn't anything there but the back way out. And I couldn't help but think it was odd, and I didn't know about Michael Feyre then, that he was dead."

"What time was it?"

"It was about nine, or maybe nine fifteen or nine thirty. I don't really remember, but somewhere in there, because when the carillon rang ten I came back home. But the carillon had rung nine. I stopped to listen to it. And the whole thing was nuts, really. It was below zero."

"It was minus nine," Philip said.

"Well, then," Marta said, "why would she want to go out the back door like that? There's nothing out there except Maverick Pond, and she couldn't have been going skating at that time of night. But that's the way she went, looking like Batgirl in that ridiculous cape."

"She wasn't with anybody?"

"Not when she was in my office, no. Oh, I don't know," Marta said. "I feel completely stupid. I mean, who cares what she did. Maybe she's got another boy. Maybe that's why Michael killed himself, because she'd thrown him over—"

"I don't think I'd say that if I were you," Philip said. "Peter would go crazy, and so would the newspapers if they ever heard a rumor like that. It's a damned miracle the newspapers haven't gone crazy yet."

"But it doesn't matter, right?" Marta said. "It doesn't matter where she was or why she was there. Maybe she wasn't anywhere. Maybe it was all part of the mystique, or maybe she made a mistake about which way to go and didn't want to admit it to me. Who knows why she does what she does? And if it doesn't have anything to do with why Michael died, there's no point in being all worked up about it."

"But you *are* worked up about it."

"Yes," Marta said, "yes, I am. I'm worked up about her. I'm worked up about Mark DeAvecca. I'm worked up about being here. I have no idea what I'm doing here. Did I tell you that? Sometimes I wake up in the morning and I don't even know where I am. I sit up in bed and for half a minute I think I'm back in my apartment in New Haven."

"Would you rather be?"

"I don't know. It wasn't too pleasant at the end there. Everybody was getting jobs, but I wasn't. I've got to ask myself about that, too. Why I wasn't. I don't know. Maybe I'm obsessing about Alice because I don't want to admit that I'm sitting here in February without a hope in hell of being anywhere but here next year—if I'm even asked back next year."

"You'll be asked back."

"Don't you hate it though? Don't you hate the uncertainty of it? It's that way for the students, too. You never know from one year to the next whether you can stay on. They don't either. It's all so up in the air. And the standards are all so—fuzzy. In graduate school it was just a matter of grade-point averages. As long as I maintained a B average, I could stay. Here it's about things and I don't even know what they mean: meaningful interaction, dedication to the mission of the school. Nonsense."

"You'll get asked back," Philip said again. "Maybe you shouldn't come back. Maybe you ought to go out and do something else, something besides teaching, something besides academia."

"I wouldn't know what to do. This is what I've always been good at."

"Teaching?"

"No," Marta said. "School. Even when I was very little, that was what I was good at. I don't think I've ever been really uncomfortable in a school before, not even in my freshman year at Wellesley. And I don't understand it. If I could have invented a place for myself, if I could have put together a group of people, it would have been just like here. And I hate it. And all I can think of is that it's all about the job. I don't know."

"Drink your tea," Philip said. "It's going to get cold."

Marta looked down into the cup and saw the tea bag still floating there. She hadn't taken off her coat either. All of a sudden it felt heavy and hot on her shoulders. She stood up and shrugged it off.

"We all spend too much time thinking about Alice Makepeace anyway," she said. "I don't know why we do it."

2

Cherie Wardrop had spent the first two days after Michael Feyre died doing what she was expected to do: staying in her apartment in Hayes House or in her office in Ridenour Library, waiting for students to come to see her and pour out their hearts. No students had, but she hadn't expected them to. She thought that the school's near mania on the subject of therapy was silly in the extreme. Most people grieved by doing something moronic in a spasm of emotion and then forgetting as much as possible the thing that had made them grieve in the first place. Most of the students would not have been grieving for Michael Feyre in any case. He hadn't been well liked or even well-known. What they really felt was shock and titillation, the same emotions they would have felt if somebody had had to have an abortion or leave school because he'd been caught stealing from the campus store. The students weren't upset or traumatized; they were excited. You could hear the revved-up energy in their voices wherever they gathered together, even when you couldn't make out the words. They were excited and almost pleased, the way they would have been if the news had been about a celebrity instead of a fellow student. Or maybe not. These kids were not impressed with celebrities. Too many of them had celebrities for parents. Still, Cherie thought, their reactions would have been different if Michael had been murdered instead of the victim of suicide. Their reactions *had* been different in those short twenty-four hours when the cause of death had still been in doubt.

Now Cherie pulled into her parking space behind President's House and shut off the engine. She'd done what she was expected to do for as long as she could, but today it had just been impossible. She'd gone to her office, sat waiting and staring out the window for half an hour, and then decided that she'd had enough. She'd packed up her things, gone back to the apartment, and gotten Melissa out of bed. Melissa was an anomaly, an artist without discipline. She maintained a schedule when Cherie maintained one, but as soon as Cherie was at loose ends, Melissa was sleeping in until noon. Cherie had had to pull the covers off her to get her to move, and even then she'd had to threaten a bowl of cold water. Only once she'd heard the sound of the shower going on had Cherie felt free to settle down in the living room. She was distressed to find that Melissa's small stack of papers next to the computer—the collection of short stories she was writing under contract to Woman Vistas Press—hadn't grown by a single sheet since the night Michael Feyre had died.

They were all too wound up, that was the problem. The boy was dead. The administration was dealing with it by canceling classes and behaving as if they were all in a public service announcement about mental health maintenance, and nobody wanted to admit the level of anxiety they were feeling, not only about the trauma itself, but about the possibility that the school might not survive the firestorm. There was going to be a firestorm, and Cherie knew it. Even though it hadn't happened yet, she could feel it coming. It made it impossible for her to do the petty housekeeping chores, the house accounts, the student accounts. Edith Braxner had scolded her more than once for the mess her accounts were in. She couldn't make herself take them seriously, and today, trying to focus on them in the wake of Michael's dying and the unbearable nervousness that affected everybody and anybody, she'd finally just given up on them and tossed them into the back of a drawer.

Cherie prodded Melissa, fast asleep in the passenger seat. It had been a very good day. They had gone into Boston and seen the first in a daylong film marathon of women's independent productions. Then they had ducked out of that and gone to eat sushi at a little place they knew in Cambridge. Then they'd dropped in at the New Words Bookstore in Cambridge and melted plastic until they'd felt guilty about it. Then they'd gone back to the film marathon and seen a movie about a woman coming out in India, which in the end had been too bloody and violent for them to enjoy watching. They were, Cherie thought, completely American. They wanted their endings happy and their heroines' quests triumphant.

Cherie prodded Melissa again. Outside the car, it was almost dark. Lights were on in President's House. Cherie thought that if she were Peter Makepeace—or Alice—she might have been happier with all the lights on, too. She prodded Melissa for a third time. Melissa moved.

"Wake up," Cherie said. "We're home. And I've been thinking about Sodom and Gomorrah."

"What?" Melissa stretched.

"I've been thinking about Sodom and Gomorrah," Cherie said. "I was thinking about what we'd talked about the other night, do you remember? About how the scandal would get out eventually, and the school could be forced to close, and how everybody knew that but everybody was trying very hard not to notice it?"

Melissa opened her eyes. "Christ, Peter's got that place lit up like he's never heard of an energy crisis. What's wrong with him?"

"Maybe it's Alice. Maybe they're both looking over their shoulders. I'd be scared as hell if I was either one of them."

"That's still no reason to waste electricity."

Cherie sighed. "I was thinking about Sodom and Gomorrah," she said again. "I was thinking about how this place could be shut down, and that it wouldn't be such a bad idea, that it was like Sodom and Gomorrah. That this place is so—filthy—that maybe shutting it down is the only thing that could clean it."

"Filthy?" Now Melissa was thoroughly awake. She sat up straight in her seat and stared. "What's this about? Are you going Midwest on me again? Are you having guilt feelings about not playing by the midwestern married lady book?"

"I don't think so," Cherie said. "I mean, I thought I might be at first, but then it occurred to me that I don't think the place is filthy because it lets us get away with what we do. It isn't about that. It's about Mark moving back into his room."

"The room where Michael Feyre died?"

"That's the only room he's got," Cherie said. "We got the news this morning from administration. Well, from Peter, really, even though nobody ever said so. It's incredible the way they hold tight to information around this place. But that's the idea. The police are finished with the room. The staff is going to go in there and clean. They want Mark back in the room before the end of the week because there's no place else for him to stay. It's nonsense, really; he's staying with Sheldon. Sheldon doesn't want him around anymore. Nobody wants him around, but that doesn't mean they should be sending the kid back to the room he found a dead body in."

"Don't suggest having him live with us," Melissa said. "It wouldn't work."

"They wouldn't allow it in any case. They wouldn't allow it because we're women and he's a boy."

"God, they're impossible around here. Don't you ever wish you could find some normal people? And why is it that practically everybody anywhere who's ever had anything to do with a place like this is completely nuts?"

"I don't think it's true that they're all completely nuts," Cherie said. She popped open the door and was immediately cold. This was the coldest winter she could remember since she moved out east from Michigan. "Back to Sodom and Gomorrah. It wasn't us I was thinking about; it was Alice. Don't you think it's incredible that Alice has gotten away with the things she's gotten away with?"

Cherie got out of the car and slammed the door shut, locked. Melissa got out her side and began putting her jacket on. Melissa always took off her jacket in the car.

"Look," she said, "I know I was the one who said Alice Makepeace was dangerous, but I think you're taking this one too far. The verdict is in, last I heard. It really *was* a suicide. She didn't kill him."

"I know she didn't kill him, at least not in the ordinary sense of the term 'kill.' Oh, I don't know. It's not just the people she sleeps with. It's the whole thing. The way she is. The way she insinuates herself into everything, every decision, every issue. And the longer this goes on without there being any fallout, the more I wonder if there's going to be any fallout at all. We think it's inevitable that the papers will get hold of it, but we've got board members who own newspapers or big chunks of them. This place has connections everywhere. Maybe nothing will happen. Maybe she'll get away with it."

"I don't think so. I think that at the very least Peter will end up getting fired. The board will have to do that to cover its ass."

"Maybe," Cherie said. Then she looked up at President's House. "Maybe they're in there right now listening to everything we have to say. I've always thought Alice would do that if she could, spy on everybody, I mean. Not for any reason, but just because she likes to know things. But that's what I mean, you see. It's as if there's something basically *wrong,* and I always knew it was there, but I never realized it mattered until Michael died."

"Let's get back over to Hayes," Melissa said. "I don't believe anybody has spy cameras, but I wouldn't put it past them to be listening at windows."

Melissa went around the side of the car to the walk, and Cherie followed. It wasn't a long walk from here. Hayes was just down the pathway in the middle of the Main Street side of the quad. When they came into the quad proper, Cherie saw that most of the dorms were lit up almost as spectacularly as President's House was. Maybe everybody needed more light than usual to get through the evenings these days.

They pushed out onto the walk, past President's House, past any conceivable danger.

"Anyway," Cherie said. "The police have finally gone and aren't coming back, as far as I know. I hated all that questioning, and everybody keeping their mouths shut about Alice. Everybody. I was really impressed. I thought somebody would have to go at it, if only out of spite. And nobody said a word."

"Maybe they thought it would shut the place down, just like you, and they didn't want to risk it."

"There are people who wouldn't have cared. Marta Coelho. God, I know we're supposed to show solidarity with all women, but that one really blows my corks. Oh, it's just too, too tragic. There she is, with her fine mind and her doctorate from Yale, stuck in this wretched, tenth-rate place."

"You're exaggerating."

"Not by much. She wouldn't care if this place was shut down. She wouldn't care about getting Alice in trouble either. She can't stand her."

"You can't stand her."

"It's not in the same way," Cherie said. "Marta—resents her. Do you know what I mean? It matters like hell to Marta, all that East Coast crap, the old families and the everybody knows everybody and all that bullshit. She'd stab Alice in the back if she could. I can't believe she didn't say anything when the police were here."

"Did the police even interview her? I thought it was just those of us in Hayes and Michael's teachers. Is she one of Michael's teachers?"

"I don't know. But even if she isn't, she could have asked to talk to them, gotten one of them aside on one of those days when they were crawling all over campus. It's the kind of thing she would do, don't you think?"

"I haven't spent that much time thinking about Marta Coelho," Melissa said. "I just thank God every once in a while that she isn't gay. Are we intending to go home? Because if we are, we ought to turn in here."

Cherie looked around. She'd missed the turn-off in the path for Hayes House. She backtracked and began going up the walk to the back door. It bothered her no end that the Houses were arranged like this, with their back doors facing the quads. Yes, the front doors faced roads that cars could travel on, but the quad was the true face of the campus, and Cherie thought the front doors should face that. Besides, the front of the library faced the quad.

If you stay at a boarding school long enough, you'll start thinking in trivialities, she thought. She got out her key and opened up, letting herself into the long back hall. The lights were on here, too, although they rarely were unless someone was passing through directly. She wondered if people were forgetting to turn them off or if they had left them on deliberately to drive out the dark. She took out the key to their apartment and began fiddling with it—it stuck, as usual—as Sheldon came around from the front and saw them there.

"Oh, good," he said. "We've been looking all over for you two. Have you seen Mark?"

"Mark DeAvecca?"

"He's the only Mark we've got in this house."

The key caught. Cherie pushed the door open. "We've been in Boston all day. We haven't seen anybody. Why? Has he gone missing?"

"He didn't sign the book this afternoon. And it's nearly five."

Cherie put the key back into her bag. "People fail to sign the book all the time," she said. "You know what afternoons are like around this place. He's probably over in the library or the Student Center. He's probably just trying to stay out of your hair."

"I'm all in favor of him staying out of my hair, but Peter's adamant. Everybody has to sign the book. It's the police and all that. He doesn't want us to look lax."

"Not having a fit when a sixteen-year-old boy doesn't check in at home some afternoon isn't looking lax. It's not looking hysterical."

"It doesn't matter," Sheldon said. "I don't give a damn one way or the other. That kid is the single most irresponsible student I've ever seen, never mind the obvious, which is that he's far too screwed up most of the time to function. I wish they'd throw him out of here, although I don't suppose there's any chance of that now. The school would look like God knows what if they threw him out in the wake of this."

"He's probably around somewhere. He'll be in for curfew. Just relax."

"I can't relax," Sheldon said. "Peter isn't relaxed. And you don't have Mark staying in your apartment."

Sheldon turned around and walked off. Cherie watched him go without regret. He was not one of her favorite people, and he was not the person she would have chosen to share a campus house with if she'd had the choice of who would get what apartment where.

She went into her own apartment, waited until Melissa came in after her, and closed up. It was only then that it occurred to her that what Mark DeAvecca really seemed to be most of the time was not stoned, but depressed, and that depressed people sometimes committed suicide.

FOUR

1

Somewhere in the world, *there is sanity,* Gregor Demarkian thought, sitting by his window looking out on the Main Street of Windsor, Massachusetts, while Mark took the longest shower in history. Windsor itself looked very sane—too sane, really, the kind of sane where people assume that everybody will naturally be "intelligent" about their "choices" and always choose not to engage in "inappropriate" behavior. There was a streak in him, Gregor knew, of the kind of rebellious teenager who wrecks his life just to make the locals tear their hair. It was interesting that it had only shown up in his fifties. When he'd actually been a teenager, he'd been very straight arrow and conscientious. On the other hand, the world in which he had had to be straight arrow and conscientious had not been like this one. None of his teachers would ever have talked about "choices" or worried about what was "appropriate." If he'd acted like an idiot, they'd have told him he was acting like an idiot. If he'd done something they didn't like, they'd have told him he'd done something they didn't like, and why, and he'd have been free to tell them why he thought they were wrong. That was, he thought, the key. He got the feeling in places like Windsor that the game was rigged. For all the talk about choices, the people who ran places like this didn't actually believe in choice. "We teach students to evaluate all the options and make the choices that are right for them." That was a line from the Windsor Academy material he'd gotten from the guidance counselor. He had a feeling it wasn't true. In fact it was something worse than not true. If students were really supposed to evaluate *all* the options and to make their *own* choices, then some of them would choose to stay drugged to the gills most of the time, and others would have sex and maybe babies at fifteen, and others would drop out of the whole college admissions game and become carpenters. Gregor was fairly sure that neither the school nor the parents would put up with any of that. What was wrong, he wondered, with admitting that adolescents didn't always know what was good for them, that they had to have their choices cut off, sometimes just to make sure they could make it through to the next phase of their lives? What was the point of pretending to an equality that you had no intention of allowing to exist? His old-fashioned school was more—honorable—than this, and in its way more respectful of him than this kind of thing could ever be. At least it had accepted him as a fully human being who had a right not to be manipulated.

I'm making all this up out of nothing, he thought, looking down on Main Street some more. There were too many cars. Traffic was barely moving. In spite of all the care that had been taken to make Windsor look like a real small town, there was no disguising the fact that it was a suburb of Boston. He really was making all this up. He knew nothing at all about Windsor or Windsor Academy. He was extrapolating not even from what he'd read, but from the feeling of unease it gave him. There were suburbs like this outside Philadelphia, too. They weren't the best suburbs, where serious old money lived. Those places were as bald and unapologetic as the worst of Philadelphia's bad neighborhoods. The suburbs he was thinking of were the ones—

There was a knock on the door, and he went to answer it. The knock on the door was room service. A young woman wheeled a cart in and unloaded it on the small, round table near the window he'd been looking out of. He gave her a dollar and she thanked him in a cheerful, uncomplicated way that did a lot to calm his nerves. He checked the soup tureen and looked under the cover of the plate of sandwiches he had ordered. They were the oddest, most precious sandwiches he had ever seen, little bite-sized triangles, carefully composed. The roast beef had something that looked like horseradish on it, except that the horseradish had little flecks of green in it. The tuna salad had little flecks of green in it, too. He wondered where the recipes for this sort of thing came from. Maybe there really were people who took Martha Stewart seriously, even outside the SEC. He wasn't making sense again. He wasn't making sense at all. The simple fact was that places like Windsor made him angry in an elemental, primal way that could not be explained, or controlled, by reason, and he really didn't know why that was.

The bathroom door opened and Mark came out, looking fifty times better than he had and trying, without much success, to dry his hair on a towel. Mark had a lot of hair—not because he'd left it long; he could have used a haircut—but only because he looked ragged, not because his hair was at his shoulders, but because it was so thick. Gregor had a memory of his mother saying that Mark didn't need his hair cut so much as he needed it mowed.

Mark let the towel drop to his shoulders. "Sorry to take so long," he said. "I zoned out a little."

"What does that mean, 'zoned out'?"

Mark shrugged. "Zoned out. I sort of lost track of time, and of where I was, that kind of thing. I've been doing it a lot lately."

"You look a lot better than you did, and you looked very bad."

"I know," Mark said. He walked over to the table and raised the lids on the soup and sandwiches.

"Have a sandwich," Gregor told him.

Mark reached in and took one of the roast beef with horseradish. "They must get this place to cater for events over at school. They have these sandwiches all the time. The roast beef ones are good."

"You could eat a little. You look thin."

Mark swayed a little and then blinked. He put his hand on the back of a chair to steady himself and then sat down, abruptly, as if his legs had given way beneath him. "Sorry," he said, "I'm just tired."

"You looked dizzy."

"I was dizzy. Am. Am dizzy. Sorry. It's just that I'm tired, really. I can't seem to sleep up here, or at least not much. I'm running on caffeine and adrenaline half the time, and even that doesn't help more often than not. Thank you for coming up here. I needed somebody to talk to."

"You used to be able to talk to your mother."

"I can still talk to my mother. I just don't want to at the moment." Mark shook his head. "Not that I'm not going to have to," he said. "She's going to hear about this eventually. Then she's probably going to ride into town in a tank and blow some things up. Did I tell you she really hates Windsor Academy?"

"No, but it doesn't surprise me."

"She came up for Parents Day in October and nearly brained my adviser with a plate. Not that I really minded much, you understand. My adviser makes my skin crawl."

"Maybe you should get a new adviser."

"It's not that easy," Mark said. "Look, the thing is, I've been up here since

September, right? Okay, I don't like it much, it was probably the wrong place, but, you know, anybody can do anything for a year. What's the sense in cutting and running before the year is over? What's the sense of quitting?"

"It's not cutting and running to recognize the fact that you're sick," Gregor said. "And if you're telling me the truth and you're not taking drugs—"

"I *am* telling you the truth. I'd never take drugs. In the first place, I'm not stupid. In the second place, my dad would probably come back to haunt me. He made it through the sixties in college without ever taking a toke on a joint."

"You know the lingo."

"Everybody knows the lingo. And Michael—Michael Feyre, my roommate—he was the biggest dealer on campus. You have no idea."

"There are a lot of drugs on this campus?"

Mark shrugged. "There are more than I'm used to. At Rumsey Hall you'd hear rumors about people sometimes, but I never actually saw anybody using the whole eight years I was there. Up here there are people who come to class stoned, and everybody knows it, even the teachers."

"And they don't do anything about it?"

"You don't go accusing people of being drugged out if you can't prove it," Mark said. "Especially if their parents are wealthy and not averse to taking you to court. They do something if they actually catch someone with the stuff on them. Not otherwise."

Gregor considered this. "If your roommate was a dealer, wouldn't he have had the stuff on him, at least sometimes?"

Mark picked up the cover of the sandwich tray again and got another roast beef with horseradish. "Can I have one of these Perriers?" he asked. Gregor nodded, and Mark opened a small Perrier bottle and poured half the contents in one of the clear water glasses that had come with the tray. "The thing about Michael and his dealing," he said, "is that we came to an understanding right away. Michael didn't bring that stuff into our room—ever. He probably wouldn't have anyway because of the searches—"

"Searches?"

"They search your room," Mark said. "They don't tell you about it, and they never talk about it unless they find something, but they search it. They're not that good at it either. It's easy to tell. They put all my stuff back in the wrong places. Never assume that just because somebody's a slob, he doesn't remember where his stuff was."

"When they searched your room, they were looking for Michael Feyre's drugs?"

"Hell, no. They were looking for *my* drugs. They all think I'm using, too. Either that or they think I'm stupid."

"I know. I called your mother."

"I expected that. That's okay. She'll come up, and I'll talk to her. Anyway, Michael and I had this deal. I don't know where he kept his stuff, but he was making anywhere from five hundred to a thousand dollars a week—"

"*How* much? How big *is* this school?"

"We've got maybe three hundred fifty kids. But we've got faculty, too, you know."

"You think there were faculty members buying drugs from Michael Feyre?"

"Yeah," Mark said. "But the big business was speed. Michael talked about it all the time. He didn't like speed. He said it made him nervous. He couldn't see why anybody bothered. I could. They do it for the same reason I drink coffee. There's a lot of work here. People load themselves up with AP courses and honors courses—"

"AP?"

"Advanced placement. It's essentially a college course you can take in high school, and then you take a test from the same people who do the SATs and if you get a good-enough grade you get credit from whatever college you go to. People use them to get rid of the distribution requirements the colleges all have so that they can take stuff they like instead of stuff they just have to take. Starting junior year, people take three or four of them at a time. They don't have time to sleep. And then, you know, if you take speed, it keeps you up; so you need downers if you want to sleep at all. Michael was making a mint."

Gregor considered this. "Did the police check that out? Drugs in his system? People he might have been connected to? Where did he get the drugs to sell?"

"I haven't got a clue," Mark said. "My best guess would be Boston, but he's not from there, so maybe not. He's from some place in Connecticut, but not a town I know."

"What about the suicide?" Gregor said. Mark had abandoned his second sandwich only half-eaten, and that was nearly impossible because the sandwiches were only about two inches long. "Did it make sense to you that Michael would commit suicide? Had he been depressed?"

"Not exactly. Maybe. It's hard to explain."

"Were you surprised?'

"Was I surprised to find his body hanging from the ceiling of our room?"

Mark asked. "Hell, yes, I was surprised. You'd have been, too. I had no idea—they don't show what it really looks like in movies. And they don't show . . . he'd sh—— God, I have no idea what the right word for it is. He'd shit himself. Sorry for my language."

"That's all right. I expect he'd pissed himself, too."

"Right," Mark said. "If I ever get to make movies, I'm going to show it the way it really is, and it's ugly as hell. I went out in the hall and got sick, but all I'd had was coffee and so mostly I just dry heaved. I think I did it for hours."

"I think that's perfectly normal. I didn't mean were you surprised to find the body; I mean were you surprised to hear that Michael Feyre had killed himself."

"Oh," Mark said. "I don't know. He was . . . uh . . . he was having an affair with Alice Makepeace."

The name sounded vaguely familiar but not familiar enough. "This was another student?"

"Alice is the headmaster's wife," Mark said. "She's, well. I don't know. Maybe you'll get a chance to meet her. She's something else."

"Young?"

"In her forties, I'd think. Madonna is in her forties. That can be all right."

"I'm sure it can. Did he tell you he was having this affair with the headmaster's wife?"

"He didn't have to," Mark said. "Everybody on campus knew about it. And I do mean everybody. Peter Makepeace must have known about it, too. It was practically up on a billboard. Except nobody ever talked about it directly, if you know what I mean."

"I think I do," Gregor said. "Was there a reason for this? Was Alice Makepeace using drugs?"

"Maybe," Mark said, "but I don't think that was the point. According to the rumors, this wasn't the first time and Michael wasn't the first kid. She makes a habit of it."

"A habit of sleeping with students?"

"A habit of sleeping with a particular kind of student—with scholarship students. The last two were African American."

"But Michael Feyre wasn't a scholarship student, was he? I have a contact in Boston who said that Michael Feyre's mother won—"

"The Powerball, yeah, for like three hundred million dollars or something. I met her. She's nice. But Michael was like a cliché, for God's sake. White trash nation. Right down to the air guitar concerts to Lynyrd Skynyrd."

Gregor had no idea who Lynyrd Skynyrd was, but he didn't think it was a good move to say so. "So you think he might have been depressed enough about this affair with Alice Makepeace to commit suicide?"

"I think he might have been if she'd wanted to break it off," Mark said. "The thing is I don't think she did want to break it off. I mean, I didn't talk to her about it, but he wasn't acting like that. And he was obsessed with her. More white trash nation. It was like one of those stalker movies."

"People who are stalked don't usually want to be," Gregor said.

"She did," Mark was adamant. "She used to send him messages on the voice mail. I'd get them sometimes by mistake if I got back to the room before he did. She set up the meetings more often than he did. I think she wanted to talk to me about it."

Gregor was curious. "You only think?"

"She came down to the computer room this morning when I was there alone. I was blasting space aliens out of the sky to get rid of my aggression, if you catch my drift. She came to the door and waited, and I pretended not to see her."

"Why?"

"Because she creeps me out. She's one of those people. It's like talking to a pod person. And I really didn't want to talk about Michael to her. It just seemed wrong." Mark blinked twice and then put his head in his hands. "I'm sorry," he said. "I really was having a good day, and now I'm dizzy again. It's just the sleep. I can't sleep."

Gregor leaned closer to get a better look. Mark's face had gone as white as chalk. Gregor had heard that cliché a thousand times, but this was the first time he'd ever seen a person who fit it. Mark's pupils were dilated, too, and the whites around them were shot through with red. The muscles in his shoulders were twitching.

"Mark," he asked, "are you sure you didn't take something? Just before you met me, maybe, or while you were in the bathroom?"

"No. Christ. I wish they'd just do a drug test and get it over with. I'm not taking anything. I'm not—I'm just like this. Almost all the time now. It just is."

Mark was swaying in his chair. Gregor pulled at his arm.

"Come on," he said. "Lie down. You look like you need to."

Mark swayed to his feet, blinking. "My head is full of fuzz. All the time. And I can't read. Did I tell you that? I sit down with a book and read the page, but I can't remember what's on it. I finish the page and it's as if I'd never read it and that's nuts because it used to be that I didn't even have to pay attention.

I could read the page and then later I could sort of remember what it looked like. I could sort of project it on the back of my eyelids and read it again. Like that. And now I can't remember anything, and I can't understand anything. At least not most of the time. I don't know what's wrong with me."

Gregor pushed Mark over to the bed and then onto it. "Try lying down for a while," he said, but he might as well not have. Mark hit the bed and seemed to be instantaneously asleep. Gregor would have thought he'd passed out if it hadn't been for the fact that his breathing was more regular than it had been at any other time in their conversation today and the further fact that he was snoring.

Gregor sat down on the edge of the bed and checked him over. He was sleeping, that was all. He was as soundly and thoroughly asleep as Rip Van Winkle.

2

At first Gregor thought he would wake Mark DeAvecca before he had to go out to his dinner meeting; but when the time came, he found that impossible to do. It wasn't that Mark wouldn't wake up. If that had been the case, Gregor would have canceled his dinner appointment and called an ambulance. It was more that he couldn't bear to wake him. The boy looked healthier and more peaceful than he had all day. Gregor wondered why he couldn't sleep in the normal run of things. He was certainly sleeping now.

Gregor picked up the phone and called the Windsor Police Service, just to make sure they knew he was coming. Then he called the desk to ask that somebody call the room at seven-thirty to wake Mark. That school had to have a curfew of some kind, although Gregor was slowly beginning to accept the possibility that Windsor ran on very different assumptions than most of the rest of the world. He found an extra blanket in the closet and threw it over Mark's body, thinking that the kid was built like a defensive linebacker. Even the underweight didn't disguise that.

Gregor went downstairs, left his key at the desk, and then headed out the front door to Main Street. It was, if anything, worse than he'd thought when he'd first seen it. It was the epitome of the sort of place built by people who recoil in horror from "suburbs," by which they mean places with housing subdivisions. There was a bookstore. Its windows displayed hardcover books in matte jackets with muted impressionistic paintings used as the backdrop to titles that made no sense: *Electric Pumpkins, Love in Aspic, The Poetics of Dystopia.* A sign near the door said: THE EXCELLENT BECOMES THE PERMANENT.

A few doors down there was a candle store, and a few doors down from that was a clothing store for women showing models in the window wearing good tweed skirts and cashmere sweaters. Gregor thought that if he stopped a dozen people at random, one right after the other, he'd find out that all of them listened to National Public Radio and owned a copy of *Chocolat*.

He checked the note he'd written to himself with the directions to the police station, walked up four blocks, and stopped for a moment to look across the road. That was the Windsor Academy campus right there. No gates set it off from the town proper, and no security service seemed to be active to keep the locals out. With the exception of one large, college Gothic building off toward the left, the Windsor Academy buildings were all large and studiously "Colonial," the kind of thing that might have served as a mansion in pre-Revolutionary Massachusetts, except that they were all larger. Some of them, though, were probably authentic. The ones on Main Street proper almost certainly were. The rest of the campus had been configured to blend in with them. No, Gregor thought, he really didn't like exaggerated respect for history.

He checked his directions again, walked down another block and a half, and turned left into a street full of large, Colonial houses set back on wide lawns. If you really want to know if a house was built in Colonial America, Bennis had told him, check out how far it is from the road. Real Colonial houses have no front lawns. They sit right up against the thoroughfare. These houses, Gregor decided, were reproductions, or at best from the early nineteenth century, when lawns had come into fashion.

He went down three blocks, checked the street sign—Muldor—and turned left again. The police station was a small, brick building hidden tastefully behind a box hedge nearly tall enough to obscure the building completely. The only way to tell that a police station was behind that hedge was to read the sign at the end of the drive.

Gregor walked up the drive to the front door. It was a very modern brick building, but it had a steep, pitched roof, as if that would be enough to make it look like a residence. Here was another way to tell the difference between a suburb and a real small town. In a real small town, the police station would have been right out front on Main Street, next door to the Town Hall and the public library. Well, the public library was on Main Street here; it was right across from Windsor Academy.

Gregor gave his name to the young woman at the desk, and she spoke quietly into a microphone. A moment later a large, beefy man in a badly fitting black suit came out of the corridor behind the desk and held out his hand.

"Mr. Demarkian? I'm very glad to meet you. I'm Brian Sheehy. Walter Cray can't stop talking about you."

"I'm not sure if that's good or bad," Gregor said.

"Well, Walt's impressed, and that's not usual. Look, I'm just getting off, I'm starving, and I need a beer and I need a cigarette—" The young woman at the desk clucked, and Brian Sheehy ignored her. "There's a place about three blocks down and around the corner, if you wouldn't mind. And you don't mind a place where they allow smoking."

"I don't mind," Gregor said.

"It's not one of those places on Main Street," Brian Sheehy said. "No sprouts. No spinach salads. You don't look like an organic vegetable guy to me."

"I'm not."

"I'm going up to Doheney's," Brian told the young woman at the desk, "then I'm going home. I'm on my cell phone."

"Okay," she said.

Brian shooed Gregor toward the door. "Only thing is, I want to make one thing clear up front. There's a lot going on with this, but what isn't going on is a murder. Walter said you understood that, right? We checked into it every way we could, and there's nothing there that even makes a murder possible. You can see the reports if you want. This one is not a doubtful case."

"I do understand that," Gregor said, as he found himself outside on the front steps again. He kept forgetting how dark it got and how early in February in New England. "I haven't come to investigate a murder. I haven't come to investigate anything. I came because Mark DeAvecca asked me to."

"Yeah, the roommate," Brian said.

"What do you think about the roommate?"

"Serious stoner," Brian said automatically. "Whacked to the gills practically all the time. Someday he's going to start convulsing, and then it's just going to be a matter of whether they get him to the hospital on time."

They were out on the street again. There was snow on the ground, but even in the darkness it didn't look soft. "The thing is," Gregor said, "I know the kid."

"Don't you ever think that," Brian said. "I've heard it a million times. Even the ones you know get caught, more often than you'd think."

"I know that," Gregor said, "but I've also just spent the last hour and a half talking to him. He knows everybody thinks he's using. He offered to take a drug test."

"When he offers where he's likely to get taken up on it, get back to me."

"I will. It may be soon. I called his mother. When she gets here, she may insist."

"I don't get this boarding school thing," Brian said. "It's bad enough when they're eighteen and want to go away to college. Why would you want your kid to go away when he was only fourteen?"

"In this case I think it was the kid who wanted to go away," Gregor said. "Get out. Be independent. He's that kind of kid. But the thing is, I did talk to him for over an hour. And the way he is, the way he behaves—yes, I can see the presumption that he's using. But the more I watched him, the less that seemed like what was going on. I hate to tell you what did seem was going on."

"What?"

"Alzheimer's disease."

"In a fourteen-year-old kid?"

"He's sixteen," Gregor said. "He turned sixteen in January. But yes, I understand. I don't really mean I think he has Alzheimer's disease. I meant that if you spend enough time with him, that's the way he comes off. Not like somebody who's drugged. He goes in and out of focus, for one thing. He'll be just fine, and then ten minutes later his mind will start to wander and his speech will get thick. Then ten minutes later he'll be fine again. Unless you know of a drug that works on a time-release basis, that doesn't sound like substance abuse."

They were suddenly outside a small building close to the street with a plain, plate-glass storefront. If Gregor had had to make a bet on it, he would have said nothing that looked like this remained in the town limits of Windsor. There was gilt stencil lettering across the plate glass: DOHENEY'S RESTAURANT. It looked less like a restaurant than a bar.

"Here we are," Brian said, opening the glass door to let Gregor go in ahead of him. Doheney's Restaurant was as dark inside as the street was outside and maybe darker. The few lights were low and concealed behind amber globes. Brian went to the back and slid into a wooden booth.

"I'm impressed," Gregor said, sliding in on the other side. "I would never have guessed you could find a place like this in this town."

"There're still a few of us here from the old days," Brian said, waving at a waitress. "Those of us who go to Our Lady of Grace instead of the First Unitarian Church. I don't get Unitarians any more than I get boarding schools. Here's Sheila. You want a beer?"

Gregor hadn't had a beer in ten years. "Sure," he said, "whatever they've got on tap."

"They've got rat piss on tap," Brian said. "Sheila, get the man a Heinecken. And get me a hot pastrami on a roll with Russian dressing. You want something like that, Mr. Demarkian?"

"Gregor," Gregor said automatically. "How about a cheeseburger and fries?"

"Cheeseburgers come with fries," Sheila said. Then she thought about it for a moment. "Everything comes with fries."

"Right," Gregor said.

Sheila waltzed off, and Brian began moving the sugar cannister around on the wooden table. It was an old-fashioned diner cannister, made of glass with a stainless steel top. "So what is it?" Brian said. "If he's not a stoner, what do you think is wrong with him?"

"I don't know," Gregor said. "That's what I came up to find out really. I like the kid. He's not acting like himself. He worries me."

"If I liked the kid, I'd worry about him, too," Brian said, "but I'd worry about—"

"Drugs, I know. He did tell me some interesting things though before I came out this evening. He said that Michael Feyre was dealing drugs. Is that true?"

"Yeah," Brian said. "We couldn't have proved it, but I'd bet anything. Not that we could have done anything about it."

"Why not?"

Brian laughed. "Look, this place is backed by serious money, you understand? Rockefeller money. Vanderbilt money. Roosevelt money. Some of the Kennedy kids went there. When they want to hush things up, they don't bother to schmooze around with me; they schmooze around with the governor. Or better. We stay off that campus. We have to. And if we pick up one of the kids in town, we go by the book, keep the papers out of it, make sure he gets probation, and then they just send him home."

The beers came. Sheila put them down next to two clean glasses and walked away again.

"But this Michael Feyre," Gregor said. "He wasn't old money, was he? Walter Cray said that his mother—"

"Won the Powerball, yeah. Have you met her?"

"I've never even seen her," Gregor said. "I'd never even heard of her until I talked to Walter Cray."

"Well," Brian said, "she's a gas, really. She's real young for having a fifteen-, sixteen-year-old kid. She must have been sixteen herself when she had him. And she looks like just what she was, except that her clothes are better. She looks like a high-school-drop-out single mother who works in a convenience store. And she's ignorant as hell in a lot of ways, but she's not stupid."

"She sounds more interesting all the time."

"Oh, she's interesting all right," Brian said. "And what's better is, she's here. She's been here for a couple of days. She has to arrange for her son's body to get back home for one thing, but I don't think that explains it. I think she's looking for something."

"Looking for what?"

"I don't know exactly. Maybe an explanation. Maybe she doesn't believe he committed suicide. Although, let me say again—"

"I know, there's no question."

"Right, there really isn't one. But she's his mother. Mothers aren't always rational about sons. If they were, they'd probably kill them at birth."

"So she's here, and she's looking for something. And Mark DeAvecca is here, and he's looking for something too, he just doesn't know what. And he's acting very oddly. And Michael Feyre was dealing drugs, and nobody could catch him at it. And I'm here. What's wrong with this picture?"

"What's wrong is that the press isn't here," Brian said. "They're good at covering things up over there, but this is a miracle. You know what the scary thing is? If they're careful, the press may never be here."

"Are they careful?"

"Not particularly. It's a weird place over there. I don't like it. Almost nobody in town does. They talk a really good game about 'diversity' and 'inclusion,' but it's money that talks at that place, and they don't ever let you forget it. If you've got the cash, you can be a drugged-out crack addict with a D average, and they'll do everything but change your underwear to help you to stay; but you come in on a scholarship, and they'll *find* a way to get rid of you if they have to, unless you're one of those ultimate scholastic stars that could have gotten into Harvard without bothering with high school at all. It used to be a girls' school, did you know that?"

"No."

"I liked it better when it was a girls' school. It was still stuck-up as all hell, but it was a kind of stuck-up I could get. It didn't tell you how wonderfully committed to fairness and social justice it was while stabbing you in the back."

"You, personally?"

The food had arrived. Gregor sat back a little to let Sheila put his cheeseburger in front of him. It was the size of the old Volkswagen bug and buried in a mountain of french fries that could have shown up on satellite pictures from space. Brian asked for another beer.

"Not me personally," he said, studying his pastrami sandwich. "It was a nephew of mine. Bright kid. Lived down on the other side of Boston, too far to commute really. Got himself a scholarship to come up here, covered practically the whole thing. End of his first year, he's got a B minus average, and they decided that 'he has not shown the ability to succeed in a sophomore year at Windsor.' A B minus average. Can you believe that? What's wrong with a B minus average? So I checked into it a little. There were two dozen kids in his class with averages of B minus or less. Only three were asked to leave. Every one of them was on a scholarship. And nobody on a scholarship with a B minus or less was allowed to stay. But lots of people with less were allowed to stay, and all of them had money."

"How did you get that information?"

Brian shrugged. "The secretaries live in town, don't they, and they didn't migrate here from Boston or New York. They're local. And most of them are Catholics."

Gregor thought it was probably not an easy time to be a Catholic in the Greater Boston Metropolitan Area, but he let it go. Brian was ripping apart his pastrami as if he were a saber-toothed tiger going at raw meat.

"The thing is," he said, while Gregor accepted the second round of beers from Sheila, "I've got to tell you the truth. I can't do anything about it because it would mean my job in the long run, but I'd love to see something happen that would make the shit hit the fan at that place. The sooner the better. There gets to be a point where I just don't feel like putting up with their bullshit anymore."

FIVE

1

There were very few things that James Hallwood didn't like about living at Windsor Academy, but there was one thing he truly hated, and that was the requirement that all teachers eat lunch and dinner in the common cafeteria with the students throughout the school term. His faculty apartment had a perfectly respectable kitchen. It was more than respectable. He'd had expensive apartments in Boston that had had fewer amenities and even more expensive flats in London where it had been impossible to cook at all. He objected to everything about the common cafeteria. The food was invariably bad. That went without saying. Institutional food was always bad. The public exposure was at the least annoying and often repressive. He found himself picking over wilted salads or overcooked cod, more aware than he wanted to be that people were staring at him. Students and faculty both stared. David said that was because he was "gay"—God, how he hated that word "gay"; he used it, but he hated it—but he knew it was because he was something else, something far worse in this place. Nobody at Windsor Academy cared whether he was gay or not. They cared that he was an elitist.

I am an elitist, James told himself, as he packed himself into his coat and scarf to make the trek over to the Student Center. It was egregious. If they had to make them all eat together in the common cafeteria, the least they could have done was to put the common cafeteria somewhere convenient, on the quad, instead of out in back with all the classroom buildings. The other thing they could have done was to set dinner at a reasonable hour instead of at five thirty.

He had no idea why the school—and not only this school; every school he had ever been involved with—felt the need to feed its students as if they were day laborers in Liverpool who couldn't wait for tea. He only wished that they could establish the kind of tradition here that they had at places like Exeter, where everyone ate at tables with tablecloths, and students took turns being waiters. That was probably elitism, too.

He let himself out the back door of Doyle House, then went down the path to the left and across the broad field to the Student Center. To his left, he could just see the top of Maverick Pond, down at the bottom of the slope that made it possible for the library to have an "above-grade lower level." He made a face at the memory of all those recruiting brochures and alumni bulletins and bent his head against the wind coming up from the open expanse to his left. Of course it was only relatively open. On the other side of the pond there was about two hundred feet of open ground. Then there was a high fence, and on the other side of that fence was some town building James had never understood the function of. He only knew it wasn't Windsor-Wellman High School, the local public school, which was from all reports a godforsaken place without facilities or standards. On the one hand, it was odd that a town as rich as Windsor, Massachusetts, wouldn't spend what it had to to make its high school a first-rate place. On the other, the whole situation seemed entirely typical. James had never seen the point in public schools on any level but the most elementary, and that in spite of the fact that he had gone to one.

He had a copy of *The Portrait of a Lady* stuffed into his coat pocket in the hope that he would be able to sit off by himself and read for the obligatory half hour; but as soon as he got to the Student Center's door, he saw that that wouldn't be possible. Marta Coelho was waiting for him. She must have seen him come up the walk. He made no effort to hide his annoyance. He knew he didn't have to; Marta would never pick up on it. She was one of those people who was completely tone-deaf when it came to social intercourse. At a place like this, she was worse than tone-deaf. She was every cliché he could remember: a fish out of water, a bull in a china shop, a fifth wheel. Why they hadn't noticed when they'd hired her how bad the fit would be, he couldn't understand, but he'd been around long enough to know it happened all the time. And then, some of the most unlikely people ended up fitting perfectly well, even if you couldn't figure out how or why. Look at Philip Candor. James began to unbutton his coat as he reached the door. Marta was standing just inside it, shifting from one foot to the other like a schoolgirl called in to the principal's office for cutting class and breaking school rules.

111

James stepped through the glass door. The air around him went from being much too cold to being much too warm. He got his coat the rest of the way unbuttoned and shrugged it off.

"You don't know how glad I am to see you," Marta said, looking around at the students milling and streaming through the long breezeway corridor. James looked at them, too. They looked . . . scruffy. They always looked scruffy. There was no dress code here. It would have been considered another form of elitism. The result was that the students felt free to wander around in jeans and T-shirts and sneakers. Everyone looked sloppy. Even students who worked hard at taking care of themselves looked sloppy.

James put his coat over his arm and started to move toward the cafeteria. He had no intention of spending even a minute longer in this place than he absolutely had to. "Surely it can't be that big a miracle to find me at dinner," he said.

Marta was hurrying to keep up. "I wanted to talk to you about something," she said. "Something Philip Candor told me, and then somebody else confirmed it. Edith, I think. Edith always knows everything, have you ever noticed that?"

"Everybody always knows everything in this place," James said. He had forged ahead steadily, and now he was at the back of the cafeteria line. There was a stack of plastic trays. He took one. If it had been up to him to redesign this place, he would have started by getting rid of all the plastic.

Marta picked up her own plastic tray. "I don't know that we should talk about it here," she said. "I mean, in line. Where too many people could hear."

"My dear woman," James said, "if you heard whatever this is from Philip, and then again from Edith, there isn't a person in this school who doesn't know what it is already, except perhaps for people who've been away all day or shut up at home and without contact with the rest of the school."

"Have you heard about it already?" Marta asked. "About Gregor Demarkian?"

"I've been shut up at home," James said drily. He had just been presented with the choice of entrée: fish fried in some kind of batter; chicken with a sauce on it that looked as if it had come straight out of a sump pump; large wedges of vegetarian omelet. He took the omelet. He'd have the least trouble looking at it throughout his purgatory at dinner, and then he could go home and cook something edible for himself. "I have heard of Gregor Demarkian though," he said. "He's that detective. He was on that television program *American Justice*."

"Oh, do you watch those?" Marta asked. She had chosen the chicken and the limp green beans that must have come from a can, and the glutinous rice they served with an enormous ice cream scoop. It was hard for James to watch. "I watch those, too. And *City Confidential.* And the other things on Court TV. You're right, he has been on some of those. I even heard that they wanted to give him his own show, but he turned it down. Could we go over there to that corner? There's an empty table. I really don't want to be—crowded."

No, James thought, *of course she doesn't want to be crowded.* He went toward the corner anyway. He didn't want to be crowded himself. He didn't want to talk to anybody. He put his tray down and sat in front of it. Then he very carefully began to take the plates off the tray and put them directly on the table. If there was one thing he wouldn't do in the cause of antielitism, which he didn't believe in anyway, it was eat directly off a cafeteria tray. The table itself was made of nothing known to nature, and laminated on top of that, and bolted into the wall, but there was nothing he could do about that.

Marta sat down. She didn't bother to take her plates off her tray. James hadn't expected her to. "Gregor Demarkian," she said, "is in town. Here. In Windsor. Earlier today, Edith heard that he was coming, and she told Philip, and then Philip saw him on Main Street near the Windsor Inn, which I suppose is where he must be staying."

"Really?" James cocked an eyebrow. He'd taken great pains to learn to do that when he was younger, and now he did it all the time without thinking. "That's surprising. From what I remember, Mr. Demarkian is a consultant to police departments, who call him in when they have homicide cases they're having trouble with. I thought our local police had decided without doubt that Michael Feyre committed suicide."

"Oh, they have," Marta said. "At least, as far as I know they have. The police didn't bring him here; Mark DeAvecca did."

"Did he? How did he manage that?"

"Oh, Demarkian is a friend of the family or something. You know what it's like in this place. The students. Their parents. It makes me sick sometimes, it really does. Don't mind me. I've been in a mood for days. Before Michael Feyre died really. And now I just don't know what to think. It bothers me, this Demarkian person being here."

"I don't see why," James said. The vegetable omelet was inedible, but he'd expected that. The coffee was undrinkable, too, but he forced himself to drink it because the Windsor Academy coffee had one thing to be said in its favor. It was some of the strongest coffee he had ever had outside of Istanbul. "I don't see what business it is of ours if Mark DeAvecca wants to ask a family friend to come here to visit, even if the family friend *is* Gregor Demarkian. Gregor Demarkian can't change the fact that Michael Feyre committed suicide."

"No, he can't change it," Marta said, "but there are other things, aren't there? There's all that stuff about Alice, for example."

"Marta, 'all that stuff about Alice,' as you put it, has been going on for a long time. It didn't start with Michael Feyre, and I doubt if it will finish with him."

"It will if it causes the school to fail," Marta said. "This isn't Exeter, you know. We don't have that kind of an endowment. If that kind of thing gets out—"

"If it gets out, Peter will be fired and he and Alice will go off somewhere, and we'll get a new headmaster whose wife is fifty-six and looks like a long-haul trucker. That's all. You've got nothing to worry about on that score."

"Well, there are other things, too," Marta said. "There are the things about the drugs."

"'The things about the drugs'?"

"That he was selling drugs."

"Marta, students sell drugs to each other in every school in the country. Schools don't fail over incidents like that; they just expel the students."

"But he wasn't just selling drugs to students," Marta said. "He was selling drugs to faculty. He was selling drugs to you."

It was odd, James thought, but just a second ago he had considered this room far too warm. Now it seemed far too cold. His plates were still spread out on the table. The vegetable omelet still looked heavy and wet at the same time. The coffee still looked too dark to really be coffee. There was a lot of noise. It seemed to be coming from another room, through a wind tunnel, broadcast by a bad microphone.

"I don't know what you're talking about," he said.

"Oh, James, for God's sake," Marta said. "What do you think, that I want to turn you in? If I did, I'd have done it already. And it wouldn't matter in this place anyway. You know what they're like. You've been here a lot longer than I have."

"I don't know what you're talking about," James said again. He picked up the plate with the omelet on it and put it back on the tray. It was very important to move slowly, and with seriousness, to not appear to be hurrying. He wanted to take the plate with the omelet on it and smash it over Marta Coelho's head, but it was the kind of thing he would never do.

Marta had pushed her tray away from her into the middle of the table.

"James, please, behave like a sane person. Somebody around here has to. You bought amphetamines from Michael Feyre. I *saw* you. In Ridenour Library not two weeks ago. My office—"

"Everybody's office is in that wing," James said. "You're mistaken."

"I'm not mistaken, and you know it." Marta stopped. Her voice had risen. She'd become aware of it. Nobody else seemed to have noticed. "I'm not mistaken," she said again. "I heard the whole conversation. Six something-or-the-others of crystal methamphetamine. I don't remember the word he used. Two hundred dollars. And I couldn't believe it, you know, so I went out into the hall so that I could hear better, and you were right there. You didn't even have your office door closed. I suppose you must have thought the wing was empty—"

"You're mistaken," James said again. He was saying things again and again. He was repeating himself. There was a roaring in his ears, like the sound you heard when you held a shell up to your head to hear the ocean. He put the coffee cup and saucer back on the tray. He put his utensils back on the tray. He felt as if he were proceeding by rote. He was a paint-by-numbers picture. All he had to do was fill in the outline and he would turn into a real boy.

"Michael saw me," Marta said. "He winked at me. James, will you please, please make sense here? This isn't a game. That boy is dead—"

"And nobody killed him," James said savagely. "He committed suicide, which, if you ask me, was entirely predictable. He was a jumped-up piece of white trash, and no lottery jackpot was ever going to change that. When he knew it was true, he cut himself off. I wish more of them would have the guts to cut themselves off. We'd be better off without them."

"We'd be better off without whom?" Marta asked. "What are you talking about?"

"We'd be better off without people like you," James said. The roaring was gone from his ears. The panic was gone from his body. He was simply more angry than he had ever been in his life. "Don't you think we all know what you are?" he said. "You got yourself a degree, and you think you can reinvent yourself as better than what you came from, but it's not working. You don't have the fiber. You don't even have the imagination."

Marta looked close to tears, but not so close that she was willing to stop. "There's no reason to shoot the messenger," she said, looking away from him. "Don't you realize that if I saw you, somebody else may have too? Not that day, of course, but another day. And he winked at me. He winked at me, James. He didn't care that I knew. He could have told anyone."

"If I were you, I'd go back to whatever godforsaken town you came from and get a job at a community college where the demands of your work will match your skills," James said.

Marta was still looking away. James knew she would not look back. He had his tray fully loaded. He need do nothing but bring it back to the kitchen, scrape off his plates, and leave. There it was again, that drive to egalitarianism. He couldn't abide the ritual of scraping off his plates.

"I don't know what you think you're doing," he told Marta Coelho, "but I can tell you for certain that you won't get away with it."

2

It was seven thirty when the phone in Gregor Demarkian's room at the Windsor Inn began ringing, and it rang a dozen times before Mark DeAvecca managed to get himself awake enough to pick it up.

"This is the front desk," a voice chirped at him. "This is your wake-up call. It's now seven thirty."

For a few long minutes, Mark was completely disoriented. He didn't think they gave wake-up calls in the dorm, and the world outside the windows he could see was far too dark for it to be seven thirty in the morning. Besides, he didn't get up at seven thirty. If he did, he missed breakfast or classes and spent the rest of the day in a complete mess. He sat up and looked around, feeling increasingly uneasy. There had been at least three times in the last two months when he'd woken up in his dorm room bed and not been able to remember how he'd gotten there, or why he'd gone to sleep, or when. The thing was he didn't feel now the way he'd felt on all those occasions. He actually felt pretty well. His head wasn't full of fuzz, or not as full of it as it tended to be these days. He wasn't suicidally depressed, which he'd come to think of as the background music to his present life. He *was* very tired, but a couple of hours napping wasn't likely to cure several months' worth of not sleeping, so that didn't worry him.

He turned on the light next to the bed. Then he sat up and looked around. The room service trays were still on the table near the window. He got up, went to the table, and sat down. He opened another bottle of Perrier and then another still. He was so thirsty, he was nearly frantic with it. He downed the first bottle in a couple of seconds and then started on the second. He took the lid off the sandwich plate and took out four roast beefs and another four tunas.

Then he put them back and put the lid to the side. He was going to eat them all. There was no use pretending he wasn't. He'd missed dinner, and he was suddenly completely ravenous.

When he'd finished the sandwiches, he looked at the soup. It was cold, but he didn't think he cared. He unwrapped the spoon from its napkin package and finished the soup off, too. He felt a little guilty. He would have to make it up to Mr. Demarkian. If his mother had seen him behave like this, she'd probably have killed him.

Or maybe not. Mark found it hard to tell what his mother would and wouldn't do.

He went into the bathroom and washed his face. He really was tired. He had that drained-of-blood feeling that made it hard for him to move. He didn't have the panic he'd been living with for so long though, and the way the head fuzz had abated was truly miraculous. Not that it was entirely gone. He could tell he wasn't functioning the way he remembered functioning before he'd come to Windsor, but for just this second he felt only *ordinarily* sick. He was also really glad that he'd had a shower. He didn't like feeling dirty. At home he sometimes showered twice a day. He didn't understand why, up here, he forgot about showering entirely, or remembered but felt too tired and confused to bother.

He went back into the bedroom and sat on the edge of the bed. Seven thirty must mean seven thirty at night. That meant he'd missed dorm check-in at five. That meant he was going to be in enormous trouble with Sheldon yet again. He was always in trouble with Sheldon for something. His room wasn't clean enough. He didn't socialize with the students in his own house enough. His clothes were a mess. Sheldon was one of the people on this campus he truly hated, but if he thought about it long enough, he had to admit that there were very few people—at least among the faculty and administration—that he didn't hate. Except that "hate" was the wrong word, he thought. It was the word people used for what he was feeling, but it wasn't the right one even so. It was more that there were people he felt in danger from. He had no idea what kind of danger or why it should be directed at him.

I'm acting nuts again, he thought. He got up and looked through the drawers of the nightstand and the table with the room service stuff on it until he found the complimentary notepad and a pen with the name of the Windsor Inn printed on it. He sat down and printed, very carefully, in block letters:

He looked at the note and shook his head. Here was something that had not been changed by a nap in Gregor Demarkian's room. His handwriting still looked like it belonged to a stroke victim. *I wonder what the hell is wrong with my hands,* he thought, and then, *I wonder what the hell is wrong with my head.*

He found his jacket and put it on. He put his note on the bed's pillow so that Gregor Demarkian couldn't fail to find it. Then he went out into the hall and down the stairs to the lobby and the street. He would have taken the elevator if he'd remembered there was one. He was still that tired. Whatever. It didn't matter. Nothing did.

He went down Main Street more quickly than he'd walked for months, more quickly than he'd walked since Christmas vacation, when he'd actually started to feel a lot better after he'd been home for a week and a half. He thought about going directly to Hayes House—it was right there on Main Street, one of the houses that faced the town—but he didn't have any coffee or Coke or Mountain Dew at Sheldon's apartment, and he knew Sheldon resented the hell out of him whenever he asked to borrow what Sheldon himself had, and he knew that he wouldn't be able to stay awake long enough to do any reading if he didn't get hold of some caffeine. As for Sheldon, it didn't matter either. Sheldon was going to be no more angry with him for coming in at eleven than if he'd come in at eight. He might as well go to the Student Center and get some coffee in peace before he had to face Round Thirty-seven of the Great Dorm War.

He turned in at Lytton House, cut around to the side of it, and crossed the quad. Then he ducked between Martinson and Doyle and out onto the path leading to the Student Center. It was unbelievably cold. He remembered it being cold, but not this cold, not even the other night when he'd been wandering around in his fog. That was the night Michael died, which was something he didn't like to think about but did. He found it impossible not to think about it. He wished he could read. Before he'd come to Windsor, he'd spent nearly all his time reading. Now he could barely understand the words on a page of a Terry Pratchett novel.

If he hadn't been so tired, he'd have run. He tried to force walk, but that didn't work either. His joints ached. He settled for pushing himself just a little to go just a bit faster, and then he was in the breezeway in the warm and he could see the big stainless steel coffee servers lined up against the back wall, standing on clean white tablecloths.

He went into the cafeteria proper and suddenly felt enormously tired, so tired he could barely remain standing. He sat down in the nearest chair and tried breathing slowly and deeply. Sometimes it helped. Sometimes it didn't. He didn't understand why the head fuzz was better, but the fatigue was worse. He put his head in his hands and tried to count. He had no idea what he thought that was going to do. He just needed to work up the energy to get across the room to where the coffee was.

"Mark?"

If he'd had to pick the voice he least wanted to hear, at this moment or at any other, he would surely have picked this particular voice. He didn't have to look up to see who it was. Nobody on earth sounded like Alice Makepeace except Alice Makepeace. That was true even though her accent was a boarding-school cliché.

"Sorry," he said, taking his face out of his hands. "I know I didn't show for check-in. I'll explain it to Sheldon when I get back to Hayes. I just wanted a cup of coffee. I don't have any back at Hayes."

"You don't look like you can make it across the room to get coffee," Alice said.

"I'm a little tired."

"You're always tired." She stood there, not saying anything. Mark had the impression that there was something he was supposed to do, but he didn't know what. "Look," she said, "I'll get you some coffee. Black you take it, don't you? And sugar?"

"As much sugar as I can get," Mark said. "And one of the big cups. Thank you. I'm sorry I'm not really functioning here."

Alice Makepeace made no comment on that. Nobody here ever made any comment when he said things like that, and he knew why. They didn't think he wasn't "functioning," and they didn't think he was tired; they thought he was either drugged up or screwing off.

The jacket he was wearing felt too hot. He didn't know why he hadn't noticed it before. He took it off and put it on the back of his chair. Only half the lights in the cafeteria were on. He didn't like this room. He missed the cafeteria at his old school in Connecticut, Rumsey Hall, which was big and open and shabby in the way that places got when they were regularly overrun with small boys. How long did it take to get a cup of coffee? What did Alice Makepeace want from him?

He looked up and she was back, holding a large coffee in one hand for him and a small one in the other for herself. Hers would probably be decaf. She was one of those people who was always very careful to eat and drink in a "healthful" way and to make damned sure that everybody around her knew it.

She sat down. He swatted at his coffee with the plastic stirrer she had brought him.

"So," she said. "I've been wanting to talk to you."

"Everybody wants to talk to me," he said. "No offense, but I've already told the police *and* Mr. Makepeace everything I know. Michael was my roommate, not my clone. I didn't really know that much about him. And I didn't see much of anything when I—when. You know when. It all happened really fast, and I wasn't noticing much. I just wanted to get out of there."

"You noticed enough to think it might not be a suicide," Alice said.

Mark took a long drink of coffee. It scalded his throat. "I don't think it wasn't suicide. The police said it has to be suicide."

"But you don't think so."

"No, that's not right. Michael committed suicide. Of course I think Michael committed suicide."

Alice stared at him. She had a truly awesome stare. It was eerie in a way. He didn't like it directed at him. He did know what Michael had been thinking to sleep with her though. She was beautiful and one of those people who were always the center of attention. "People who glow in the dark," his mother liked to call them. They walked into a room, and nobody wanted to look at anybody else.

Alice took a sip of her coffee. "I find that hard to believe," she said. "If you didn't think there was at least a chance that Michael may have been murdered, why did you bring that Mr. Demarkian to Windsor?"

"Not to investigate a murder," Mark said quickly.

"But that's what he does, isn't that true? He investigates murders."

"He does when he's working," Mark said. "He doesn't all the time."

"And he's not working here?"

The head fuzz was back. Mark could feel it. He looked down at the coffee and saw that he'd already drunk half the cup. He was going to have to get another one before he went back to Hayes. Alice Makepeace was staring at him again. He felt sick.

"Look," he said, "he's here because I needed somebody to hold my hand, and I didn't want it to be my mother because I thought she'd get all upset and want to haul me out of school. She *is* all upset. I've talked to her twice."

"And you don't want to be hauled out of school? I find that a little surprising. You don't seem to like it here."

"I like it fine," Mark said. He didn't know if that was true.

"Most of your teachers think you're completely out of place here, and I have to say I agree. You don't fit the school very well."

"Thank you."

"You must know that we talk about it. And evaluations are coming up. It will be part of the meeting the faculty has on you."

"I'm sure." He shifted in his seat. The coffee was almost gone. He was sucking it down like air. The head fuzz was back in force. So was the feeling that he had lost control of all his muscles. He was twitching. "I've got to get more coffee and go back to the house," he said. "Sheldon's going to have a fit as it is. I might as well not keep him waiting."

"I want to talk to you," she said again.

"You *are* talking to me," Mark pointed out. "You've been talking to me. You've been telling me I don't fit the school."

"I was thinking that there might be another reason for you to ask Mr. Demarkian here. Not because you had reason to think that Michael was murdered, but because you wanted to expose me."

"*Expose* you?"

"I know that you were . . . a little jealous . . . of Michael's relationship with me," Alice said, very carefully. "I know it felt like favoritism to you, that you would have taken his place if you could have. He told me—"

"He said I had the hots for *you?*"

"I don't think 'had the hots for' is an accurate description of what he meant or of what I saw. And I did see it, Mark. It was impossible to miss, even if you've never admitted it to yourself."

Mark started to get up. "I have to get another cup of coffee," he said. "I've finished this one. I've got to go back to Hayes House."

"Sit down, Mark."

"I'm not going to continue this conversation, Mrs. Makepeace."

"Alice. You know to call me Alice."

"I don't want to call you Alice. I don't want to call Miss Wardrop Cherie. I don't want to call Mr. Hallwood James. I just want to get my coffee and go back to my dorm. Get out of my way."

121

"You can barely stand up," Alice said. She put the palm of her hand against his chest and pushed gently. He sat back down again. "You're dizzy as hell."

"I haven't been feeling well all day."

"It matters that you don't fit in at this school," Alice said. "You don't have the loyalty to it that we expect of students here. And that's what worries me. That you're angry with us; that you'd like to see us fail—"

"Fail at what?"

"Fail as a school. Close down. Or be mired in an enormous scandal. That's why you've brought Gregor Demarkian here, to bring the attention of the press on the school. To tell tales about what may or may not have been going on between Michael and myself."

"For Christ's sake," Mark said, "my mother writes a regular column for the *New York Times*. She's a talking head on CNN three times a week. If I wanted to bring the attention of the press on Windsor Academy, I wouldn't have to go round about by bringing Mr. Demarkian here. I could just call Dan Rather and talk to him. He was at my christening. And my last birthday party. And everybody knows what was going on between you and Michael."

"I don't think they do, Mark, no. I think they thought as you do, that it was merely a physical thing. It wasn't. Michael was very important to me."

"I have to go back to Hayes House."

"Have you any idea how hard it is to find somebody who completes you, who makes you the human being you thought you never would be able to be, and to have that someone be beyond your reach? Repression and social convention are terrible things, Mark. They're much more tyrannous than dictatorships, or poverty, or war. They're worse because they come from inside yourself."

"I can't believe you think that you're worse off because people would laugh at you if you left your husband for a sixteen-year-old kid than you would be if you'd lived under Hitler."

"It's one of the reasons you don't really belong here," Alice said; "you don't understand the hermeneutics of oppression. You really don't. We've tried to teach it to you, but you resist it. You're like so many people. You aren't willing to give up your white skin privilege, your white male privilege. Michael wasn't like that."

"Michael was in way over his head," Mark said carefully. "I don't know what you want from me."

"I want you to promise that you will not tell Gregor Demarkian about the relationship between Michael and myself."

"What if I already have?"

"Then there's nothing I can do about it, is there? But I don't think you have. I think if you had told him, I'd know about it already. The news would be out."

"The news is going to be out one way or the other, sooner or later," Mark said. "I'm not the only one who knows. Everybody knows."

"Nobody else would tell."

"And Michael's mother is here. She'll tell."

"Michael didn't tell his mother about us. I asked him not to, and he gave me his promise, and I'm sure he wouldn't have broken it. You don't understand that either, but we were so close, so perfectly in touch with each other, not only physically but in every other way—we were so perfectly matched. We trusted each other without reservation."

"How very nice for both of you."

"You ought to learn not to be envious of other people, Mark. It isn't a very attractive trait in someone like you, someone who's had all the advantages. It's not as if you've done anything to deserve the things you've had. It's all been handed to you. You ought to take it in good grace when other people sometimes get a few of the crumbs from your table."

The head fuzz was more than back in force. It was completely out in the stratosphere. The only reason he wasn't twitching anymore was that he'd willed himself not to. He kept seeing a vision of himself and his mother and his little brother, Geoff, in the cabin they had rented on Lake Candlewood the year after his father had died, when they were all out of money and his mother wasn't working, and the whole world seemed to have gone to hell, and his life seemed to be effectively over. He'd been ten years old at the time, and he could still see them sitting on chairs with their feet up because the cabin flooded with an inch of water in every bad rain. He could still see the Christmas with no tree and no stockings and nothing for presents but boxes of Russell Stover candy that his mother had managed to get hold of he never knew how. He did not mind those memories. His life had been much more complicated than Alice Makepeace would ever understand. He did mind Alice's soft, sad, condescending smile.

"I have to go back to Hayes House," he said again, again trying to get up.

Alice's smile grew more pitying as she pushed him down yet again. "Please," she said, "let me get you your coffee."

SIX

1

Gregor Demarkian found the note from Mark DeAvecca on his bed when he returned to his room, but he had expected that. He only read the note with enough attention to be sure that Mark had gone back to school, something he'd only half expected him to do. Mark was not the sort of boy who "hated" school and spent his time playing truant or hiding a Game Boy Advance behind the upraised back of his textbook in biology class. Gregor was willing to bet that, until this year, Mark hadn't ever wanted to be somewhere else in the middle of a school day. He revised that. There were times when any sane human being wanted to be somewhere else in the middle of a school day. What he meant was that he had always thought, before this visit, that Mark DeAvecca was a lot like he himself had been at the same age—a boy who truly loved books, and whose mind was the most noticeable thing about him, but not a "bookish" boy. *There is a difference,* Gregor thought, *between intelligence and scholarliness.* He didn't know if "scholarliness" was even a word. But there was a difference, and he had never been scholarly. He had loved to read, and he had read everything, from *Popular Mechanics* magazines to Jean-Paul Sartre novels that had been stupefying in their nihilism. He had loved school because in school, for at least some of the time, he was out of the maelstrom that was Cavanaugh Street in the days before everybody had enough money to turn tenements into town houses. School and the public library were his two most distinct memories of growing up, but the background music for both was the sound of people arguing, men shouting, women crying, the crash of rickety wooden chairs and cheap crockery against the walls of apartments too thin to contain either the sound or the anger. He had read those articles in the *Philadelphia Inquirer* bent on "celebrating ethnic Philadelphia," and he had wanted more than once to talk some sense into the writers who produced them. He would say:

Ethnic Philadelphia was like ethnic everywhere else. The people who came here were poor, and ignorant, and scared to death. They came from a world where women were not much better than cattle in the social scheme of things, and men expected to have authority whether they had earned it or not. They came to a world where men have authority only as the result of striving and achievement, and women sometimes have authority, too. The schoolteachers were women. The family court judges were women. They went back to their neighborhoods and their wives and their children after a day of working in the Anglo-Saxon world, and they were running on panic and rage.

He had no idea why he was thinking about all that now: Cavanaugh Street in the early fifties; his own father, usually the calmest of men, breaking out at least twice a year in fits of fury so irrational and so uncontrollable that there was nothing for him to do but hide in a closet somewhere until it was over. And then it wasn't bad. His father never did much more to his mother than slap her. He wasn't a brutal man. Howard Kashinian's father was a very brutal man, and at least three times before Howard was eight, his mother had landed in the hospital with bones broken and worse. The absolute worst was that Howard's mother always landed on a charity ward. She had to. The Kashinians had no more money than anybody else on Cavanaugh Street in those days. Mikhel Kashinian was a steady worker at the kind of jobs men got when they knew little or no English and had no education even in their native tongue. He was a day laborer at times, a driver of light trucks in local markets, a ditch digger, a man who hauled dirt and debris at construction sites. Gregor remembered him as an enormous man, built more like an ox or a yak than a human being, with hands the size of shovels. When Howard's mother would be in the hospital, broken and bleeding from what Mikhel had done to her, Mikhel would not go to see her. He did not want to feel sorry for what he had done, and he would not show his face on the charity ward, where the utter, uninhibited evidence of his failure at all things American would be impossible to avoid.

That's what Gregor would tell the writers who wanted to "celebrate" "ethnic Philadelphia," including the ones who were building nostalgic dreams of the lives of their own grandparents and great-grandparents, people who had lived in a world that the writers themselves had never had any real contact with. People come to America to build a better life, and it is the genius of America that most of them are able to do it; but the better life they build is one that their children and grandchildren live. For most immigrants, life in the United States is one long litany of failure, one long, twisted fairy tale of never being able to meet the standard because the standard keeps moving. Gregor guessed that the circumstances of Mikhel Kashinian's life on Cavanaugh Street were no worse than what he had had in Armenia and probably better. No matter how awful those old tenements had been, they'd been better than the huts and hovels the Kashinians and the Demarkians had left behind in the villages outside Yekevan. There were central heating and running water and indoor plumbing. The Kashinians had to use a bathroom in the hall, but Gregor couldn't help believe that that had to be better than a privy in the yard. Mikhel would not have done more interesting work in Armenia than he did in Philadelphia. He was a beast of burden. It was all he had been trained for. It was all he would have known, no matter what the place.

Still, if his relatives from the village could have seen Mikhel and his apartment and his family full of children going every day to a free school, they would have considered him rich; and if he had been able to keep their perspective, he would have considered himself rich, too. The problem was that he couldn't keep their perspective. His children went to school with children whose families owned whole houses on pleasant, tree-lined streets. His daughters wore plain dresses from Montgomery Ward, while the girls they sat beside in class had Bobbie Brooks and Villager. The exodus to the suburbs had begun. "Successful" men—real Americans—didn't stay in Philadelphia. They took their families out to subdivisions where their children would have real lawns to play on and school buses to pick them up every day with their Howdy Doody lunch boxes in tow.

Howdy Doody lunch boxes, Gregor thought. It had been years since he'd remembered Howdy Doody lunch boxes. He had no idea why he was suddenly on this tear about the "old" Cavanaugh Street. He doubted if Howard himself remembered much about it, although he just might. Howard being Howard, Gregor, like everybody else, often didn't give him much credit; but there was this to be said about him. He'd absorbed the ethic of America as thoroughly as any of them; and when he'd turned sixteen and realized that he'd grown larger and heavier and more powerful than his father, he put an end to Mikhel's fits of rage and his mother's trips to the hospital, charity ward or not.

He'd been thinking about Mark DeAvecca, that was it. He had been thinking about how much he and Mark were alike—or had been alike, a year and a half ago, when they'd first met—and that had made him think about the ways they were not alike at all. He didn't think Mark had ever seen the kinds of things he had, never mind seen them on a regular basis, so that they felt entirely normal. He wondered if Mark had ever approached any place the way he himself had approached his local branch of the Philadelphia Public Library. Other people believed in God and prayer. He believed in the Philadelphia Public Library. It was the place he went to feel that there was a way to make his life more like what he wanted it to be.

I'm making no sense at all, he thought, sitting down on the side of the bed and staring at the phone. He thought about calling room service, but that didn't feel right. He'd just eaten, and the last thing he needed was more coffee. He thought about calling Bennis, but that didn't feel right either. He didn't think he could face the wall of coldness he was expecting from her. It was just the wrong night for it. It was something about that school, he decided, something about Brian Sheehy's visceral anger at all things Windsor, about Mark's scattershot descriptions, about his own gut instincts just walking through town. Somehow, Windsor Academy and the old days on Cavanaugh Street connected. He just didn't know how.

I'm not only not making any sense; I'm positively incoherent, he thought. He picked up the phone, considered his options, and dialed Tibor. He got a message that said the number had been disconnected and he had to dial again. He kept forgetting. Tibor's apartment had been destroyed in the explosion that had destroyed Holy Trinity Church. Tibor was now living in Bennis's old apartment on the second floor of Gregor's building. That meant Gregor had to call Bennis's number to get Tibor because . . .

This whole thing is beginning to sound like a sitcom, Gregor thought. Besides, it might all fall apart in a week or two. If Bennis continued to be not much interested in talking to him, she probably would be not much interested in going on living with him. He wondered what she would do if that day ever came. Would she move back to the second floor, or would she leave Cavanaugh Street altogether and go back to the Main Line world she'd come from?

The thought of Bennis leaving Cavanaugh Street made his stomach lurch. The phone rang and rang in his ear, making him think that Tibor had gone out somewhere, to the Ararat, to old George Tekemanian's to play cards. It was only eight o'clock.

He was about to put the phone back on the hook and try to think of something else to do with himself for the evening when Tibor picked up.

"Is Kasparian," Tibor said.

That was new. In the old days all Tibor said when he picked up the phone was, "Hello."

"It's me," Gregor said. "I called your old number first. I don't know why I can't get used to this."

"Nobody can get used to this, Krekor. Three or four times a day, I have phone calls from people looking for Bennis, and people who should know better: Lida, Hannah Krekorian."

"Bennis," Gregor said.

Tibor cleared his throat. "You are all right where you are? You have determined that the suicide was really a murder?"

"I'm fine, but the suicide was almost certainly a suicide. I talked to the chief of police today. He took me to dinner. He gave me chapter and verse. I can't see why he'd lie to me."

"To protect the people at this school maybe? You said when you left it was a rich school."

"I know, but Brian Sheehy hates the place. I don't think he'd do a thing to save it embarrassment. No, it was definitely a suicide."

"Then you will be coming home," Tibor said.

Gregor hesitated. "I don't think so, no. Not right away."

There was the sound of rapid-fire typing on the other end of the line. Gregor thought Tibor must be on the Internet. "Why are you staying if there is no murder?" Tibor asked. "It's what you do, looking into murders."

"I know. Right now I'm looking into Mark DeAvecca."

"The boy."

"Exactly, the boy, who is a complete mess. I don't know how to describe it. You didn't meet him last spring. I did. He's done a one-hundred-eighty-degree personality turn, for one thing."

"This is drugs, Krekor?"

"He says not, and my instinct is to believe him. I don't know why, but it's not the kind of thing I think he'd lie about. The trouble is, if it's not drugs, he's got to be sick. Really sick. So I called his mother."

"Why didn't he call his mother?"

"Because he's afraid she'll take him out of school, which would be giving up."

There was a very long pause, no typing. Tibor said, "Krekor, that is not sensible."

"I agree, but it's what he says. And I think I understand the basic thrust. Anyway, Liz will be up here tomorrow, first thing, if she's not up here late tonight. She made me book her a place at the inn where I'm staying. And I've been walking around. For some reason or the other, this place makes me think about Cavanaugh Street in the old days—before you'd ever heard of it. When Lida and Howard and Hannah and I were all children."

There was more typing. Tibor must be on RAM. The typing stopped and Tibor said, "This is a poor place you are in, Krekor? A, what, inner city?"

"Hardly. It's one of the richest suburbs I've ever seen in my life. And it's precious to the point of being lethally so."

"I don't understand 'precious,' except in 'precious metal.' That isn't what you mean."

"No," Gregor said. "It's hard to explain. It's a famous place in American history. Battles were fought here in the American Revolutionary War. In fact, next to Lexington and Concord, it may be *the* most famous place in that period of American history; and then in the fifty years or so immediately after, it was home to a whole pack of American writers and intellectuals, people we were all forced to read in school during the time when that sort of thing mattered."

"I see. So this is a place precious to American culture."

"No," Gregor said. " 'Precious' in this sense means—quaint, but worse. I can't explain it. They've turned the town into a parody of itself, in a way, is what I suppose it means. It's not real. It's a theme park, except people live in it. The stores on Main Street are all in clapboard buildings that look like houses and might once have been houses. The dormitories at Windsor Academy are houses, too, real ones that have been here for two hundred years. Everything is very carefully preserved, except it isn't. It's history cleansed of factuality."

"Like history without the bad parts?" Tibor said. "This is why I do not like Walt Disney, Krekor, because he makes Disney World, and there are exhibits about history but it does not show the pain."

"You've been to Disney World?"

"Twice, Krekor, yes. With Lida when I go to visit her at the house she has in Florida. I liked the roller coasters."

Gregor tried to wrap his mind around Fr. Tibor Kasparian, an immigrant refugee from Yekevan, who had been tortured and imprisoned by the old Soviet government, whirling around on Space Mountain—and found that the vision was entirely believable. He left it alone.

"They'd show the pain here," he said, "but it wouldn't be pain. They'd put it in a museum dedicated to the lives of people oppressed by gender, race, and class, and it wouldn't be pain anymore. It would be an ideological version of what you don't like about Disney World. The whole thing is staged."

"And this made you think of Cavanaugh Street when you were a child?"

"Yes. And don't ask me why. I don't entirely know. I was thinking about Howard Kashinian."

"We all think about Howard Kashinian sometimes, Krekor. We are all still in amazement about the miracle of the fact that nobody has indicted him yet."

"Yes, well. The thing is, Howard's father, Mikhel, was this huge man, this unbelievably huge man. Armenians aren't very tall, you know that—"

"Krekor, you yourself must be six three or four."

"But they're not usually," Gregor insisted, "but Mikhel was tall and broad. Built like an ox, people used to say then. He was also bone stupid."

"Then Howard comes by it honestly, as Bennis would say."

"Oh he was a lot stupider than Howard," Gregor said, "and it wasn't just education. He was slow. It was Howard's mother who had the brains, but of course in those days and among those people it didn't matter if she did. He never adjusted. Mikhel, I mean. A lot of those men never adjusted. They were angry all the time. Mikhel used to blow up at least twice a month. There was a bill he couldn't pay. Something had gone wrong at work. He'd lost another job. No reason at all, maybe. When he blew up, he'd beat the hell out of Howard's mother—"

"*Tcha,*" Tibor said.

"Are you going to try to tell me it doesn't happen in the old country all the time?"

"No, Krekor. It does happen in the old country all the time, and it is tolerated there far more than here. But not so much now as it was thirty or forty years ago."

"And this was longer ago than that. So he'd beat her up, and a few times she'd end up in the hospital, and when she did she'd always land up a charity patient, and that would make everything worse. I remember one time when Mikhel came out of his apartment while she was coming up the stairs with the groceries, two big, brown paper bags in her arms, and when she got to the landing he swiped the bags onto the floor and punched her in the eye. Just like that. Right there. We lived underneath them for a while, and we'd hear it. He'd pick her up and throw her on the floor. He'd break furniture. My parents would sit in our living room and get very still. My mother would sew. My father would read the newspaper. They'd give no indication at all that they heard any of it."

"Because you do not interfere between a husband and a wife."

"Exactly," Gregor said. "And that was what I was thinking about with Howard. Because he got big, you know, as big as he is now, as big as his father was. And one day he was sixteen or so and not only just as big as Mikhel but twenty years younger, and he was playing football, so he was in shape. We were coming home from school together one afternoon in early May, a beautiful afternoon, even places like Cavanaugh Street was then looked good, and when we came around the corner into the neighborhood, Mikhel and Howard's mother were standing out in front of our building. I have no idea what happened or what started the fight. With men like that there isn't much need to start one. I don't know that Howard knew what started it either. We came around the corner, and just as we did Mikhel grabbed Howard's mother by the front of her dress and hit her in the side of the head with his fist. It was insane. There had to be a dozen people on the street. Nobody did anything. Mikhel had a grip on her dress and he was pulling her toward him and then hitting her away over and over again, and there was blood coming out of her ear and her head was whipping back and forth—"

"*Tcha,*" Tibor said again.

"And Howard didn't run. He didn't shout. He just walked up to them, dropped his books on the ground, picked his father up from behind, by his belt and his shirt, just lifted him up into the air and threw him across the street—all the way across the street. Mikhel landed on somebody's stoop. It might have been the building where Lida's family lived. He slid down the stoop stairs to the sidewalk, and Howard walked over to him, picked him up, put him back on his feet, and said, 'Enough.' That was it. 'Enough.' We never heard Mikhel beat that woman up again, and we never saw her hurt again, ever."

"That is the first creditable thing I have ever heard about Howard Kashinian," Tibor said.

"There are lots of creditable things about Howard," Gregor said. "You just don't want to let him near your stock trades. He's a crook. But the thing is, that's what Windsor reminded me of, the town of Windsor and what I've heard so far about the school. It reminded me of the day Howard Kashinian took on his father."

"And this is supposed to make me feel better, as if you were making sense?"

"I think so," Gregor said. "I think it's the key to what's wrong with Mark DeAvecca and what's wrong with this place and what's wrong with the country. How's that for megalomania?"

"I think you should get Bennis to talk to you again, Krekor; you are becoming a crank."

"Maybe. But I do know that I've decided what I think I'm supposed to be doing up here. I've got a mission."

"Which is?"

"Which is to get Mark DeAvecca to drop out of school. He can drop back in next fall. He needs to get away from here."

"And do you think his mother will agree with you about this?"

"She will when she sees him," Gregor said. "Celebrating diversity. That's the problem."

"You are once again making no sense, Krekor."

"Never mind. I'm glad you were in. It helped to talk to you."

"It would help you more if you could talk to Bennis, Krekor. She would even understand the things you are saying."

"She might, but she wouldn't talk back."

Tibor said something that sounded like *tcha* once again, except that his tone was even more negative. Gregor hung up and stared at the phone for a moment. He should call Bennis. He knew he should. He should call precisely because she wasn't talking to him, and he didn't know why. There was something deeply dangerous about letting this go. He tried, one more time, to consider the possibility that Bennis would leave Cavanaugh Street, put all her things into boxes, call for a moving company, buy a train ticket to Bryn Mawr or a plane ticket to Paris. He thought of the other side of the bed empty and the apartment under his feet with nobody but Tibor in it, ever, or a stranger to replace Tibor when the church and its rectory apartment were rebuilt. He got a pain in his stomach again but no answers. He wished he knew what Bennis wanted of him. He couldn't make himself ask.

He put his hand on the phone, picked up the receiver, listened to the dial tone in his ear. He put the phone back and stared at it. It was a green phone, "avocado" in decorating terms. It matched the wallpaper and the quilt spread out on the bed. It did not match the pen holder, which was made out of wood and not plastic, as it would have been in any ordinary hotel. He got up and walked over to the window.

"Bullshit," he said, out loud.

He had no idea if he was talking about Windsor, Massachusetts, or himself.

2

In the end Gregor went out because he had nothing else to do and because he was not the kind of person who took pills or drank seriously in order to calm his nerves. It was only half past eight, and he was as revved up and restless as he had been after breakfast this morning. He was not tired. He thought he ought to be exhausted, considering the day he'd had, all the traveling and all the stress. He couldn't stop moving. He paced back and forth across his room until he began to worry that whoever had the room under him would call the desk to complain. His mind jumped from Windsor to Howard to Mark to Bennis and back to Mark again. He tried to stand still looking out on Main Street at the traffic moving slowly, bumper to bumper, from one end of the area he still thought of as "precious" to the other. He found himself craning slightly to his left to catch the start of the Windsor Academy grounds, as if he expected something revelatory to happen there: Mark bursting out of one of the gates screaming, "Free at last!" at the top of his lungs; Brian Sheehy finally giving in and torching the place; Liz Toliver showing up on her white charger to do . . . what? He didn't know what he expected Liz to do when she got here. He only hoped she'd take her son home, whether he wanted to go or not.

Gregor got his coat, put it back on, and went out into the hall again. He wanted to walk. It would clear his head. He went downstairs, left the key at the desk for the second time since he'd checked in less than five hours ago, and went back out onto Main Street. This time, though, he didn't stay on the inn's side of the street. He crossed at the nearest crosswalk, which was not hard, because the people in cars seemed to assume that the pedestrian right-of-way was absolute. As soon as he stepped into the zebra walk, traffic came to a halt. He crossed without having to wait.

On the other side there was a pharmacy, then a video store, then the first of the enormous Colonial houses that were the town-side face of the Windsor Academy campus. He tried to count along the street to see how many there were, but he couldn't see far enough. Windsor was curiously flat for a New England town. Some of the houses were Greek Revival and had pillars meant to mimic the facade of the Parthenon. Some of the houses were older than that and as plain as the plain thinking that the old Massachusetts Unitarians had put so much store in. Most of the windows in the houses were lit up. Gregor supposed that most students would be in their rooms studying at this time of night.

He came to a wrought-iron fence and a sign that said EAST GATE, but it wasn't a gate. There was only an opening in the bars beneath a wrought-iron arch, a stylized gate, not a real one. That seemed terribly symbolic in some way he couldn't figure out. He let it go and went through into a small parking lot along one side of a large, gray building discreetly marked with a sign that said ADMISSIONS.

He went through the parking lot into what was obviously a standard campus quadrangle and waited. Surely there were guards here somewhere. There didn't appear to be. Nobody came out to challenge his presence on campus. Nobody stopped him from walking into the quad's center and looking around. He looked at the buildings on every side. It was their backs that fronted the quad, which he found very odd. He wasn't all that familiar with campuses— he'd been a commuter student at the University of Pennsylvania, and too over-loaded with work at Harvard Business School to pay much attention to Harvard Yard—but he'd always had the impression that buildings faced quads. The arrangement here felt slightly off. So did the big Gothic building to his right, which didn't look as if it belonged on the same campus.

He walked through on the path, between two large white houses and out to the other side. The path continued to his left until it reached a large building with several articulated wings. To his right there was open space that went down to a midsized pond. The building with articulated wings was relatively new, but it had been designed to "blend" with all that authentic Colonial. The pond was frozen over and obscured by thick stamds of evergreens. He looked but didn't see any sign of sports facilities. There were no cages for batters to stand in for baseball. There were no goalposts for football. There was nothing that looked like it could have held a basketball court.

He walked a little ways toward the building with articulated wings and then stopped. He could see no point in going there. He didn't know what it was; and although it was lit up, it seemed to be deserted. He went back into the quad and paid more attention to the Gothic building. It said RIDENOUR LI-BRARY on the front. He knew the name Ridenour from somewhere; he wasn't sure where. The library looked as deserted as the newer buildings. Only the Houses looked inhabited, and he assumed they were all dorms.

I wish I knew what I was doing here, he thought. Then he remembered something Mark had told him and tried to figure out which of the houses was the one Mark lived in. It was one of the ones that fronted on Main Street, he re-membered that. It was the one next to the one next to West Gate. He remem-bered that, too. West Gate defined the western end of campus, so the last house on the other side would be that one, and the next one closer to him would be Hayes, where Mark lived. Gregor went down the path in that direction.

When he came to the house he thought was Hayes, he hesitated. It wasn't late, that was true, but he wasn't sure that students were allowed to receive vis-itors on school nights or at all if the visitors hadn't been cleared in advance. If he was running a boarding school for teenagers, that was the kind of rule he'd put in force. On the other hand, if he was running a boarding school for teenagers, he wouldn't leave the campus open to the town the way this one was.

It surprised him that they hadn't had a murder here yet or a kidnapping. A serial killer could waltz in at will and snatch anybody he wanted to. There would be no way to stop him.

He mounted the two shallow steps to the back door and stopped. He could hear noise inside, shouting, anger. For a split second, he was having that flashback to the old Cavanaugh Street all over again. Someone was furious and not doing anything to hide it. Nothing seemed to be breaking though. No furniture seemed to be flying. He went right up to the door and found the bell and rang it. The shouting was much closer now. Whoever was angry was angry on the ground floor, not upstairs in one of the rooms.

He was just about to ring again, sure that nobody had heard him the first time because of the noise, when the door was yanked open by a small man with thinning hair.

"Who the hell are you?" he asked. "What the hell are you doing here at this time of night?"

"I'm Gregor Demarkian," Gregor said. "I'm looking for Mark DeAvecca, if it isn't too late to talk to him."

"You're looking for Mark DeAvecca," the small man said. "What the fucking hell."

An even smaller woman came running out from somewhere toward the back of the house. "Sheldon, for God's sake. You've got to do something."

"I *will* do something," Sheldon said. "I'm going to kick that little asshole's ass from here to New York."

"Sheldon, *please*."

"I've come at a bad time," Gregor said. "I'm looking for Mark DeAvecca. I was just wondering—"

The small woman looked at him, her eyes wide. "You're Gregor Demarkian," she said. "Edith and I were just discussing you. Edith Braxner. I'm sorry. I know I'm not making any sense. Come in. Please come in."

"You can't let some idiot off the street into the house because you talked about him with Edith," Sheldon said.

"Shut up," the woman said. "Oh, God. I don't know what we're going to do, Mr. Demarkian. I'm Cherie Wardrop. I'm Mark's biology teacher. Mark is—"

"Mark is throwing up all the hell over my bathroom and you know as well as I do that he's not going to clean up after himself," Sheldon said. "Gregor Demarkian isn't going to clean up after him either. There is vomit all over my bathroom. There's vomit on the goddamned ceiling in my bathroom—"

"Projectile vomiting?" Gregor asked. "Bad enough to reach a, what, twenty-foot ceiling?"

"Come with me," Cherie said, grabbing him by his arm.

Gregor let himself be pushed along, down a narrow hall lined with coat hooks and littered with snow boots, to a small door that stood open at the end. By now he was aware that they had an audience. A little crowd of students was clutched together near the door where he'd come in, spilling out of a corridor that would probably lead to the main rooms of the house and the stairs to the bedrooms upstairs. Gregor paid very little attention to them.

Cherie pulled him through the door at the end and into Sheldon's apartment. Gregor noticed that it was small and meticulously neat, but not much else about it. If Sheldon had taste, it was not the sort of taste that leapt out at you.

Cherie pulled him into another narrow hall and then into a bathroom, and right from the beginning Gregor saw two things completely clearly. One was that Mark had indeed been vomiting, and there was indeed vomit everywhere, even on the ceiling. There was vomit all over Mark, too, down the front of the sweatshirt he had borrowed from Gregor, down his arms, on his hands, on his shoes. The bathroom was the kind of mess that couldn't be cleaned up without professional help.

The second thing Gregor noticed was that Mark was not vomiting any longer. He was convulsing. His eyes were bugging out of his head. His body was arched and snapping as if he were being electrocuted, over and over again.

"Call nine-one-one," he told Cherie. "Do it now."

He got to his knees and grabbed Mark in the middle of a snap. It was hard as hell to hold onto him. He was whipping around like a rag doll and stiff and dangerous at the same time. Gregor grabbed his head and got it wedged between his arm and his side. He forced Mark's mouth open and grabbed the tongue, then held it down with his thumb.

"Jesus Christ," he said, "what's wrong with you people?"

"I can't call nine-one-one," Cherie said, "I have to clear it with President's House first. Those are the rules, and we can't—"

"Call nine-one-one or I'll do it for you, with one hand if I have to," Gregor said. "Can't you see he's not sick to his stomach? He's having convulsions. He could die from them. He could be permanently brain damaged. How long has he been like this?"

"He's was fine ten minutes ago," Cherie said frantically. "He came in and he wanted a cup of coffee, but he didn't want to ask Sheldon because Sheldon, Sheldon—"

"Because Sheldon is a selfish prick who didn't want him to think that just because he was bunking in Sheldon's apartment he could have free rein with Sheldon's stuff," Sheldon said, "and Sheldon was right as rain because this kid is a selfish asshole slacker who thinks the world owes him a living."

"He was fine," Cherie said, in tears. "He wanted some coffee, so I made him some, and he took it back here because he's been staying here since Michael died, and then the next thing I knew Sheldon was screaming and Mark was throwing up and everything was a mess and I don't know what to do. I don't know what to do."

"Call nine-one-one," Gregor said again.

Mark's body had stopped snapping. This wave of convulsions was over. That didn't mean another wave couldn't start in thirty seconds or less. Cherie stared down at Mark's inert body. Mark's chest was rising and falling, rhythmically and deeply. Gregor thought that was the best sign he'd had since he'd walked into this room. Cherie bit her lip.

"I've got to call President's House," she said. "I have to. And I will. But I'll call nine-one-one first."

The man named Sheldon said nothing. He had the kind of look on his face that people have when they think they're the victim of a con. Gregor realized that if Mark DeAvecca had shown every sign of collapsing with a heart attack, this man Sheldon would have thought it was just another ruse.

PART TWO

The inventor of the mirror poisoned the human heart.
—FERNANDO PESSOA

Human beings know neither how to rejoice properly, nor how to grieve properly, for they do not understand the distance between good and evil.
—SAINT JOHN OF THE CROSS

We're on a mission from God.
—ELWOOD BLUES

ONE

1

By the time Liz Toliver showed up to find out what was happening to her son, it was nearly midnight, Mark was "resting comfortably," and Gregor Demarkian thought he was going to fall over from exhaustion. He should have gone back to the inn an hour ago. He could have taken a comfortable seat in the lobby and waited for Liz to arrive. It would have been at least as compassionate as what he had done and far more sensible. This way Liz had had to arrive at the inn's front desk to be given a note about Mark and how to find him, and the note would of necessity have been brief and uninformative. Gregor didn't know how uninformative, since he had had to phone it in from the hospital once Mark was out of danger and he could think about something besides what he would say if Mark died and he had to tell Liz about it. He had been careful to give the desk clerk at the inn a complete and exhaustive text to pass on, but he didn't trust it. The desk clerk was one of those people—he was running into more and more of them in Windsor—who seemed to run fueled by a barely concealed resentment of the school and all it stood for. There was no way to disguise the fact that he was "connected" to the school, even though it was only to the extent of being the friend of the family of a student. When he wasn't worrying about Mark, Gregor couldn't help noticing that it was a nasty situation. The police and the firefighters would do their jobs because, by and large, they would be the kind of men for whom the job mattered more than the worthiness of the people receiving its benefits. There were other people to be considered though. The school couldn't survive without support services, and support services were delivered by dozens of men and women, the vast majority of whom seemed to be of the opinion that they'd be better off if the school and all its people vanished from the face of the earth. Gregor had seen it every place he went, on his two brief walks up and down Main Street. He had seen it here, in the hospital, in the way the nurses' faces got blank and the emergency room doctor's spine got stiff as soon as they all understood that Mark was a Windsor Academy student. The emergency room doctor was a solemn, intelligent, and very young man who had obviously come to America from India or Pakistan. His distaste for Windsor and all its works was palpable. There was something about him that made Gregor trust his professionalism, but that was all that made Gregor confident that Mark would be well served in this place. *No,* he thought now, *that's not fair.* Nurses and doctors, like policemen and firemen, usually valued the job more than the worthiness of the people receiving its benefits.

It didn't help the situation that Gregor had not been left to wait for Liz on his own. Peter Makepeace, Windsor's headmaster, had decided to wait with him. Gregor had no idea if this was what Peter Makepeace was expected to do as headmaster, or if he'd decided it was something he had to do as long as Gregor was there. In any event it made for difficulties Gregor wasn't prepared for. Left on his own, and given an hour or two, he could probably have managed to get the nurses to talk to him. He was good at that sort of thing. If he hadn't been, he would never have risen as far as he had in the FBI. The nurses would not talk in front of Peter Makepeace. They would barely stay in the small waiting room with its molded blue plastic seats screwed into stainless steel bars and anchored into the walls. When there was news, they came just as far in past the swinging fire doors as they had to. Often, they held one of those doors open for the sake of quick escape. Then they would deliver whatever line they had been given to say and dart out again, unavailable for questions.

No nurse had come in for over an hour now. There really was nothing else to say this evening. Mark had had his stomach pumped. He was sleeping. They had done tests. The results would be available in the morning. Gregor guessed that the results would be available a lot earlier than that, but that it was going to be damned near impossible to get anybody to tell them what they were.

It was a typical hospital waiting room. Gregor had been in dozens of hospitals in his life, as a patient and a visitor, and the waiting rooms were always the same. The floor was some kind of linoleum or vinyl. No matter how often it was scrubbed clean, it looked stained. There were bits and pieces of paper garbage in the corners and up against the walls: candy wrappers, Popsicle sticks, stray cigarette butts. No smoking was allowed here, but people had been smoking nonetheless. The smell of it was in the air. The windows looked out on a part of Windsor Gregor would not have believed existed if he hadn't seen it. There was a women's prison, and a big brick building he thought might be the local high school. Neither building looked as if it belonged in a town as rich as this one.

Peter Makepeace looked as out of place in this room as a Japanese rice paper print would have looked on the walls of a Neanderthal's cave. He was, Gregor thought, almost unreal in his perfection of the stereotype he had been hired to represent. He was tall and lean and athletic; but more strikingly, he was elongated. Even his face was elongated. He was all angles and edges, as uncompromisingly aristocratic as a Plantagenet prince. It was there in his air of entitlement, too, which was more than just confidence. Gregor was confident that, once Liz got here, he could get the people he needed to talk to him to talk to him. Peter Makepeace gave the impression of believing that his access to information was a matter of right.

I'm being unfair this time, too, Gregor thought, and that was true. He was making assumptions about Peter Makepeace just as he had been making assumptions about the hospital's nurses. God only knew Makepeace seemed to be nervous enough. He had been pacing nonstop for most of the time he'd been in the waiting room, and Gregor got the impression that he'd go on pacing until something forcibly stopped him. Gregor would have paced himself except that he was too tired to move.

Peter Makepeace stopped in midpace and looked down at him. "Did you say you were a friend of the family? That's what you're doing here?"

"I'm acquainted with Mark's mother," Gregor said.

"And he asked you down here," Peter said. "Yes, I know about that. The whole school knows about that. It's been the subject of gossip for days. He shouldn't have done that. There's been enough conspiracy talk about Michael's death as it is. Now everybody and his brother will assume that Michael Feyre was murdered."

"I don't see why," Gregor said. "I've got no information that would indicate that Michael Feyre was murdered."

Peter Makepeace smiled. It was a thin, bitter smile. "Excuse me if I feel that you're very naive no matter how many years you spent in the Federal Bureau of Investigation. You investigate murders. If you're here, somebody must have been murdered. The only likely candidate is Michael Feyre. He's the one who's dead. Of course, now there's Mark."

"He's not dead."

"No, he isn't, but I think there's reason to say he could have been. People will just say it was attempted murder, don't you think?"

Gregor stretched out his legs. It was difficult because he was very tall, and Peter Makepeace was standing up close, towering over him, intimidating.

"What do you think *did* happen to Mark DeAvecca tonight?"

Peter shrugged. "Drugs, I'd expect. My guess is some kind of speed, which is what Michael sold. Did you know that Michael sold drugs?"

"I didn't know that you did."

"Oh, I couldn't prove it. If I could have proved it, I'd have sent him packing with no ceremony whatsoever. As it is I would have gotten rid of both of them at the end of the year. We issue contracts, you know. Students have to get a new contract every year. We don't always give them if we think the student is unsuitable."

"And you thought both Michael Feyre and Mark DeAvecca were unsuitable? On what grounds? Were they flunking out? Were they discipline problems?"

"Ah, that's the beauty of it," Peter Makepeace said, "we don't have to have grounds. All we need to do is say that we think they're unsuitable. They don't fit the school. They're not comfortable here. We think they won't be able to succeed."

"I find it hard to believe that Mark DeAvecca would have trouble succeeding anywhere."

Peter Makepeace turned away and went back to the window end of the room. He looked out, probably on nothing. "Yes, I know. I've heard that. And I've checked his papers. He's got a truly spectacular set of papers. And God only knows, he's not flunking out even now, in spite of the mess he's made of himself. I think he's averaging about a C plus."

"In my day that was a perfectly respectable showing."

"It's a bit low for this place, but I agree. It's nothing to have a fit about. That makes it all the worse really. Think of how well he'd have done if he hadn't gone off into the world of chemicals."

"I talked to Mark earlier this evening, you know. He says he hasn't been taking drugs."

"They all say that, don't they?" Peter Makepeace replied. "They never admit it straight off. But I've been around a long time, Mr. Demarkian. That kid was on speed half the time and on tranquilizers at least sometimes. I know all the signs."

"He offered to take a drug test."

"They'll take him up on it in here," Peter said. "Screening for drugs is probably the first thing they did after they pumped his stomach. And they'll screen what came out of that, too. If that damned doctor wasn't such a martinet, we'd know already what the kid was on tonight."

"He can't just give information to anybody and everybody," Gregor said. "There's a federal law at the very least about medical privacy. I knew Mark before, you know. I'd have said he was the last kid to end up on drugs."

"Yes, well," Peter Makepeace said, "that's what everybody says about every kid, or at least every kid from a well-heeled family."

"I don't think I'm subject to that kind of prejudice," Gregor said. "I've spent a lot of my life in law enforcement. I know what goes on. But I did meet Mark, and I'd be surprised if they find drugs."

Peter Makepeace turned around again. "Have you seen him? The way he is? What was he like when you talked to him today?"

"He was a mess."

"Did you think he was on drugs?"

"At first, yes."

"There, then."

"But only at first," Gregor said. "And I didn't change my mind only because he told me he wasn't or offered to take a blood test. Some of the things he was telling me don't make sense as drug symptoms."

"What things? That he couldn't remember anything? That could be drugs. That he was having blackouts? Everything he's ever reported to the infirmary could be drug related—everything. And it's been worse since Michael died. I'd be willing to bet everything that Mark knows where Michael kept whatever he was selling."

"I think it's interesting that Mark reported his symptoms to the infirmary," Gregor said. "Why would he do that if he was taking drugs?"

"Why do they ever do anything?" Peter Makepeace said. "Have you any idea what it's like trying to run a school like this? Half the boarding students are only boarding because their parents want to get rid of them. If you ever repeat that, I'll deny that I ever said it, but it's true. The level of hostility between some children and some parents is unbelievable. The other half are here for a variety of reasons, but they rarely like being here. They may think it's a good idea because their parents live in Zimbabwe or the Ivory Coast and boarding is the only way they can get a decent education, or because we have a program they like and can't find closer to home or for a million other reasons. And we screen. We screen until we're blue in the face. It doesn't matter. There are always some kids, like Mark, who just shouldn't be here."

"Shouldn't be? Why not?"

"A million reasons. I saw it at orientation though. He just didn't fit. We should have seen it in the interview. We didn't. I knew the minute he walked on this campus that he wasn't going to last more than a year. Now it seems he's going to last less."

"You don't expect him to recover from this sufficiently to return to classes?"

"I expect at least one of those drug tests to come back positive, and when it does I have every intention of expelling him. The only reason I haven't expelled him yet is because I had to be careful about the legal situation and about the reputation of the school. A woman like Elizabeth Toliver can do us a lot of damage if she wants to."

"She could still do it."

"Of course she could. But it doesn't matter anymore, does it?" Peter said. "You know and I know that after this there's going to be no hope that we can keep it all out of the papers. It was hard enough to keep Michael's suicide out. But Jimmy Card's stepson takes a drug overdose and nearly dies in his dorm at Windsor Academy? Please. We're about to become a national sensation. And I'm about to become unemployed."

"Was it a drug overdose?" Liz Toliver asked.

The two of them both turned toward the swinging fire doors at once. Gregor thought, rather uselessly, that he had never seen Liz in winter clothes before, and at the same time that these were probably not the clothes she wore in New York. She was dressed in jeans and L.L. Bean hunting boots and a big quilted jacket in an odd color that was neither red nor orange. Her hair was pulled back at the nape of her neck. She was wearing no makeup.

Peter Makepeace nearly leaped forward and held out his hand. "Ms. Toliver, I'm so sorry. I don't know if you remember me, but I'm—"

"You're Peter Makepeace. You're the headmaster. I remember you. Gregor? Was it a drug overdose?"

"I don't know," Gregor said, "the doctor isn't telling us anything. He probably shouldn't; I don't know if he'll tell you."

"The nurse said he was all right," Liz said. "Do you think that?"

"Yes," Gregor said. "That I can definitely tell you. He's not dead, and from what they've told us, he's not likely to suffer permanent damage; but he's in bad shape."

"Right," Liz said.

"Ms. Toliver," Peter Makepeace said.

"Mr. Makepeace," Liz said, "right this second, between what I heard from Mr. Demarkian earlier this evening on the phone, and what I've heard since about Mark's trip to this place, I'd suggest that it was far and away the better part of valor for you to just shut up. I'm going to take Mr. Demarkian here. We're going to go in to see my son. Then we're going to talk to the doctor. You are not welcome in either place; and I'll discuss the details of the lawsuit I'll be filing against Windsor Academy at some later date. Have I made myself clear?"

"I don't believe the doctor will talk to you," Peter Makepeace said. "I think his position is that you'll need to hear anything that is to be heard from the regular ward physician when he comes on in the morning."

Gregor saw Liz give him the kind of look God probably gave souls trying to bullshit their way out of purgatory. She then turned back to the swinging doors.

"He'll talk to *me*," she said, dragging Gregor behind her.

2

Liz Toliver was not usually a high-handed woman. In fact, in Gregor's experience, she was usually anything but. This was not a usual circumstance, and Gregor did not blame her for using what clout she had to get the answers she needed about Mark. It was, though, truly remarkable to behold her operating at full-tilt boogie. He'd never seen her that way before. She pulled him up to the nurses' station, spent less than thirty seconds arguing with the nurse on duty about calling the doctor out of emergency, and then started down the hall in the other direction to find Mark's room.

"I want him moved to a single as soon as possible," was the last thing she said to the nurse. "My husband's due up here in the morning. My husband's Jimmy Card—"

The nurse looked startled.

"—the musician," Liz went on, "and as soon as he arrives a complete circus of press is likely to arrive with him, so there are going to be issues of security. Get Mark moved within the hour."

Gregor had no doubt that the nurse would get Mark moved within the hour, and probably faster. He followed Liz down the hall. The rooms all seemed to be full, with two patients each. Everybody seemed to be sleeping.

They got to the door of the room where the nurse had said they would find Mark. The door had been left slightly open, and the lights were off inside. Liz hesitated for a moment, gave Gregor a look, took a deep breath, and went inside. It turned out that Mark might as well have been in a private room. There was no other patient bunked in with him. The bed closest to the door was empty. Liz went past it to the bed by the windows and motioned Gregor to come along.

Mark was lying in bed, breathing normally, seemingly no worse than asleep. Gregor reminded himself that he had no reason to think that Mark was anything but asleep. It was just that he'd seen the kid in convulsions, and this complete return to normalcy seemed odd and out of place. Mark actually looked good. He looked a lot better than either of the times Gregor had seen him tonight.

Liz went over to Mark and ran her hand through his hair. "It's stiff with sweat," she said. "I wonder if they've given him a sedative."

"I don't know," Gregor said.

"You know I'm not one of those mothers who sends her children off to boarding school and then pretends they don't exist. I hated the idea of his going away to school so soon. I did everything I could to prevent it. And there are a couple of very good places within commuting distance of where we live in Connecticut. He could have stayed home."

"I take it he didn't want to."

"Windsor has a film department," Liz said. "It's a very famous one, actually. They've got a man running it who's actually won an Emmy and works in the field. That's what Mark wants to do in the long run—film. There was that. And this place has a decent record of getting people into USC, too, which is where he wants to go."

"USC?"

"University of Southern California. That or UCLA, which I think would be the better place. Oh, I don't know. It's the kind of thing you think of when you send your child to a school. And he loved this place the minute he laid eyes on it. He completely loved it. Oddly enough, I hated it."

"And you let him go anyway?"

"He was the one who had to live with it," Liz said. "And I didn't hate it because I thought it was full of irresponsible jerks, which apparently it is. I hated it because it was so, so—eh. Who knows what to call it? So *smug*."

"I'd think any rich private school would be smug," Gregor said.

Liz laughed, just a little. "True enough. Self-righteously smug, I guess is what I really want to say. And I should have known he would never have fit here any more than I would have. But I thought it was his life, and it is. And

I thought that there was no harm in trying it out for a year. Anybody could get through a year of anything; and even if you end up hating it, you've learned something. And now look."

"I think it's going to be all right," Gregor said. "I wouldn't insist on that until we've heard from the doctor, but I do think it will."

"He'll need to take a post-grad year if he wants to get into USC now," Liz said. "His grades are mediocre at best. Grades. My God. What am I thinking of? My grades sucked most of the way through high school. Tell me what he was like when you found him. Tell me what it was that got you to make them bring him here."

Gregor was very careful. Liz had a good memory. He knew that if he elided too much, it would come back to haunt him. She would find out what needed to be known. She would bring it back to him. He told her about Mark's coming to the Windsor Inn to meet him and taking a shower and falling asleep on the bed. He told her about walking through the Windsor Academy campus and going to Mark's dorm on a whim. He told her about the convulsions.

Liz listened in eerie stillness, only her arm and hand moving as she stroked Mark's hair. When Gregor was done, she shuddered.

"They're right," she said, "it does sound like drugs."

"It does and it doesn't," Gregor said. "I didn't see him for long, Liz, but the fact is that all it took to make him look almost infinitely better was a shower and some Perrier. That doesn't sound like any drug I've ever heard of. And he went to sleep. He didn't pass out."

"But something must be wrong with him," Liz said. "He was shaking and sweat was pouring off him. That doesn't sound psychological. I suppose it could be, but—"

"I think it might be a good idea to at least consider the possibility that he's ill," Gregor said. "I doubt if he has Huntington's chorea—"

"What?"

"I think he found it in a medical book. He says it fit his symptoms. He can't have it since neither you nor his father did. But those symptoms might be typical of something else, maybe of several something elses. And I'd think that it would be a very good idea to find out what because Mark was not well when I saw him."

"You mean the shaking and the sweat."

"I mean the inability to remember anything and the blackouts, or what might be blackouts, and the problem he has with reading."

"*Mark* has a problem with reading? My Mark?"

"He says he reads a page and when he gets to the end of it he has no idea what it says."

"For God's sake," Liz said, "the kid could read before he was three."

At the other side of the room, the door slid open, and the South Asian doctor came in, a small, rigidly formal, very young man in a white coat. Gregor tried to read the name on his identification tag, but could only make out the last one, which was spelled "Niazi." He had no idea how to pronounce it and an uncomfortable tendency to misread it when he saw it as "Nazi."

Liz left Mark's side and crossed the room with her hand held out. "Doctor, thank you so much for coming. I'm very sorry to be so insistent, but I don't know what's going on, you see, and I'm his mother."

Dr. Niazi took Liz's hand and shook it. "There is no difficulty," he said, just as formal in expression as in looks. "You have an understandable concern, and I am about to go off duty now in any case. If you could come down the hall to the conference room where we could talk? Your son is sleeping, but he is not unconscious."

"All right," Liz said. "I'd like to have Mr. Demarkian here come with us."

"Of course," Dr. Niazi said. "And the gentleman in the waiting room? Should he be asked to come, too?"

"No," Liz said.

If Dr. Niazi found this strange, he didn't indicate it. He went back to the door and held it open while Liz and Gregor walked out. Then he motioned them farther down the hall in the direction away from the nurses' station and the waiting room. Moments later he was ushering them into a small room almost entirely occupied by a square conference table and its attendant chairs, each chair upholstered in a nubbly fabric that was hideously, relentlessly purple.

Dr. Niazi motioned for them to sit down. Liz sat in the chair nearest the door. Gregor sat beside her. Dr. Niazi sat at what could arguably have been called the head of the table and put down a thin manila folder Gregor hadn't noticed he was carrying.

"So," Dr. Niazi said, "the first of what I have to say is to reassure. Your son is not in danger. He will not die. He will not have permanent brain damage or damage to his organs. I should not be so confident so soon, but I am confident. I have had a chance to speak to him. He is normal."

"He spoke?" Gregor said.

"For a few moments after we had pumped his stomach and given him some water to drink. He is not in a coma. He is not incoherent. We have given him a very mild sedative to help him sleep."

Liz took a deep breath. "Well," she said, "then there are the obvious questions. What happened to him? Why did he go into convulsions? Was he using drugs?"

Dr. Niazi shot her an odd look. Gregor caught it, but he didn't think Liz did. "Was he using drugs?" Gregor asked. "Everybody at the school seems to assume so."

"Yes, we do understand that that is always an issue with adolescents," Dr. Niazi said. "But I can say with some certainty that this is not the case here. We have tested for several drugs, including marijuana, some few forms of amphetamines, heroin, cocaine."

"Some of those leave the body fairly quickly and without a trace," Gregor said.

"This is true, but they do not leave the body in an hour or two, and it was less than an hour before we took his blood. There were no signs of drugs. We have yet out some tests that take longer to read, but I do not expect to find positive results there either."

"But," Liz said.

Dr. Niazi nodded. "Yes, I do know. But. I spoke to Mr. Demarkian here and to several other people when the boy was admitted, and based on some things they said I did a test for caffeine toxicity. You know what caffeine is? It is in—"

"Coffee," Liz said. "Drinking coffee could give him convulsions?"

"No," Dr. Niazi said. "Sensitivity to caffeine varies among people, but even for those especially sensitive to it it does not cause convulsions or death from the amounts found in drinks, no matter how much the patient drinks. You must understand this. Most people eliminate caffeine very quickly. Some small group of people retain it much longer, and there is a tendency then for the caffeine to build up in the system and to cause symptoms, difficulty concentrating, difficulty sitting still, high levels of anxiety."

"Oh," Gregor said.

"Yes," Dr. Niazi said. "From what I have here, I would have expected him to show such symptoms. They occur even in people who eliminate caffeine normally if such people drink more than they are used to or drink coffee or tea that is stronger than what they are used to. In someone with a particular sensitivity, the symptoms would be pronounced, and they would extend longer than the few hours they would in people who eliminate normally. A single cup of coffee could cause symptoms for most of a day. I am under the impression that this boy was drinking more than a single cup of coffee a day?"

"He said he was mainlining it," Gregor said.

Dr. Niazi looked puzzled.

"It means he was practically living on the stuff," Liz said. "I know just what he means; I was like that in college. I almost didn't eat. And I couldn't ever seem to stay awake for the amount of time I needed to work. So I drank tea practically all day, except I used to steep each cup for twenty minutes, so it probably had more caffeine in it than coffee. I mean, that was the idea. I just didn't like the taste of coffee."

"In this boy's case," Dr. Niazi said, "he liked the taste of coffee. Mr. Demarkian, and Mr. Makepeace, and several other people have said to us that he was drinking coffee before he began to convulse, so I decided to check. It is not as uncommon as you might think in students, although we do not usually see high school students in this state. It's more often college students. Especially here. In Greater Boston. And in Boston itself. Because of the universities, and the level of the work required of them."

"But you said that he couldn't have had convulsions from drinking coffee," Liz said, "but he did have convulsions. Mr. Demarkian saw him."

"Yes," Dr. Niazi said, "we understand that. However, he did not have convulsions here. The convulsions seem to have come and gone in a very short time, and that in itself would be consistent with caffeine poisoning."

"Caffeine poisoning," Liz said. "It's possible to be poisoned by caffeine. That's new to me. But you're still contradicting yourself. You said he couldn't have gotten convulsions from drinking coffee. Or tea or Coca-Cola, I'd expect."

"He could not have gotten convulsions from drinking, no," Dr. Niazi said, "but there are other ways to ingest caffeine. There are caffeine pills."

Gregor sat up a little straighter. "Tablets," he said, "caffeine tablets. Like NoDoz. I remember those."

"So do I," Liz said. "Was Mark taking NoDoz?"

Dr. Niazi flipped through the folder. "He had most certainly had some kind of caffeine tablet or pill in the last several hours before his convulsions," he said. "We analyzed the contents of his stomach from the pump, and also some of the matter from the vomit on his clothes. In the vomit on his clothes there were pieces of these tablets. Many pieces. It will be a day or more before we can have an understanding of how many of these tablets he might have ingested during the evening before his trouble. When the attending physician takes over, I will give him a complete report, and I will put him in touch with the laboratory people for the complete analyses. I will tell you what I can. The level of caffeine in his blood when he was admitted here was close to fifty times higher than is considered safe—"

"*Fifty* times?" Liz said.

Dr. Niazi gave no sign that he'd heard. "That in and of itself could have caused him difficulty and might have brought on convulsions. It is not unknown for elevated levels of caffeine to bring on stroke or heart attack in people susceptible to such things. Your son is young and healthy and without any known family medical history of these illnesses, and he is not considered at risk. Unless the medical records are incomplete? Unless you have something to add?"

"Well, his father's family had a lot of heart disease," Liz said, "but they didn't have it young. And they weren't like Mark. They were mostly very overweight."

"As so," Dr. Niazi said. "The level of caffeine toxicity in the material analyzed from the vomit on his clothes was two hundred and fifty times higher than is considered safe."

"What?" Liz said.

"Jesus Christ," Gregor said.

"Precisely," Dr. Niazi said. "There is no question that the level of caffeine toxicity found could have brought on convulsions. The same is the case for the vomiting. One has to assume the logical result of such ingestion to be at least both and possibly something much worse. It is my opinion that your son will be found to have a particular sensitivity to caffeine, and that that is what saved him. His system could not handle the caffeine he had taken in, and so it got rid of it in vomit. It is a very good thing. If those caffeine tablets had been able to dissolve fully and get into his bloodstream, he would now be dead."

"Dead," Liz said, looking stunned.

Gregor sat back and watched Dr. Niazi gather up the folder and get to his feet. He looked exhausted and more than a little disapproving.

"It is not a shameful thing," he said suddenly, bending over Liz. "It is not these drugs that are such a waste, such a moral disaster. It is only a student too conscientious for his own good. You should not forget that. You should not punish for what was only an attempt to achieve what would bring respect to himself and his family."

Gregor bit his lip. It was the first note of levity in what had been a long and depressing day, but he knew better than to let the solemn Dr. Niazi know he found anything about the situation funny.

Liz then stood up herself. "I'm not going to punish him," she said, "I'm going to kill the bloody idiot."

TWO

1

Alice Makepeace knew there were 101 things she ought to do this morning, 101 things required by her "position," which Peter had been reminding her of ever since he came back from the hospital at one in the morning, looking exhausted and annoyed and, underneath it all, scared to death. Alice was not scared, although she knew she had good reason to be. The conscious side of Peter thought that he would be able to come through to the other side of this thing unscathed. Even if he was not able to stay on at Windsor—and he must have known, as soon as he heard that Mark DeAvecca had been taken to Windsor Hospital, that that would be impossible—he would be able to move on to another school in another state, another part of the great network of private schools where everybody knew everybody else and the man who was headmaster in one place one year was the man at the head of the History Department in another the next. There was a usefulness to those networks. Alice knew that. Schools were odd places, and parents were odd people to have to deal with. Colleges and universities had much more latitude. By then the students were mostly over eighteen, and the policy of in loco parentis had ended decades ago. College administrations did not, and did not have to, placate hysterical mothers convinced their precious sons were reincarnations of Galileo, both great geniuses and the victims of persecution. The best colleges didn't have to do that even for the children of their biggest donors. It was a great advantage to have an endowment in excess of a billion dollars. It was, Alice thought, a great advantage to be Harvard.

Windsor, of course, was not Harvard. It was not even Andover, where the endowment was almost as large. It was one of those places, one of about two dozen, that took only the best candidates in an ever-widening pool made up, not only of the children and grandchildren of those people who had themselves been to boarding schools, but the children and grandchildren of what Alice persisted in thinking of as the New Incredibly Rich. There were lots of them out there. Not all of them were Incredibly Rich, although so many were that she found it disorienting when she encountered them. A combination of the rise of new industries like computer hardware and a Republican tax policy that seemed to be a repeat of Herbert Hoover's had thrown up hundreds of people, maybe even thousands, who thought nothing of buying Hummers as second cars and vacationing for six weeks in the winter on private islands in the South Pacific. There were other people though, the people who worked for those people, the lawyers in firms that had once been white-shoe and restricted to candidates with all the right bells and whistles, the accountants in the big national firms that had once been the same, people who had grown up in small towns and middle-class suburbs in midwestern cities and made it into a "good" university and from those "good" universities to "good" jobs, and who now wanted to mark their distinction with something palpable. What they chose to mark their distinction with was their children, who were expected to "get into" the right boarding school and then the right college, to provide stickers to put on the backs of cars. A Range Rover looked good with "Windsor Academy" and "Yale University" on the back of it. It looked less good with "Local High School" and "State College." These were people who came to schools like Windsor and expected to get results. The only results that mattered were the ones that came in college admissions packets around the fifteenth of March every year.

What Alice knew she should do was go to the hospital and visit Mark DeAvecca. It was the kind of thing the headmaster's wife was expected to do, and in this case it was triply important because Mark was the son of a prominent person who could be expected to contribute significantly to the general fund. Windsor was not Andover. Its endowment was fair, not spectacular. There was a hundred million dollars or so in the bank, not enough to ensure the school's survival if the tides ever turned and the numbers of applicants were greatly reduced. Things were already a little dicey because of the stock market collapse. People who might have considered Windsor when they had more money than they knew what to do with sometimes decided to learn to live with the public school in town when not to would mean giving up something they considered more important, like vacations in the Bahamas or a new Porsche. There were times when Alice thought her head would explode. When she was growing up, she had decided that the people among whom she had been born were the worst in the world. They were handed power and privilege and money for no effort of their own, and they thought they somehow deserved it. She had decided since that these other people, the ones who started without but made the climb by themselves, were far worse. They thought their money gave them a halo. They expected to control the world. Worse yet, they had no respect for the things that ought to be respected, for art and music that wasn't mass-produced and mindless, for films that challenged the mind and soul instead of movies that provided two hours of special effects after dinner at a chain restaurant, for the well made instead of just the expensive.

It was the hardest thing for Alice about living at Windsor, these people who had invaded the places where she had been a child and a girl and which she had always considered her own, the places that should have been reserved only for students of the kind she had once been and for the most disadvantaged, the truly hard cases with whom it was necessary to make alliances if the world was ever to be put right. That was the key, the thing that mattered more than money, in the days when there *had* been anything that mattered more than money. Decent people were dedicated to the spread of fairness and social justice. These people were dedicated only to themselves.

She had a pile of Elizabeth Toliver's books sitting on the small deal table that sat against the living room window that looked out on the quad. Peter had put it there for her to look through, along with a videotape of Ms. Toliver on some CNN talking-heads program where she appeared a couple of times a week. Alice had seen the program on and off and made note of Ms. Toliver, since she was the mother of a student. Peter had not left her any CDs by Jimmy Card, probably because he didn't think she needed them to be familiar with Card's work, which was true. Alice didn't like the music Jimmy Card had produced in the days when he'd been a real, genuine, not simply has-been rock star, and she didn't like the music he produced now, when he seemed to think he could turn himself into a classical composer a hundred years after the form had died in a mess of atonal aesthetic theory. She wondered if he even knew the theory. These people tended not to. She didn't need to look through any of the things on this table. She'd met them both at orientation in September, and then again at Parents Day in October, and she had been about as impressed with them as she'd been with the one and only chicken fajita salad she'd eaten at a Chili's restaurant—meaning, not at all. She'd known people like both of them in college, the people who'd worked too hard and dressed too well to ever really belong in the places they'd managed to scramble their way into.

If anybody were able to hear me think, they'd call me an elitist, Alice thought, but she knew it wasn't that. It was exactly the opposite. They were the elitists. They believed it all mattered, the "polish" they got from a good education, the "achievement" of spending their lives doing things that were worth nothing to anybody, while the people who did the necessary work—who planted the crops and cleaned the sewers and filled the potholes in the roads—existed only to give them somebody to look down on. There was a nobility in poverty. There was no nobility in what these people were. Alice thought that she herself, if she had found herself born into the wrong circumstances, would have opted for living on the street or on welfare rather than grubbing away at schoolwork and a "good" job. She would not have played the lottery; and if she had, and if she'd won it as Michael's mother had, she would have taken the jackpot only to give it all away again to the people who were working so hard to abolish all lotteries. She would not have been brainwashed into believing that qualifying for a mortgage on a three-bedroom, one-and-a-half-bath house in a subdivision in New Jersey was "success." She would not have been so drunk on the power of money that she thought thirty-five thousand square feet in Scarsdale was "success" either. She would have seen what Michael had seen, and what his mother had not. She would have understood that wanting that subdivision house was no different than wanting that Scarsdale one or a mansion in Malibu. It was all corruption, and the only way to remain authentic and fully human was to walk away from all of it.

The books were still sitting on the table. The window was still looking out on the quad. The weather looked as awful as it had for weeks. The sky was slate gray and showed no signs of getting better anytime soon. The air was that odd color it got before they had a truly impressive snow, and they'd already had three or four this winter. She didn't like thinking about Michael. She was sure she had done what she had to do in that case, right up until the end; but it was hard to think about, even so, and harder to think about when she put Mark DeAvecca into the same picture. It was too bad that Michael had had to room with that particular boy. Almost anybody else would have been better and less of a problem in the long run.

What she remembered, what stuck in her mind, was her last vision of Michael, only hours before he died, on that last night. He was standing out by Maverick Pond behind the hedge of trees that curved along its bank closest to the library, his hands stuck in his pockets, his arms held tightly against his chest, and she had suddenly thought how wrong it all was. He hadn't escaped the brainwashing, not all of it. Everything he was wearing had logos on it. Even his jeans had a big leather patch on the back meant to let strangers know he'd bought a brand and a famous corporate one at that. She'd been thinking about ripping the patch off with her bare hands, and then it had been his bare hand she'd noticed, stripped of its glove, plunging up the front of her sweater, through the layers made by her cape and her camisole, his fingers pricking at the tips of her nipples as they got hard under the touch. The shock had been so immediate and so total, she'd almost given into it. She'd wanted to drop to the ice just as she was and open her legs to him without reservation, the way she'd done the first few times they had been together in her own bedroom in President's House, while Peter was away at his conference and the campus had not suspected anything yet. She remembered those first few times quite clearly, even now, when thinking about Michael too often made her imagine, against her will, the process of fucking a dead body. That last night she could have made love to him in the frigid open air, risked frostbite for herself and for him, and exposure of a more lasting kind as well. For a few seconds before her sanity returned, she had reached for him as he had reached for her. She had put her hand down the front of his jeans and found his penis stiff and resistant against her hand. She'd had no idea if she was cold. She didn't think he did either. His hand had moved away from her nipples and gone downward, down and down. His finger was right at the very tip of her clitoris when there were suddenly sounds in the quad. They were far away—the quad was light years away from the pond, she'd thought at the time, although of course that wasn't true—but for some reason they were distinct and immediate, as if they were being projected over a very good speaker system. They both felt as if those voices were right beside them. His hand froze against the mound of her pubic hair and then retreated. Her own hand came up into the cold without her willing it. It happened because it had to happen, because the one thing they could not do, not either of them, was let the rest of this campus know that what everybody suspected was true.

Now she wondered. Everybody did suspect. They suspected even now, when they wouldn't talk about it, because Michael was dead. Mark DeAvecca might even know, if Michael had talked to him. Alice had no idea if he had or not. She knew Mark was dangerous to her, but that was not the way in which he was dangerous.

Everything was dangerous to her really. She knew that. She knew that they would not be able to stay at this school after what would happen in the next week or so. Everything was already out of hand. She didn't care if they stayed here or not. It wasn't the school she needed, and it wasn't her position as the headmaster's wife she needed to preserve.

She did think, however, that since there was no hope for it on any level, there was no need for her to go to see Mark DeAvecca in the hospital. They'd be gone whether she did or not, and she had never been able to stand that kid for longer than it took to shake his hand at official functions.

2

Edith Braxner had decided, in a rush of irritation at herself and exasperation at the campus, that there was one thing and only one thing that mattered, and that was doing what she had an obligation to do. The rumors around school this morning were as thick as poison gas. Mark DeAvecca had taken a drug overdose. Mark DeAvecca had been the victim of an attempted murder. The papers had been silent this morning, but then they would be. Whatever had happened had happened yesterday evening and not really been resolved until late at night. That much Edith had managed to pick up in the cafeteria at breakfast. The local news had been silent this morning, too, but she knew that would not last long. There was another piece of information she'd managed to pick up in the cafeteria, and that was the fact that Mark's mother was already here and Mark's father was on the way. They weren't Madonna or the Backstreet Boys, but they brought publicity with them wherever they went. It would take a little time to jump-start it, that was all. This was Tuesday. By Thursday it would all be everywhere. The only question was the nature of what would be out. Michael Feyre's suicide would be out, of course, but it was impossible to tell what the media would say about Mark. That was because the one person who would know what had really happened, besides Peter Makepeace, was not at breakfast at all, in spite of the fact that all faculty were required to take their meals in the cafeteria with the students. Edith had gotten to breakfast with the first opening of the doors because she did so every day, and then she had waited until the breakfast hour was over, in order to catch Cherie and feel her out. There had been no Cherie. There had been no Sheldon either. Edith had been reduced to listening politely while James Hallwood unleashed a tedious meta-analysis of everything from Windsor's policy of having students call their teachers by their first names to Mark DeAvecca's failings as a Member of the Windsor Community.

Edith understood, exactly, the importance of making sure that every student and faculty member was a Member of the Windsor Community, and she understood as well why so many people here thought Mark DeAvecca wasn't one and could never be one. At the moment, however, this was not a topic she was interested in. She was back in her apartment in Lytton House, and she knew that if she stayed here she would learn nothing she could count on about what was going on. She would learn nothing in her office, either, because she was sure that Cherie had no intention of occupying hers. Edith had brought her tote bag full of work to breakfast. She left it on her desk without bothering to repack it and started back out again. She hadn't even bothered to unbutton her coat.

Out on the quad, it was mostly quiet. Students had not taken this opportunity to catch up on their classwork. They were all staying up late and sleeping in. There had been very few of them this morning at breakfast. Edith went down the diagonal path that would have taken her to Barrett if she'd followed it long enough. Then she turned at the center crossing and went down to Hayes. It looked no livelier than any other House, although surely the students there must have witnessed whatever had happened to Mark in the night. Edith didn't believe they'd all slept through it.

She got to the back door of Hayes and let herself in. Every faculty member knew the codes to get into every House. Edith was sure that every student knew them, too. She looked around the back hall and caught a fleeting glimpse of Sheldon at the door to his own apartment. He shut it quickly as soon as he saw her, which didn't surprise her at all. From what she'd heard in the cafeteria—assuming she could trust any of it, which she thought she could, especially where it concerned Sheldon—he was about to be in a great deal of trouble. Sheldon hadn't ever quite been a Member of the Windsor Community either. He'd just been better at hiding it and more difficult to get rid of than a student.

Edith went through to the other hall and then around the side to Cherie's apartment. She knocked softly and waited. She could hear sounds in there, Cherie and Melissa, music playing on a radio or a CD player. It was Pachelbel, she thought. Pachelbel was the school obsession this year. Every year there was a classical composer, or baroque, or medieval, whom very few people had heard of, who became the school's icon of genius. Nobody ever bothered to play Beethoven in this place. Beethoven was far too obvious.

Nobody was coming to the door. Edith knocked again, a little more loudly this time. Still nobody came. The voices had ceased, but there was no sound of footsteps.

"Cherie," Edith said, "it's Edith Braxner. I need to talk to you."

161

This time there were footsteps, maybe because Edith's voice sounded as loud to Cherie and Melissa as it had sounded to Edith in the hall. It was odd what high ceilings and empty halls could do to acoustics. The footsteps on the other side of the door were quick and heavy. The door opened, and it was Melissa, not Cherie, standing there.

"Edith, listen," Melissa said, "we know you're curious. We know everybody is curious, but we're very upset. And Peter's asked us to say nothing to anybody."

"I rather doubt if it matters what Peter says now," Edith said. "Can't you tell that it's all fallen apart already? You don't really expect him to be headmaster a month from now."

"I think Cherie would like to have a job a month from now."

Cherie came up behind Melissa. It was obvious to Edith that she'd been crying. Her eyes were as puffy as doughnuts. Her nose was red. She gentled Melissa out of the way and came to the door.

"Come on in," Cherie said, stepping back to let Edith through. "I'm going crazy in here. We're not supposed to leave. Peter told us not to. He wants us 'instantly available at all times.' And I couldn't face the cafeteria. I really couldn't. I don't know what to do. Do you think the police will be called in? He looked like he had been poisoned."

Edith went down the narrow front hall into the apartment proper. It had a big living room that had been left to go to mess much longer than Mark DeAvecca had been in the hospital. Edith leaned over and took a pile of magazines off a chair and sat down.

"First things first," she said. "I take it that Mark is not dead."

"Oh, no," Cherie said, the blood draining out of her face. She sat down herself, abruptly, on the couch. The couch was as littered with magazines as the chair had been. "No, no, not at all. Peter said that he was quite fine really."

" 'Out of danger,' is what Peter said," Melissa said, "whatever that means. He isn't exactly being forthcoming."

"He was forthcoming about one thing," Cherie said. "Well no, not exactly forthcoming, but he said it. They did drug tests. Mark wasn't on drugs."

"Ah," Edith said.

"Well, it settles that," Cherie said, sounding despairing. "I never believed that gossip. It was all wrong. It was—too easy. He was behaving oddly and it was the easiest way of explaining it. Sometimes I think we've got only two explanations we're willing to accept at this school, drugs or attention deficit disorder."

"But he was behaving oddly," Edith pointed out. "Did Peter have an explanation as to why?"

"No," Cherie said.

"He really didn't say much of anything," Melissa said, "except to tell us to keep our mouths shut. I don't know what he thinks we're going to say. We were out in Boston yesterday and when we got back, well, we'd been back a little while—"

"An hour or so," Cherie said.

"An hour or so," Melissa agreed, "well, there he was, having another fight with Sheldon. I'm telling you, Edith. You have no idea what it's been like since they moved that kid in with Sheldon. Sheldon resented the hell out of it. And he didn't like Mark."

"Not many people like Mark," Edith said.

"True," Melissa said, "but this was really awful. And of course Mark is something of a slob. And Sheldon's anal retentive beyond belief. And it went on and on, day after day, so that Mark spent as little time in the House as possible because he didn't feel comfortable with Sheldon there looming over him. I wouldn't have either. God only knows where Mark was spending his time during the day."

"Does it matter where he was spending his time during the day?" Edith asked.

"It depends on what happened," Cherie said. "That's why I asked about the police. He really did look as if somebody or something had poisoned him, Edith. You should have seen him. And if it wasn't drugs, then what was it?"

Edith thought about this. "It could have been something he ate. It could have been food poisoning."

"The vomiting could have been food poisoning," Cherie said. "But the convulsions couldn't have been. Is that all over campus already, that he had convulsions last night? Like a grand mal seizure, but worse, much worse, than any of those I've ever heard about. It was like he was being electrocuted. I thought he was going to die."

"But he didn't die," Edith said.

"No, he didn't," Cherie said, "and if you can believe Peter Makepeace, he isn't even much the worse for wear. No, that isn't right. That isn't what Peter said exactly. He was just so *relieved*."

"Peter was?" Edith asked.

"Peter was," Cherie said. She looked cold. Edith did not think it was cold in this room, but she hadn't taken off her coat. Cherie rubbed her hands together. "Peter asked if I'd seen Mark drinking coffee."

Edith stood up, unbuttoned her coat, and took it off. Hayes House was not her favorite dorm. The main living room was too small, and the windows were too small throughout. "Mark is always drinking coffee," she said. "I don't think I've ever seen him without his coffee. He even brings coffee to class, and he isn't supposed to."

"I know," Cherie said. "And of course I did see him drinking coffee last night. I brought him a cup myself right before all that craziness started, and Sheldon was behaving like an idiot. The whole thing is so unbelievable. Maybe somebody did poison him. Maybe somebody put the poison in coffee, and they know that. That would make me a suspect."

Edith shook her head. "That doesn't make sense," she said. "Why would Peter sound relieved if Mark DeAvecca had been poisoned?"

"Oh," Cherie said, looking a little less likely to start crying again.

"Attempted murder would be worse than successful suicide," Edith said, pursuing the thought. "A successful suicide is the result of a psychological problem on the part of the person who commits suicide. It isn't usually an indication that there's a danger to anybody else. Except in the case of suicide pacts, of course, but I don't think there's any danger of Mark having made a suicide pact with Michael Feyre. They didn't like each other all that well. It must be something else. It must be something that gets Peter out of at least some of the trouble he's going to be in."

"I don't see what could get him out of trouble after this," Melissa said. "It may not have been attempted murder, and Mark may be alive, but his parents are in town. His mother got here last night. Peter said so over the phone—"

"That piece of information was all over the cafeteria this morning," Edith said.

"—and," Melissa went on, "his stepfather is going to be arriving today. The publicity is going to be awful no matter what happened to Mark. I'm surprised it hasn't started yet."

"Maybe," Edith said. "Did you ever wonder, though, what Mark DeAvecca knew about Michael Feyre's relationship with Alice?"

"Everybody knew about Michael's relationship with Alice," Cherie said.

"Of course they did," Edith said, "but Mark was Michael's roommate. Michael could have talked in his sleep for all we know. I know Michael didn't seem the type, but you never know. Or they could have confided in each other."

"Michael could have confided in Mark?" Cherie said. "It's more likely that they made a suicide pact. Mark stayed away from Michael as much as he could. That's one of the reasons why I never believed that Mark was on drugs. Drug addicts don't avoid the best dealers in their vicinity; they cultivate them. But Mark could never stand to be around Michael, not even for a few hours."

"Still," Edith said. Then she shook her head. "Maybe the answer is something much simpler. Maybe it's just that this latest . . . event . . . takes the spotlight off Michael Feyre and anything he might have done while he was here. Maybe it just changes the subject, and that's enough for Peter."

"I can see it now," Melissa said. "Peter secretly poisons Mark DeAvecca's coffee in the hopes that in the wake of this dramatic new death, public scrutiny will be distracted from the serial depredations of his own wife. . . ."

"No," Cherie said, "there you go again. If the coffee was poisoned, things would be worse for Peter and not better."

"There's also the obvious," Edith said. "If you wanted to poison somebody to take the public's mind off your wife's love affairs, you'd poison somebody other than your wife's lover's roommate."

"They weren't love affairs," Cherie said, "not really. They weren't that clean. I don't believe they were even about sex."

"Whatever," Melissa said.

Edith shifted a little in her chair. "It must have been something that happened by accident," she said, "or that he could make seem as if it had happened by accident or by Mark's intention. It could be another suicide attempt. It would fit. Mark has been depressed for months."

"Two suicides would be better than one? I thought you just said they wouldn't be," Cherie said.

"No, I said that attempted murder was worse than successful suicide," Edith said, "but it's hard to tell how the board will react in cases like this. And of course Peter hasn't just to think of his job here. He has to think of where he'll go in the long run, what the next place will be. There's a difference between not being able to go on at Windsor and not being able to stay in the network at all."

"Does Peter want to stay in the network?" Cherie asked. "I think it's incredible the way we all are. We get into this place, and it's as if we forget that there's life outside it."

Edith shrugged. "There aren't all that many jobs that are congenial to do or that many where you can be with people you respect. Everybody can't teach in one of the better universities. Have either of you seen Alice today at all?"

"We haven't been out at all," Melissa said.

"I thought you might have seen her through the window. She wasn't at breakfast. It was the oddest breakfast. It was better attended than breakfasts usually are, probably because people wanted to find out any news they could, but the two of you weren't there, and Sheldon wasn't there, and Alice wasn't there, and Peter wasn't there either. I suppose Peter has some excuse. He must have been up until the early hours of the morning."

"I think we had an excuse, too," Melissa said.

Edith didn't argue with her. Cherie's apartment looked out onto the quad, and at just that moment Alice Makepeace had come out of President's House, her enormous black cape wrapped around her body like a heavy wool blanket around a victim fished out of a river in winter, her red hair gleaming like rouged bronze even without the help of the sun. She dyed it, of course, Edith thought, but it worked nonetheless. It took people's attention away from her face, and her words, and her attitude. Alice went around to the side of President's House to where the parking lot was. Edith supposed she was going to her car.

"There's Alice on her way out," she said. "Maybe she's gone to pay the obligatory call on the student in the hospital."

"If she is," Cherie said, "I hope Mark throws her out of his room."

3

Diagonally across the quad, in Barrett House, Marta Coelho saw Alice Makepeace leave, too, although it took straining and leaning to follow her movements to the parking lot, and even then Marta only managed to be sure that she could see the bright red hair. Then she withdrew into the Barrett living room and counted to one hundred with potatoes, the way they used to count seconds when she was a child. The last thing she wanted this morning was to run into Alice in any capacity at all. In the last few days, Marta had been feeling more and more as if she had to leave this place, no matter what the consequences. Even going home would be better than staying here, even though she knew she would die at home. She could no more go back to living that life among those people than she could sprout wings and fly. The problem was she couldn't stay here either, not without losing her mind. She thought she might have lost her mind already.

She also thought that it might all be a hat trick. She hadn't had anything to eat this morning. She'd gone to the cafeteria first thing, but she'd no sooner gotten there than she had heard the news about Mark DeAvecca, and the speculations about him, too, as if whatever had happened had been an episode on a soap opera. *The ultimate reality TV,* she had thought, and then realized that she'd never actually seen any reality TV. It seemed to fit anyway, and it made her feel a little sick. They were talking about how he had vomited on Sheldon's ceiling and gone into convulsions that looked as if he were being electrocuted, and they were doing it in the tones they might use to discuss Martha Stewart's problems with the SEC. Nobody was even talking about counselors, or the trauma the students were likely to feel, and those were usually the first two things anybody at Windsor thought of when anything untoward happened. It didn't even have to be something untoward happening to one of their own.

She hadn't been able to eat. That was all there was to it. She hadn't been able to sit still in that room and listen to everybody talking about Mark and the vomit and the convulsions and the possibility that Mark's mother and stepfather would descend, a plague of locusts in their own right, to make a mess of the Windsor Academy campus and everything it stood for. She didn't like the boy. In many ways she truly hated him. She thought he was the picture of everything a school like Windsor should refuse to have anything to do with. She still didn't think they ought to talk about him like that when he had nearly died.

She'd come back to Barrett House and tried to make do on her own. For some reason she had no food in the house to speak of. She had a little cluster of grapes and some mineral water in the refrigerator. She had a bag of organic blue corn tortillas on the counter next to the stove. She'd tried to eat the tortillas and been forced to admit, in no time at all, that they were completely awful. She had never gotten used to the food these people ate, the food she was supposed to eat now that she was one of them. She'd lost twenty pounds since coming to Windsor from the simple fact that she could not allow herself to be seen in public eating things like cheeseburgers, and half the time she couldn't force herself to stuff down vegan tarts and organically grown beet salad no matter how hungry she was. What she needed to do now was to run into Boston to a diner where nobody knew who she was. That way she could eat french fries until she was sick and not have to explain herself to anybody.

She was just coming out of the quad-side front door when she saw the woman coming in from what must have been East Gate and start across the long, diagonal path in the direction of what Marta was sure would eventually be President's House. She put aside her annoyance at the name—why call something "East Gate" when there was no fence for it to be a gate of?—and stopped to stare. There was really no way to mistake this woman, in spite of the fact that she wasn't dressed in heels or covered with makeup the way she was on CNN. This was Elizabeth Toliver, Mark DeAvecca's mother. She was walking very quickly. Marta had the impression that if she could have, she would have run.

Marta had no idea what got into her. She wasn't a celebrity hound. Elizabeth Toliver wasn't even somebody whose work she respected much. Marta felt propelled by forces beyond her control down the porch steps, into the quad, along the path most likely to intersect with Ms. Toliver on her way to whatever she was going to do at Peter Makepeace's house. They collided at the quad's center, the place where the center paths all came together. Ms. Toliver hadn't been paying attention. She looked startled to see anybody else in the quad.

"Excuse me," she said.

"Excuse me." Marta thought she sounded lame. "I'm sorry, I don't mean to bother you. You're Ms. Toliver, aren't you?"

"Yes," Liz Toliver said. "I'm sorry I can't stop to talk, but I have an appointment."

"Oh, I didn't mean to bother you," Marta said. "I'm Marta Coelho; I'm Mark's history teacher."

Liz Toliver stopped looking as if she were about to take flight. "Oh," she said, "yes. Mark's told me about you."

It was a noncommittal line. Marta had the uncomfortable feeling that what Mark had told his mother was not good, but how could it be otherwise? She was getting used to the fact that when students didn't do well, they blamed their failures on their teachers and not on their own lack of commitment to academic work.

Marta shifted to the other foot. "Well," she said, "I didn't mean to keep you. I just meant to say that I hope Mark is recovering from, well, whatever it was. They haven't really told us much of anything, you see, except that it wasn't a drug overdose. Food poisoning, somebody said in the cafeteria this morning."

"Mark's fine," Liz Toliver said, "I just came from his room. He's had a very quiet night. There doesn't seem to be any chance of permanent damage from the incident last night."

"Well, good," Marta said. "I mean, he's been so sick so often this term, hasn't he? Much sicker than most students are, even in a bad winter. And that thing with the shakes, you know, and the tremors—"

"What?" Liz asked.

Marta blinked. "The shakes," she said. "I told the infirmary about it. I thought they must have told you. He'd come to class and he'd have the shakes, and there would be sweat coming off his forehead in waves really. We do have a number of first-year students who have hygiene problems, but Mark was the worst I've ever seen. Although of course I've only been here this one year—"

"Why is having the shakes a hygiene problem?" Liz Toliver asked.

"What?" Marta asked.

"Never mind," Liz Toliver said. "Do you think you were the only one who noticed it? Was it just in your class?"

"Oh, no," Marta said, "it wasn't in class at all necessarily. He had them the night, the night—yes. Well, the night his roommate committed suicide. I don't know if you know about that, if Mark told you—"

"I even got a formal notice from the school. Yes, I heard about that. He had them the night the boy killed himself? Why did you see him at night?"

"It was in the library," Marta said. "I've got an office in the faculty wing in the library. He came through."

Liz Toliver turned around until she was looking at Ridenour. "That's the library?" she asked.

"Yes," Marta said. "Yes, of course. But there's no reason to be upset, Ms. Toliver. It's just another indication, you see, of why Mark isn't really suited to be here. We've all discussed it this year. He just doesn't fit. And the hygiene problems, and the getting sick, well, they're symptoms. I don't mean last night was a symptom. That sounds like it was a terrible accident. We warn them about keeping food in their rooms when it could go bad, but they never listen of course. But the other things—"

"I have an appointment," Liz Toliver said again, moving in the direction of President's House. "Mark is going to be quite well. I'll convey your good wishes."

"You should take him out before we're forced to ask him to leave," Marta pushed on. "You must see it would be better. What good is it going to do to insist on keeping him here when he's not really suited for this level of academic work? There's no shame in admitting that he's just not bright enough to compete on this level. It's—"

But she was gone. Marta had no idea how long she had been gone. She was more than halfway to President's House, but she moved very quickly. Maybe it had been no time at all. Marta's mouth felt dry. Her lips felt chapped. She was sure she had said things she should not have said. She'd only told the truth though. She was sure of that.

She'd only told the truth, and she thought somebody around here ought to start telling it, all the time, to everybody.

THREE

1

Gregor Demarkian was not a man who "slept in," not ever, not even when he'd been up most of the night before. He could remember mornings in his early days at the FBI, when he'd been on kidnapping detail all night, when he'd insisted on showing up at the office on time to file his paperwork and only going home later for a short nap. He could remember mornings in that last sad year when his wife was dying of the uterine cancer they had caught far too late to do anything about. There would be a crisis, and he would go to her hospital room and sit, hour after hour in the darkness. Her small square of the room would be closed off by a white curtain. Behind the faux–Danish Modern chair he sat in would be a half wall of windows, looking out on the cemetery that every hospital seemed to be built beside. Her breathing would be labored but steady. The machines would wink and blink and let off small hiccoughy beeps at random intervals. Then the sun would come up, and the day nurse would check in to see how everything was going, and Gregor, reassured yet again that Elizabeth was not likely to die anytime in the next few hours, would go off to the coffee shop on the first floor to put enough coffee into himself to keep going. And he had kept going. That was the thing. It had never occurred to him in that year to reset the alarm clock for a later hour, even though he was on leave and had no office to go to. Productive people got up at five thirty or six and started the day. He had always been a productive person.

It was quarter after nine when Brian Sheehy's call came through to Gregor's room at the Windsor Inn, and Gregor was still fast asleep across his bed and still dressed in the clothes he'd worn the night before. It had been after three by the time he'd gotten in. Even Liz had left earlier, waiting only long enough for Mark to waken slightly so that she could tell him she was there. Mark hadn't woken for long. He'd barely opened a single eyelid, and he hadn't seemed to be surprised that his mother was next to him, running her hands through his hair. Gregor thought Mark didn't know where he was. He woke to find his mother beside him and assumed he was in his own home in his own bed. Gregor didn't blame him. Mark went back to sleep. Gregor went back to waiting for Dr. Niazi's replacement to give him some idea of where the tests that took longer to read were heading. At three, he'd finally given up. Not only was he annoying the hospital staff—although he tried to do as little of that as possible; he wasn't *nagging*—but the results that were coming back in dribs and drabs all said the same thing, and that was that there was no sign of anything in Mark's body but the caffeine.

"He does have strep throat," the second-shift doctor told Gregor at one point, trying his best to be polite when he was far too busy to be discussing test results with the patient's mother's designated "representative." "It's a very bad strep throat, too, and he's probably had it for weeks or even months. His throat's so sore, I'm surprised he was able to talk."

Strep throat was not the kind of thing Gregor was looking for. As far as he knew, it wasn't possible for one person to give another strep throat in an attempt to weaken or kill him. The longer he thought about the amount of caffeine in Mark's system, however, the more sure he was that Mark hadn't ingested it all by himself, not even accidentally. It wasn't impossible that a student of Mark's age and ambition would take caffeine tablets in an attempt to stay awake long enough to get extra work done or to study more thoroughly for a test. What seemed impossible to Gregor was that a student of Mark's intelligence wouldn't know that he risked injury or death by taking what appeared to have been a handful of the things. Gregor was sure that Mark had not been intent on committing suicide. There was nothing suicidal about the kid who had turned up to greet him at the Windsor Inn yesterday, no matter how much of a mess he was otherwise. There was nothing stupid about that kid either. The problem was that Gregor couldn't understand how somebody could have given Mark those tablets without Mark knowing he was taking them.

In the end he'd been too tired to think anymore. He'd called the police and left a message, very urgent, on Brian Sheehy's voice mail. Then he'd loosened his tie and sat down on the bed for what he'd thought would be a rest just long enough to get his shoes off. As the phone rang in his ear, it became obvious to him that he had never taken those shoes off. They were still on his feet, and they hurt. He rolled over onto his back and stared at the ceiling momentarily. The ceiling had molding on it, the way a lot of eighteenth-century ceilings did. It had cherubs and small bunches of grapes with leaves that looked broad enough to belong to marijuana plants. He reached for the phone and wondered, absently, why people had thought it so important to have bumpy representations of fruit on their ceilings at all.

He picked up and said, "Yes?"

Brian Sheehy said, "I had four phone calls this morning, all about the same thing. I answered yours. You want to tell me what's going on?"

"Yes," Gregor said. He sat up. His back ached. His neck ached, too. He'd been joking about getting old for so long, but now that the state seemed to be visited on him, he did not find it funny. "Meet me somewhere for breakfast. There's got to be somewhere for breakfast in this town that won't serve alfalfa sprouts with the toast."

"Don't bet on it. I'm in the middle of a workday, you know. Granted, there's not a lot of work to the day here at the moment, but I'm informed on the best possible evidence that there's about to be. It seems a certain Mr. Jimmy Card has been spotted checking into the Windsor Inn. It's going to be a circus."

"I agree, but it isn't going to be one immediately, and I want to lay it all out the best I can," Gregor said. "Meet me somewhere for breakfast. Pick a place and I'll find it."

"The Aubergine Harpsichord on Main Street."

"The what?"

"The Aubergine Harpsichord. Don't ask. You wanted breakfast. They do serve alfalfa sprouts with the toast, and some specialty herb teas that would make a dog puke, but they also make a decent omelet, so have that. I've got a couple of things to clear up. Meet me in twenty minutes. Go down to your lobby, turn right when you get out the door, it's just at the end of the block. You'll know it because it has one of those big wooden signs hanging out over the sidewalk with an eggplant on it. That's what an aubergine is; it's an eggplant."

"Right," Gregor said.

They hung up, and Gregor decided he had just enough time for a quick shower. He stripped, threw himself under the water, and stepped out again exactly seven minutes later, timing the operation by his travel alarm clock. He gave a fleeting thought to the fact that Bennis had given him this alarm clock,

173

and then, in a hope that gave evidence of more desperation than he knew he felt, called down to the desk to see if he had any messages. He'd picked up his messages when he'd come in the night before, but he told himself that he'd been asleep for a few hours. The idea that Bennis would call him after three o'clock in the morning unless somebody had died was absurd, but he tried it anyway. There were no messages. Tibor had learned long ago not to call him in the early hours of the morning with news about the people on his Internet newsgroups.

Gregor threw himself into clean clothes, made sure he had his wallet and keys, and left the room. In the hallway outside, there was nothing but quiet and a few small stacks of dishes waiting by one of the other doors. He might not like to sleep in, but presumably most other people who came to stay at a place like the Windsor Inn preferred to.

2

The Aubergine Harpsichord was indeed at the end of Gregor's own short block, just past an art gallery selling what looked like children's drawings rendered in oils and earth tones and a store with no stated purpose at all but with a beautiful pewter tea set in the window. Gregor had no idea who bought teapots. Bennis owned a beautiful ceramic one but never used it. He thought she had received it as a gift. The Aubergine Harpsichord's front windows were made to look as if they were divided. Gregor could tell that they were, in fact, plate glass with cosmetic dividers pasted over them. He went in through the divided wooden door and saw that the restaurant itself was very nearly a political statement. There were posters on the walls, carefully framed, of the kind that particularly intellectual college students favored: Barishnikov in midleap, Alice in Wonderland, Che Guevera. There were two posters of the kind Gregor thought of as "fat letters, caught drunk." They had mud brown backgrounds, and the letters themselves were black, plump, and sort of wandering all over in different sizes, the text swooping around the sides, nothing made straight or easy to read. LIVE SIMPLY THAT OTHERS MAY SIMPLY LIVE, one of them said. The other said, RACISM: RANDOM ACTS OF BLINDNESS. Gregor had no idea why those posters irritated him so much. He didn't disagree with them. He thought people who piled up mountains of stuff and spent their money on things they wouldn't want in six months' time were stupid beyond belief, and he had never had any patience with racism at all, not even in his early days at the Bureau when it had still been considered both "natural" and "inevitable" that African

Americans would never become full-fledged agents. For some reason the posters brought out the anarchist in him. He was sorry he wasn't able to drive up to the curb in a gigantic SUV, and that in spite of the fact that no sane person allowed him to drive anywhere where there might be traffic.

He found a seat at a table near the window and sat down. He looked at the menu—more fat letters curving around the front cover, these saying WAR IS HARMFUL TO CHILDREN AND OTHER LIVING THINGS, as if whoever had opened this place had found it impossible to escape from 1968. He found the section of the menu with "beverages" on it and paused. There were at least fifty different kinds of tea listed there, and two dozen kinds of coffee. The waitress came up, dressed in what looked like a burlap apron over a shirt made out of something similar that flowed to the floor, and he said,

"Could I have some coffee to start? Just plain coffee, with a little milk in it."

"We have Bana Tiryu coffee. It's grown and harvested by native peoples on their own cooperative in the Brazilian rain forest. The Aubergine Harpsichord participates in the boycotts of Brazilian and Colombian corporate-harvested coffee and of all GM coffee wherever it is grown—"

"What's GM coffee?"

"Genetically modified."

"Ah," Gregor said. He still had no idea what she was talking about. "Is this Bana—"

"Bana Tiryu."

"Yes, is that regular coffee? Not flavored or noncaffeinated or—"

"It's plain coffee, yes. But you don't have to worry about that kind of thing here. We don't serve artificially flavored coffees or teas of any kind. If we offer vanilla coffee, it's because we've ground the vanilla beans and flavored it ourselves."

The front door opened. Gregor looked up and was relieved to see Brian Sheehy, dressed in yet another badly fitting suit with nothing more than a down vest over it, in spite of the fact that it was still cold enough so that it hurt to breathe outside. The waitress saw him come in and backed away from the table a step or two. Brian sat down on the other side of the table and said,

"Good morning, Alexandra. Give the man a cup of plain coffee, will you please, and not a nervous breakdown. Give me a cup of plain coffee while you're at it."

"A little cream," Gregor said.

"You should consider the facts of dairy farming before you decide to have

175

cream," Alexandra started; but Brian shot her a look, and she shrugged. "I'll leave some pamphlets," she said, taking off.

"It's like being in a time warp," Gregor said.

"Not really," Brian told him. "I remember hippies, and these people are not hippies. Alexandra is taking a year off to work before she starts a master's degree program at Tufts in sociology. Nobody around here is going back to the land and giving up their possessions. They just all drive minicompacts and vote for Nader."

"Right," Gregor said.

Alexandra was back with the coffee, in two white ceramic mugs that looked a little uneven. "These are hand thrown by the Joy Hope Women's Cooperative in Lagos, Nigeria," she said. "The Aubergine Harpsichord supports women's cooperative enterprises throughout the developing world."

"You hungry?" Brian asked.

"A little," Gregor said.

Brian handed Alexandra both the menus. "Give us a couple of western omelets." He turned to Gregor. "They're vegetarian but not vegan, so no ham but a lot of cheese." He looked back at Alexandra. "And no more lectures, sweetheart. Please."

Alexandra rolled her eyes and wandered off, and Gregor noticed that she hadn't written down anything they'd said. Didn't waitresses carry order books anymore?

"Can you grow coffee in the Brazilian rain forest?" he asked Brian.

"How should I know?" Brian said. "If you really want an answer, you should talk to Kitty, who owns this place. She actually knows what she's talking about. Alexandra is, well, Alexandra."

"I see." Gregor took a sip of his coffee. It tasted like coffee. He knew people who could tell the difference between coffees, and who treated drinking coffee like some people treated drinking wine, but he wasn't one of them.

"So," Brian said, "you want to tell me what's going on exactly?"

Gregor nodded. "Mark DeAvecca, the boy I came up to see, was admitted to the hospital last night. I was there when he convulsed by the way. I'd gone to his dorm to see if I could ask him a few more questions, and when I got there he was throwing up everywhere and whipping around like he was being electrocuted."

"Drug overdose?"

"No." Gregor reached into his pocket, got out his wallet, and got the folded-up sheets of paper he had put in behind his credit cards the night before. They were bad notes, but at least they were notes. He flattened out the papers against the table. "At least as of three o'clock this morning," he said, "every drug test done on Mark DeAvecca came back negative, except for one."

"Ah," Brian said.

"And that one was for caffeine."

Brian Sheehy blinked. "You did say caffeine."

"Yes, I did, and it's not as trivial as it sounds. I wrote down all the numbers, but the bottom line is that he had enough caffeine in him to kill him. The only reason it didn't kill him was because he vomited out a lot of it. In chunks. In the form of pieces of caffeine tablets, the kind of thing kids take to stay up during exam week."

"Jesus Christ. What did he think he was doing?"

"Well," Gregor said, "what he wasn't doing was getting high. I need to find out exactly what sort of symptoms caffeine can cause, but I've been wondering, ever since I heard this, if caffeine could explain everything people have been saying about Mark up here. The high anxiety levels, for instance, and the sweating. And the memory losses. And the blackouts."

"I've never heard of anybody having blackouts from too much caffeine," Brian said.

"Neither have I, but we're both thinking of people who have been drinking lots of coffee, not people who've been ingesting these tablets. Maybe wholesale. We're talking about a level of caffeine use here that exceeds even the worst coffee habit by a factor of ten."

"But what did he think he was doing?" Brian asked again. "Did he decide he never wanted to have to sleep at all? What?"

"I think we should consider the possibility that he didn't take them on purpose," Gregor said.

"You mean he took some and forgot about it and then took more?"

"Maybe," Gregor said, "but I'm thinking more along the lines of somebody giving them to him without his knowing it or without his knowing what they were."

Brian took a deep breath. "Is that what he says happened?"

"No," Gregor said. "At the time I left, he still hadn't said anything except hello to his mother and then only for a split second. I'm speculating here."

"It doesn't make much sense," Brian said. "I'm going to have to look up the particulars on caffeine poisoning, if there is such a thing, but the simple fact is that people drink coffee by the gallonsful without dying from it, or having convulsions, or having any of those other symptoms you were talking about. Except for the anxiety maybe. The coffee jitters."

177

"I know."

"Did he have some kind of allergy to the stuff?" Brian asked.

"The tentative answer to that is yes," Gregor said, "at least according to the emergency room doctor I talked to. He thought that Mark had enough of a sensitivity to caffeine so that he had a violent reaction to what he ingested last night, which is what caused the projectile vomiting, which is why he lived. I do want to stress that. Both the emergency room doctor and the floor physician who came on afterward were adamant that, given what they managed to find in the vomit on his clothes and in his stomach, he should have died last night. He got very lucky."

"Still," Brian said.

"I know," Gregor said, "but hear me out here, all right? For months, apparently, everybody in Windsor, Massachusetts, has been assuming that Mark DeAvecca was on drugs and lying about it. You assumed that. Well, we now know that he wasn't on drugs, and he wasn't lying about it. Yes, I do realize he might have taken some on and off sometime in the last however many weeks. But the behavior people saw and interpreted as drug use was not caused by drug use. If it had been, it would have showed up in the drug tests that were done last night. So far so good?"

"Yes," Brian said. "All right. Fair enough. We owe the kid an apology."

"The kid may be owed more than that," Gregor said. "There obviously has been something wrong with him. Something seriously wrong with him. I saw it myself when I met him at the inn yesterday, hours before he convulsed. Now the doctors were saying last night that the possibility of permanent damage from caffeine poisoning is remote. The immediate problem is death, and he didn't die. Even so, the fact is that he's been physically a mess, and nobody up here did anything about it that I can tell. Did I tell you he also had strep?"

"No, you didn't," Brian said, "but you can't tell me you think somebody gave him that on purpose."

"No, I don't, but it's indicative of another part of the problem. According to the doctor I talked to, this was the floor phycisian, Mark not only has strep, he has *bad* strep. They put him on some ridiculously high level of antibiotics, something like four times the normal dose. That bad. The doctor said he thinks Mark may have been walking around with the strep for weeks."

"So?"

"So," Gregor said, "what's going on over at that school? What's wrong with those people? I can't believe Mark's never checked into the infirmary feeling bad. Didn't they do a throat culture? Didn't they even look down the kid's throat? The floor physician told Liz Toliver that Mark's throat was red and raw enough to be mistaken for meat in a butcher shop."

"Even so," Brian said, "you can't give somebody strep in an attempt to kill them, not unless you're a mad scientist type with access to all kinds of things, and I don't think we've got mad scientist types at Windsor Academy. And strep doesn't usually kill."

"Granted," Gregor said, "but the fact is, their system over there is so lax, and so cavalier, at least where Mark is concerned, that anybody could have been doing anything to him and nobody would have noticed. They just assumed he must be on drugs, and they just assumed that they weren't going to do anything about it. Although why not—"

"I've told you why not," Brian said. "They couldn't prove it. And if they accuse without proof and they're wrong, they've got lawsuits."

"I know. But they should have done something when he started to look that bad. And you know it as well as I do. The first thing is, though, to ask him if he was taking caffeine tablets. And to believe him if he says no."

"He could lie, you know," Brian said.

"I know," Gregor said. "But, as I've told you, I've met him before. He's not a natural liar. And he's in the situation he's in at the moment because he did not lie, and everybody refused to believe he was telling the truth. This time we should assume he's being straight with us."

"All right. Also fair enough," Brian said.

"The second thing we should do is proceed on the assumption that this was an attempted murder."

Brian shook his head. Alexandra was back with the omelets. They were enormous, even if they didn't have meat in them. Gregor was a little disappointed, but not surprised, to see that the cheese was a pale white and not the orange of what he considered "normal" cheddar. It was too much to ask that The Aubergine Harpsichord have artificially colored cheese.

Brian waited until Alexandra went away and then said, "You really can't do that, you know. We don't have evidence of an attempted murder here. Peter Makepeace may be in a lot of trouble when the going gets tough, but he's still got connections. The school still has connections."

"Liz Toliver and Jimmy Card have connections."

"Not those kinds of connections," Brian said. "And be reasonable. Even if this really is an attempted murder, it's going to be damned near impossible to prove. You'd have to hope for a real piece of stupidity, somebody charging half a dozen boxes of those tablets on a credit card or buying an armful in a store

179

where they're known. And if Mark DeAvecca has ever bought a box of those things himself, if anybody even comes forward and says they saw him with a box of his own, it's all going to go to hell. The incident is going to be written off as accidental, and there's going to be nothing you can do about it."

"I know," Gregor said, "but there's something else."

"What?"

"Well, I was sitting in that hospital last night watching Mark breathe, and even Liz had gone back to the inn to bed, and I got to thinking. I don't know what the symptoms of caffeine poisoning are, never mind chronic caffeine poisoning, if there is such a thing. But those symptoms sure as hell are familiar. The whole thing about the memory loss, and not blackouts, but 'coming to,' which is how he put it."

"That's different than blackouts?"

"I think so, yes," Gregor said. "I think it's more like being distracted to the point of thoughtlessness rather than literally blacking out. And, like I said, it's all very familiar. The loss of appetite. The trouble in his hands. The inability to write. The joint pain."

"He had joint pain?"

"Something like that. He kept saying his hands didn't work right. You should get a look at his handwriting sometime. It looks, well, what came to mind was the way people's handwriting looks after strokes. And that's when it hit me, while I was sitting in the hospital. There's definitely something that can cause all those symptoms."

"Lyme disease?" Brian asked helpfully.

"Maybe," Gregor said, "I don't know much about Lyme disease. What I asked the doctor to test Mark for was arsenic."

FOUR

1

The first thing Mark DeAvecca saw when he woke up was his stepfather standing against a wall whose upper half was made entirely of windows, signing an autograph for a woman who appeared to be dressed in hospital whites. The woman towered over Jimmy Card. Mark found nothing strange in that. Most people towered over Jimmy Card, except for Mark's mother, who was only five four herself. Mark thought Jimmy might be five six. Even if the woman wasn't wearing heels—and she wouldn't be, would she, if she was in a nurse's uniform?—there was a good chance she could make Jimmy look like a midget.

The light from the windows was blinding. All the Venetian blinds had been pulled uncompromisingly to the top of their frames. Mark decided that he must be in a hospital of some kind, although that made less than good sense since the last thing he remembered was his mother bending over him and running her hands through his hair, which he thought must have meant he was at home. His throat was dry and scratchy. He needed to use the bathroom. He wanted to sit up. He tried to move around a little in bed, and both Jimmy and the woman in white nearly jumped out of their skins.

The Woman in White was a novel by Wilkie Collins. It had been one of Mark's father's favorites, and Mark himself had read it half a dozen times. He was now making no sense at all.

Jimmy and the woman in white came to the edge of the bed. The woman peered into Mark's open eyes and said, "He seems to be awake."

"I want to go to the bathroom," Mark said. It was not the first thing he'd thought of to say. He was a very polite boy, trained that way by a mother who did not put up with rudeness in her own children. The problem was, his throat was more than scratchy, it was downright sore. It hurt him to talk.

"The bathroom," the woman in white said, as if she'd never heard of such a thing.

Mark almost panicked. Maybe this was a dream, and in this dream there would be no bathrooms, and the result would be waking up to find he'd wet himself. That was all he would need. Sheldon would throw him out in the snow, or worse, and the story would get around campus in no time at all. He struggled to sit up. It wasn't easy to do when you were lying flat on your back. Jimmy came over and held out an arm. Mark grabbed it and pulled himself forward.

"Water," he said, and then, with enormous effort, "please?"

There was water in a pitcher with ice in it on a little side table, and a glass beside it. Jimmy filled the glass and handed it over. Mark took it. His hands were shaking. His arms were shaking. It took a conscious resolve of will to get the glass to his mouth without spilling any water, but he did it, and as soon as he did his throat felt better.

"Thank you," he said again. It wasn't so difficult this time. "I've got a sore throat."

"You've got strep," Jimmy said. "You had an IV full of antibiotics when I came in, but it's gone now."

"Bathroom," Mark said again. He threw his legs off the side of the bed and almost fell over. The woman in white offered her arm and Jimmy offered his. Mark took both of them and allowed himself to be steered into what he saw with relief was a bath private to this room. The bed that should have belonged to his roommate was empty. He shook off his helpers at the bathroom door— he really wasn't ready to have his own stepfather wipe his behind for him—and went in on his own. The bathroom was like the room it served. There was too much in the way of tile.

Mark did what he needed to do and then, deliberately, spent a long time at the sink washing up. He washed both his face and his neck. He washed his hands twice. He was in a hospital gown and a pair of boxers, which didn't bother him, since he tended to hang around the dorm in boxers and a T-shirt. That was something else that got him into trouble with Sheldon and the Dean of Student Life, who was a fat, pompous giant of a man whose social development seemed to have been arrested at the age of twelve. Washing his face felt good. He did it again. He looked at himself in the mirror and decided that he looked dead. The odd thing was, he didn't feel dead. He felt creaky. He felt ridiculously tired. His muscles ached. His head itched. Even so, he felt better than he had even when he'd been talking to Gregor Demarkian yesterday, and that was the best he'd felt in—

Gregor Demarkian, Mark thought. *Michael Feyre.* The body hanging from the sprinkler system pipe in the middle of his dorm room, swinging slightly in the breeze Mark had made when he'd opened the door.

Mark opened the bathroom door and went back into the hospital room proper. Jimmy and the woman in white were still standing more or less where he'd left them.

"I'm in Windsor," he said. "I couldn't remember where I was."

"You're in the hospital," Jimmy said.

"Why?"

"You don't remember?" the woman in white asked.

Mark wished he could figure out if the woman in white was a nurse or a nurse's aide or what. He hated not knowing, even though he wasn't sure it would do him any good if he knew. He walked back over to the bed and sat down on the side of it. He didn't want to lie down. He would have used the chair if it hadn't meant that Jimmy would have no place to sit himself.

"I'm starving to death," he said. "Can I have some breakfast? Can I have some coffee?"

"No," the woman in white said.

"What?" Mark said.

"He could have a milkshake, I'll bet," Jimmy said. "Mark's always liked milkshakes."

"Of course he could have a milkshake," the woman in white said.

"Great," Mark said. "A chocolate milkshake. That would be—"

"No," the woman in white said.

"Is this a joke?" Mark said. "Because my throat hurts, and I ache, and I don't know how I got here, and I'm in no mood."

"Get him a vanilla milkshake," Jimmy said. "He liked those the last time I talked to him."

"One vanilla milkshake," the woman in white said. "And I'll page Dr. Holloway and let him know Mark is up."

The woman in white left the room, still clutching the small square piece of paper Jimmy had been signing for her when Mark first opened his eyes. Mark watched her go with relief. He had the feeling that she was more of a hindrance than a help to his finding out what was going on.

"So," he said, "I'm in the hospital for strep throat? Is that usual?"

"To tell you the truth," Jimmy said, "you probably could be here for strep throat. According to what the doctor told your mother last night, you've had it for weeks, untreated. Didn't you feel sick? How could you walk around for weeks with your throat looking, to quote your mother, like raw hamburger, and not get some help for yourself?"

"I went to the infirmary just last Tuesday," Mark said. "They checked me out. They didn't find anything."

"Did they look in your throat?"

"I don't remember."

"Did they do one of those throat tests where they use the huge Q-tip and stick it down behind your tongue?"

"No, they didn't do that," Mark said. "That I'd remember. They took my temperature, though. I remember that. If I'm not in the hospital for strep throat, what am I in the hospital for?"

Jimmy sat down in the plastic-upholstered chair near the window. "Well, I only got in about two and a half hours ago, and I've only heard all this second-hand from your mother, so take whatever I say with a certain amount of caution, okay? The best guess this morning seems to be caffeine poisoning."

"Ah," Mark said, "that's why no coffee."

"Right. Also why no chocolate, which is apparently full of caffeine, too. No caffeine at all of any kind for at least thirty days."

"So what happened? Did I pass out?"

"You started by vomiting on some guy's ceiling—"

"On his *ceiling?* What guy? Where?"

"At your dorm. Then you had convulsions. Then you passed out. Demarkian showed up in the middle of the convulsions and got them to call nine-one-one, which they were apparently not thinking of doing. Nine-one-one brought you here. Your mother got in about an hour or so later because she'd already started up because Gregor had called to say that you looked like you were dying—"

"He called from the inn while I was there," Mark said dismissively. "I know. Wait. Mom's here, right? I saw her last night, but I was still out of it and I thought I was home."

"She's got meetings over at the school."

"Whoo boy. Is she suing everybody on the planet, or has she skipped that part and gone directly to homicide?"

"She's got a meeting this afternoon with the Boston contact firm for Shelby, Dredson and Cranch."

"Right," Mark said. "You've been in Hayes House, haven't you? The ceilings are twenty feet high. How did I vomit on the ceiling?"

"Don't ask me," Jimmy said. "I told you; I've just wandered in. I wasn't even coming originally before you ended up here. Liz was going to come down, assess the situation, and decide if you needed to be pulled out of school and brought back home."

"She decided that before she'd left, did she?"

"Pretty much," Jimmy said.

"She's always hated this place," Mark said. "Not this place. The Windsor Academy. Crap, I don't know. I asked Mr. Demarkian down here, did you know that?"

"Yes, he told Liz and Liz told me."

"I don't think Michael was murdered or anything. It's not that. It's just that this place is so odd, and I wasn't thinking straight and I couldn't figure it out. Except that I am thinking straight today. I mean, I'm a little fuzzy, but mostly I'm okay. And I was mostly okay over at the inn last night with Gregor. Except I'm more all right now. I can't read anymore, did I tell you that?"

"No," Jimmy said, "how can you not be able to read anymore?"

"I don't know," Mark said. "I try to read but nothing makes sense. So I just sort of make myself, but when I finish the page I don't understand what the hell I've read. It's been going on for months. It was going on at Christmas—"

"You were pretty damned strange at Christmas. Your mother and I thought you were—"

"On drugs," Mark said, "but I'm not. I'm—"

"Relax," Jimmy said, "that much I know. They did tests. You're clean. Except for the caffeine. That's something I know about, too. I mean, for Christ's sake, Mark. Drink a little coffee to keep yourself awake, but those caffeine tablets are murder. I know, I used to do that to myself when I still thought I was going to get a college education, pop a couple of those and stay up all night trying to study, but the thing is—"

"What are caffeine tablets?"

"NoDoz. Vivarin. That kind of thing. They've got generic ones. I've seen them in the drugstores. They're a stupid way to go. They've got as much caffeine in one of them as in a cup of strong black coffee, and everybody takes five or six. You apparently took about thirty."

"I did not," Mark said. "I've never taken a caffeine tablet in my life."

"Well, there were pieces of the damned things in your stomach when they pumped it, kid. And in the vomit on your clothes. Your mother, speaking of homicide, is ready to kill you."

"I've never taken a caffeine tablet in my life," Mark repeated. "And if this gets to be like the drug thing, where nobody believes me, I'll scream. Or break something. I'm big enough to break something serious these days. I mean, for Christ's sake, Jimmy, what do you take me for? I know I've been behaving like an irresponsible jerk this year, but I'm not an idiot. I've been drinking a lot of coffee, yes, okay, maybe too much, maybe about ten cups a day. I shouldn't have done that, thinking about it sounds pretty stupid itself. But I don't pop pills. I won't even take Tylenol for a headache most of the time."

The woman in white came back in, carrying a very large, tall glassful of milkshake. Mark thanked her and reached for it, but she insisted on putting it down on the table, taking the straw out of its paper wrapper, and putting the straw in the milkshake herself. She reminded Mark of a waiter in a very, very, very pretentious restaurant who had been trained to believe that diners were incapable of putting their own napkins in their own laps. Mark took a long drink of milkshake. The woman in white nodded appreciatively and walked back out of the room again.

Mark put the milkshake back on the side table. "Listen," he said, "that's why I asked Gregor Demarkian up here. Because nobody would believe me. Nobody would believe me about anything. If it's going to get like that again, I don't know what I'm going to do. I didn't take any caffeine tablets, not one. If they found them in my stomach, then somebody slipped them to me when I wasn't looking. And if you can't take my word for it, then to hell with you."

"If somebody slipped them to you when you weren't looking," Jimmy said, "then that somebody was trying to kill you. Unless you're suggesting it was a joke. Do you really think somebody is trying to kill you?"

"No," Mark said, "why would they? But I didn't take them, and that's final. And I told everybody I wasn't taking drugs, and they didn't believe that either, and now you've got the proof that I wasn't lying after all. God, I don't know what's happened to my life. I really don't. People didn't use to think I was lying practically anytime I opened my mouth. What's the deal here? Have I suddenly grown horns and a tail I can't see in the mirror?"

"Of course not," Jimmy said. "Calm down. You're yelling at the wrong person. I'm an innocent bystander. Did you really get Gregor Demarkian all the way up here just because people wouldn't believe you when you said you weren't on drugs?"

"Of course not." Mark had more milkshake. He'd drunk nearly the whole thing, and he wanted more. He couldn't remember the last time he'd been this hungry. He thought he might never have been this hungry. He was ready to eat the mud beige, wholly inadequate blanket that covered his bed. He pulled his legs up under him, crossed in a not-quite lotus position. "Hey, Jimmy," he said, "you got your car up here? Driver and everything?"

"Of course I have the driver and everything. Why?"

"Because I'm starving," Mark said, "and all the food in Windsor sucks dead rats, and you know the hospital food won't be any better. What I want is three crispy chicken sandwiches from McDonald's and a supersized fries and, I don't know. Another milkshake. Like that. The thing is, the only way you can get that that I know of is if you go out to exit 30 on I-95 north in, I think it's Lexington. It may be Concord. But you have to get off exit 30 going north, because the McDonald's is on the exit. It's a weird sort of arrangement. It's not off the exit in town, it's on this long access ramp. Oh, and I want ketchup. That doesn't have caffeine in it, does it?"

"I don't think so. I used to be able to eat like that without getting sick. It was a long time ago."

"Will you do it?"

"I suppose," Jimmy said, "but I still want to know. If you didn't get Gregor up here because nobody would believe you weren't taking drugs, why did you get him up here?"

Mark shrugged. "Because of something I saw on the night Michael died or maybe something I didn't see. I could have been hallucinating it. I could have been wrong. I saw it out the window of the library from the catwalk. And it was dark."

"You've been hallucinating?" Jimmy said.

"I don't know," Mark told him. "I really don't. It was just so weird. And I tried to tell a bunch of people, Cherie Wardrop, even Philip Candor, although he hates the hell out of me, but he's the kind of person people tell things to. And nobody would listen. Even the police wouldn't listen. So I thought Gregor Demarkian would, and if I was just hallucinating he'd find that out, too, and I could just check myself into a loony bin. Except I don't feel like I need to be in a loony bin anymore. Are you going to go get me something to eat? We've got to do it before Mom gets back because she'll make me eat broccoli and stuff. Except she won't if the food is already here. You know."

"You sound better than I've heard you in months," Jimmy said.

Mark felt better than he'd felt in months. He had no idea why, and he didn't care. He just wanted to eat something and do it soon.

2

It was noon, and that meant it had now been at least two hours since some of the particulars of what had happened to Mark DeAvecca had begun to filter through the Windsor Academy campus. Philip Candor would never have accused Peter Makepeace's secretary of listening at doors or, better yet, at intercoms, but he knew she did it, and so did everybody else. That was why the news was out within minutes of Liz Toliver's meeting at President's House, that Mark's drug tests had come back negative, not only the quick ones that had been done when he was first admitted, but the more accurate ones that had taken until this morning to be read and interpreted. Mark was not on marijuana. Mark was not on speed. Mark was not on heroin—not that Philip had ever suspected that one. Heroin made people calm, not wired and frantic. Of course, Mark was not on cocaine either, which was a much more interesting finding. Philip would have bet his life that that kid was pickled in cocaine, even if he didn't snort it through his nose or leave dustings of powder on the hardwood surfaces of his dorm room.

The gossip had been somewhat more hazy about just what had been wrong with Mark when he'd vomited all over Sheldon's ceiling and collapsed in convulsions on the bathroom floor, but the best guess was an overdose of caffeine tablets of the kind kids used to stay up to study for exams. There was no question that Mark had been found with the half-digested remnants of several of these tablets in his stomach when he was admitted to the hospital, and Philip supposed that it was not impossible that Mark had taken them. Drugged or not, the kid had been making no sense for most of the time he was on this campus. Unlike most of his colleagues in the cafeteria, however, Philip knew enough to be sure that caffeine pills weren't likely to explain the projectile vomiting, never mind the myriad other symptoms they'd all been watching for months on end. There was something seriously wrong here, and it was likely to get even more wrong in the next few days. Jimmy Card had arrived. Liz Toliver had been around for twelve hours. The one thing Philip had spent most of his life avoiding had arrived, and he was uncomfortably aware of the fact that there was nothing he could do to escape it. His best chance lay in staying out of sight as much as possible and in making sure that he was prepared for any eventuality. That was why he was cleaning and loading his stainless steel Colt Anaconda. It was not a gun he liked very much. It had only a six-round chamber, and it was too heavy for most of the purposes for which people wanted handguns. At the time he'd bought it, however, he hadn't had much choice, and he hadn't had the time to go shopping. He'd only been back in Idaho for the week.

He saw Alice coming up the walk before she knocked. He could have put the gun out of sight if he'd wanted to. He knew that no matter how easily he'd strong-armed the Windsor Academy administration over the matter of his smoking, he would not be able to strong-arm them on the matter of this gun. They would insist that he get rid of the gun or get himself out of faculty housing. He wanted to do neither.

Even so, he opened the door to Alice without putting the gun away. It was lying out in the open on the coffee table when she walked in. She took off her cape and stared at it, truly shocked. Philip thought it was the only time he had ever seen her shocked. Then he amended that. It was the only time he had ever seen her show a thoroughly genuine emotion. Alice was always on stage. She was like that remarkable hair of hers: overblown, overcolored, overwrought.

"Well," she said, "you got paranoid very fast. I wouldn't have expected that of you. What did you do, go into Boston last night and pass a man a hundred on a street corner?"

"No." He sat down on his own couch and went back to loading the chamber. "I bought this gun in 1998."

"And you've had it here ever since? In the dorm?"

"That I have."

"The trustees will have a complete fit. They won't let you keep it, you know. And I don't understand why you have it in the first place. It's not as if Windsor is a high-crime area."

"No." There was more crime in Windsor than she knew, but that was one of those things Philip had long since ceased trying to explain to the faculty of Windsor Academy. He finished loading the chambers and tried siting at his reflection in the wall mirror. Alice Makepeace shuddered.

"I'll be happier when they make you get rid of it," she said. "I don't know why you want it here to begin with. Especially not now. God only knows what's going to happen around here now that we're in the middle of this mess. Don't you hate what it's like around here? When the institution is threatened, I mean. Peter gets insane. You should see him."

189

"I'd expect that Peter is afraid for his job."

"Of course he is. And of course we're going to have to leave. That's inevitable. If it wasn't when Michael decided to kill himself, it was as soon as that poisonous Mark DeAvecca starting flopping around Sheldon's bathroom like a rag doll. That woman came to see Peter this morning, you know. Mark's mother."

"Liz Toliver. I've seen her on television."

"Yes, well, so have I. That hardly matters, does it? Anyway, she's breathing fire and when she breathes fire, the *New York Times* breathes fire along with her. The whole thing is such a mess, I don't know where to start. That's why I came. Maybe you can tell me where to start."

"Where to start what?" Philip asked. "Explaining yourself? Getting Peter another job?"

"People come to you and tell you things. I know that. Everybody knows that. You're everybody's father confessor, except mine."

"That's quite all right, Alice. I wouldn't want to be your father confessor."

"I don't have one," Alice said, "I know better. But people talk to you, which means you know what they're thinking."

"They don't talk to me as much as you think, Alice. And they don't tell me their secrets. If that's the kind of thing you want, hire a private detective and have them bugged."

"I want to know what they're saying. About Michael. About me."

"Like I said, have them bugged."

"It wouldn't do any good to have them bugged now, would it? They've already done their talking. I don't think you realize the seriousness of what's been going on here."

"Oh, I realize the seriousness, Alice," Philip said, "I just don't evaluate it the same way you do. Are people talking about the affair you had with Michael Feyre—"

"I didn't have an 'affair' with Michael Feyre."

"—then yes, they're talking about that. They've been talking about it for months. Why should it matter to you that they're talking about it now?"

"People don't understand the problems a boy like Michael has finding himself," Alice said. "They're used to their own comfortable lives, and they just don't realize how repressed somebody like Michael is. How oppressed. Oppressed by false consciousness, really, thinking that the system is just fine, really, it's all their own fault if they constantly screw up. You have to give them back their self-respect if you're going to teach them to see the world clearly, if you're going to make them understand that they're the victims here."

"And you do that by fucking them in broom closets in the off-hours on weekends? Alice, try to make sense for once. You like to star in your own movie. You like to be the center of attention. You do it every year, and you're only going to stop doing it when those lines on your face get deep enough so that the boys can't help noticing."

"I don't have lines on my face."

"Yes, Alice, you do, and in a year or two you're going to face the choice all fair-skinned women do. You're either going to have to go in for surgery or Retin-A, or you're going to have to give it up. I'm betting on the surgery myself. You'll never give it up, and Retin-A would mean no more long afternoon walks in the sun."

"Michael," Alice said, choosing her words carefully, "was a misguided but very intelligent boy. He could have become a great leader, a truly authentic leader—"

"Michael," Philip said, "was a thug. He was a thug when he came to Windsor, and he was a thug when he hung himself. His mother could see him for what he was. He was a thug without pretensions, at least until you got to him. He was better off where he was."

"He was better off as a thug?"

"Yes," Philip said, "thugs rehabilitate themselves sometimes. I've seen it happen. Thugs with pretensions, though, they're hooked worse than any junkie ever was."

"If he was hooked, as you put it, why would he have killed himself?"

"I have no idea why he killed himself."

"You really don't understand," Alice said. She was pacing. Philip thought she had been pacing for a long time, but he hadn't noticed. His eyes were always going on and off the gun. It was fully loaded by now. She could pick it up and use it. He knew she wouldn't.

She stopped at the wall mirror and checked herself out. She kept her back to him and said, "There's a whole world out there that has nothing to do with the trivialities you concern yourself with. There's a whole world that has nothing to do with equations and geometry proofs and logic templates or whatever it is you call them. There's a world of people."

"I'm aware there's a world of people, Alice. I'm more aware of it than you are."

"There's a world of history, too," Alice said. "History is marching on whether you choose to acknowledge it or not. History is not on the side of this place and the people in it—people like you."

It was a measure of the extent of the radical change that had taken place since Mark DeAvecca collapsed in Hayes House that Philip was tempted, even if only for a moment, to deliver a lecture on "people like" himself, a lecture so detailed and explicit that even Alice Makepeace would have no way of misinterpreting it. He stopped himself just in time, but he couldn't deny that he'd tapped a vein of recklessness in himself that he'd thought he'd exorcized forever a very long time ago. His cigarettes were on the table next to the gun, two kinds of coffin nails huddled together for warmth in the icy moralistic air of a progressive school. He stuck a cigarette in his mouth and lit it with the plain blue plastic Bic lighter he kept next to the ashtray. He had Bic lighters all over the house. They were the only kind he used.

"You know," he said, "there are people out there, people in this country, who take revolution seriously. They're not playing a game, and they don't deal in concepts like 'false consciousness.' They just do what they do. They're very dangerous. You wouldn't like them much. You'd approve even less."

"I want to know if anybody saw me talking to Mark last night in the cafeteria."

"People like Timothy McVeigh," Philip said.

Alice turned away from the mirror. She looked like she was forcing herself. "Leave it to you to call a fascist like that a revolutionary."

"He was a revolutionary, Alice. He was a home-grown, working-class American revolutionary. If the proletariat of the United States ever rises up to overthrow the capitalist hegemony, that's what they're going to look like: Timothy McVeigh, Eric Rudolph. Take your pick. And you do. Take your pick, I mean. You picked Michael Feyre because he had no interest in revolution at all."

"I picked Michael Feyre because he was one of the most intelligent and tortured souls I'd ever met."

"And the one last year? Alex Cowby. He was an intelligent and tortured soul, too. Until he became too obviously disappointing."

"You can't save everybody," Alice said. "They're so damaged by the time they get here, saving them isn't always possible. They buy into the whole thing, into the big corporate lie. Into the idea that having things and making money are what they should be after."

"Alice, for God's sake. We've got a Socialist Club and a Communist Youth League. We've also got a nice little sprinkling of working-class kids on scholarship. Not one of them wants anything to do with—"

"Why are we going into this again?" Alice said. "What's your point, Philip? Is there some reason that this is all you can ever talk about? I asked you a question. I asked if you'd heard anybody say they saw me in the cafeteria with Mark last night."

He took a deep drag on his cigarette and leaned forward with his elbows on his knees. "Why? Were you trying to seduce him, too?"

"Don't be ridiculous."

"Then why?"

"Because I want to know," Alice said, "that's all. Because I want to know. There've been rumors all day about the caffeine, about caffeine pills or tablets or whatever you call them. Maybe he took them last night while I was there, and I just didn't notice. Maybe something. I don't know. I want to know."

"All right." The cigarette was nearly out. Philip put it down in the ashtray and got another. He rarely chain-smoked; it made his lungs hurt. Now he found he wanted his lungs to hurt, if only because the sensation would have a reality to it that he could not make come clear in this room. He had always found Alice ephemeral in some odd way. He'd never been able to accept her as solid. She seemed to him to be a mass of affect and confusion: that electric red hair, that way of carrying her body that showed she had always known that men admired it—and women too, that mass of drivel that poured out of her mouth every time she talked. Freud had once asked: "What do women want?" Philip was willing to bet that if he'd ever met Alice, he would have been completely stumped.

"You're not going to tell me what I want to know," she said, coming to sit down on the edge of the chair across from him.

"I don't know the answer to the question you've asked. Nobody has said anything to me about it. That's the best I can do."

"People tell you everything."

"I doubt it."

"Peter was saying this morning that we should never have admitted Michael to Windsor. We knew what his problem was with drugs. He had an arrest record. But it isn't Michael we shouldn't have admitted; it's Mark DeAvecca. He's going to ruin everything."

"I doubt that, too."

Alice stood up, and Philip thought she was going to come over to him. She'd done that once, when he was first at Windsor, after one of those long-winded faculty parties where too many people had drunk too much cheap sherry and at least two of the men had had to be talked out of lecturing the assembled company on The Mission of Education in the Twenty-first Century. He had thought at the time that her move was calculated as well as practiced. She had done it before with other new male faculty members, maybe even with female ones; and she was doing it again, not out of desire or necessity, but almost as a kind of insurance. She had snaked one arm around his neck and the other between his legs. He could feel her long, strong fingers outlining the mound of his stiffening penis and probing carefully for his balls. He stared into her face with bemusement, not sure how she expected him to react. She had tried kissing him. He had allowed her tongue into his mouth without much interest. He had not closed his eyes. He didn't know her, and he could see for himself that she was truly beautiful, but she left him absolutely cold.

Maybe she remembered that. She stepped a little away from him and reached for her cape. Philip always found that cape more than a little ridiculous.

"You know," he said, "you ought to take me seriously. You can't go on doing what you're doing much longer. It doesn't even work all that well anymore. It never worked on me. My guess is that it doesn't work on Mark DeAvecca either. Which raises him in my estimation more than you know."

"Nothing could raise him in my estimation," Alice said. "He's a disaster. And he's going to blow this whole place up, not just me. Doesn't that matter to you?"

"No," Philip said, surprised to realize that it was true.

"I'll leave you to it then," Alice said. The cape floated in the air and settled around her shoulders. She could still do that trick. It was fun to watch. She looked down at the gun, still on the table. "Be careful nobody ends up shot. You'll be a ready-made suspect with that thing hanging around."

Then she turned on her heel and stalked out, the picture of a stage heroine in high dudgeon, the star of one more performance. Philip watched her go first out his door, then, a few moments later, out of Martinson and into the quad. She had the hood of the cape down around her shoulders in spite of the cold. Her red hair shone and shimmered and danced. Philip thought of all the American revolutionaries, the rich and poor ones who'd joined liberation armies; the lower-middle-class ones who'd joined militias; the real ones who "went sovereign," as the saying goes, and cut themselves off from everybody and everything, cut themselves off even from electricity and running water; the true lunatics in their mountain cabins with their arsenals and their Bibles and their ears tuned to the sound of creeping footsteps in the brush around the edges of their yards. It was the arsenals that were the weak links in those chains, and Philip knew it. It was the arsenals that were the weak links in all the chains because in the end there was no way to consider yourself a revolutionary and not be willing to kill somebody. He wondered who Alice Makepeace was willing to kill, and how she'd go about doing it.

Then he got up and went to the chest of drawers in his bedroom. He pulled it out a little ways from the wall and found what had also been taped there, along with the gun and its ammunition. He pulled out the shoulder holster and fixed it on his left shoulder. He had to adjust it twice. It had been years since he'd worn it, and he was definitely growing both older and wider. He thought about putting the gun in the small of his back and rejected the idea. He'd seen too damn many idiots shoot themselves in their butts.

Alice Makepeace had disappeared from the quad. Philip had no idea where she'd gone. He got the gun settled in the holster and then went looking for a jacket to cover it. It was just a precaution, but it was a precaution he'd decided to take when he first came out East from Idaho, and he still thought it was a very good idea.

FIVE

1

Gregor Demarkian didn't think he had ever been this calculating about any other case in his career. Even at the FBI, where, especially in his early days, when Hoover was still holding down the fort in the main office, Machiavellian intrigue was accepted as a matter of course, he had insisted on sticking to the straightforward and out-front. There was something fundamental to his nature that recoiled from the backroom underhandedness that characterized the informal power structure of most organizations. Sometimes he tried to convince himself that this fastidiousness was a virtue. Maybe he was more honest and less manipulative than other people. Most of the time he recognized it as a weakness. There was no virtue in being unable to accept the reality of human nature or being unable to deal with it either. He had been very lucky to be able to advance without pulling the kinds of strings most people would have had to to get anywhere above the level of field agent. It had been a stroke of luck, completely outside his control, that he had both landed and then solved one of the first of the notorious serial killer cases, and a further stroke of luck that he had been the object of a great deal of publicity because of it. He didn't want to say that it was also a stroke of luck that Hoover had died only a few years before, but it was, and in ways that had nothing to do with the course of his own career. Gregor Demarkian had not been one of Hoover's loyal acolytes, and he was not the kind of man to idolize the director just because he'd lasted so long in office that he'd become a "legend." The legend covered a lot of unpleasant business, and not just the obvious things like blackmailing Congress, persecuting anybody whose politics he didn't like, and wearing women's underwear. Gregor had spent his first decade in the Bureau knowing that Hoover did not consider him a "real" American, and that he wasn't the only one Hoover had marked out for "foreignness" in a crew of men and women almost every one of whom had been born in the United States. Some people wanted to go back to the fifties. Gregor Demarkian wasn't interested in any period of American history before May 2, 1972, when Hoover had died.

Gregor had been made head of the new Behavioral Sciences Unit because the new director was at sea, because the Bureau had just moved to a new building, and because he'd had so much publicity that appointing him looked like a good piece of PR. It had been a grace to all concerned that he had also been competent. That's why not being able to engage in office politics was not a virtue. If competent people didn't engage in office politics, incompetent ones would, or worse, competent ones with ulterior motives, with agendas both personal and ideological, with their eye on the prize. Gregor only wished that most people who lusted after power did so because they wanted fame, money, and luxury. People who wanted fame and money could be bought off. Even people who wanted power for power's sake could be bought off, at least up to a point. The real killers were the ones who wanted to change the world. Gregor Demarkian was not a conservative and couldn't be. He was a child of an immigrant tenement neighborhood, and his own mother had kept a picture of Franklin Delano Roosevelt in an icon frame right next to her icon of the Black Madonna. He did share one idea with the conservatives though, and he thought it was a sensible one. He did not think it was ever possible to make human beings perfect, to rid them forever of greed and lust and avarice and pride. He distrusted the hell out of people who thought they could.

He was able to do the Machiavellian thing in this case because he was truly convinced that somebody had tried to murder Mark DeAvecca and because he had cleared the whole thing with Brian Sheehy beforehand. There was nothing like getting the cooperation of the person you wanted to manipulate to make manipulation feel like high morality. He had no idea if Brian took him seriously or was merely indulging him, but the result was the same in either case, and the result was all that Gregor cared about. Brian, in the meantime, cared mostly about embarrassing the school. Gregor would be happy to oblige him.

The call from the hospital came less than half an hour after he'd left Dee Feyre at the inn's front door. She had a room there, too—there wasn't anywhere else to get a room in Windsor unless you went out to the Interstate, to Concord or Lexington—but she wanted to get "some things done," as she put it, and Gregor hadn't wanted to ask her what. He'd gone back up to his room to think, and to think about calling Bennis, when the phone rang and he was put through to a pleasant female voice speaking against a background of conversation and random noise. He wondered where she was calling from. It wasn't an office. Was it that distractingly loud at a nurses' station?

"Mr. Demarkian?" she said. "This is Carol Alberani at Windsor Hospital. I'm the head nurse on Two West. Dr. Copeland asked me to call you."

"Thank you," Gregor said, wondering if he'd been completely off the wall. Her voice did sound pleasant and unconcerned. Would it be unconcerned if what he'd suspected was true?

"Dr. Copeland said to tell you that what you suggested turned out to be true and to thank you for suggesting it. He wouldn't have thought of it on his own. He'd like to talk to you in person, along with Mark's parents, later on this afternoon. Say about two o'clock? He said he knows this is short notice, but under the circumstances—"

"No, no," Gregor said. "It's fine. I'm grateful he can see me that quickly."

"From what I know of Dr. Copeland's schedule, that's the end of his rounds for the day. He'd like you to meet him on the floor at the nurses' station at two, if you could."

"I'll be there."

"I'll tell him. Thank you very much, Mr. Demarkian."

"Don't mention it."

She hung up in his ear. Gregor stared at the receiver for a moment and then put it down. It was already well after noon, and it wasn't all that easy to get out to the hospital. He'd have to arrange for a cab ahead of time. He put in a call to the front desk and asked them to do that for him. He hung up and stared at his hands. He needed Bennis, that was the truth. He always needed Bennis, but he needed her especially in cases like this one, when something about the case itself, or the place it happened in, or the people involved in it, started tripping all his wires. He couldn't seem to make his mind stop drifting into his own past, his childhood, his career, his memories. Maybe "drift" was the wrong word. Drifting implied randomness. There was nothing random about the way his mind was working. He knew, by now, just what it was about Windsor that drove him so completely up the wall—that hermetically sealed, pristinely smug self-righteous bubble that adopted "liberalism," not because of liberal convictions, but because of the sense that only stupid, vulgar, ignorant people were anything else. It was not the liberalism his mother had embraced when she became an American, and it was not the liberalism of somebody like Bennis, whose support for government health insurance and rejection of the death penalty had nothing to do with morality and everything to do with what she thought of as practical necessity. Hell, he thought, it wasn't even the liberalism of initiatives and programs. He suddenly realized what it was all these people reminded him of. They were the liberals of conservative caricature, born into the flesh and made real on a stage of their own choosing. This was a place where care would be taken to choose only those foods that could be imported from workers' collectives in the third world by the same people who had only contempt for the everyday, middle-class kids who made up the population at the local public high school.

It was, Gregor thought, a symptom of something, of the same something that had resulted in the destruction of Holy Trinity Armenian Apostolic Christian Church, of something that was neither liberal nor conservative except superficially. No wonder so many people were turned off of politics these days. It wasn't politics anymore. It wasn't about how best to fill the potholes or how best to make sure that everybody could see a doctor if he needed to or how best to build a system of defense that would neither leave the country vulnerable to attack nor bankrupt it. This was politics as total lifestyle choice, a kind of armor people put on to proclaim their superiority to every other person, and Tom DeLay did it just as surely as Barbara Boxer did. This wasn't even politics about candidates. He had no idea who the people of Windsor, Massachusetts, had voted for in the last election, and he didn't think it mattered. This was the politicization of everything. It was no longer possible to decide you liked beer instead of wine without that choice becoming a declaration of just which side you were on.

Personally Gregor thought he was on the side of sanity, but he could see how at least some people might argue that point. He dragged the phone as close to him as he could without putting it on his lap and stared at it. If he called and got the answering machine, he would not be able to leave a message. He knew that already. The sound of Bennis's voice on the answering machine tape would make him mute. If he called and she was still cold to him, he didn't know if he'd be able to talk then either. What he really wanted was for her to show up in Windsor on her own, the way she had in Hollman, Pennsylvania, when he had been involved in the mess that had first introduced him to Liz Toliver, Jimmy Card, and Mark. The chances of her doing that now were slim to nonexistent. If he was honest about it, he knew they were only nonexistent. He knew he was going to have to call.

He took a deep breath. He dialed for a long-distance line. He dialed his own number on Cavanaugh Street. He had Bennis's cell phone number, just as she had his, but for some reason he didn't want to talk to her on her cell phone. He had no idea why that was. Maybe he just wanted to be sure she was sitting down somewhere and able to pay attention to whatever it was he might have to say. He didn't want to try to talk to her while she was driving or with a lot of people or in the lobby of an art movie house getting ready to go in to see one of those films he always begged off of because they were so damned bizarre. Here was something about Bennis he didn't understand. She liked movies, preferably in foreign languages, where really odd things happened. There was a Fellini movie with a fashion show of religious garments that included, toward the end, skeletons in veils and lace. There was a German film where people faded in and out of reality for no good reason he could see. First they were standing there, solid, and then they were dissolving like ghosts, but there didn't seem to be any actual ghosts in the film. Fortunately, she would also go to "real" movies with Tibor, but Gregor had to admit he didn't like most of Tibor's movies either. Tibor's movies ran heavily to space aliens, wizards in beards longer than most bridal veils, and desperate races to save the world. Whatever happened to movie movies, where ordinary people had love affairs or tried to save the family business or learned the real meaning of Christmas? On that last one, Tibor had had an entry, and Gregor had gone along for the afternoon. It was called *The Grinch,* and everybody in it was made up to look like—Gregor didn't know what.

Bennis would understand what he meant about politics that wasn't really politics, Gregor thought. At least, she would have understood as of a few weeks ago because she was both very active politically and mostly driven to distraction by what she had to put up with in order to be that way. She would know what he meant by the unreality of places like this, too. Bennis had been in a lot of unreal places in her life, and she'd been to a school like this one. Or had it been like this one? Maybe it had been a conservative enclave instead of a liberal one. His palms were sweating. So was his neck. His stomach was one enormous knot, as hard as a bowling ball and as comfortable as if he had swallowed one. He hadn't been this afraid of Bennis when they'd first started seeing each other.

The phone rang and rang. After a while Gregor was sure she was out, and that he ought to hang up and try again another time. Instead he just sat there, listening to the ring. There were three phones in his apartment. One was in the bedroom, on the night table on the left side of the bed. One was in the living room, on the wicker side table to the right of the couch that faced the big window looking onto Cavanaugh Street. The last was on the wall in the kitchen, next to the refrigerator. There was no place in the apartment, any-where, where it took more than a few seconds to get to a phone.

He was just about to put the receiver back into the cradle when he heard her pick up on the other end, and then the sound of her voice, not talking to him but to somebody with her in the apartment.

"I got flour. It's in that bag with Tibor's Pizza Rolls in it," she said.

Suddenly everything Gregor had wanted to say disappeared from his head. There was something about politics, but he couldn't remember what. There was all the news about Mark DeAvecca. He could remember that, but he couldn't think of the words he needed to explain it.

"Hello," she said, in that flat, unconsciously upper-class voice he'd found so off-putting when they'd first met and hardly ever noticed anymore.

He took a deep breath, trying to give himself time to think, but he couldn't think. He was frozen solid. He had a terrible intuition that his breath was very heavy though, that he sounded like one of those men who call phone numbers at random until they get a female voice they can talk dirty to.

"Hello?" she said again.

He tried to cough. He couldn't do it. He tried to speak. He couldn't do that either. Everything was wrong. He couldn't imagine his life without her. He couldn't imagine what he was supposed to say to make it all right between them. He couldn't imagine what he'd done that had been so damned awful that it had led to this, so that she hadn't called him even once since he'd been out of town and hadn't seen him off when he left Philadelphia.

"Christ," she said, her voice turned away from the receiver again, "I've got a breather."

"Wait," Gregor started to say, remembering at the last moment the whistle he'd given her for just such occasions as she thought this was.

Fortunately or unfortunately, she didn't use it. She just hung up.

Gregor sat staring at the phone in his hand, wondering what the hell was the matter with him. He'd never been this awkward with a girl, not even in high school. He'd never been this scared in his life.

2

By the time Gregor got to the nurses' station on Two West at ten minutes be-fore two, he was thoroughly disgusted with himself and in no mood to put up with anybody else's nonsense. He came out of the elevator with his mind still on Bennis, and for the first few moments as he walked ahead toward the big curved wooden desk, he didn't realize that he knew at least half the people standing in front of it, arguing. The other half were doctors, a tall, angular young man with too much hair and a nose that could have served as a hood ornament, and a slight, middle-aged woman who exuded tension the way the Cookie Monster ate cookies. She was, Gregor thought, the single most defensively hostile person he had ever seen in his life. Then he realized that she was standing next to Liz Toliver, and that he was about to have to deal with her.

It wasn't the most promising situation he had ever walked into in his life. The small woman might be angry and aggressive, but Liz was in that unnatural calm that Gregor had learned to associate with the prelude to one of her nuke attacks. Both Jimmy Card and the male doctor were standing just a little away from the two women, as if both of them knew that something was about to blow.

"It is my professional opinion that this course of action is very inadvisable," the small woman was saying. "Very inadvisable. I haven't even had a chance to go over these results. I don't know how accurate they are—"

"I don't see why you should go over these results at all," Liz said. *Very calm,* Gregor thought. She was very calm. He winced. "You are not Mark's doctor, and you are not Mark's mother. I'm that."

"I'm the doctor for the school," the small woman said, "and you signed an agreement when Mark came to Windsor that he would be treated by me—"

"In the event that he got sick up here and the school had to make arrangements for his care," Liz said. "Yes. But the school doesn't have to make arrangements for his care now. I'm here."

"You're risking his health and his recovery by delivering information to him that is very disturbing and that, as far as we know, is completely inaccurate. I'm sure Dr. Copeland is very talented, but he's still a resident and he does not have the experience—"

"Excuse me," the young male doctor said.

"This entire idea is ludicrous," the small woman said. "I must be concerned first and foremost with Mark's well-being. He's still a child, and he's not able to interpret—"

"Jesus Christ," Liz said.

"Adults often have to insist that children do what is best for them because they will not always know what is best for them themselves," the woman plowed on.

Gregor pulled up into the little group and coughed. They all turned to look at him, Jimmy Card with relief so pronounced it was comical. "Hello," he said. "Hello, Liz. Hello, Jimmy."

"This is Gregor Demarkian," Jimmy said.

The young male doctor stuck out his hand. "Mr. Demarkian. I'm Lloyd Copeland. It's good to meet you."

"It's all *your* fault," the small woman said, rounding on Gregor. "You're the one who gave them this ridiculous idea. I don't know what you think you're doing, but if you're getting a lot of publicity for yourself by jeopardizing that child's health and sanity—"

"That child," Liz said, "is six feet tall and built like a tank. I'd be surprised as hell if he was a virgin, considering the fact that he spent half his life backstage at rock concerts last summer. He's got an IQ in the one hundred and sixties, and he hasn't exactly been living in a nursery school for the last sixteen years. I resent your attempts to treat him like a mental defective, and I resent even more your attempts to get me to manipulate him. I have never been anything but honest and honorable with Mark, and I don't intend to start being less than either now."

"I haven't asked you not to be honest," the small woman said. "I've merely pointed out that children need to be given information in doses they can handle, not dumped into a cold bath of bad and frightening news as if they were miniature adults."

"Mark isn't a miniature anything," Liz said. She turned to Gregor and said, "This woman is Brenda Elliot. She's the doctor attached to the school. She's also an idiot. I'm going to go talk to Mark."

She walked off down the hall in the direction of Mark's room, and Gregor looked at Jimmy Card.

"Don't ask," Jimmy said. "It's been a very long day."

Brenda Elliot straightened the jacket of her good wool suit. "I suppose I'll have to come along. Somebody has to look after that child's interests. He's already been fed food he shouldn't have been and thrown it all up. It took the hospital staff half an hour to get that room back into shape."

"He was throwing up again?" Gregor asked.

Dr. Copeland smiled. "Understandably. It seems he woke up this afternoon and he was hungry, and he prevailed upon Mr. Card here to make a run out to McDonald's—"

"Three crispy chicken extra value meals supersized with vanilla milk-shakes," Jimmy said. "And he ate it all, too, but then—"

"Irresponsible," Brenda Elliot sniffed.

She was, Gregor thought, exactly the sort of woman who would sniff. He turned away from her and gestured down the hall in the direction of Mark's room.

"Right," Jimmy said. "This ought to be interesting."

Gregor led the way. It wasn't a long walk. When they got to the room, Liz was standing by herself at the windows, and Mark was sitting up in bed talking away on a cell phone. He did not look as if he had recently been sick. He did look a million times better than he had the day before.

Mark nodded to Gregor as he came in, said, "I've got to go" into the phone, and switched it off. "I was talking to Geoff," he said. Then, looking around and not too sure of who knew what, "He's my little brother. He's got Grandma wrapped, by the way. She's letting him play video games and eat TV dinners nonstop."

"I told her she could," Liz said.

"Cool," Mark said.

Dr. Copeland waved the folder he was carrying in the air. "Well," he said, "we ought to get started. Mark, I want to warn you, right now, that what you're about to hear is probably going to be very disturbing. Dr. Elliot is of the opinion that you should not be told about it at all."

"I shouldn't be told about my medical condition?" Mark said. Now he *did* look sick. "What's wrong with me? Is it terminal?"

"I told you this was irresponsible," Brenda Elliot said.

Gregor knew what it was Mark was worried about. "Relax," he said, "you've got no serious medical condition, terminal or otherwise, except maybe an allergy to caffeine; and then it's just a question of staying off. It's not that kind of news."

"So what kind of news is it?" Mark asked.

Dr. Copeland plunged in again. "We did a number of standard tests," he said, "and they all came out negative, except for the caffeine toxicity, which was abnormally high. High enough to have killed you on its own, by the way. Now, some of the symptoms you've been reporting—high levels of anxiety, for instance, and abnormal sweating—can be traced to the caffeine allergy coupled to the fact that you seem to have been ingesting a lot of the stuff you're allergic to."

"Do you know what's been going on here?" Liz asked, addressing herself to Brenda Elliot. "Teachers saw him in class with body tremors and sweat pouring down his body and nobody even sent him to the infirmary. He went to the infirmary on his own power with a strep throat bad enough to take over Taiwan, and they didn't even do a throat culture."

"Excuse me," Dr. Copeland said, "some of the symptoms are unlikely to be the result of caffeine poisoning alone. Oh, they could be if the caffeine poisoning were as acute as it was last night, or close to, but if it had been, he'd have been hospitalized long ago. I'm thinking of the memory losses, and the body tremors, and the blackouts. We did test for Parkinson's disease."

"Jesus," Mark said.

"And the tests came back negative," Dr. Copeland went on. "You really don't have anything medically wrong with you. I'd be interested in knowing, though, when those symptoms started: the tremors, the blackouts, those."

Mark thought about it. "After Christmas," he said finally. "Before then I was nervous all the time, and I couldn't pay attention to anything, but that was about it. And it was that way all through Christmas, too—"

"Were you drinking a lot of caffeine over the Christmas break?" Dr. Copeland asked.

Mark looked sheepish. "Yeah, well, but not intentionally. I mean, I was drinking Mountain Dew, and I didn't know it had caffeine in it until the vacation was nearly over, and I'd been drinking nearly a case a day."

"What?" Liz said.

"Well, it was in the pantry," Mark said.

"Go back to the symptoms," Dr. Copeland said. "You say they started after Christmas."

"Yeah, right, after Christmas break. First I was just sick a lot. I'd get stomach cramps something awful. Then I lost my appetite. I didn't want to eat anything. I'd have coffee and put a ton of sugar in it and that would be it most of the day. Then about a week or so later it got really weird. I mean, really, really weird." He looked at Gregor. "Like it was yesterday when I saw you," he said. "Only worse, sometimes."

"All right," Dr. Copeland said, "then we have to assume that this started soon after you got back to school after Christmas break. We're going to want to take a few locks of your hair for analysis."

"My hair, why?"

"Because it will give us a fair idea of how long this has been going on and to what extent," Dr. Copeland said. "Mind you, this isn't my area of expertise. If you'd asked me the day before yesterday if I expected ever to encounter a case of this kind throughout my entire career, I'd have said no. But here we are."

"Where are we?" Mark said.

"I still think we should wait until we have these results analyzed by experts," Brenda Elliot said. "It's ridiculous to get the boy worked up over what may very well be a false alarm."

Dr. Copeland stepped in. "When you were brought in last night, after the danger was passed, Mr. Demarkian suggested to the doctor on duty that we should screen you for arsenic poisoning."

"Arsenic? Somebody has been giving me arsenic?"

"Yes, that much we know for sure," Dr. Copeland said. "The issue now is, how much arsenic and how long have they been giving it to you. The human body can take quite a bit of arsenic if it's delivered in small doses over time, and it will develop a tolerance for it. The symptoms you've been reporting, and the ones Mr. Demarkian also reported on seeing you yesterday, do seem to indicate a slow and steady delivery of—"

"Somebody's been poisoning me with arsenic," Mark marveled. Then he brightened. "Cool!"

Liz stared at the ceiling. "Dr. Elliot's of the opinion that you're a child. I'm of the opinion that you're impossible."

"We do have to check," Dr. Copeland said. "Arsenic can cause long-term problems, especially in the liver and kidneys. And you're not going anywhere for the next couple of days. For one thing it's going to take a while for that stuff to work its way out of your system. I know you feel better. You probably feel a lot better. If you've been getting doses of arsenic at least daily for weeks, then going a day or so without one is going to make you feel better. You're not going to be better, though, for weeks and maybe not months. So that's the first reason I don't want you to go back to school."

"What's the second reason?" Mark asked.

"Well," Dr. Copeland said, "arsenic is not a child's toy. I suppose it's possible that somebody gave it to you as a prank, but it's not very likely, is it? Most people do know that arsenic is a poison, and that it can kill you. I think we have to assume either that somebody wanted you dead, or that they wanted you very sick and didn't care if they risked making you dead as a consequence. We're having more tests run on what we pumped out of you last night. I think we're going to find a really big dose of arsenic, enough to have killed you in the ordinary course of events. You were very lucky."

"I'm the world champion upchucker," Mark said. "Ask any of the nurses on this floor."

"Be grateful," Dr. Copeland said.

"You're all jumping to conclusions," Dr. Elliot said. "The idea that somebody at Windsor Academy would feed a student arsenic over the course of weeks is absolutely ridiculous. You're blowing what's probably a mistake into a first-rate scandal, and if you think that's to Mark's benefit, you're quite wrong."

Everybody ignored her. Liz went over to the bed and began stroking Mark's hair again. When she didn't look ready to kill him, she looked as if she adored him. Mark looked as if he knew it.

"You know," Mark said, with beaming satisfaction, "this is really awesome. I mean it. This is the coolest thing that has ever happened to me."

3

It was nearly three quarters of an hour later before they were all ready to leave. Brenda Elliot waited until Dr. Copeland left and only then departed, shaking her head and muttering all the way. Her back was stiff with disapproval. Her face was a mask of anger. She was not a woman who took well to people questioning her authority, and she was not a woman who felt all that secure in what authority she had.

It was darkening in the outside world again. Gregor couldn't get over how quickly the sun faded, even this close to spring. In the dimming light, he could see the start of an early March snow, random flakes floating downward lazily. It didn't look like the start of a serious storm. One of the nurses had delivered a trayful of carefully bland foods. Mark had complained of being hungry again, but even Jimmy had rejected the idea of another run to McDonald's. The tray had clear chicken broth, dry white toast, and what looked like vanilla pudding. Mark picked at it without much enthusiasm. Liz and Jimmy talked quietly by the window. Gregor sat in the green plastic upholstered chair, thinking.

"We're going to go get something to eat," Liz said finally. "We've got an idea we want to talk over. You'd be welcome to come with us, though, Gregor, if you're hungry. Or you can stay and keep Mark company until we get back."

"I'll stay and keep Mark company," Gregor said.

"Try to talk some sense into his head," Liz said. "It never works when I do it, but I figure there's always a chance."

She went over to Mark's bed and kissed him on the forehead, which he responded to mostly by ignoring it. Jimmy waved, without expecting Mark to wave back. Gregor waited until they were safely out in the hall.

"Well," he said, "do you really think it's 'cool' that somebody gave you arsenic?"

"Hell, yes," Mark said.

"You could have died."

"But I didn't, did I?" Mark sat up a little straighter and pushed the tray table away. "Look, I'm not going to last at Windsor past the end of this year. If Mom has her way, I'm not going to last past the end of this week. But the thing is, even without all this crap, it was all wrong. I'm all wrong. I don't fit, and they can't stand it."

"They? You mean the school?"

"Yeah," Mark said. "I've been thinking about it. I mean, mostly, the last few months, I've just been depressed about it. The general consensus around here is that it was a fluke I ever got in. I'm not all that bright, and I'm a slacker. And maybe it's true, but there are people like that here, and they don't have any trouble. I have trouble. I don't think like the people here. Well, I mean, the faculty and the administration. I just don't. I think they pretty much decided back in November that they wanted to get rid of me. I could tell. I just couldn't admit it."

"You don't mean that you think somebody at the school would poison you to get you to leave?" Gregor said. "That's hardly sane, is it? All they'd have to do is trump up an excuse to expel you. I doubt if it would be that hard."

"They wouldn't even have to do that," Mark said. "They don't have to have any excuse at all. They just have to say that they think you're 'unsuitable' and not ask you back for the next year. Everything is contingent here. There aren't any standards, you know, regular ones like you'd have in a college, where if you had a C average you'd be okay and if you had a D you'd be flunking out. There's a story that they got rid of a girl last year who had straight As and boards in the stratosphere, but who wanted to go to one of the service academies and wouldn't change her mind and opt for the Ivy League. I don't know if it's true."

"If it is true, it's a very nasty story," Gregor said. "But this still doesn't deal with the poisoning. And you *were* poisoned, Mark. There had to be a motive for that."

"I know. I'm just saying, if I have to go out anyway, I want to go out in a blaze of legend, if you know what I mean. Except they will probably ask me back now because they'll be afraid that Mom will sue them if they don't. But Mom won't send me back, so the issue is decided anyway."

"Do you have any idea why somebody would want to kill you?"

"For real?" Mark said. "Of course I don't. I don't even have enough property to leave a will. I don't have any enemies that I know of. There's no reason for anybody to kill me."

"But somebody wanted to."

"Apparently, yeah."

"More than apparently," Gregor said. "Of course, there's always the possibility that the idea was just to disable you. Either way, it sounds pretty desperate. Did something happen after you came back from Christmas break?"

"Happen how? Lots of things happened."

"I mean did something change," Gregor said. "I'm told that Michael Feyre sold drugs, that he was having an affair with the headmaster's wife, that he was something of a bad actor, but I don't really know what was going on. You might. You roomed with him."

"You think that's what this is about? Michael?"

"Don't you?" Gregor said. "There may be no reason for anybody to want to kill you, but a drug dealer has lots of people with knives out for him. It goes with the territory."

"I guess," Mark said. "I don't know what you want me to say. Michael and Alice were not exactly discreet, but they never were. Alice was doing that thing, you know, talking politics instead of talking dirty. Like that Woody Allen movie. He was selling stuff to at least one of the teachers, did I tell you that?"

"No," Gregor said. "Do you mean he was giving drugs to Alice Makepeace?"

"Well, yeah, maybe," Mark said. "I mean, that goes without saying. But no, he was selling to at least one member of the faculty and maybe more. He told me about it one night after lights out. About how one of the teachers had to get high to get it up. Sorry, but that's what he said. He didn't say which teacher."

"And what about last night?" Gregor asked. "What was different about last night?"

"Nothing," Mark said. He looked suddenly and irrevocably tired. "The only thing that's been different since Michael died is that I called you. It got around. People weren't happy. And, you know, it made me think—about the hallucination."

"What hallucination?"

"I told you yesterday. The night Michael died I saw this thing, only it didn't seem real, it seemed like an hallucination. That's why I wanted you to come. I figured you could find out if it was real or not. Only now that I mostly feel better—well, no. I'm not sure it was real. I'm just not so sure it probably wasn't."

"If what was real?" Gregor asked, patiently.

"What you need to do," Mark said, "is go to the library and go up to the second floor to the catwalk. If you go along the catwalk, it ends at this little window space, this arched space, that looks out over Maverick Pond. I was there the night Michael died. I was trying to read but I wasn't getting very far, and I looked out the window there and I saw what looked like a body lying on the ground under this little stand of evergreens at the end of the pond. It was freezing. It was way below zero, actually. And it was Friday. I thought that whoever it was had had too much to drink or, you know, something else, and had passed out; and if somebody didn't do something, he'd freeze to death out there. So—"

"So?"

"So I went out to wake him up," Mark said. "I figured I'd push him until I could get him moving, and then when I saw who it was I'd know where he was supposed to go. Only when I got out there, he was gone."

"You're sure it was a he?"

"No," Mark said. "I'm not even sure it was a student. Whoever it was was dressed all in black, but that isn't odd because there are lots of people here who do that kind of thing, you know, to show how different they are. People around here like to show how different they are."

"Do they?" Gregor said drily.

"And whoever it was was too big—no, that's not it. Too solid. It's not that he seemed tall. You couldn't really tell with him lying down like that. But whoever it was seemed big somehow; solid; it was odd. But then I went down there and no one was there, and there wasn't any sign anyone had ever been there. I mean, you know, maybe there wouldn't have been because the snow was hard out there, and you wouldn't get footprints. I don't think I left any, but still . . ."

"You have any idea what bothered you so much about it that you thought you needed me here?"

"Was it wrong to call?" Mark said. "I thought it was pushing it myself, but I was scared to death. I thought I was going crazy."

"No, I'm glad you called me," Gregor said. "I'm just wondering what it was about that particular incident that bothered you so much."

"I don't know." Mark yawned. "I'm sorry, Mr. Demarkian. I'm falling apart here. At least I don't feel like I'm going nuts. But I don't know what it was. You might talk to Mr. Candor about it. I saw him on my way back to Hayes House and told him all about it. He probably remembers what I said better than I do."

"All right," Gregor said, but Mark was already asleep, sitting up in bed and yet completely relaxed, asleep the way children sometimes fell asleep, with complete and unreserved abandon.

Gregor got his coat and made some calculations in his head about just how hard it was going to be to get Brian Sheehy alone in the next forty five minutes.

SIX

1

Peter Makepeace had lived at President's House for a decade, but he'd never taken the time to really look at it before. It was, as headmasters' houses went, neither all that large nor all that impressive. At some of the more prestigious boys' schools, the headmaster got a house made of stone and built to resemble an Oxford University college. Windsor, on the other hand, had started its life as a girls' school, and it suffered from many of the things that had made the girls' schools less impressive and imposing than the institutions the very same parents had supported for their sons. There was, for instance, the conceit that the dorms were really houses, and the school itself really a home. The only building on the entire campus that was not built to ape domesticity was the library, which had been given by Margaret Milbourne Ridenour, who had bitterly resented her exile to Windsor in the days when no coeducation was available and children were shipped off to boarding schools whether they liked it or not. There was a portrait of old Margaret in the library's foyer. Peter honestly believed he had never seen a sourer, less satisfied human being. He didn't think she'd be any less sour if she were sent to Windsor today, with its commitment to progressive education, its self-conscious egalitarianism, its pride in the interest its students took in all forms of political causes. Old Margaret was something of a fascist and even more of a traditionalist. She had wanted Windsor to look like, and be like, the Exeter her brothers had been sent to. It hadn't then. It didn't now. It never would.

It was odd, but he'd spent the entire day thinking about the Mission of the

School. He'd never done that before, not even when he was prepping for his interview back when he was only hoping he would get this job. By then he'd known all about Alice, of course. He'd known that she liked to sleep with students; and that if students were not available, and sometimes even if they were, she liked to sleep with faculty instead. He'd known she used sex as a means to politics and politics as a means to sex; and that politics for her meant not the day-to-day grubbiness of compromises on the Highway Transportation Bill and half measures in pursuit of Welfare Reform, but grand visions of apocalypse and redemption, the one sure cure for the boredom of a life in which there was no need to make much of an effort about anything. People thought it was only the rich who found themselves caught in the web of meaninglessness that came with not having to work for what they had, but it wasn't true. There were dozens of upper-middle-class housewives just like Alice, with husbands who were doctors and lawyers and campus-star university professors, who didn't need to work even if they decided they wanted to, who couldn't think of anything to care about, who had to make it all up. Lots of them took to alcohol or children. They came to places like Windsor in droves, driven and furious, insisting that Susie or Johnny would be admitted to Harvard or they'd die trying. Peter had long ago learned to spot the haunted look of those adolescent stand-ins, the children who were supposed to be everything their mothers had not had the courage to be ambitious for themselves. It was the mothers, too, not the fathers. The fathers dealt with it differently. They absented themselves from home and family. They put their desperation into their work. There were a lot of people out there who had not found a place of peace or a plateau of satisfaction. It wasn't only Alice.

Maybe this was why he was thinking about the Mission of the School and about President's House and what it looked like. He was standing on his own front steps—except that they didn't really belong to him; they belonged to the school; headmasters only lived here while they were serving as headmasters—looking into the blackness of a sky whose details were obscured by the haze caused by the lights that were everywhere: coming from the houses, lining the quad, making the world safe on Main Street. Snow was coming down on him in thick, wet flakes. It had started falling an hour ago in the lazy way that made it seem as if no storm could be coming, and now it was gentle but relentless, the beginning of something far more serious. This house, he thought, was just like the house it had been meant to imitate, and just like the man who had once lived in that house, who had defined for all time the role of the American radical manqué. Peter had never had much use for Ralph Waldo Emerson. Even

213

the name grated on him. The idea that this fool—this utter dilettante with his third-rate mind and his enthusiasms, his wooly-headed flights into the nether reaches of incoherent antitheology—was supposed to be the very foundation of American literature made Peter angry to the point of violence. There had been a time when he had spent hours of work trying to prove that it wasn't true. He'd done his master's thesis on just that subject. Now he thought that there was nothing truer. Old Waldo's spirit was alive and well and walking the Main Street of Windsor, Massachusetts, just as it had walked the Main Streets of Lexington and Concord and all the towns in between. Waldo would have liked Windsor Academy's Mission Statement, with its dedication to educating "the whole person" and its paeans to creativity, intelligence, and "spiritual excellence." He wouldn't have known what it all meant any more than the trustees had, but Peter doubted if he'd known what half the things he'd written himself meant.

President's House was, indeed, a perfect replica. There was the hipped roof, the twin brick chimneys, the squared-off entry portico with its thin, Greek Revival columns. Peter wouldn't have been surprised to find that this house had been built to scale. The three women who had founded Windsor Academy had been fond of that kind of historical voyeurism. They had been less interested in what Emerson had had to say than they had been in celebrating a peculiarly *American* standard. It was a time when being American was more fashionable than it had become now.

He went up the front steps and let himself in the front door. He had seen Alice through the front windows, sitting at the desk in his study. He thought that if he got fired—which he almost surely would be—he would spend some time digging up the floor plans for the original Emerson house or even going down to Concord to visit it. He was pretty sure it was still standing. He'd be surprised if it wasn't a shrine. Emerson had lived there for years, and Thoreau had taken over the place when Emerson went to Europe. Everybody from the Daughters of the American Revolution to hippies with an itch for civil disobedience ought to treat the place as if it were hallowed ground.

He went through the hall to the door of the study and stopped. The door was not locked. Alice would not hide what she considered to be something she deserved to do by right. He looked in on her seated at the desk, jimmying the lock on the long center drawer. Then he cleared his throat and waited until she looked up.

"You could always just ask me for the key," he said. "It would be easier."

"Would you give me the key?" Her red hair shone in the muted light from the desk lamp. It was such an improbable color, and yet Peter knew for certain that there had been a time when it was completely genuine.

He came forward with the key in his hand. "I won't give it to you, but I'll open the drawer," he said. He half expected her to grab it out of his hand while he bent forward to slip it into the lock, but she didn't. He opened it up and stepped back. "Go ahead. Take a look."

She sat staring at him for a moment, emotionally blank. Then she pulled out the drawer, found the manila envelope, and pulled that out, too. She was, he thought, curiously without affect. She showed only those emotions she wanted to, meaning none of the ones she actually had. She dumped the contents of the manila envelope on the green felt desk blotter and spread them out under her hands.

"Well," she said.

"You can keep them if you want to," he told her. "For a long time I thought of them as insurance. I'd use them if I ever had the guts to divorce you, and you wanted to make trouble over it. But I've realized, these past few days, that I don't want to divorce you."

"Worried about your reputation in the field?" Alice said.

"No," Peter told her. He thought he ought to sit down. It would have a better effect. He couldn't make himself do it. "My reputation in the field is shot, and you know it. There isn't going to be another headmaster's job after this one. I'll have to retire to New Hampshire and live on what's left of my trust fund. You'll have to do what you want."

"I thought you said you didn't want to divorce me."

"I don't. But I don't intend to force you to stay with me either. You can do what you want to do. You can take those with you."

"They're a form of pornography, aren't they?" Alice said. "Did you masturbate to them?"

Peter went over to the window and looked out onto the quad. The snow was beginning to come down very heavily. People were walking along the paths in the direction of the Student Center and the cafeteria. They both ought to be on their way over right now.

"I want to know the truth," he said. "I want to know if you tried to kill Mark DeAvecca."

"Are you crazy?"

"No, Alice, I'm not crazy. I've been cut out of the loop on the official end. His mother can't stand me, which under the circumstances I think makes a good deal of sense. Even so, it's not that easy to keep me from getting the information I want, and I do know what's been going on at the hospital all this afternoon. Somebody poisoned Mark with arsenic. Not a single dose of arsenic, apparently, but several weeks' worth of smaller doses—"

"You don't necessarily die of arsenic."

"True enough," Peter said. "That's another of the possibilities they're considering, that somebody was just trying to make Mark ill. If that was what they were looking for, I'd say they got it, wouldn't you?"

"I don't believe it," Alice said. "He hasn't been sick. He's been doped to the gills—"

"Not according to the lab tests."

"—and treating this place like it was a residential party. He's all wrong for Windsor, Peter, and you know it. He's not serious."

"He may not be serious, Alice, but what has happened to him is; and there's no way around it, at least not from what I've heard. He was found with arsenic in his body as well as enough caffeine to have killed him. There's arsenic in his hair. A lot of it, apparently. Which means he was being poisoned for weeks at least—"

"Or poisoning himself," Alice said quickly.

"What for? Alice, let's leave the realm of the ridiculous here for a moment. Let's leave the realm of that *Hustler* centerfold you like to turn yourself into when the occasion arises and look at what we have here. We were nearly out from under the problem caused by Michael Feyre's suicide, a suicide you almost certainly had something to do with—"

"Don't be an idiot."

"I'm not. I'm being practical. If you weren't the reason Michael committed suicide, you could be made to look like the reason. But that was all right. We were almost clear from that one. Now we have this. And we aren't dealing with Dee Feyre anymore, somebody with a lot of money but without sophistication or education or connections, we're dealing with Liz Toliver. And I've seen her, Alice. She's on the warpath."

"She can be on the warpath all she likes. She can't do anything. You've said yourself that we're not going to be asked to stay on after all this. What difference does it make what she does?"

"It makes a difference if she lands you in jail, Alice. I don't think you're going to like the women's correctional facility in Concord."

"She can't land me in jail," Alice said. "I haven't done anything to get landed in jail."

"You were sleeping with a minor and a student, that could land you in jail."

"He was sixteen."

"It doesn't matter; he was under eighteen. That's the law, whether you intend to recognize it or not."

"Those laws were passed to prosecute male predators who abused female
children," Alice said. "They have nothing to do with teenaged sex, for God's
sake. Teenagers have sex with each other all the time; they don't get prosecuted."

"They don't get prosecuted if they have sex with each other. But never
mind. It doesn't matter. What does matter is whether or not you're going to
find yourself arrested for attempted murder, and the possibility does exist. You
were feeding Mark coffee last night. You were seen. In the cafeteria."

"I wasn't feeding him," Alice said. "I just got him a cup. He asked for it."

"Two cups."

"Whatever. We were talking."

"About what?"

"About Michael. Why shouldn't we talk about Michael? For God's sake,
Peter, everybody has been talking about Michael since it happened. Until today, I mean. It's only natural. It's a small community."

It was the word "community" that stopped him, that catch-all word meant
to impose order and cohesion on random collections of people. Windsor was a
"community." They said it all the time. He went back to the desk and swept up
the photographs and the manila envelope. The photograph on the top was of
Alice sitting astride some boy whose name Peter no longer remembered. It was
a younger Alice. Even in black and white, her hair looked thicker and more
glossy; her breasts looked firmer. They had no children and because of it, and
of the fact that they were small, Alice's breasts had lasted much longer than
women's ordinarily do. Still, it was coming to her as it came to all women everywhere. That was the problem for a woman who had based her life on sex.

Peter walked across the room to the fireplace and threw the envelope and
photographs inside. It was a gas fireplace, easy to turn on and just as hot as one
that burned with wood. He flipped the switch and watched the flames leap, in-
stantaneous and deadly.

"I'd have thought you would want to keep those," Alice said.

Peter was watching it all burn. "I was thinking about Ralph Waldo Emerson, did I tell you that? This house is a replica of Emerson's house in Concord."

"That was in the material they gave us when you were applying for this
job."

"I know. I was thinking about it. And about Emerson himself and all those people—the New England transcendentalists. The original American 'radicals': Thoreau, Margaret Fuller. I was thinking that Windsor was just their kind of place. They would have liked it here."

"Thoreau didn't even like schools."

"He didn't like the schools he was used to. He wanted to encourage creativity and expressiveness and getting in touch with the greatness of the universal spirit, or however he put it. It was all very vague. We're like that, aren't we, Alice? We're very vague. We don't know what we're talking about; we only want to feel special."

"I don't think it's a small thing to celebrate diversity, do you?"

"No," Peter said. The photographs were almost gone. Nobody would be fooled if they came to look, however. There were ashes in the grate now, and gas fires didn't leave ashes. He stood up. "It's not a small thing to 'celebrate diversity.' It's just that to the extent that we know what it means, we don't do it; and to the extent that we don't know what it means, it doesn't matter. We haven't got the faintest idea of what it means to live with the differences in people. We're very careful, every year, to make sure we have the right number of African Americans and the right number of Hispanic Americans and the right number of students from abroad, and we pick them all very carefully to make sure that they fit this place just as much as we do. When we're faced with someone we really don't understand, we don't behave too well. Do you know how I know that?"

"Please," Alice said.

"I know that because I realized, in the middle of this afternoon, while I was panicking about what was going to happen now that Jimmy Card has arrived and Liz Toliver would very much like to shut us down—I realized that Mark DeAvecca is the first student we've had here for years whom I cannot anticipate. I have no idea what he's going to do next. I have no idea what he thinks. I have no idea what he's going to say. And I further realized that there are lots of people out there whom I do not understand, but none of them are connected to this school in any way. Unfortunately, a lot of them are essential to this school's surivival."

"You're not making any sense," Alice said.

"It's Ralph Waldo Emerson's two hundredth birthday this May twenty-fifth. We ought to get the school to celebrate it, if we're still here and the school's still here. We can mount events around the lives of Emerson and Thoreau. We can stage readings from Emerson's essays. We can show the world how little

218

we've changed since that man was bleating on about all the drivel we've since adopted as dogma. Back to nature. Eastern religions. The all-compassing wisdom of the Oversoul. We even use the same language."

"You really *aren't* making any sense," Alice said, and now she was finished. She pushed the drawer back into place and stood up. "We'd better get over to dinner. We've both been ducking appearing in public for days. Wouldn't you usually call that irresponsible?"

Peter didn't know if he was being irresponsible or not. He didn't think he cared. She had been really beautiful, Alice. When he'd first known her, she'd been as perfect as the miniature Renaissance madonnas he had loved to go to see at the Metropolitan Museum of Art. Exquisite and rare, she had been her own reason for existing; and like all truly beautiful people she had been almost a force of nature, like a hurricane or a tornado. Beauty is a compelling thing, and he had been compelled, unable to look at anything or anybody else, unable to reason calmly about who and what she was under that flawless exterior shell. Now the shell was no longer flawless, and it stunned him to see just how small the imperfections needed to be to wreck the majestic power of the whole. She was still a beautiful woman, in the sense that the lines and angles and shadows of her face and body made up an aesthetic ideal, intellectual and cold. She was no longer a beautiful woman in the sense of beauty as power. In the half-light cast by the study's lamp, he could see darkness and hollowness under her eyes, under her cheekbones, along her jaw. Even surgery could not replace what she had lost because it depended so heavily on the impression that she carried within herself the secret to eternal life, lived as someone forever young.

If she wondered what he was thinking, she gave no indication of it. She just brushed by him and went out the door, into the hallway and the rest of the house. He thought she might be going to the cafeteria. He didn't care.

2

The first thing James Hallwood had done after his conversation with Marta Coelho was to take the rest of the crystal meth out of its hiding place behind the medicine cabinet and flush it down the toilet. There wasn't much of it left, and for the time being it would be safer to indulge in that sort of thing at David's apartment rather than here. David would have said it served him right for insisting on staying here, where he was treated as a child almost as much as the students were. For James, the issue was more complicated. He'd seen his share of true crime documentaries. If there was an investigation and he became the target of it, they would surely find traces of crystal meth in his apartment and probably traces of cocaine, too. It was nearly impossible to erase all evidence of the stuff once you had used it because powders scattered. Their individual grains were too small to be seen, but not so small they couldn't be discovered by chemical tests. At first this seemed to be his biggest and most important problem: the possibility that they might find the drugs and along with the drugs the things he was not so proud of, the things that he at once associated with his own homosexuality and rejected on account of it. This was not something he could talk to David about because this was not something David had much sympathy with. David's tastes in sex were strictly vanilla, the way his tastes in music were strictly for the bourgeois classical. If he had been born in England instead of the United States, he might have ended his life as an Anglican bishop. James had never had vanilla tastes in much of anything. The homosexuals he had sympathized with, in literature, while he was growing up had been the ones like M. Charlus in Proust, who had been first and foremost men of great dignity and culture. There was something to be said for those Anglican bishops. The world was not worse off for having men in it who understood the human drive for perfection in form and language. The problem was, he himself could never have been one of those men because he himself could never force himself to be attracted only to the nobility of the human being. In private, what he was attracted to was anything but nobility. He thought he might be the only man in history to suffer from a madonna/whore complex about himself.

"After all"—David would say, after they'd discussed it for the twentieth time, and David had acquiesced for the evening or not, depending on some standard of decision making known only to David himself—"it's not as if you invented the taste for leather. It's not even as if the gay community invented it. Think of the Marquis de Sade."

James did think of the Marquis de Sade, and that was what bothered him. It was self-evident to him that no completely sane person could read de Sade without repulsion. De Sade loved not just the "bondage and discipline" so favored by the owners of Web sites and specialty stores, he loved pain, real pain, complete with blood and great gashing holes in the skin, holes that would cause scars and sometimes death. Sadism was not "bondage," and it was not "discipline." Sadism was not playacting either. It lived not on suburban streets where middle-class couples made videotapes of themselves pretending to be masters and slaves, but in the soundproofed back rooms of skid-row storefronts, where you could buy the literature in the front and everything else you wanted in the back. He had been in a room like that exactly once, during a terrified trip he had taken to New York City while he was still in college. He had known in no time at all that he would never be back, in spite of the fact that it had been the best and most obliterating sex of his life. He was not David, and he would never be David. He would not call himself "gay." He would not start "coming out" and campaigning for "gay rights." At the same time he felt he owed it to the whole history of men like himself not to be what the straight world expected of him, and what he'd seen in that back room was far too much what the straight world expected of him. It was the dignity of his position that mattered to him. He had an obligation to preserve it for himself and to maintain it for the sake of everybody else who might want to occupy a similar one.

The second thing James had done after he'd talked to Marta Coelho was to gather up all the leather things from their different places around the apartment. He had been much too nervous about having them to have felt comfortable about keeping them together in one place. They were scattered around in drawers in the bedroom and the living room both. They were hung up in the closets, safely hidden in opaque cleaner's bags that zipped shut and couldn't be taken off their hangers without a struggle. He had laid them all out on his dining room table and gone through them with painstaking concentration to make sure there was nothing on them that could be traced to him. He couldn't imagine what there could be, but he didn't put it past David to do something cute, like etch their initials in the soft underside of one of the restraints. There was nothing, and he had realized only at the last minute what a mess he would have been in if somebody had knocked on his door while he was in the middle of checking. Nobody had—but then, nobody had been knocking on anybody's door much in the last few hours, since noon, when the first news began to trickle back to campus that something far more serious than a drug addiction had been going on with Mark DeAvecca.

He'd put the entire collection into two plain brown grocery bags, bags without so much as a few lines of printing on the sides, anonymous bags that could have come from anywhere. He had gone into Boston and taken them to The South End. He had never understood the lure of stores like the ones he saw there. There was something infinitely sad about the way the lights jumped and hammered, all to take the attention of their viewers away from the fact that there was nothing here but failure and resignation, the natural habitat of men who had given up. He had put the bags in two separate garbage cans, moving aside fast-food wrappers and cigarette butts and used condoms to make sure that his own garbage was not in plain sight of people on the street. He thought about the news stories that appeared from time to time about babies left in Dumpsters, and body parts discovered in antilittering receptacles, the police baffled, the public up in arms. When he got back to Boston proper, he stripped off his gloves and discarded them in the first garbage can he saw. They were good gloves, black leather lined with cashmere, but they had been in too much muck today. He didn't think he would ever be able to wear them again or to trust them. Then he'd come back to Windsor, feeling infinitely tired. It had started to snow. The campus looked hyped up and jittery. The few people moving around it moved as if they had nothing to do.

He went back to his apartment and got his second-best gloves from the top drawer of his dresser. He looked around his bedroom and thought with some satisfaction that anybody who entered it would find nothing but the possessions of a man who took himself and literature seriously. There would, of course, be no question about his "sexual orientation," as they put it these days, but the indications of it would not be shameful, and they would not be stereotypical. Here was a man who liked Proust and Eliot, Dante and Raphael, John Donne and Emily Dickinson.

He was about to go out again to the cafeteria and to dinner. He knew that Peter Makepeace would think it was important, in a desperately crucial time, for all the faculty to show their commitment to the best interests of "the Windsor community." He also knew that Peter Makepeace was unlikely to be defining those best interests any more than a week from now, but there would be somebody new, and that somebody would be watching for the smaller signs. He started to get a book from the shelf to read while he ate, and then stopped, thinking of something. He didn't usually bring his work home from his office. He liked to keep things in their places, and correcting papers should be done at his desk in the Student Center, not at home, where his private life was. He had brought these papers home because, with all the mess caused by Michael Feyre's death, he hadn't been able to concentrate in his office. Besides, people kept going in and out. Everybody wanted to talk. Everybody wanted to say something meaningless but profound.

He had brought this set of papers home in a plain folder and left the folder on top of the bookcase to the right of his fireplace in his living room. He got the folder now and put it down on his coffee table. He unbuttoned his coat and sat down. This was the only piece of creative writing he had assigned in his sophomore English class. He didn't like doing it because, as far as he was concerned, the vast majority of high school students knew no more about writing fiction than they knew about the government of Burkina Faso. The school insisted, though. It had its reputation as a haven for the arts and for the artistic students to consider. He had assigned the story and then had had a hard time making himself read what his students handed in.

He went through the papers now and pulled out first the one written by Mark DeAvecca and then the one written by Michael Feyre. The story was supposed to be four to five pages long. Mark's was over seventeen pages, and James had been able to tell, from the first paragraph, that it was an assignment he had done while deliberately ignoring every instruction he had been given for doing it. James suspected that that was the way Mark did most of his homework, except that in every assignment before this one he had done far less than he had been asked to do. James had put it down to laziness and bad attitude. This story was an example of neither. It was, instead, an assertion of integrity so forceful and uncompromising that there was no mistaking it. Mark DeAvecca might or might not be a scholastic slacker. James was willing to give him the benefit of the doubt now that it was known for certain that the boy hadn't been on drugs and had been seriously ill at least some of the time. What Mark DeAvecca was, without question, was a writer, with as strong a narrative voice as James had ever seen anywhere. It was astonishing in a boy of his age, and what was more astonishing was the fact that it was obvious that, at least on some level, Mark knew exactly what he had. Knew it, James thought, and had no intention of violating it for the sake of jumping through hoops to get an A on an English paper. *Quite right,* James thought. He'd even give the boy his A, in spite of the fact that it wasn't the kind of fiction he liked or even found possible to appreciate. James had an ear, and that ear knew when it was hearing the real thing.

Michael Feyre's paper was only three and a half pages long, and it, too, was astonishing. It was not the work of a writer but of a savage, and of a savage with a streak of brutality so wide and deep that he should have been locked away for his own safety long before he'd decided to hang himself. James had made the obligatory forays into the red light districts of half a dozen cities, in the United States and abroad. He had read his share of filthy pulp novels that existed only to prove that it was possible to extend a sex scene written in excremental slang for 181 pages. He had never seen anything like this: raw, nasty, lethal, feral. After the first time he'd read it, he hadn't wanted to touch it with his bare hands. Once he'd made himself get over that, he'd found himself not so much reading it for a second time, as counting off the number of times Michael had used the word "cunt." It was second only to the number of times he used the word "fuck," and that was due to the fact that the second word could be used in more ways than the first and in more ambiguous circumstances.

But it wasn't only the words. James had had students attempt to shock him with words before. It was the revelation of a mind for whom all human relations had been reduced to rape. You raped or were raped. There were no other choices. There were no other explanations for why two people might spend any time together doing anything. There were no other explanations for why one person might be emotionally committed to another, even a mother to a child.

Everyone at Windsor treated Michael Feyre as a cipher. He was the paradigmatic Poor Boy from a Miserable Background who needed only Love and Attention to bring out his better qualities. Those qualities would include sensitivity and tolerance and a zeal for social justice. James knew for a fact, from the very pages of this very short story, that this fairy tale had had nothing to do with the Michael Feyre who had really existed among them this school year. The real Michael Feyre had not been a misunderstood genius or a juvenile delinquent or even a street thug. The real Michael Feyre had been an out-and-out psychopath.

If James had read this paper before Michael committed suicide, he would have made copies of it and sent them to Peter Makepeace and every member of the Board of Trustees. No school could tolerate this kind of person for long and especially not a boarding school. James was surprised as hell that there hadn't been some kind of incident. Michael wouldn't have felt much compunction about grabbing one of the girls or threatening a teacher. Maybe the affair with Alice had kept all that at bay. Still, it was surprising there hadn't been an incident with Alice, that Michael hadn't beaten her to a pulp one afternoon while they were shacked up during study hall or risking exposure in a faculty bathroom during sports trials on a Saturday afternoon. James was fairly sure that Michael was no stranger to beating people into pulps. That was in this short story, too.

Of course, in the meantime, Michael had died. James had to wonder if psychopaths committed suicide. It seemed to him like a contradiction in terms. Psychopaths didn't want to die; they thought they were the center of the universe. One way or another, though, Michael was dead, and James had responded to this paper only a few days ago by putting it at the bottom of the stack and deciding to forget about it. He hadn't thrown it away because he had wanted to make sure Michael's mother had it. For some reason it had seemed very important to him that Michael Feyre's mother know the kind of human being he was.

That aside, though, there was now another consideration. From what he had heard so far on campus, somebody had tried to murder Mark DeAvecca, unless Mark DeAvecca had been administering arsenic to himself, which was not impossible but highly improbable. That made these two papers interesting in another way, one having nothing to do with their revelations about their writers' personalities. The interesting thing was that these two stories were about the same series of events. They took as their starting point the same set of facts. Everybody on campus thought they knew what those facts were. People like Marta Coelho—who thought she knew everything—believed they knew as much about them as either of the principals.

Any quick reading through these two papers together, though, and it became clear that everybody had been deceived. Mark presented what "everybody" knew, but what Michael presented was a variation on the theme, not the theme itself, and that variation might matter. Nobody would kill Mark DeAvecca for fear that he'd tell the world that his roommate was sleeping with the headmaster's wife. Everybody on campus knew that Michael was sleeping with Alice. Only Alice herself might be deluded enough to think otherwise. If you were going to kill everybody who knew, then you were going to have to turn Windsor into a graveyard. The same was true of Michael's drug selling. Everybody knew, even though they hadn't been able to catch him at it. You didn't murder, or attempt to murder, somebody to hide something that was already generally known.

James ran his hand across the first page of Michael's paper. He'd read the damned thing through twice and never realized that he was reading his own assumptions into it. Then he'd decided that his confusion was the result of Michael's bad writing. Then he'd known better, but he hadn't known what to do about it.

He picked up both papers now and put them into the pocket of his coat. Safety required not keeping secrets, and this was one secret he had every intention of putting into the hands of the first policeman he ran across.

Either that or he was going to give them to that Gregor Demarkian, who might have more than the minimum of sense.

SEVEN

1

Gregor Demarkian was sure he was not having a change of heart. He was not interested in going back to work. He was not interested in investigating a murder. He was interested in making sure Mark DeAvecca was all right and stayed that way; and although he admitted that that could be done just by convincing Liz to take him out of school immediately and keep him out, it was a matter of principle not to allow Mark's tormentor to go free without so much as an inconvenience. Besides, there was always the old truth that someone who committed murder once was always at risk of committing another. It was the kind of "old truth" Gregor sometimes took exception to. Most people who committed murder didn't so much commit it as fail to commit self-control. They got liquored up or got stuck in the house for days by a storm or shocked into some kind of knowledge they weren't expecting—that ancient scenario, catching his wife in bed with another man—and just blew up. If there hadn't been a gun or a knife or a great big rock available, if they'd been small men instead of large ones with well-developed muscles, they would have pitched a fit and the whole thing would be over in a heartbeat, with no other consequences but the fact that they'd have to look silly every time the outburst was mentioned for the rest of their lives. Gregor believed sincerely and fervently that stupidity was at the heart of most lives, even the lives of people who were supposed to be very intelligent. It was certainly at the heart of his life, and Bennis's, at the moment; but he didn't like to think about that because he hadn't decided yet who was being the stupid one.

She is, his brain whispered—but that could be stupidity, too, his own, that eternal human tendency to absolve oneself and blame whatever problems might exist on anybody and anything else in the world. Gregor thought there must have been a lot of comfort in primitive religion, where there were gods for even small things like kitchen spills. "Ibdru made me drop the soup all over the floor" had a much better ring to it than, "I was eavesdropping on Lili and Marti and not looking where I was going and tripped over the doorjamb."

With Mark, impulse was not a consideration. The preliminary tests on his hair had come back from the lab, and it was quite clear that the boy had been given poison for weeks, and maybe longer.

"I understand your concern about the Christmas holidays," the lab investigator had told him, in one of those infinitely patient voices that meant she found Gregor both importunate and overwrought, "but all I can tell you is what I can tell you. We've got a lot of arsenic here. Best guess at the moment, a minimum of eight weeks."

Gregor had put it out of his mind to get back to later. If the poisoning had begun before the Christmas break, then either he had been sent home with something that was contaminated, or he should have appeared better over the course of the three weeks at home. Liz and Jimmy kept saying that Mark had not been well over Christmas, but it was impossible to tell if their "not well" was the same as "just like he's been lately," since they hadn't seen him lately. He had been here in Windsor at boarding school, and they had been back in Connecticut and New York. Gregor had a feeling that was about to change. Liz was making the kind of noises that mothers make when they are willing to brook no arguments. It might be the custom among the people they knew to send their children to boarding schools, but there were *perfectly good* private schools in New York and he could live at home.

The final issue was to establish some kind of official connection to an official investigation. Gregor really hated those detective novels where the intrepid private eye rushes about the city digging into a murder the police don't want him to touch. In real life that private eye would be arrested for obstruction of justice and stripped of his license. Gregor didn't have a license—his refusal to get one, or to call himself a "private detective," had brought a note of curiosity to half the articles ever written about him in the press; the other half simply ignored the inconvenient fact of it and called him a private detective—but the rule remained. He needed an official connection. It was fortunate that in this case there would be no difficulty in getting it.

"We've got to get the permission of the mayor," Brian Sheehy said, "but it's not going to be any problem. Especially not for a dollar. Isn't that what you usually charge?"

Gregor routinely charged ten thousand dollars or more, if he was charging at all. In this case he would have preferred not to charge at all, but he understood the legal problems. Many states and municipalities, like the federal government, had rules against using people on an unpaid volunteer basis. That was why so many of Franklin Delano Roosevelt's men had had to take that dollar a year in order to serve in the Brain Trust. They might have wanted to give their time and talent freely to the country during the Depression, but the law wouldn't allow it. The law wouldn't allow it in Windsor either. Gregor agreed to take his dollar and suppressed the thought that it was going to cost Windsor more than that to process the paperwork and write the check. There were things it made sense to argue about when it came to government, and things that it didn't.

"The mayor's a guy named Frank Petrelli," Brian Sheehy said. "I've been filling him in on and off since you got here. There's nothing he'd like better than to give that place a black eye."

"Do the people at the school realize just how much they're hated in this town?" Gregor asked. "It seems to me that they couldn't avoid knowing, but if they know I don't understand why they don't do something about it."

"There's town and there's town," Brian said. "They're not hated by the people who live here to commute into Boston to work in advertising and publishing and that kind of thing. And I don't think they care much for the rest of us. They probably think we vote Republican."

"Do you?"

"My name is Sheehy, and I live in Massachusetts," Brian said. "What do you think? I vote for Kennedys."

Gregor didn't know if it was being Irish or being Catholic that made that decision for Brian, but he didn't like to ask. Instead he waited at the long table in the Windsor Police Service conference room for the call to come from the mayor's office, and while he did he made notes about what he knew so far. So much of it was hazy. He had done no investigating. Aside from wandering around the campus of Windsor Academy on the night Mark had gone into convulsions, he had had nothing to do with the people who might have reason to want Mark dead. He had interrogated no one. He had viewed no crime scenes or even event scenes. He could hardly call his role in getting Mark to the hospital last night "viewing" anything, since he hadn't been paying attention to what was where or how Hayes House was set up. He'd been trying to get that fool woman to call 911.

Even so, he knew a few things that mattered and one thing that was absolutely crucial. It was truly remarkable how often "solving" a case came down to a few small details, mechanical and precise. Those detective novels wanted the reader to believe that knowledge of personality and closeness to people made all the difference. Gregor supposed it could, but often it didn't matter at all, except in the end, when you needed to hand something to the prosecutor that he could go into court with. Juries like personality and people. They were never comfortable with bare facts. They wanted it all to be clothed in "motive."

Gregor didn't have a clue as to motive, although he could imagine a few, given what he'd been told about Windsor, and Mark, and Michael Feyre. From what he'd heard so far though, there were more people with motives to kill Michael than to kill Mark; and as far as he knew, nobody had killed Michael.

Brian came in just after six, bustling happily, followed by a tall, thin, angular woman with closely cropped salt-and-pepper hair, wearing no makeup, and dressed for all the world as if she were about to go gardening.

"Frank is delighted to have you aboard," Brian said. "You could practically hear him gloat. I've got one of the girls to stay late—"

The angular woman cleared her throat, glaring.

"Okay, okay," Brian said, "one of the women. Excuse me, one of the secretaries. June Morland, to be exact. She's going to stay late and file all your paperwork just so that you're completely legal, no problems from the litigious ones up the street. This is Kay Hanrahan. She's one of our pathologists."

"A town like this has need for more than one?" Gregor said.

"Drugs," Kay Hanrahan said. Then she held out her hand to him. "How do you do?"

"How do you do?" Gregor responded automatically, shaking what felt like a skeleton in a skin bag.

Kay Hanrahan sat down and threw a pile of papers on the conference table. "I've been looking over these since the hospital sent them," she said, "and they've given me several hair samples to analyze on my own. On our own, I should say. And I'm coming in late here. But I must say, from a cursory look, this is truly extraordinary."

"The arsenic makes it truly extraordinary?" Gregor asked.

"It's not the arsenic per se," Kay said, "it's the apparent trail of dosages." She fanned the papers out in front of her. "I have to caution you that I'm interpreting somebody else's test results. I'm not going to be completely sure I know what's happened here until I've got results of tests we've done ourselves.

But I do know the lab at the hospital, and it's generally very reliable. I don't know them ever to have had a problem with raw results. For the moment let's assume that these numbers are reliable."

"All right," Gregor said.

"The note here says that Mark received a 'massive' dose of arsenic last night," Kay says, "but that's not entirely accurate. People can develop a tolerance to arsenic, and Mark must have had one, if the analysis of the hair samples is to be believed at all. The amount of arsenic found in his stomach contents and in the vomit on his clothes indicates a dose that would have killed him without that tolerance but not necessarily a dose that would have killed him with it. The interesting thing to me is that he was given enough to throw up, but not enough to be sure he'd die. You'd think that anyone who had gone to all the trouble of habituating him to arsenic over a period of two months minimum would know better. Either that or have had a reason for getting him to vomit."

"It could have been a miscalculation," Brian said. "Whoever it was could have been intending to murder him, or just to keep him sick, and misjudged the dose."

"I agree," Kay said. "In fact it's most likely to be a miscalculation. I just want to point out that the circumstances are curious. The other problem is that even with a tolerance in theory, the tolerance in fact will depend on a number of factors peculiar to the immediate circumstances. For instance, if he'd eaten more or less than usual that day, or if he'd had more or less sleep. Or if he'd had more or less caffeine, for that matter. This," she flicked her hands at the pages, "seems to indicate quite a bit of caffeine, enough to kill him on its own. Does he have anything to say about why he was ingesting all this caffeine?"

"His mother says he claims not to have taken the tablets at all," Gregor said, "and I want to stress something here. For the last several months, people have assumed he's been using drugs, and he's been insisting he wasn't; and from what we know, he was telling the truth. It makes sense to me to believe what he has to tell us."

"I agree," Kay said, "at least in this preliminary stage. But if he didn't take the tablets himself, then somebody must have given them to him, either at the same time as the arsenic or immediately before or after. The issue, you see, is why. What was the person or persons trying to accomplish? It's all well and good to say that somebody wanted to kill this boy, but if that were the case, it would make as much sense to give him a whopping dose of arsenic the first time and get it over with. And it leaves in question the matter of the caffeine.

You've got a very elaborate sequence of events here. What was the point? If the same person gave him both the arsenic and then caffeine, then it's hard to see what that person was trying to accomplish with both that couldn't be accomplished with one or the other. If two different people were giving him two different things—well. Now you've got a plot out of a fantasy novel. I would say it was damn near unheard of for two people to be running around trying to kill or injure the same person in an underhanded way as part of a plot to—well, you see what I mean."

"I see what you mean," Gregor said. It had been bothering him, too. But there was something else, something he thought more important, and he wanted to make sure he had that nailed to the wall. "Give me something in the way of a time frame," he said. "When did he have to have been given the caffeine that resulted in the pieces of tablets pumped out of his stomach? And when did he have to have been given the arsenic?"

Kay pulled the papers to her again, took a pen out of her shirt pocket, and made a few calculations. "The caffeine tablets, within twenty minutes or less, or they would have dissolved. The arsenic, anytime within an hour. It would act faster than that, of course, but it wouldn't necessarily kick in at full force all at once. There's the tolerance to consider. Still, I'd guess much less than an hour. I'd be happier with that same twenty minutes."

"So would I," Gregor said. He drummed his fingers on the table. There was another possibility, one he didn't like to consider, but he knew it would be brought up sooner or later. "There's always one other possibility," he said slowly. "There's always the possibility that Mark did it all to himself."

"Do you think that's likely?" Kay asked. She looked genuinely curious. "It brings you back to the question of why. Why would anybody want to do something like this to himself? It must have been excruciatingly painful at times. It must have been miserable nearly all the time. What possible motive could he have had?"

"I don't think he did do it to himself," Gregor said, "but the possibility is there, and you know it's going to be brought up. You and I might think the idea is insane, but it would be the best possible solution for the school."

Kay shrugged. "I've given up trying to understand what those people think of as a best possible solution for the school. If the local public school dealt with its drug problems the way Windsor Academy deals with theirs, it would be raided by the DEA. They get away with it because they have connections. It's a revelation, living next door to that place. You think you know how it works with connections, and then you find out you've vastly underestimated the whole process. But just because they might think that that's the best possible solution from their point of view doesn't mean it's any kind of solution at all from ours. If you want my professional opinion, it's not an impossible scenario because practically nothing is an impossible scenario, but it is so improbable as to make it legitimate that we not consider it—at least not seriously."

"They could say," Gregor said carefully, "that Mark was disturbed. That he was, is, mentally ill. He's got a history of erratic behavior, at least during this school year. That this was some kind of bid for attention."

Brian cocked his head. "You do sound like you think it's plausible," he said. "Is there something we don't know about?"

"No," Gregor said, "not at all. I'd bet my life Mark wasn't doing a thing to himself. But it does seem to me to be the tack somebody would take if they were trying to defend the school. And it also seems to me to be the possible explanation for why somebody would do what they did to Mark, assuming that the same person who fed him the arsenic fed him the caffeine tablets."

"And what reason is that?" Brian said.

"To discredit him," Gregor said. "Look, the kid was drinking enough caffeine on his own to give himself serious problems. At the very least, he'd be jittery and unfocussed and highly anxious. The arsenic would have given him stomach problems, and after he'd had enough of it it would have given him short-term memory problems, too. Put it all together and what you get is a mess of a kid who can't be relied on in any way at all. He looks like he has a drug problem, and even if that's ruled out, he looks like he's mentally ill."

"But what would be the *point?*" Kay asked in exasperation. "Why bother to do all that?"

"Well," Gregor said, "Mark was rooming with a boy who was known to be having a sexual relationship with the headmaster's wife and to be selling drugs. Maybe there were things going on that Mark couldn't help seeing that somebody didn't want him to be able to report to anyone else. Maybe the idea was to make sure that if Mark saw what he wasn't supposed to see, and told somebody about it, nobody would believe him."

"Did he see something?" Brian asked.

"My guess is that he doesn't think he did," Gregor said, "but then that would be handy, too. If you get him addled and distracted enough, maybe he won't even notice the thing you don't want him to notice."

"I think this is a really dodgy device to do that sort of thing," Kay said. "And why bother with it, really? Why not just use straightforward illegal drugs? If this other boy was selling them, couldn't whoever it was have gotten hold of some hallucinogen? Or some speed, some crystal meth, something with a kick to it. It would have done pretty much the same sort of thing, especially the hallucinogen, but it wouldn't have had the danger that you'd end up killing him. And if they found out he had LSD or something in his system, so what? They thought he had a drug problem anyway. They'd just kick him out of school, and that would be the end of the trouble whoever was having with Mark."

"Very good," Gregor said. "I've got to assume, then, that whoever it was had access to arsenic and caffeine tablets but didn't have access to illegal street drugs. That's interesting in and of itself."

"Everybody has access to caffeine tablets," Brian said.

"But not everybody has access to arsenic," Gregor said. "Would you do me a favor?"

"If I can," Brian said.

"First, check with the pharmacies in the area and find out if anybody bought anything with arsenic in it recently that can be traced. Pesticides. That kind of thing. The lab should do an analysis to look for some of the other things in those formulae. Second, I've talked to Michael Feyre's mother. Michael still isn't buried, and I've prevailed on her to forgo embalming for another day or two. She can't wait much longer, even with the boy in the freezer. Run some more tests. Check for arsenic. Check for tranquilizers and other prescription relaxants. Check for sleeping pills, both prescription and over-the-counter."

"There really isn't any way for Michael Feyre to have been murdered," Kay said. "I worked on that one myself. He definitely died from hanging, and I defy you to find a way that anybody could get a large, strong, very young man into that position and then kick the chair out under him. He wouldn't go quietly. And if he was unconscious, he'd be one hell of a dead weight."

"Well," Gregor said, "there is one other way."

"What way is that?" Brian asked.

"Sex."

2

Gregor didn't want to go charging over to Windsor Academy in his new official capacity, brandishing his credentials and demanding that faculty and students both cooperate in a formal investigation. It was just going on eight o'clock, dark and cold, and what he wanted was to look at that place in the library that Mark had told him about. Then he wanted to go back to the hospital and make the end of evening visiting hours. He wondered if Mark still thought it was "cool" that somebody had tried to poison him. Mark being Mark, he probably did.

Gregor went down Main Street without marveling at the stores. If they ever made a Hip Urban Liberal with a Social Conscience Barbie, her main street would look like this. If they made a Rural Conservative Barbie, she'd probably come with a miniature Wal-Mart. He pulled the collar of his coat high on his neck. It was snowing, steadily and heavily, and the snow was sticking on the clean sidewalks under his feet. He went down to East Gate and crossed the street in the middle of traffic. Main Street was so crowded most of the time that the cars weren't moving fast enough to hurt him when he jaywalked. He went through East Gate and onto the quad. Then he turned to the left and headed for the library.

The library building was impressive, he had to admit that. It reminded him of a church, and there was a lot of it. It was easily the largest building on campus that he could see. He went up the front steps and into the foyer and was impressed again. The ceiling was far above his head and arched. The floors and the base of the check-out desk were made of dark, polished hardwood and the surface of the check-out desk was marble. Through the arched doorway into the main reading room, he could see an enormous stained-glass window. The building had been designed to awe. It succeeded.

It was when Gregor got past that arched doorway and into the main reading room that he first sensed that something was wrong—not wrong wrong, not menacing, but *off*. He looked around at the long tables with students studying at them and the carrels with computers where students were doing everything from academic work to playing computer games, and for the longest time he couldn't put his finger on it. It was a college Gothic library. Schools all over the country had them. Saint Joseph's University in Philadelphia had the one he liked the best. He turned around and around, and then it hit him.

There weren't any books.

No, that wasn't quite right. There were some books, there just weren't very many of them. Where any other school library would have had tall shelves full of volumes, dividing the tables from each other in rows along each wall, or crammed in without tables between them at all, this one had the minimum number of bookcases, and most of those cases were at least half empty. Of the books he could see, most looked old and oddly bound, like textbooks, or library editions of standard classics. There were a lot of things other than books around: framed posters for African art exhibits and South American cultural festivals; row on row of audiotapes and videotapes and DVDS; CDs and CD players, with headphones, to listen to them on. Gregor didn't know what to think. He had seen elementary school libraries with more and better volumes than this. He was sure Father Tibor had more all by himself.

He had just about decided that he must have made a mistake, the *real* library was somewhere else, complete with the standard academic collection, when he felt a tug on his sleeve and looked down to see a smallish woman in the Windsor Main Street Uniform trying to get his attention. The Windsor Main Street Uniform consisted of a print skirt and a standard twin set. Gregor thought he was about to be ushered politely back into the quad, and that at any moment he would need to pull out those credentials he hadn't wanted to show anyone just yet.

The small woman saw she had his attention and smiled, anxiously. "It's Gregor Demarkian, isn't it? I've seen your picture in magazines. Everybody's been wondering when we'd see you on campus."

"I was looking for something called the catwalk," Gregor said. He wasn't about to apologize for his presence before he had to.

The small woman looked around. "It's up there," she said, pointing above their heads. "You take the spiral staircase up to get there. But I don't know what you'd want that for. Nothing has happened there."

"There's supposed to be a window at the end of it," Gregor said. "I wanted to look out that window."

"Ah, I see," the small woman said. "Of course, that's one of the places Mark likes to go to be alone. He's supposed to have supervised study hall every night because his grades are awful. He's very irresponsible. But he ducks out of it and goes up there where nobody can see him. He probably plays video games."

"Are there facilities up there to play video games?"

"Of course not," the small woman said. "We don't approve of video games at Windsor. There's not a lot we can do to eradicate them, but we do try to keep them out of the library. But Mark probably brought his Game Boy or something like that. It's the kind of thing he would do. He had no dedication to work. I never did understand how he'd managed to get admitted to this place. He wasn't serious."

In Gregor's memory Mark was one of the most seriously dedicated teenagers he'd ever met, but he let it go for the moment. He looked around again. "Where are the books?" he asked. "Is there another room, more stacks somewhere, something?"

The small woman bristled. "We have a perfectly adequate collection," she said. "We don't spend the kind of money some schools do on volumes, it's true, but there's a public library right across Main Street, one of the best in the state, and the students are welcome to use that one whenever they need to. That leaves us with the budget to invest in truly innovative teaching tools, interactive learning, that kind of thing. It's all very state-of-the-art."

Gregor suppressed his immediate need to tell this woman that the state of the art for schools was and always would be books, and said instead, "You know my name, but I don't know yours. You are—?"

"Marta Coelho," the small woman said. "I teach history. I teach history to Mark DeAvecca, to tell you the truth. And it's only my first year here, but I find it very easy to understand what the problem has been—with Mark. I realize that we were wrong, you know, to think that he was taking drugs. There's been talk all day about how they found out in the hospital that that wasn't true, but you can see how we thought so."

"Of course," Gregor said. "I thought so at first."

"There then," Marta said. "I don't see what anybody expected us to do about it. And arsenic. I heard that somebody had given him arsenic. Somebody had tried to poison him."

This was interesting, Gregor thought. He wondered how the news had gotten around so fast—and then he didn't wonder. Peter Makepeace would have been informed. Unless he'd kept his mouth completely shut, telling neither his secretary nor his wife, the news was likely to be all over the school in no time at all.

"He had quite a bit of arsenic in his system, yes," Gregor said. "We don't really know how it got there at the moment."

Marta Coelho looked away. She was, Gregor thought, almost painfully uncomfortable here. He couldn't tell if she was uncomfortable because she was talking to him or uncomfortable at the school. Her defense of the library had been elaborate but delivered without conviction. Her eyes kept darting around as if she expected to be attacked at any moment. Maybe there was a directive out that faculty and students should not be talking to him, or to the police, without a lawyer present.

Gregor looked around the main reading room one more time. "I'd like to get up to that catwalk if I could. Could you show me?"

Marta bit her lip. "I don't see it as sensible," she said, "that somebody would try to poison Mark. Why would they bother? It was different with Michael. Michael Feyre, you know. He was an evil kid. We aren't supposed to say that sort of thing. They don't like talk about evil around here, but it was true. He was an evil kid. Mark is just—well, Mark. He's a loser, but he's mostly harmless."

Did everybody at this school believe that Mark DeAvecca was a fairly stupid, fairly harmless, slacking-off loser? Gregor thought of the Mark he had seen at the Windsor Inn yesterday and decided that the judgment wasn't entirely surprising, even if it was far from reality when you knew all the circumstances. Even so, he thought that Liz had a good reason to get Mark out of here that had nothing to do with arsenic poisoning. He didn't like Marta Coelho. She was far too rigid, and far too angry, for his taste.

"The catwalk," he said again.

"It's right along here," Marta said, moving him toward the east wall of the reading room. "There are two, really. You get to them by spiral staircases, but they're not connected to each other. And the other one is off-limits at the moment because there's something wrong with it and it's being repaired."

"Has it been off-limits long?"

"Since Thanksgiving. Somebody dropped something off it and broke part of the railing. But Mark always liked this one. There's a little study nook at the end of it. Well, that's true of both of them. But this study nook looks out over Maverick Pond. It's the closest we have in Windsor to real outdoors nature."

Gregor didn't remember that Mark was fond of nature, but he might have been. He followed Marta through the bare and meager stacks to the far edge of the room. There was a narrow break in the wall. Through it he could see the start of the circular staircase.

"It's silly, really," Marta said. "The woman who gave us the money for a library was angry because her brothers had been able to go to Andover or Exeter or wherever, and girls weren't allowed at the time. Her parents sent her here instead, and she inherited everything eventually. I don't know what happened to the brothers, but she left Windsor the money to build this. We wouldn't have a library as a separate building otherwise. If it wasn't for the terms of the bequest, we'd probably turn this building into a performing arts space. We've talked about it at every faculty meeting I've been to since I got here. But there's the legal aspect. The will won't let us."

Marta went up the staircase first. Gregor followed her. It was claustrophobic in the small circular space, a lot like he remembered in one of the buildings at the Tower of London. He had no idea why he'd remembered that. He hadn't been to the tower in years, and then he'd gone with Bennis.

They came out on the catwalk itself. It was very high in the air. Gregor had a good head for heights, but his first reaction was to feel as if he were going to be sick. The railing looked unsubstantial and far too low for safety.

"You come along here," Marta said. "I don't like being up here. Most people don't, but there are always a few students who love it. Mark loves it, did I tell you? He's up here all the time. I know you're supposed to be a friend of his family, and now he's been poisoned, or might have been, and somebody must be responsible; but I have to say that I never did like him. Mark, I mean. He wasn't a very likable kid. And I know he lies."

"Mark?"

"Oh, yes," Marta said. "I can't believe you've never noticed it. People don't like to admit they've noticed it, but they must have in this case. It couldn't have started here. He lies about everything. He lies about his work and why he hasn't done it. We put a lot of emphasis on trust in this school. He isn't trustworthy."

"I see. I thought you said it was his roommate who was the 'evil' kid."

"Oh, I did. I didn't mean I thought Mark was evil. He isn't evil. It's not that. Michael was different. He was frightening, really, and violent. When we talked about the decimation of the Native Americans and that kind of thing, Michael liked to talk about torture. To *dwell* on it. He wasn't all that bright, but he had a very vivid imagination. He could make you just see it: the pain, the blood. And he loved it. It was terrible to see. I didn't mean Mark was anything like that. He really isn't."

"I wouldn't have thought so."

"But he isn't trustworthy," Marta insisted. She had turned to face him. Now she turned again. The catwalk was very narrow. Turning wasn't easy. Gregor wished he were out in front. He thought it would be easier, less frightening, if he could see the nook ahead of them and concentrate on that, instead of having his attention constantly pulled toward the empty space under his feet.

"Oh, dear," Marta said. "That's Edith up ahead. I hope she doesn't start coming this way without checking the walk. It's awful when that happens. There isn't room for two people to pass, and there isn't supposed to be more than one person on the walk at a time. Those are the rules. More safety concerns, I think."

They were apparently nearing the end of the catwalk and the nook. Marta suddenly moved a little to the side, and Gregor could see past her into a small, high-ceilinged space just big enough for one person to sit on the floor or stand to look out the window. The older woman who took up most of that space was standing, more or less. She had her hands against the stone sides of the arched window and was bent at the waist, breathing heavily.

Gregor knew something was wrong before Marta did. Marta put her hand on the other woman's shoulder and said, "Edith? It's Marta, and I've got Gregor—"

She never got farther than that. The older woman named Edith straightened only slightly, then wheeled around on the heels of her shoes. Marta's smile was prepared and stayed on her face, frozen, for many seconds after Edith had turned fully around and begun to lurch toward them both. Gregor assessed the signs immediately: the flushed face, the labored breathing that suddenly became much worse, frantic and out of control. Gregor knew that the most important thing at this moment was to keep this woman from getting past them onto the catwalk, and he put out his arm to stop her as she swayed. He was a second too late, and she was a hair too panicked.

"Edith?" Marta said again.

Gregor's arm was in the air. Edith knocked it away from her with a single wide sweep of her right arm. Before they knew it, she was past them and out onto the narrow ledge. Gregor had no sooner turned to follow her than she went over the side, breaking the railing as she fell.

The catwalk was immediately over a set of low bookshelves. Edith hit the top of those face first, rolled sideways, and then plummeted the rest of the way to the floor.

PART THREE

Exile accepted as a destiny, in the way we accept an inscrutable illness, should help us see through our self-delusions.
—CZESŁAW MIŁOSZ

The easiest person to deceive is yourself.
—RICHARD FEYNMAN

Boring others is a form of aggression . . .
—P. J. O'ROURKE

ONE

1

Gregor Demarkian knew who she was as soon as she walked into the main reading room of Ridenour Library, even though he had never heard a physical description of her. *Somebody should have mentioned the red hair,* he thought. It was far and away the most notable thing about her, so notable that, after a split second spent admiring it, it grated on him. This was a woman who not only expected to occupy center stage, but expended a lot of energy securing her place in it. Everything about her was theatrical: the head-to-toe black of the leather trousers and cashmere sweater; the sweeping exaggeration of the hooded black cashmere cape; the hair, surely dyed at her time of life; the walk. She walked like a woman determined to command, not only attention, but obedience. And it worked. Gregor had always thought that human beings were essentially lazy. They took other people at their own word unless something significant happened to make them question it. Here they sensed her presence in the room as soon as she walked through the door and parted quickly to let her through.

Gregor was standing next to Edith Braxner's body. It was only a body now. He'd expected it to be nothing else. She was already more than half-dead when she started to fall. She was sprawled out on the floor, her back jammed into a row of chairs that were themselves jammed into the side of a reading table. Marta Coelho was standing just beyond the body, near the door to the foyer, looking sick. She had given Gregor "Edith's" last name, and then run off to call 911 when he'd asked her to. Everybody else who had been in the library at the time was still there, as far as Gregor knew. They were huddled in little groups around the reading room, staring. Most of them were students. Gregor had no idea what faculty did at this time of night, but they weren't in the library. Both of the librarians had come in and stopped uncertainly at the edge of the student groups. It was as if Edith Braxner's body had a magic circle drawn around it that no one could pass.

Alice Makepeace arrived on this scene as if it were any other scene, as if she were entering the cafeteria for lunch or dinner on a perfectly ordinary day, but a day on which she was not in a very good mood. The magic circle didn't hold her. She strode past the librarians and two little groups of students right up to the body itself. She threw the edges of her cape back over her shoulders. Gregor half expected her to take out a sword and slash an oversized Z into the library carpet.

"Oh, God," she said, "I've been telling Peter for years that those catwalks aren't safe. I knew this had to happen sometime. Why isn't anybody giving her mouth-to-mouth resuscitation?"

"Because there's nothing to resuscitate," Gregor said, "and because it wouldn't be safe. It's not very likely that there's enough cyanide left in her mouth to kill you, but it's not impossible."

Alice Makepeace looked him up and down, very slowly. Gregor had the impression that this was a technique she had used before and to good effect on other people. It had no effect on him.

"Who are you?" she said. "You're not faculty, and you're not a student. If you're not a parent, you have no right to be on this campus."

"I probably don't. My name is Gregor Demarkian. I was invited here by Mark DeAvecca. Does that count?"

"Of course it doesn't count. You ought to get out of here. Or maybe you shouldn't. Maybe we should call the police."

"If Marta over there did what I asked her to, the police have already been called," Gregor said.

Alice Makepeace whirled around, looking for Marta. Marta looked frightened and resentful. Gregor was sure this wasn't the first time Alice had tried to bully her. And bully Alice did. She was good at it.

"Marta, for God's sake, what were you thinking? You know you aren't supposed to call the police without permission from President's House. You're not supposed to call an ambulance without permission from President's House. I know you haven't been here very long, but most faculty do understand the rules of behavior in this school when they've been here far less long than you have—"

"I did call President's House," Marta said. "I talked to you. That's why you're here. And don't tell me I shouldn't have called nine-one-one without permission. You gave that lecture to Cherie just this morning because of Mark DeAvecca, and look how that turned out. He could have ended up dead. Poor Edith *is* dead."

"We don't know that," Alice said.

"We do, in fact, know that," Gregor said. Alice turned back to him. She had lost none of her arrogance. She was not afraid. That was important for him to remember. "I've checked the vital signs myself, Mrs. Makepeace. Ms. Braxner is dead."

"Alice," Alice said. "You may not realize it, but we don't use formal address at Windsor Academy. We find it distancing, and a bar to the spirit of collegiality we are trying to maintain. Learning is most effective when it is carried out among equals."

"And you're all equals here, Mrs. Makepeace?"

"Of course."

"Students and teachers both?"

"Of course."

"Then I don't understand how you function," Gregor said, politely, thinking how bizarre it was having this conversation over the body of a woman who was dead from cyanide or had at least had cyanide before she died. He could feel the groups of students staring at them, tense. "Either your teachers don't grade your students," he said, "or they do, and your students grade their teachers in return."

"They do," Alice said quickly. "We're committed to student evaluations of teaching effectiveness."

"But their positions still aren't equal," Gregor said, "unless the grading has equal weight on both sides. Unless student grades can affect a teacher's future as much as a teacher's grades can affect a student's. Is that what you do here, Mrs. Makepeace?"

Alice threw back her shoulders. "I will have to inform you that your continued use of the patriarchal form of my name will be construed by most people here as a collaboration with the white male hegemonic oppression of women and people of color."

There were no people of color in the library that Gregor could see. He said, "That's quite all right, Mrs. Makepeace. I'd much rather be convicted of committing white male hegemonic oppression than of dishonesty."

Around the edge of the magic circle, somebody burst into laughter. It was

245

tension released, but Gregor hoped it was also insight gained. It was extraordinary to listen to this flamboyant creature throw around words like "hegemony" and "oppression." She used them as if they were incantations. When her beauty failed, this was her ritual of control.

The sounds of sirens were suddenly very close. Gregor realized that he'd been hearing them for a long time. The ambulance would have to come from the hospital, which was on the very edge of town, but he didn't understand why it had taken the police so long to arrive. Then he remembered that there were no roads on the campus itself, only walkways much too narrow to allow vehicles, even small cars, to pass. The police had to know that. Both the police and the ambulance would have been called in when Michael Feyre died. The ambulance had been called again, for Mark, only last night. Then, though, they'd only had to go to Hayes House, which fronted Main Street. They hadn't had to maneuver the campus proper.

There was a commotion in the foyer and then the ambulance men came in, carrying a stretcher, in a hurry. They pushed the groups of students out of the way, and one of them knelt down next to the body. A moment later he stood up and motioned to one of the men behind him. The second man came forward with what Gregor knew was a defibrillator.

A moment later Brian Sheehy came through the crowd himself, along with a younger man in a suit as badly fitting as his own. He saw Gregor and then the body. He came over to watch.

"Think it's going to work?" he asked.

"No," Gregor said. "I saw her fall. We were up there." He pointed to the catwalk. Its railing sagged and twisted where Edith had crashed through it. "I saw her before she fell. I'd bet my life we're looking at cyanide. You could smell it."

"Crap," Brian said. He turned to the man next to him. "This is Danny Kelly. He's the detective in charge of Mark's case. I thought it would make sense to put him on this one."

"I think so too," Gregor said.

The ambulance men were running electricity through Edith Braxner's body. Every time they did, the body jumped into the air, hovered, shuddered, and fell again. It was a small body. Edith Braxner had been a small woman, but not as small as Marta Coelho. Now that Gregor thought of it, Cherie at Hayes House had been a small woman, too. The only tall woman he had seen so far at Windsor Academy was Alice Makepeace. Maybe that had been arranged deliberately. It surprised him to realize that he didn't think that speculation was entirely ridiculous.

"I've got a partner," Danny Kelly said. "His name's Fitzhugh. He's getting names in the foyer."

Edith Braxner's body jumped again. Gregor felt as if the process had been going on for hours. Surely they must realize the woman was dead, and that nothing could be done for her. He looked away and just caught the arrival of Peter Makepeace, without a coat or hat, hurrying. He looked no more confident on his own turf than he had the night before at the hospital.

Peter Makepeace came up to the magic circle and looked down at Edith Braxner's body. He did not look at his wife. "Somebody said she was dead," he said.

"She probably is," Gregor told him. "I would say definitely, but they're still trying. You can't bring back a victim of cyanide poisoning with a defibrillator."

"He keeps saying somebody gave Edith cyanide," Alice Makepeace said. "He's said it a couple of times. But he can't know. He's just guessing."

"But he does know these things." It was Marta Coelho, her voice high and thin, stretched tight with strain. "He's an expert on these things. That's why he's here. He's here because Mark DeAvecca knows something, and Michael Feyre didn't commit suicide."

"Don't be ridiculous," Alice Makepeace said, furious. "For God's sake, Marta, we've been over the death of Michael Feyre a dozen times. There's no question but that it was suicide."

"If there's no question, then why did Mark bring *him* here?" Marta pointed at Gregor. Her voice was beyond stretched now. She was coming very close to hysteria. "Why did somebody poison Mark? Why did somebody poison Edith? Edith is dead, Alice, can't you get anything *sensible* into your head? And Michael's dead, too, and from what I've heard today, Mark nearly died. He was stuffed full of arsenic. You can't just walk around pretending it's all an exercise in deconstruction and that you don't know what's going on in this place."

"*Education* is going on in this place," Alice Makepeace said, furious.

Marta pushed her way through the students toward the circle until she was right in front of Alice, close enough to touch the cape. "Edith was in the catwalk nook," Marta said. "She was in the same place Mark was on the night Michael died. There's something up there. There's something Mark saw and then Edith saw it and somebody tried to poison them both and now Edith is dead. And you know that because you were there."

"I don't have the faintest idea what you're talking about," Alice said.

"You were *there*," Marta shrieked. "I *saw* you. You passed my office the night Michael died and then you went out the wrong door. You said you were going to go back to President's House, but you went out the wrong door, the door to Maverick Pond. I *saw* you. And you were sleeping with Michael Feyre. I know that. Everybody knows that. You think you're being so damned cute, but everybody knows what you're up to. Everybody always knows. And everybody knows James bought drugs from that boy and that there's something wrong with Philip that he's trying to hide and all the rest of it. You're all trying to hide something here. You hide it behind a lot of academic jargon instead of in closets, that's all."

"That's enough," Peter Makepeace said, walking up to Marta and putting a hand on her shoulder. "Do you have any idea what you're doing? There are police here."

"So what?" Marta sounded like a banshee. "Why can't anybody in this place just tell the truth for once?"

"It's not telling the truth to engage in irresponsible speculation about matters whose facts you don't know," Peter said.

"I know the facts just fine," Marta said, "and I'm not going to go on pretending any longer for the sake of the school. I don't give a damn what happens to the school. I hate it here. I've always hated it here. And any policeman who wants to ask me what I know, I'll tell him."

"Police officer," Alice said, automatically. "You'd think they'd have trained you out of all those sexist constructions at Yale."

Gregor thought Marta was going to haul back her arm and slap Alice Makepeace across the face. It didn't happen. Marta shrugged Peter Makepeace's hand off her shoulder and said, "Get away from me." Then she pushed past Alice and out toward the foyer, through the milling students and the small crowd of crime-scene personnel waiting to get a chance at Edith Braxner's body. Danny Kelly gave both Gregor and Brian Sheehy a look and took off after her.

The ambulance men were giving up. The one with the defibrillator had gotten to his feet. The other one was still kneeling by the body, but not in order to do anything to revive it. Edith Braxner looked broken, her back bent at an unnatural angle, her face not calm as much as frozen. Gregor had never understood the things people said about corpses, or the need so many people had not to accept that a corpse was indeed a corpse. It didn't matter if they were religious believers or not, people wanted to see nobility in the human body, even when that body was devoid of life. They wanted to see beauty, and meaning, and purpose.

When Gregor looked at a corpse, he thought only that death made the human condition all too clear. Whatever it was we were, electrical impulses or eternal spirit, our bodies were victorious in the end; and our bodies did not really want to live. Descartes had had it wrong. It wasn't, "I think, therefore I am." It was, "I breathe, therefore I am," and our bodies didn't want to breathe. It was too much work and too much trouble. Our bodies were always headed for the decay that was their only rest.

2

Peter Makepeace didn't want them to treat Edith Braxner's death as a homicide, at least not right away, but his protests were halfhearted. Gregor had thought he looked like a defeated man last night at the hospital. Now he admitted that he hadn't realized what real defeat would look like. Peter Makepeace seemed to be walking through ether. He was beyond dazed and beyond resigned. His face was white. His hands were still. He was so without emotion that it was a shock to remember that he was a very large man.

Alice Makepeace was not without emotion, and she was still not afraid or intimidated. If there had been any truth to the things Marta Coelho had said—and Gregor knew that there had been, with some of those things—Alice did not expect to be affected by them.

Alice moved first after Marta rushed out. "That little ass," she said. "I can't stand people with no sense of self-control."

Brian Sheehy moved away from the body just a bit. The crime-scene personnel were coming through to do their jobs, and from now on what would happen to Edith Braxner would be technical, mechanical, and cold.

"Mr. Makepeace, Mrs. Makepeace, we really do need to have a word if we could."

"I don't want *him* there." Alice pointed to Gregor. "He's not a police officer. I don't have to talk to him, and I don't intend to."

"You don't have to talk to the police officers if you don't want to," Brian said mildly. "I'm sure you've got enough lawyers to secure your constitutional rights. Mr. Demarkian, however, although he is not a police officer, is a consultant who has been hired by the town of Windsor to serve in an official capacity in the investigation into the poisoning of Mark DeAvecca, and since this case is being treated as part of that one—"

"Why should it be?" Alice demanded.

"Because it isn't common to find two poisoners operating totally independently and from unconnected motives in the same place at the same time,"

Brian said. "In fact if that's what we have here, it will be the first case I've ever heard of. The detectives assigned to Mark's case are here. We don't need to talk to all of you this evening. It's enough that we get names and contact information for most of you. But we will talk to all of you eventually."

"Don't bet on it," Alice said. "As soon as this gets out, there's going to be a stampede. Families will be coming in from all over the country to get their little darlings out of here. There's a mad poisoner on the loose—or so you say."

Danny Kelly came back in from the foyer. "Okay," he said, "I've got a statement. I'm going to treat it as preliminary; she's a little upset."

"She was hysterical," Gregor said.

"Maybe we could find some place reasonably private and have a talk with Mr. Makepeace here," Brian said. "There are a few things we need to know immediately."

Alice Makepeace looked as if she wanted to protest yet again, but she didn't. She turned away from all of them and marched out the way she had marched in, with that inner sense of her own importance that could not have been shaken by the appearance on the scene of God Himself. Danny Kelly started to go after her, but Brian Sheehy stopped him.

"Don't bother," he said, "we know where to find Alice Makepeace if we want her."

Peter Makepeace looked relieved to have something to do. "There's a seminar room in the faculty wing," he said. "It's just through the foyer and then through the side door. We can go there."

"Fine," Brian said.

Peter gave a last look at Edith Braxner's body—they were taking fingerprints now; somebody was using a sterile vacuum to suck up fibers from the carpet where she had fallen—and then led the way out of the main reading room, into the foyer, and around the side to the wing. Back in the main reading room, the police had begun to take the names and contact information of all the witnesses and then clear them out of the immediate area. They'd take short statements from each of them before allowing them to go home. Gregor thought that the statements wouldn't amount to much.

The seminar room wasn't very far along the corridor. Peter opened the third door on the left after they came through from the foyer, and then he ushered Gregor, Danny, and Brian inside. It was an elegant room, high-ceilinged and studiously Gothic, the very image of what education was supposed to be. Gregor wondered where so many Americans, who lived in a country that had been virtually uninhabited when Gothic was the reigning style of architecture in Europe, came by that impression.

Peter motioned them all to chairs and, closing the door behind them, sat down in one himself. "This should do," he said. "This should be comfortable."

"It will be very comfortable," Danny Kelly said.

Gregor made himself sit down next to Peter Makepeace. They all seemed to be having one of those moments when nobody was sure what the etiquette was; and although Gregor did not underestimate the importance of etiquette, it had to be secondary here.

"So," Peter said, "what do you want to know? About all the things Marta said? I don't know where to start."

"At the moment," Danny Kelly said, "I think we'd like to know the more basic things. Who the victim was, for instance."

"Oh." Peter Makepeace looked as if he were radically adjusting expectations he hadn't realized he had. "Her name was Edith Braxner, Edith Delshort Braxner. She was married once, I think, when she was very young. She didn't talk about it. She taught languages, French and German. She was head of the Language Department."

"Had she been here long?" Danny asked.

"Longer than I have," Peter said. "She's one of our stalwarts, and one of the few to have lasted long after the school's mission changed. This used to be a girls' school, and a very traditional one in many ways. When the school decided to admit boys, they also decided to make some changes to the educational philosophy. Many of the teachers who had been here under the original ethos had a hard time adjusting. The headmistress at the time lasted less than a year."

"And you replaced her?" Gregor asked.

"No," Peter Makepeace said. "I've only been here eight years. This was back in the early 1980s. Edith must have been close to retirement age. I should know that, but for some reason I don't."

"But you know she'd adjusted to the new, ah, mission," Danny said.

"Not exactly," Peter said. "Edith was an odd woman out, in many ways, but she was an excellent teacher, and she made it possible for us to offer German in a very small school. Students didn't call her Edith though. They called her Dr. Braxner."

"Doctor?" Gregor said.

"Yes. Yes, she had a doctorate in comparative literature from Harvard. She got it in the days when women found it very difficult to get faculty places at colleges and universities, except at the women's colleges. I don't know why she didn't try for one of those. Or perhaps she did and still met with prejudice. There was quite a bit. For whatever reason she came here. I can't believe I'm talking about her in the past tense."

Gregor thought that there came a time when you had to talk about everybody in the past tense, except when you could no longer talk at all, and other people referred to you that way. He asked, "Was there any family? I take it she lived alone."

"She lived alone and on campus," Peter said. "As for family, I think there's a married sister somewhere. Edith used to visit her in the summers for a week before taking a group of students to Germany to study. A number of our teachers run these little summer sessions. It provides the students with enrichment they wouldn't be able to get otherwise, and it provides the teachers with a means of traveling, which they otherwise couldn't afford."

"Do you know if she was having a dispute of any kind with anyone?" Danny Kelly asked. "Was she involved in litigation, or were there bad feelings between herself and any other faculty member?"

"Do you mean, did she have any enemies?" Peter smiled faintly. "That always sounds so unrealistic to me. Do people have enemies in that sense in this day and age?"

"Some of them do," Danny said. "What we need to know is if Edith Braxner did."

"Not that I know of," Peter said. "I won't say there were never any frictions between members of the faculty, or between members of the faculty and students, because there were. It's a matter of degree. I don't think a teacher would kill another teacher over a dispute about which textbook to adopt in a freshman course or whether to offer Art History as a lecture course or a seminar."

"And were there disputes like that?" Danny asked. "Was Edith Braxner involved in them?"

"I don't know," Peter Makepeace said.

Gregor tried another tack. "When I saw her for the first time," he said, "she was standing in a little nook at the end of a catwalk that ran along one side above the main reading room of the library. There are apparently two catwalks and two nooks."

"That's right," Peter said. "They're not really completely safe. I knew that. They're narrow, for one thing, and the railings are too low. We've been warned by the insurance company more than once, and we did intend to do something about them. I hope she didn't die from that. I hope she didn't die from the fall."

Gregor was convinced she hadn't died from the fall. "I was going up to that catwalk because Mark DeAvecca told me that he had been there, in the nook, on the night Michael Feyre died. He had looked out of the window in that nook and seen something that disturbed him near something called Maverick Pond. Could Edith Braxner have been looking for the same thing?"

"I don't see how," Peter said. "You're welcome to go up and look for yourself if the police will let you. There's nothing to see. Oh, that catwalk's better than the other one. The nook on the other one is crammed right against the faculty wing so that all you see is a building on one side and a little lawn right in front of you. But even the nook you saw Edith in doesn't look out on much. There's the pond, yes, and a small stand of evergreens, and some benches. It's mostly deserted this time of year."

"Do you know if anybody on this campus would have regular access to cyanide?" Gregor asked. "What about arsenic?"

"I don't know what you mean by 'regular access,'" Peter Makepeace said.

"I mean access as a matter of course. Somebody who works with pesticides, for instance. Or chemicals. Somebody who would not have to do anything special to get his hands on poison."

"Well, the groundskeepers work with pesticides, I'm sure," Peter said. "We have a student protest or two every year over their use of them, but they do use them. In the end nothing else is practical in taking care of a property this size. And the Chemistry Department has chemicals. I'll admit I don't know which ones. I suppose some of them must be poisonous."

"Is chemistry a separate department?" Gregor asked.

"No," Peter said, "it's part of the Sciences Department. We offer chemistry, biology, and physics. We're very proud of the physics. It wasn't offered when this was a girls' school. Many girls' schools didn't in the old days. It was considered too mathematical and alienating for girls, especially since it was expected that most of them would marry as soon as they graduated from their colleges, if not before. Some of the girls' schools that have remained girls' schools don't offer physics even now."

"Who would have access to the chemicals in the Sciences Department?" Gregor asked. "Only the chemistry teachers, or all the science teachers? Or all the teachers? Or all the students? Are they locked up?"

"All the science teachers would be able to get to the science materials closet, which is where the things needed for lab courses are kept," Peter said.

253

"There's a key, but I think all the science teachers would have to have it, because it's not just chemicals for chemistry that are kept in there. I know the fetal pigs are—in glass jars. None of the other teachers are likely to have one of those keys, though, since they'd have no need to go into that closet. And none of the students would have them, unless they'd been sent by a teacher to get something from the closet. Then they'd have the key for however long the errand took and be required to hand it back when the errand was complete. We *are* careful about safety, Mr. Demarkian, no matter what it might seem like given the problems with the catwalks."

"Was Edith Braxner particularly close to Mark DeAvecca?" Gregor asked.

"I wouldn't think so," Peter said. "Nobody was, really. Cherie Wardrop was fond of him, but the consensus of most of the teachers was that he either had no commitment to academic work, or he just wasn't all that bright. He was one of our top picks last spring, too. We had doubts about some of the people we admitted, but we had no doubts about Mark. His record in his previous school was outstanding. It happens sometimes, no matter how careful you are."

"What happens?" Gregor asked.

"That you bring in unsuitable people," Peter said. "Students are a mystery. We screen until we're blue in the face, but we always miss a few of the ones we should have screened out."

"Was Michael Feyre one of the ones you should have screened out?" Gregor asked.

Peter Makepeace shrugged. "Michael Feyre was a concern from the beginning. We knew before we admitted him that he was a long shot. Sometimes you want to take long shots. In Michael's case, we were sensitive to his mother's position. His mother—"

"Won a lottery," Gregor said. "We know."

"She didn't just win a lottery, she won the biggest lottery in history," Peter said. "And she was very isolated because of it, and so were her children. We had the whole family up here when Michael applied. The younger children are adjusting well, and at least one of them is very bright. Michael wasn't adjusting very well. There was some question that he might have a drug problem, although that was never proved. But I don't see how you can say all this is connected. Michael committed suicide. He wasn't poisoned."

Brian and Danny looked away, keeping their faces expressionless. Gregor watched Peter Makepeace carefully. He was not being disingenuous. He had absorbed this piece of information as thoroughly as if he were a Catholic submitting to dogma, and it had never occurred to him to question it.

"One more thing," Danny said. "Who would be able to tell us what Edith Braxner was doing this evening before her fall? Did she eat dinner in her apartment or with the rest of you? Why had she come to the library? Why was she up on that catwalk? If there was nothing to be seen out that window but a pond and some evergreens and nothing else, why did anybody ever go up there?"

"Students go up there to study," Peter said, "or some students do. And Mark DeAvecca, I think, went up there mostly to be alone. I often felt he was overwhelmed by boarding life. I suppose teachers might sometimes go up there to be alone as well."

"But you're not sure?" Danny said.

"Of course I'm not sure. I'm not clairvoyant. I don't know what Edith was thinking. Isn't that the kind of thing an investigation is supposed to find out? Besides, I think it would be more important to find out where Edith had been before she went up to the catwalk, don't you? Unless you think somebody was up there feeding her cyanide in full view of the entire main reading room. And even then you'd have to figure out how they got down without Marta and Mr. Demarkian here running right into them."

3

Outside, the air was cold and crisp, and the snow was definitely something serious, coming down in hard-driving streams that were almost as violent as a bad rain. The body was gone and so was the ambulance. It had been parked, with the police cars, in the East Gate lot. Gregor stopped on the steps of the library to look over the quad one more time, and Brian Sheehy stopped with him.

"It's a beautiful place," Brian said. "I think part of the reason we hate it so much is that we envy it. The local high school is not, exactly, this well equipped."

"I'm sure it's not," Gregor said.

Danny Kelly had met up with his partner, and they were walking together toward the parking lot, their heads bent toward each other as they talked through the distraction of the snow. All the lights in all the windows that faced the quad were on.

"What do you think?" Brian said. "That woman who had hysterics, were they real hysterics or put on? I don't trust people who have hysterics. I tend to think they're guilty."

"She was making enough accusations," Gregor said. "Who is this Philip she was talking about, the one she said was hiding something?"

"I don't know," Brian said. "We get to know a few of the people at the school, especially if they've been around long enough, but that's not one I've run into."

"And members of the faculty buying drugs from Michael Feyre, do you think that's plausible?"

"Hell, yes," Brian said, "and not the ones you'd necessarily think either. A lot of the leftover hippies have gone organic in their old age."

"It might be a motive," Gregor said. "Get rid of Michael Feyre because he could expose you as a customer. Get rid of Mark because he'd heard about it from Michael Feyre. Get rid of Edith because she knew something that pointed to you as the killer of Michael Feyre or as Mark's poisoner. You do realize that she couldn't possibly have taken that cyanide before she went up to the catwalk? It would have worked too fast."

"Yeah, I know," Brian said. "She must have taken it on her own up there. I've already told Danny to be on the lookout for something she was carrying. Candy is traditional, isn't it?"

"It is. But it could have been in anything. A sandwich. One of those sandwich cookies with the creme filling. She could have carried it around for days before she ate it. Which I suspect was the idea."

"You've got to wonder if the same wasn't done to Mark DeAvecca."

Gregor shook his head. "Couldn't have been. The killer couldn't have been sure that Mark would eat whatever he gave him. Mark wasn't eating much. And besides, that poisoning had been going on for weeks."

"You've got a look on your face that says you know what's going on here."

Gregor looked up into the darkness. The snow came down at him in swirls and curtains, melting as soon as it touched his skin. If this went on for another few hours, the town would be snowed in. He wondered how often that happened.

"No," he said, "I don't have it all figured out. I know what *must* be true, but I'll be damned if I know how it makes any sense."

TWO

1

Marta Coelho knew that she was not behaving rationally. She had spent too much of her life holding herself in not to realize when her self-control had vanished or to understand how hard it would be to get it back. It had started last night, long before Edith had fallen to the library floor, dead and horrible looking. It had begun when she had not been able to sit in her office for one more minute. That was when she had stood up to walk around, to visit whoever else had come in to work, only to realize that she couldn't. In the last few days, she had alienated every other faculty member she had established any friendly acquaintance with. She hadn't even been aware that she was doing it. James Hallwood would barely say hello to her in passing. Philip Candor was staying out of sight, and the last time she had gone to his apartment he had made it clear that she was invading his privacy. Even Cherie seemed to be avoiding her. Marta couldn't remember what she'd said to Cherie. All of a sudden her time at Windsor seemed like a long, black tunnel where all the sights and sounds of ordinary life were blacked out. She had never reconciled herself to a year teaching in this place. She had hated it from the start, at first because of what it said about her—*not good enough,* the words kept ringing in her mind, *not good enough for a real job*—and in the end because of what it was. She hadn't wanted to stay in the world in which she had grown up. That was true enough. She couldn't have stayed there, if only because her interest in books and ideas and scholarship was natural. It was not something she had taken on in order to escape the pointlessness of the existence she had seen in the lives of all the people around here. But there was pointlessness here, too, and it was a hundred times worse. The people she had grown up among did necessary work. They built things and fixed things and cleaned things. It all had to be done if the world was going to function. The people here did nothing that anybody would miss if they stopped doing it. Even the "education" they provided was a hothouse flower that had very little to do with the real world in which most people had to live, in which they themselves had to live. It was an education in attitude, not in ideas, and like all educations in attitude it produced people proud of what they were instead of what they did.

The last straw, however, had been Edith; and now that it was daylight again and Marta could look out over the quad at the snow, still coming down in thick curtains, and the Houses and the trees, she had to admit that what scared her the most was that she thought she was about to die. She'd read a few mystery novels in her time. Wasn't she the perfect candidate for the next dead body? She knew too much about everybody, and she'd been running around like an addled chicken for days, letting everybody know just how much she knew. She knew more than she'd said, too, and just how much more had been on full display in the library last night when she'd blurted out her protest to Alice Makepeace like a character in a bad movie, a parody movie, not even one intended to be serious. If this *had* been a movie, she would be lying dead on her own kitchen floor right this minute, her head smashed in by the edge of her microwave oven. Except, Marta thought, that this murderer did not use household objects. This murderer used poison. The only question was how he had used poison on Michael Feyre.

It was eight o'clock, and Marta couldn't stand the idea of staying in her apartment one more minute. The cafeteria had been running on weekend hours all week. That meant there was a buffet set out every morning from eight to ten, to allow both students and faculty time to sleep in. Theoretically, they were all "engaging" each other over the "events" of the last few days. Originally, they were supposed to be "engaging" each other over the emotions unleashed by the suicide of Michael Feyre. Marta wondered what the students were saying now, when so many of them had witnessed Edith's fall, and the police, and all the rest of it. She couldn't stand the idea of walking into that and having to eat breakfast on her own, as if she were still in high school and the town pariah, too odd and studious to fit into any of the existing social groups.

I have to get out of here, she thought, and then she realized she didn't have to go out onto campus at all. Barrett faced Main Street. She just had to go out the front door and into town. Her hair was still wet from her shower. She didn't own a hair dryer because she hated the way they made newly cleaned hair feel instantly dirty again. She got a wool snow cap out of the pile of things on the bench near her door. She had to unearth it from under scarves and gloves. She didn't wear hats normally. Then she circled back to her bedroom and changed into jeans and a sweater. It was interesting how easily she could be transformed from Upper-Middle-Class Professional Intellectual Woman back to Marta from the Neighborhood. She felt like one of the mice that had been pulling Cinderella's carriage, for a few moments transformed into a magnificent horse, now transformed back again and never to be returned.

The House was quiet. If students were up and about, picking apart the death of Edith Braxner, they were not doing it in the Barrett House common rooms. Although Barrett fronted on Main Street, its front door didn't open there, but to the side. Marta went out onto the side porch and looked around. There was a lot going on, much more than she had expected. The street seemed to be even more clogged with people than it was usually. She came around to the front and made her way onto Main Street proper, and then she saw what was going on. There were half a dozen large vans parked in the middle of the road down at Hayes House. They were blocking all traffic on Main; and although the police were out in force, trying to do something about the situation, they didn't look ready to move. Marta saw two women holding microphones, and then, looking more closely, paying attention finally, a few men carrying cameras on their shoulders. *Press,* she thought. She should have realized there would be Press. You couldn't have a murder at an expensive private school, where lots of famous people sent their children, without attracting attention from the media. The question was why they were at Hayes House instead of down here at the other end, at the library. Edith had died in the library.

Marta's immediate thought was that somebody else had died, and nobody had come to tell her. If she had been a member of the media, she would have called Hayes House the "locus of evil" or something like that. Maybe "locus" was too esoteric a word for a mass audience. Still, Michael Feyre had died in Hayes House. Mark DeAvecca had been poisoned in Hayes House. Now, if there was another one, it would be like one of those serial killer/slasher movies that had been all the rage while she was growing up.

She moved a little closer and saw that, although there were plenty of cameras and men and women with microphones and media vans and people asking other people to speak into audiotapes, there was no sign of an ambulance or of the pile of police vehicles that had been at the library last night. It wasn't likely that anything new had happened. She pressed even closer, trying to hear somebody saying something sensible, but nobody was. The media people were speaking in generalities and not even sensible generalities. There was a tall man in a long, formal coat right in front of her. She pressed against him, trying to get past.

He had turned around and was already holding out his hand to her before she realized who it was: Gregor Demarkian, the detective or consultant or whatever he was who had wanted to see the nook in the library where Mark DeAvecca used to go to read. Marta had no idea if she was happy to see him. He was there, just as he had been there in Ridenour. He did not make her feel intimidated, or frightened, or shy, which she often did with people she didn't know well, and especially with men. She took his hand, feeling a little embarrassed for him because he was holding it out like that. He didn't seem to be embarrassed for himself.

"It's Marta Coelho," he said, polite, not questioning.

She nodded. "It's Portuguese," she said. "My name, I mean. Coelho is a Portuguese name, and my family named me Marta instead of Martha because Marta is the Portuguese form."

"Mine's Armenian."

"Yes," Marta said. She thought they both sounded like idiots. "I came out to walk. I didn't realize all this was going on. There hasn't been another . . . another death, has there?"

"No," Gregor Demarkian said, "the media has just caught up with us, that's all. It had to happen eventually."

"Everybody's been saying that for days," Marta said. "They even said that when Michael died, and then it didn't happen. You never got what you wanted last night, did you? A view out that window. Although I still don't see what you could have seen, even if you had looked. There's nothing there."

"So everybody keeps telling me," Gregor said. "Edith Braxner wanted to look though, didn't she?"

"Did she?" There was actually a CBS van in the street—not just the local CBS van, with the local CBS reporter, but a national one. She looked around and caught sight of John Whateverhisnamewas, the very pretty one who sat in for Dan Rather from time to time on the evening news. "Maybe Edith was just up there," she said. "People did go up there every once in a while. Not a lot of people. The catwalk made people dizzy. But some people did. Maybe Edith just went up to read for a while."

"Maybe," Gregor agreed. "Do you know what she was doing before she went up there?"

"I don't know," Marta said. "I was in my office. Not that I was getting a lot of work done. I've been distracted beyond belief this week. But I was there for over an hour. She was at dinner though."

"Oh? Did you eat dinner with her?"

"No," Marta said. There was no reason to tell him that Edith had barely been speaking to her, or that not much of anybody else had been either. "She was sitting with Cherie Wardrop and Melissa, Cherie's partner. We're very tolerant at Windsor Academy. When Cherie and Melissa came, they got their pictures in the school magazine and a whole story about how they met."

"That's not a bad thing, surely?"

"Oh no," Marta said. "No, it's not a bad thing at all. It's just one of the things that surprised me when I first came here. I went to an ordinary public high school, you know. I didn't know much about schools like this. I thought they were much more conservative."

"Did you know if Edith looked odd in any way during dinner? Did you pay that much attention to her?"

"She looked normal enough," Marta said. "But then Edith always looked very stern in a way. Very disapproving. She wasn't like that, really, but that was how she looked. Anyway, she had dinner with Cherie and Melissa, and then when she was leaving James Hallwood was coming in, and she had a talk with him at the door, and then, of course, there was Alice."

"Of course?"

"Well, Alice is everywhere. It's as if she can clone herself. She came into dinner late and she didn't look happy, so I was hoping she wouldn't notice me for once and she didn't. They had words, Alice and Edith did. I didn't hear what they were."

"How did you know they 'had words,' then?"

"Because of the way they looked, talking to each other," Marta said. "Edith was definitely not part of Alice's fan club, not that too many people are around here. Alice is a force of nature, and they all do what she tells them to do, but they don't like it. Maybe that's why I've always had so much trouble. I haven't always done what she's told me to do."

"What kind of thing does she tell people to do?"

"Oh, nothing outrageous," Marta said. "She organizes things. We had a Winter Solstice party, for instance, because Alice fancies herself as a pagan, and she thinks pagan rituals are more environmentally sound than Christian or Jewish ones. Things like that."

"And you had objections to a Winter Solstice party?"

"No," Marta said. "It's not that I've ever objected to anything in particular; it's more that I've not been very happy with the whole tone of the place. I didn't even realize that until today. I mean, I probably did realize it. I just hadn't realized it consciously. And now of course I've killed any chance I'd ever had of staying on next year. They're very big on loyalty around here. They won't forget that performance I put on in the library last night."

"It was a very informative performance," Gregor said.

Marta shrugged. "I've been scared to death all night. I feel like I've set myself up to be the next victim. I'm the perfect target, the Woman Who Knows Too Much."

"I doubt it," Gregor said. "It's not common in real life, you know. Outside of organized crime, it's very unusual for murderers to run around killing people just because they think those people will say something inconvenient to the police. It's different, of course, if the witness actually knows. You didn't give the impression last night that you do actually know. Or do you?"

"Do you mean, know who murdered Edith?"

"Know that, yes, or know who might have murdered Michael Feyre, or who poisoned Mark DeAvecca. Actually know, actually have evidence. Not just speculate."

"Of course I don't know," Marta said. "I'd be surprised if anybody did."

"Could Edith Braxner have known, and not have told the police about it or a neutral person?"

"I don't know who a neutral person would be," Marta said. "The Board of Trustees, maybe. But not even then. They wouldn't be neutral. They'd want to protect the school. Everybody does around here. The institution comes first. They like to say it doesn't, but it does."

"I think that's normal, too, for institutions."

"Maybe," Marta said. "This is the first school I've ever been at where I wasn't a student. This is the first time I've ever not been a student. You can't count summer jobs, or jobs in the term, can you, because you're still a student even though you're temporarily doing something else. Do you know what I was thinking? Half the people in this place have never been out of school. Not ever. They've been students and they've been teachers, but they've never been anything else. Their whole lives have been caught up in grading and being graded and in semesters and in years that start in September. For most people, the year starts in January. You should hear us all talk. Cherie Wardrop said the other day that she really hoped that next year would be better than this one because she'd had so much trouble as a houseparent this year, and she wasn't talking about the things that have happened since Christmas. She was talking about the things that have happened since September. James Hallwood said the same thing. And Philip." Marta shrugged. "Cherie probably hated it the worst, what with Michael in her house, but everybody's been complaining. They were complaining before Michael Feyre ever died."

Marta was sure Mr. Demarkian was about to tell her that complaining was perfectly natural, too, but she already knew that. She trained her attention on John Whoever, now set up and talking in front of Hayes House's big front windows, looking appropriately solemn while reporting a story in which two people had died. The snow had been very bad overnight. It wasn't only media vans that were blocking traffic on Main, it was snow dunes as well, created by a road clearance department that liked to make big piles of white stuff in what were supposed to be parking spaces.

Marta just wanted to go home—not to Barrett House, or even back to Yale, but *home.*

What worried her was that she didn't think such a place had ever existed.

2

Mark DeAvecca was bored. He was screamingly bored. He was outrageously bored. He had the television on in his hospital room and was sitting up in the visitor's chair with a tray of hospital food in front of him, and he felt *fine,* except, of course, that he was starving. It was impossible to get them to give you enough to eat around here, and he didn't need another lecture about how badly he'd handled the McDonald's Jimmy had brought for him the other day. Yesterday. It was only yesterday. His mother had brought him a copy of *Don Quixote,* which she said was one of his father's favorite books. That was good, especially since he was able to read again, but it wasn't enough to keep him from going crazy. Now there were all these news stories, and camera crews and television reporters standing right outside Hayes House, and he was stuck here staring at a little cup of tapioca pudding that the hospital nutritionist insisted on calling a "portion." The woman was insane. A portion was half a gallon of ice cream, or one entire extra large sausage and pepperoni pizza, or three or four of those Triple Play appetizer samplers you could get at Chili's. Mark's mother was not very fond of Chili's, but Jimmy absolutely loved it; and when they were all home in Connecticut, Mark and Geoff could get Jimmy to take them out to the one in Waterbury. Mark thought there was nothing on the planet he wanted right now more than he wanted to go to Chili's.

A reporter on CNN was saying, "Edith Braxner was born in 1948 in . . ."

Mark didn't catch where she'd been born, only the date. She was even more ancient than he'd thought she was. He poked at the tapioca pudding with his finger. It was a very odd consistency. He'd never had tapioca pudding before. He'd decided to hate it without trying it.

There was a cough on the other side of the room. Mark looked up from the chair and saw Gregor Demarkian standing in the doorway.

"Oh, good," he said. "I'm so bored, you wouldn't believe it. Couldn't you tell these idiots it's okay for me to go? I feel fine. I really do. And it's not like I'm going to go drinking any more caffeine. Even I can get the message of 'it was enough to kill me.' I'm not stupid."

Gregor came all the way into the room and sat down on the edge of Mark's bed. They never had put Mark into a single room, they'd just failed to fill the other bed in this one. Mark thought Gregor looked tired.

"I *am* fine, you know," he said. "There's no reason to keep me cooped up here going stir-crazy while the only interesting thing that's ever happened at Windsor is in full-tilt boogie. All I want to do is go back to my dorm."

"And give the person who tried to kill you another shot?"

"I promise not to eat any of the food at school at all," Mark said solemnly. "I won't take so much as a Life Saver from any person on campus. I'll have everything I eat brought in on delivery. I'll double-check the seal on every can of Sprite. How's that?"

"I think you ought to consider the possibility that your mother isn't going to let you go back to school at all, not even to finish the year," Gregor said. "That's been the general drift of the conversations I've heard."

"Yeah, I know," Mark said. "It's stupid though. I mean, okay, under the circumstances, I can see my not coming back next year, if they'd even have me, which I don't think they would. But does it make sense to make me repeat my sophomore year of high school because my mother wants to blow this place up?"

"She's got good reason to want to blow this place up. And there might not be much of a year left for you to finish. I take it you've been watching the news."

"Yeah. Somebody killed Dr. Braxner."

"Poisoned her, yes. The usual result of this sort of thing is that parents take their children out, even once the murderer is caught and there is no more danger. It wouldn't be surprising if the school was forced to close down."

"It won't be," Mark said. "There's way too much money behind it. Just watch."

"I will. Do me a favor and answer a few questions for me since you think you're feeling so much better."

"Shoot. It's got to be better than sitting here waiting to see if they declare Windsor a war zone and send in Christiane Amanpour."

Gregor stood up and went to the window. He was, Mark realized, very tense. He just hid it well so that it showed up only in the stiffness of his back. Mark began to feel a little uncomfortable. He wasn't as irrepressible as he was trying to appear. He was scared to death on about seven levels. He just didn't want to live his life that way. Fear caught up to you eventually, if you let it get to you at all. He'd seen that more times than he could count.

"Tell me again about the night Michael Feyre died," Gregor said. "You were in the library, in the same nook where Edith Braxner was last night. You were doing what again—reading something."

"Reading a medical encyclopedia," Mark said. "Yeah. Well, you know, I didn't know I was being poisoned; I thought I was sick."

"And you were sick, that's right, isn't it? You weren't feeling well, and you weren't thinking well."

"Right," Mark said. "That's why I thought what I saw could have been a hallucination. I mean, I'd never had a hallucination before, but with everything else that had been happening to me, I thought it was perfectly possible. And I didn't know the half of it. It's only in the last twenty-four hours that I've realized just how odd I had been. People around here must think I'm a real idiot."

"We'll deal with that later," Gregor said. "You saw this figure on the ground, dressed in black. You went out to see who it was. You found nothing. Who did you tell about it?"

"Philip Candor, like I said," Mark said. "I ran into him going back to Hayes House. And then I got confused, like I said. I was sort of wandering around, and I'd forget where I was going. And I went back again. I think I talked to half a dozen other people."

"Edith Braxner?"

"I don't remember."

"Who else?"

"Well, I talked to Cherie when I got back to the dorm, right before I went up to my room. That's because Sheldon was screaming at me again. I was back late or not acting the way I was supposed to act or something. I didn't go into a lot of detail, or anything, I just sort of mentioned that I thought I'd seen somebody passed out in the snow because otherwise I just looked like an irresponsible jerk. You know. So I said I'd seen somebody and gone to look, and I didn't think I was bad. And then, you know."

"You went upstairs and found the body."

"Right. I think of a body as something on a slab, you know. But I guess that's what it was—Michael's body."

"Do you know what autoasphyxiation erotica is?"

"That thing where guys hang themselves so they can jerk off?" Mark said. "Yeah, I know what that is, and don't ask. Yeah, I think Michael did that, sort of. But only sort of. According to him, masturbation was for losers."

"Masturbation was for losers, but he practiced autoasphyxiation?"

"Not exactly. He got girls to do things for him. While he was, you know. This is according to what he said, though, and you can't trust that. I mean, let's face it, guys lie all the time, especially about sex. Michael said he'd get girls to tie him up like that and then blow him, you know. So it wasn't just him himself. He'd blackmail them into it."

"Blackmail them how?"

"Well," Mark said, "he sold drugs to people, right? At least he said he did, and other people said they bought them from him, so I guess we can believe that. He'd threaten them and tell them he'd tell the administration and they'd get expelled or something, you know. And not just the drugs. He had dirt on just about everybody. But it can't be that autoasphyxiation thing anyway, can it? Not even if he was doing it to himself."

"Why not?" Gregor asked.

"Well," Mark said, thinking that if Gregor was the great detective he was supposed to be, he should already know, "if there had been, there would have been semen, wouldn't there? And his dick would have been hanging out. Excuse my language. But his dick wasn't hanging out when I found him. If it had been, I'd have noticed it. And I haven't heard anything about there being semen."

Gregor looked impressed. "Very good. There was no semen mentioned in the medical report, no. As for his, uh, penis being exposed, if he was engaged in the act with another person, that person could have—"

"Not possible," Mark said. "He couldn't have gotten a girl up there. We have parietal hours on Saturday and Sunday afternoons from two to five. That's it. Otherwise, no members of the other sex allowed in the Houses above the first-floor common rooms. And don't tell me he could have sneaked her in there or that she could have sneaked out. Go look at Hayes. There's one stairwell going up three floors, and there are doors opening on it all the way. Weekend nights, the place is full of people running back and forth. There aren't even any fire escapes except for one at each of the sides, and you have to go through the bathrooms to access those. He couldn't have gotten a girl up there without somebody seeing, and she couldn't have gotten out again without somebody seeing."

"Maybe it's not a girl we're looking for," Gregor said.

"Wrong again," Mark said. "Michael was not a decent human being. I mean, okay, I think we get a little too trite and silly with all the hymns to tolerance at Windsor, but once I'd known Michael for a while I could almost see the point. He hated homosexuals. He truly and sincerely hated them. It wasn't homophobia and all that stuff people talk about. It was pure hostility. He might have raped some guy in the butt if he was feeling particularly vicious, but he wouldn't let another guy do something to him; and he really wouldn't have let some other guy get him tied up."

"Sometimes, what people protest most—"

"Please, Mr. Demarkian. I've heard it all before. But I knew Michael Feyre."

"All right," Gregor said. "Let's try a couple of nights ago, the night you ended up in here. You fell asleep on the bed in my room. You woke up. Then what?"

"I went back to campus," Mark said, "and I went to the Student Center to get some coffee because I was tired and I didn't want to go to sleep right away. Oh, wait. I ate the food in your room that room service left you."

"I noticed that. That's all right. What about when you went back to campus?"

"I went to get coffee," Mark said, trying to think, "and I wasn't moving too well. I was really tired. I don't get tired like that anymore. Do you think that was the arsenic?"

"Maybe. It could have been the caffeine."

"But caffeine is supposed to hype you up," Mark said. "Okay, never mind. I ran into Alice Makepeace, and she got me a cup of coffee. A big one. Don't go jumping to conclusions. I asked her to. A big one with sugar. And she sat down with me for a while and said, well—" Mark had no idea how he was supposed to put this. It was always difficult to tell what adults would take in stride and what would make them go ballistic. "She accused me of being jealous of her, uh, relationship with Michael. She said I brought you here to hurt the school and hurt her because I was jealous."

"Were you?"

"Hell, no," Mark said. "I mean, she's gorgeous to look at, you know, I'm not dead; but she doesn't do it for me at all. She makes my skin crawl. She's one of those people who uses 'appropriate' all the time. You know what I mean? She finds Johnny and Susie screwing on the dining room table right in the middle of lunchtime and she says it's 'inappropriate.' The word drives me nuts."

"So you had coffee with her and listened to her lecture," Gregor said.

"And that was it," Mark said. "I got really upset. I mean, wouldn't you be? So I got up to get myself another cup of coffee, and she got snide and said in the shape I was in I'd never make it, so she went and got me the second one, too, full of sugar. And then I left the cafeteria and took the coffee up to the lounge to drink it in peace because there isn't ever anybody there at that time at night, and then when I was finished with it I threw the cup away and came back to Hayes House."

"And?"

Mark got out of his chair. He was not only bored, he was restless. "And," he said, "I was in trouble again. Welcome to my life at Windsor. You're supposed to stop into the House before dinner and sign in, as a sort of check that they know you're around somewhere. I forgot about it when I went to see you. Actually, I was with you longer than I expected to be and then I fell asleep and *then* I forgot about it when I woke up, but it didn't make a damned bit of difference what had happened because Sheldon was after my hide on any excuse. So I came back in and there was a big fuss, and Cherie took me to her apartment to get me out of Sheldon's way while she tried to calm Sheldon down, which wasn't easy. And I was still hungry, you know, so she let me have one of these prepackaged ice cream sundae things she keeps in her freezer. And then I wanted another cup of coffee and she made me one because Sheldon never lets me use his kitchen. He won't even let me use my electric kettle. He says it's a fire hazard."

"Is it?"

"I've been using it all year and nothing's happened yet," Mark said.

"So she gave you the coffee," Gregor said. "Then what?"

"Then I took the coffee back to Sheldon's apartment. And he started in on me practically immediately. I was going to spill it. I was going to ruin his carpet. It isn't his carpet in the first place. It belongs to the school. I was a big problem to have around. I was invading his privacy. Yada yada yada. So I gulped the coffee down and brought the cup back to Cherie's apartment because Sheldon didn't want it in his sink. Ask him why. I'd stopped listening. Then I went to my room and closed the door and tried to read. I just sort of sat around for a while. Maybe ten minutes. Then Sheldon came barging in on me to tell me to turn the CD player off, except that it wasn't on. He just needs to think he can hear it even when I have the earphones on. Except this time I didn't even have the earphones on. It was off. He comes barging into my room, and all of a sudden I felt really sick to my stomach. So I jumped up and pushed him out of the way, and he fell against the door. And he yelled at me. And that's all I remember. Really. I started throwing up, I remember that. But I don't remember anything else until I woke up here in the middle of the night and thought I was home because I saw Mom. It was not good."

"No," Gregor said. "I can see that it wasn't good. Do you mind if I ask why it is you want to continue the year in this place? I know you somewhat. I remember you very well from that time in Holman. You've got a lot more going for you than anybody here seems to recognize. Why put up with this nonsense?"

"Because," Mark said, "if I don't, they win."

Gregor Demarkian sighed. Mark could tell Gregor had no idea what he was talking about, but in a way that was all right. His own mother didn't get it exactly either. Sometime during their conversation, Gregor had shrugged off his coat and left it on the bed. Now he stood up, picked it up, and put it on.

"I've got to go," he said. "Your mother and stepfather are supposed to be on their way here, but it may take them a little time. The media have discovered Windsor."

"It must be a zoo," Mark said.

"Let's just say that there isn't any actual moving traffic on Main Street," Gregor said. "That's why you're getting all those wonderful pictures of Hayes House on CNN. Just sit around and rest some more, Mark, will you? It won't be all that much longer before we get this cleared up. Then you can work things out with your mother any way you want. In the meantime, it isn't safe for you on that campus, and you should know it."

"Of course I know it," Mark said politely; but he was lying, and he knew that if his mother could have heard the sound of his voice, she would have known he was lying.

Gregor went out. Mark waited for a while, hearing his footsteps in the hall. Then he started thinking. He would have to be very careful. His mother was supposed to be on her way here; and even with the mess caused by a full-blown media blitz, it wasn't impossible that she was already down in the lobby. It would be just his luck to come flying out of the elevators only to come face-to-face with Jimmy, who would sympathize but not be much help. It would be almost as bad, if not worse, if he made it out of the hospital and started hitchhiking back to school, only to be spotted by both Mom and Jimmy as they drove in the other direction on their way to see him. Then he'd be subjected not only to capture, but to capture in full view of the American television public, who'd probably just love the sight of a pampered rich kid being hauled off to purgatory by his very own mother. He just wanted to get out, that's all. He just wanted to be out in the open air, walking around in the real world, instead of cooped up in a place where they treated french fries as lethal weapons.

Besides, he had this terrible feeling that if he didn't get back to school, he'd end up missing the whole thing. There he would be, the only living star of this drama, and he wouldn't know anything about it because he wouldn't have had a part in it. He didn't believe what Mr. Demarkian said about the murderer trying to get at him a second time. He knew that somebody must have tried to kill him once—otherwise, he wouldn't have been full of arsenic—but since it seemed to him to be self-evident that he was both completely harmless and completely clueless about whatever had been going on with Michael Feyre, he had trouble taking it seriously. And he would be careful this time. He wouldn't eat anything on campus except stuff from vending machines or in secure packaging, and he'd check the seals. He wouldn't drink coffee at all.

What he couldn't do was sit around here any longer. He'd been feeling awful for months, and worse than awful ever since he'd gotten back from Christmas break. Now that he felt like himself again, he saw no reason at all to watch life pass him by as a badly reported fifteen-second clip on *Headline News*.

THREE

1

Gregor didn't see Liz or Jimmy on his way out of the hospital and didn't spot them from the cab as he was making his way back to Main Street, although he did look out for them. He didn't trust Mark on this particular thing. He'd have trusted him to keep his mouth shut and to back him up in a fight—not that he ever got into physical fights these days; the popular culture image of law enforcement in the United States was ridiculous to tell the truth, but Gregor had been sixteen once himself. He knew that gleam in the eye when he saw it. Mark was bored, and there was nothing more dangerous on this planet than a sixteen-year-old boy who is bored.

Since there wasn't anything he could do about it, and since he had more to do to finish up here than he liked, Gregor put it out of his mind as soon as he got out of the cab in front of Barrett House. He would have gotten out in front of Hayes, but although the worst of the traffic jam had been cleared, there were still vans parked there. They came accompanied by little knots of men and women standing around with nothing to do. They were here only on the hope that, this close to the crime, something else would happen. Gregor always wondered what these people wanted to happen. Didn't they think one murder was enough? Maybe they expected the perpetrator to reveal himself in a dramatic on-air surrender and the case to be cleared on the spot. Probably they were just hoping for an arrest, Gregor thought. Arrests played well on air. So did perp walks. At least it was something to show and not tell on the evening news.

He walked through East Gate and looked around. This House immediately to his left was Barrett. To his right and a little ahead of him was Ridenour Library. That made the House immediately across the quad Doyle, and the one to the left of that on the same side Martinson. It was Martinson he was looking for. He took his notebook out of the inside pocket of his jacket and checked it again. Last night, when he'd finally had time to sit and think after the mess of Edith Braxner's death, he'd written down everything he needed to know and everyone he needed to talk to. He'd come to the same conclusion he'd come to many hours before, and that had only been reinforced since: there was only one person in this cast of characters who *could* have done all the things that needed to be done to kill Michael Feyre and poison Mark DeAvecca, and in the end it was the death of Michael Feyre that was the key to understanding what had happened here. Unfortunately, he didn't know the why of any of it, and without the why he knew he couldn't get Brian Sheehy to agree to an arrest.

He crossed to the center of the quad and then down the parallel walk to Martinson. He tried opening Martinson's front door and found it locked. *Well, he thought, it would be.* There was nothing to stop anybody who wanted to from coming in from Main Street. He found the button for the bell and rang.

It was the middle of a weekday. If nobody had answered the door, Gregor would have put the lack of response down to everyone being out, although he found that rather odd for a day with no classes and a lot of boarding students. He rang the bell again, just for good measure, and was surprised to hear the sound of footsteps and shuffling behind the door. A moment later it was opened, and he was standing face-to-face with a tall man in chinos, black T-shirt, and good tweed blazer. The wire-rimmed glasses were, he thought, the perfect touch. Whoever this man was, he could pose for the cover of *Esquire* in the role of Hip Urban Intellectual.

The man stood very still, watching him. He had steady blue eyes and an expression of bemusement on his face. Gregor couldn't get past the feeling that he had seen this man before, somewhere, and that the where had not been a pleasant place.

The man stepped back and said, "Mr. Demarkian, I was wondering when you'd show up here. I expect Mark told you about our conversation on the night Michael died."

"You're Philip Candor, then?" Gregor said.

"I'm Philip Candor." Philip smiled, very slightly, and that wave of conviction passed over Gregor again. He *had* seen this man before. He just couldn't remember when.

"My apartment's this way," Philip said.

Gregor followed him down a narrow hall to the right, thinking as he went that the school Houses had been similarly designed to accommodate faculty and students. Philip opened a door at the end of the hall and ushered Gregor through. This apartment was like the one belonging to Sheldon in Hayes, but far less pretentious, and because of it far more masculine. There were hundreds of books, stacked two deep in all the bookcases and littering all the tables and surfaces. They reminded Gregor of Tibor back on Cavanaugh Street, especially because the books looked read. There was a CD player and a tall stack of CDs in a cheap, plastic revolving case. The CDs included everything from Mozart to Johnny Cash to Lynyrd Skynyrd to Miles Davis.

Gregor took a seat in a club chair without waiting to be asked. Philip Candor stayed standing.

"Would you like me to get you some coffee? I always seem to be offering coffee to people who come here."

"Thank you, but no," Gregor said. "Have some yourself, if you'd like, of course."

"I would, if I liked," Philip said. Then he came around and sat down on the couch, close enough so that his knees would have touched Gregor's if he leaned only a little forward. He leaned back instead. "Mark's all right from what I've heard. That's a relief."

"Yes, it is," Gregor agreed. He took his coat off. He reached into his jacket and took out his notebook again. He knew what questions he needed to ask. He couldn't get started because he couldn't get past the increasingly intense conviction that he knew this man's face. He looked at his notes again. He looked at the face again. Philip Candor was still smiling.

"Dear God," Gregor said suddenly, "you're Leland Beech."

"Very good, Mr. Demarkian, but you're slipping. I've been sitting here for days, expecting you to walk through my door and recognize me immediately."

"It's been a long time," Gregor said. "It's been, I don't know—"

"Coming onto twenty-five years. If I'd stayed in jail, I'd have had another ten to go before I could be considered for parole. But of course I wouldn't be considered for parole, not seriously, not in this climate."

"I remember the escape," Gregor said. "I didn't realize you'd never been picked up again. But how did you get here? What are you doing here?"

"Teaching mathematics. I've been teaching mathematics here for more than a decade."

"Do you know anything about mathematics?"

"Of course," Philip said, "I've got a very good degree. Two of them, to be accurate. A bachelor's from Williams. A master's from Tufts. About a year after the escape, I took the GED in Massachusetts and passed with flying colors. My father may have been a lunatic, but he did make sure we were all literate. Then I took the SATs and did very well indeed. I applied to Williams and they took me. I didn't really lie, you know, about anything but my name and my arrest record."

"That's a lot to lie about," Gregor said.

Philip shrugged. "I told them the truth as far as it went. Growing up with a survivalist lunatic who'd gone sovereign before I was six years old. Growing up living off the land and learning to read from the Bible and those amazing books he had. I still remember those books. I even have them. My own copies, of course. The originals were destroyed in the firebombing. Everything was destroyed in the firebombing. I wasn't sorry to see it go."

"You did your best to defend it at the time," Gregor pointed out.

Philip dismissed this. "Look at it in context. Nobody ever does anymore, but you should. I was two days past my eighteenth birthday. I'd never seen more than four or five people who weren't directly related to me since my father had taken us all out of town and set us up in that cabin. I'd been brought up to believe that the entire world was plotting against us, not against the United States or against the people of Idaho, but against us, the Beech family, we were the big prize the FBI and the CIA and the Vatican and everybody else you can think of meant to wipe off the face of the earth. And then what happened? The FBI showed up at our front door and started shooting at us."

"That's not the way it happened, and you know it," Gregor said.

"But it is the way it happened," Philip insisted. "At least, that's what it looked like from the inside, and I was on the inside. You can show me all the evidence you want that my father was stockpiling weapons and doing God knows what else up there. I heard all the evidence about that at the trial. But that isn't what it looked like from the inside. What it looked like was a bunch of guys with helicopters and machine guns ganging up on us. And even now, even after all this time and everything I know, it still looks like that to me. What difference did it make if he was stockpiling weapons? There were just the six of us. He was too much of a loner even to band together with other loners. We weren't a threat to the security of the United States. We weren't even a threat to the peace and safety of Dubran, Idaho. We were just up there doing our thing and not bothering anybody."

"He bought three rifles and enough ammunition to take out the state of Illinois from a federal officer," Gregor said.

"No better than entrapment," Philip said. "I've been out in the real world for a long time now. I don't have any of my father's peculiar ideas about politics or people. Hell, I'm probably a pretty standard issue political liberal. But I've never understood what went on up there that day. I've never understood why it was necessary. Dubran. Ruby Ridge. Waco. What's the point, really? Why do people find it so hard just to let their neighbors be a little eccentric?"

"You shot and killed two federal officers," Gregor said. "I was there. I saw you do it."

"I shot at them because they were shooting at me," Philip said. "I did not start shooting first. Neither did he. The whole incident was manufactured and, worse than that, it was manufactured for television. It's why I didn't major in sociology, did you know that?"

"How could I?"

"True enough. It *is* why I didn't major in sociology though. My sophomore year at Williams, I took an upper-level course called American Rebellions. It covered things like the antiwar movements in the sixties, but it also covered people like us. I barely made it through to the final exam. People on the outside really don't get it at all."

"But you're not on the inside any longer," Gregor pointed out. "You didn't go back to Idaho. You didn't, what did you call it?"

"Go sovereign."

"That."

"No, I didn't," Philip said. "At first I didn't because I knew that's what the authorities expected me to do. It's what people like me do do when they escape from the federal penitentiary. So I came East instead and moved into an apartment in Boston and went to work doing day labor and did all the other things I told you about. Took the GED. Applied to Williams. They would never have thought to look for me at a place like Williams. Of course, Williams would never have accepted me if they knew I was Leland Beech."

"But it wasn't just for convenience," Gregor insisted, "or even as a smart way to stay away from the law. You never went sovereign. You built an entirely different life. And my guess is, you couldn't go back to what you were now even if it was the only way to save yourself from going back to prison."

"Don't bet on it, Mr. Demarkian. I have no intention of going back to prison."

"That may not be up to you."

Philip smiled again. It was one of the eeriest smiles Gregor had ever seen.

"You came to ask me about the night Michael Feyre died. Why don't you ask me?"

Gregor was aware that something was wrong here. Philip Candor—he had to think of this man as Philip Candor; he was too unlike the boy Leland Beech had been to share the same name—was hiding something. Gregor wondered if he'd taken that name, Candor, on purpose. He probably had.

"All right," Gregor said. "The night Michael Feyre died, Mark DeAvecca was in the library, in the catwalk nook we found Edith Braxner in last night just before she fell to her death. He says that he looked out the window there and saw somebody lying under a small stand of evergreens, somebody wearing black from head to foot. He came out of the library and went down to see who it was because, he said, he thought the person might have been drinking and passed out, and it was cold—"

"It was freezing," Philip said. "It was under nine below."

"Quite. Mark got to the evergreens and found nothing there. He then came back through the faculty wing of the library and stopped for a moment to talk to Marta Coelho. Then he came on out the front and started to cross the quad and ran into you. He said he told you all about it."

"He did."

"And did you believe him?"

"No," Philip said. "He wasn't in good shape. We've heard all about the caffeine and arsenic poisoning now, but at the time I simply assumed he was wasted. And hallucinating. But just in case, after I sent him back to Hayes House, I went out to check."

"Did you? Did you find anything?"

"No," Philip said. "There was nobody at or under the evergreens when I looked, and there was no sign that anybody had been there. No footprints in the snow. Nothing like that, at least that I could see. Of course, even if somebody had been there when Mark looked out from the library, there might not have been any traces left behind. The ground was solid with ice. We'd had a couple of bad storms right before."

"So you thought, what? That Mark was hallucinating?"

"I thought he was behaving fairly normally for a habitual druggie. He may have been hallucinating. He may just have seen something and misinterpreted it. My only concern was in case there really was someone passed out there because in that weather they could easily have frozen to death if they'd slept there overnight. So I checked, and there was nothing."

"What about the description Mark gave? Somebody all in black, from head to foot."

"It sounds like Alice, doesn't it?" Philip said. "You must have seen her by now, last night if not before. She's always wandering around in that cape and black leather pants as if she thinks she's about to be cast in a movie with the young Marlon Brando. But it needn't have been Alice. Black is very fashionable around here. People think it distinguishes them from the rah-rah cheerleader types they came here to escape. They think it's intellectual."

Philip Candor would not be susceptible to that kind of symbolism, Gregor thought. He switched directions. "According to Mark, Michael Feyre had a habit of blackmailing people, specifically women, by threatening to expose the fact that they'd bought drugs from him and taking payment for the blackmail in sexual favors."

Now Philip looked very, *very* amused. "You mean in blow jobs? Yes, Mr. Demarkian, I'd heard all about that. But it wasn't just blackmail about the drugs, and it wasn't just women, and it wasn't just sex. Michael was an out-and-out psychopath, the proverbial bad seed. He had no conscience at all, and he had a limitless appetite for sadism."

"Did he find out about your secret? Did he threaten to expose the fact that you are actually Leland Beech."

"No," Philip said. "I'm not a fool, Mr. Demarkian. I don't keep reminders of that part of my life lying around loose for people to find. There's nothing to connect me to Leland Beech here or anywhere else in the state of Massachusetts. To expose me, Michael would have had to be someone like you, someone with a connection to the case, or a true-crime buff who watched all the little documentaries on *Court*TV and A&E and the *Unsolved Mysteries* episodes. I've—well, we've, my family and myself—we've been the subject of one of those episodes and of an episode of *City Confidential*. I watched them both. More stupidity."

"And Michael had not watched them?"

"Michael's tastes in entertainment ran mostly to the pornographic. He was not all that bright, Mr. Demarkian. And he had nothing at all in the way of cultural literacy. He didn't read newspapers. He would have looked on *City Confidential* as just another newspaper, even if it is a television show. And I'm way out of his league. A lot of people here weren't though."

"Weren't out of his league?"

"Exactly."

"Such as who? Who do you think Michael Feyre had information on?"

"James Hallwood, for one," Philip said. "He was definitely pushing Hallwood on the drugs, if nothing else. There's no other way to explain the grade he got in English. Hallwood is not a pushover. He's never heard of grade inflation. Michael should have been flunking that course. He wasn't coming close."

Gregor checked his notebook. "Hallwood is Mark's English teacher?"

"And Michael's, yes. He does most of the sophomore English classes."

"Who else?"

"I don't really know, Mr. Demarkian. I only know who was nervous, and I probably don't know everybody who was nervous. Marta, for instance, was very nervous. But I can't see her buying drugs, and she doesn't strike me as the kind of person who has a deep, dark secret."

"What about Alice Makepeace?"

Philip laughed. "Michael was already getting everything he wanted out of Alice, and probably more."

"She was sleeping with a student. She would have been rightly afraid of having that exposed."

"Maybe," Philip said, "but I don't see why she'd suddenly be afraid of that with Michael when she was never afraid of it before. Michael wasn't the first one. There're been a string of them. It's what she does. I always thought she'd be happier than not to get thrown out of this place. I don't think her idea of a good time was growing old as a headmaster's wife."

"What about the houseparents in Hayes? Cherie Wardrop and Sheldon—nobody has ever used any name for him but Sheldon."

"Sheldon LeRouve. No, nobody does use any other name for him. A bitter, small-minded, spiteful man. The first time I ever had any sympathy for Mark DeAvecca was when he got stuck rooming with Sheldon. Cherie is gay and lives with her partner, Melissa."

"I know that. I've been in their apartment."

"So you must have been," Philip said. "They seem nice enough. They're school hoppers, though, which never makes administrations happy."

"What's a school hopper?"

"A faculty member who hops from school to school. Schools are like businesses. They like to keep a stable workforce as much as possible. And most teachers like to find a congenial place and stay in it. Some teachers get restless and move from school to school. They want different areas of the country or different educational philosophies or different people to talk to. It's a way of relieving boredom, mostly. With Cherie, I think Peter Makepeace thought that since she'd be able to share faculty housing with Melissa, which wasn't the case in most schools, she'd be more likely to stay here. It might be true. It also might be that it is Melissa who wants to move and not Cherie. Cherie's got a good degree in biology and a good teaching record. She could probably find a job anywhere except a religious school that wouldn't tolerate her sexual orientation."

"And any other school would?"

"She may just not have mentioned it," Philip said. "She'd have been living in faculty housing, and Melissa would have been living on her own. They could have kept it a secret if they wanted to. But they don't need to keep it secret here. So that couldn't be a reason for Michael Feyre to blackmail her."

"What about Edith Braxner?" Gregor asked. "Could Michael have been blackmailing her?"

"Not likely. Edith was our resident saint. She's the only person in the history of Windsor Academy ever to turn in house accounts that actually balanced."

"House accounts?"

"The houseparents have to turn in house accounts," Philip said. "We've got operating budgets for the Houses for things like Christmas parties and birthday parties for the boarding students and that kind of thing. They're not large and they're not important, but Edith kept them down to the penny. The student accounts, too. That's what our boarding students do for money. They have House accounts they can draw from. The houseparents act as bankers, and we're always shelling out cash and forgetting who we shelled it out to and having to backtrack. There's a memo from administration every month, but Edith never got one. Her student accounts were perfect. And she was a demon about maintaining the heirlooms."

"What are the heirlooms?"

"Go into the common room here and see," Philip said. "We've got at least four pieces of seriously expensive furniture, art furniture, really. Lytton, where Edith lived, has a table that belonged to Henry David Thoreau. It's worth thousands of dollars. All the Houses have antiques. The insurance company must have a cow knowing they're around where students can get to them. But Edith's House always has the best ones because she's the only one of us who really is diligent about caring for them. Was. I'll admit it, she's one of the few people I know here I'm sorry to see gone."

Gregor stood up. "You've been very helpful," he said. "I need to know where to find Doyle House. That should be the next one closer to the library from here, yes?"

"Yes," Philip said.

"I will have to tell the police where you are and who you are."

"I know," Philip said, "I didn't expect anything else. But you've got no way of holding me here against my will, Mr. Demarkian. I'm younger than you are and stronger than you are, and if it ever came down to a fight, I'd win. So I suggest that you leave here and make your call from next door. And I'll do what I have to do."

"If you're thinking of staging some kind of confrontation, it would be very foolish."

"I gave up staging confrontations years ago."

"If you're thinking of running, that would be very foolish, too."

"Would it? Well, it probably would be. Good-bye, Mr. Demarkian. I hope you found it interesting."

Gregor was about to say he had when he found himself deposited unceremoniously onto the porch. Philip Candor had ushered him out of the apartment and out of Martinson House so adeptly that he'd hardly noticed he was moving.

2

Gregor made the call to Brian Sheehy and then to the federal fugitive hotline from his cell phone, but what Philip Candor had said was true. He had no way of holding him against his will, and not much he could do to keep Philip from leaving if he wanted to leave. Even if he stood here in the quad and watched the door he'd just come out of, Philip could probably go through a different door or out a window or a fire escape. He stood for a moment or two, looking at Martinson House, but in the end he felt silly. He thought it mattered enormously that Philip Candor be returned to his identity as Leland Beech and sent back to prison. He just didn't see that there was anything else he could do to make it happen.

He made his way along the frozen paths to Doyle House's front door and rang that bell. He'd barely put his finger to the button when the door was flung open and he found himself staring at a tall, thin, elegant man in impeccable tailoring, holding a sheaf of papers in one hand.

"Mr. Demarkian," the man said. "Mr. Demarkian. I went over to the inn a little while ago looking for you, but you'd already gone out. I'm James Hallwood."

This was almost too convenient to be believed, but Gregor didn't think he ought to turn down good luck. He didn't have that much of it. James Hallwood was standing back and motioning him inside. Gregor went, wondering what the papers were. James closed the door behind them both.

"It's very difficult to know what the right thing to do might be," James said. "You think and you think. And, of course, if I'd received this paper, Michael's paper, at any other time, I would have brought it to the attention of the administration. Ever since Columbine, we're all very careful to focus on any sign of impending violence. But then he was dead. You can see that, can't you? There was no point making a fuss of it if he was dead. It would only have hurt his family to no good purpose."

Gregor noticed that James Hallwood was not leading him into an apartment. He had opted instead to go to the large Doyle House living room, a gigantic empty space with more couches than Gregor would have thought any room needed. There was also a television set, tucked in between the shelves of a built-in bookcase. It was not a large television set, and it had dust on it. James motioned for him to sit down.

"Don't worry," he said, "they're not anywhere around at this hour of the day. On days when class is in session, they're not permitted in the Houses after breakfast until two thirty. That's to make sure that none of them hide. There are no classes today, of course, but they're all at an assembly at the moment. We'll have the grief counselors in any minute now."

"Other faculty members can be here, can't they?" Gregor said. "Houses have more than one houseparent, as far as I can tell."

"Yes, yes they do," James said. "But you don't have to worry about that either. Linda and Donald Corby are away for the day. They've gone to visit Linda's mother. About to jump ship, if you ask me, although I don't expect there's going to be much of a ship to jump by the end of the week. The news is out now. It's all over the place. This school will be on the verge of collapse by tomorrow morning. I wanted to show you these, both of them. The first one is Mark DeAvecca's. The second one is Michael Feyre's. They're short stories they wrote for my English class a few weeks ago. Take a look."

Gregor sat down on one of the big couches, took off his coat again—this was what he hated most about winter, getting in and out of all the extra clothes—and read the first few paragraphs of the story on the top.

That year the snow came down in thick white mats like lace doilies, shutting out the mountains. Martin Francis thought he had reached a place in life where only good things could happen to him, and the best of those things was Andrea Marl. It didn't matter to him that Andrea Marl was twenty years older than he was, any more than it mattered to him that she was married. He cared only that she ask him into her bedroom every Wednesday afternoon during the study break, and that her husband always be away in Boston until very late on Wednesday evening.

"That's remarkable," Gregor said. "Mark wrote this?"

James Hallwood nodded impatiently. "Yes, yes. Whatever else we may all want to say about Mark DeAvecca, he writes like a professional. Better than his mother does, and she's been at it and getting paid for it for longer than he's been born. But that's not the point. Look at the other one."

Gregor ran through page after page—Mark had written a very long story—and finally came to the last few, badly typed and almost illegible under a cascade of inkjet printer smear. The first few lines were impossible to read. The next few were not, but he wished they were.

. . . take an axe straight to her cunt smash it open and see it bleed
and fuck the whole slimy garbage of entrails and pussy and . . .

Gregor put the papers down on his lap. "For God's sake."

"It's hard to read, I know it is," James Hallwood said. "It took me three tries before I managed to get through it. But I did get through it. And that's when I realized."

"Realized what?" Gregor said. "That Michael Feyre was apparently deeply mentally disturbed? I think everybody knew that already."

"They did," James Hallwood said, "but that's not the point either. The point is that those two, uh, papers, are about the same thing. Or they're supposed to be. They're about Michael having sex with a faculty member. And Michael's paper is so awful that you don't pay attention to details after a while because your mind is reeling. But if you do pay attention to details, you see it. Mark wrote his paper about Michael and Alice. Michael wrote his paper about himself and someone else."

Gregor looked down at the papers on his lap again. He didn't want to read any more of Michael Feyre's. James leaned forward, impatient.

"Look at that," he said, flipping to the next to the last page and pointing to the middle paragraph. "Look at it. He says he wants to take an Exacto knife to her tattoo, do you see that?"

What Gregor saw was a sentence that had that information in it, but a lot of other words as well, most of them obscene.

"I see it," he said.

"Whoever it is, she has a tattoo on her inner right thigh. A tattoo of numbers: 75744210. He says it right here."

"It might still refer to Mrs. Makepeace," Gregor said.

"No, it couldn't. Alice does not have tattoos, and I know she doesn't have them on her inner thighs. We have a pool here, and I've seen her swim."

"It could refer to someone he knew before he ever came here," Gregor said, "or someone he knows in town rather than in school. Or it could refer to a student."

"No," James said again. He grabbed the papers and rifled through them another time. "Look here. *Sit in class and watch her teach see her naked tell her next time she should strip right there and then get the knife, get something serious and cut her eyes . . .* It sounds like one of his teachers, doesn't it? One of his teachers here."

"Maybe," Gregor said cautiously. "Did Michael have many women teachers?"

"He had Edith," James said. "Not that I think for a moment that this could be Edith. She's not the type to give in to sexual blackmail, and she's not the type for a boy like that to want to, well, to do what he's suggesting he did here. And I can't imagine Edith had a tattoo, although they'll find that out at the autopsy, won't they?"

"Yes," Gregor said, "if there's a tattoo, they'll make a note of it."

"I think the best bet is Marta Coelho," James said. "She's his history teacher. Was his history teacher. And she's new this year. Nobody's seen her at the pool or walking around in shorts. She could have a tattoo. I wonder what the numbers mean."

James's eyes were gleaming. He looked, Gregor thought, like a man who had just spied a prize he'd wanted desperately or an addict about to score a fresh fix. His hunger was so intense it was difficult to stay in the same room with him. Gregor was suddenly more aware than he liked of the utter silence of the House around them.

"Here," James said, thrusting the papers at him again. "Take them. They may help you."

"They may help me what?" Gregor asked.

"They may help you," James insisted. "It's too late for the school, of course.

It doesn't matter what Peter Makepeace thinks. He's not God and he's not Superman. The school is finished. But that doesn't mean she should get away with it."

"She? Do you mean Marta Coelho?"

"Of course I mean Marta Coelho," James said, impatient now. "Do you know what she's been doing for days? She's been running around campus, accusing people—accusing people of things. Spreading rumors and gossip about people. Trying to make all of us look guilty."

"Guilty of what exactly?"

"Of trying to poison Mark, that's what," James said. "At least that, if not more."

"But nobody knew Mark had been poisoned until yesterday."

"Then of causing Michael to kill himself," James said. "What difference does it make? Not that I ever believed Michael killed himself, not for a moment. He wasn't the type. Homicidal maniacs don't kill themselves; they kill other people."

"What makes you think Michael Feyre was a homicidal maniac?"

"Well, look at that thing," James said. "Don't tell me you don't think he wouldn't have ended up a serial killer if he hadn't died here. He's got the mind of a serial killer. He spent enough time working out the methods of attack, too."

"I don't understand what you're getting at," Gregor said. "Are you trying to tell me that Michael Feyre was murdered, and Marta Coelho killed him?"

"It's possible, isn't it?" James said. "It's entirely possible."

"How?" Gregor said.

"What do you mean, how?"

"How did she kill him?" Gregor insisted. "You know the particulars of Michael Feyre's death, I presume. From what I understand, they were common knowledge. How did Marta Coelho kill Michael Feyre?"

"She knocked him out with something, strung him up while he was unconscious, and then staged the rest."

"Very good. Not plausible," Gregor said, "but very good. Unfortunately, that particular scenario won't fit the autopsy report. But never mind. I can think of a scenario that would. Tell me how she managed to get into Hayes House without being seen on a night when most students and both houseparents were at home."

"How am I supposed to know?" James said. "That's not my job. It's your job. Maybe she was seen. Maybe nobody has mentioned it."

"There was a death and an autopsy and a police investigation," Gregor said. "If somebody had seen her on the third floor of Hayes House, where she had no business being either as a resident—which she wasn't, she's a resident of Barrett—or as a visitor, somebody would have mentioned it. It would have been in the autopsy report, or Mark would have said something, or one of the other people I talked to would have said something. If the descriptions I've heard of that House on that night are in any way accurate, she could not have been on that floor at any time between dinner and when Mark found the body without having been noticed, and she was not noticed."

James turned away. "So maybe Michael did commit suicide," he said sullenly. "Maybe she was poisoning Mark because he knew something about her sleeping with Michael."

"Maybe," Gregor said.

"You should see the way she's been behaving," James said. "Going on and on. Making accusations where anybody could hear them. Making accusations in front of half the student body in the library last night, from what I've heard. What could possibly be the point of that except to deflect suspicion from herself?"

"I don't know," Gregor said. "Some people like to gossip. What could possibly be the point of this display you've put on for me today except to deflect suspicion from *your*self?"

James Hallwood froze. "I don't know what you mean," he said. "I don't have the faintest idea what you're talking about."

He really was an elegant man, Gregor thought. He could play the part of an Oxford don or a Nobel Prize winner in a movie aimed at the sort of people who thought of Indiana Jones as brainwashing. Gregor gathered up the papers—he would keep those; he wasn't an idiot—and stood himself.

"It has been suggested to me," he said carefully, "that you bought drugs from Michael Feyre."

James snorted. "Suggested by Marta, I suppose. That's what she's been going around saying. And not only about me."

"I didn't hear it from Marta Coelho."

"Then you heard it from somebody who heard it from Marta Coelho," James said. "I don't buy drugs, Mr. Demarkian. And if I did, I wouldn't buy them from a student. I'm not a fool."

"Maybe not, but the idea that you do buy drugs is current on this campus, and I have to wonder, if you don't buy them at all, why that's so. I also have to wonder about the possibility that Michael Feyre knew you bought them and threatened to expose you for it. He was a blackmailer."

"He was a blackmailer for sex," James said, "and he blackmailed women."

"Maybe he blackmailed men for money."

"He had more money than all the faculty combined. He had more money than the school's endowment, most likely. He didn't need money."

"Psychopaths need things in ways much different than normal people do. He may not have needed money in the usual sense, but he might have needed to extort it."

"If he did, he didn't extort it from me."

James was glaring. Gregor didn't blame him. He'd come into this interview convinced he could make Gregor move in the direction he wanted him to go, and Gregor wasn't going there. James turned away and stared out the living room windows onto an expanse that ended in a large clapboard building Gregor thought might be the Student Center.

"If you've come here to trap me into saying something that you can use to arrest me, I won't have any part in it," James said. "You might as well pack up and go."

"All right," Gregor said.

"You mean you don't want to interrogate me any further? You don't have a thousand clever questions that will prove I broke Michael's neck with my bare hands and strung him up like a sausage in his own bedroom? I'm disappointed in you."

"I'd like to keep these papers, if I could."

"Do what you want. I have copies."

"All right."

"She's going to get what she wants after all," James said. "She's going to get to see one of us arrested, and she's going to stand by and gloat. And you're going to help her do it."

Gregor didn't think he was helping anybody do anything, but he knew there was no point in arguing with somebody in the mood James Hallwood had sunk himself in. Gregor left James standing with his back to the rest of the living room and let himself out Martinson House's back door. He had to remind himself again that the school Houses did not face the quad. They backed onto it.

He didn't think that was significant, but it was the kind of detail it was much too easy to ignore until it tripped you up.

FOUR

1

Cherie Wardrop had to admit it. It only made sense. It was a matter of practical reality. Windsor may have been the best place they had ever had, and the only school where they had stayed more than two years, but all good things must come to an end. Even without murders and publicity, they would have been on their way next year or the year after. It got boring to stay in one place for too long. It also got difficult. It got to the point where you knew everything about the place, and it knew everything about you. After that, things always got to be a little tense.

"I know the normal thing would be to stay to the end of the year," Melissa said, "but I don't think there's going to be any school to stay at in a day or two. And what would we do here? Answer questions from the police. There's that. But we can answer questions anywhere. We don't have to be sitting here in an empty dormitory for five months while Gregor Demarkian figures out that he doesn't know what he's doing."

"The dormitory isn't empty," Cherie pointed out.

"It's not empty now," Melissa said, "but give it a minute or two. We've already had, what, six calls today? The entire third floor is due to be picked up before evening. The only reason there will be anybody left on the second is that all three of the Korean boys are there, and their parents don't have any place for them to go yet. At the most we have a week before this building will clear out. It will only be the middle of March. You really don't expect those students to come back for this school year, or ever?"

"If the police make an arrest," Cherie said.

"If the police make an arrest in the next hour, the kids are going to go," Melissa said. "Let's face it. Half these people wouldn't recognize their own children if they passed them in the street. And even if they would recognize them, they don't like them. But they all feel guilty about it, Cherie. Every last one of them. So when something like this happens, they panic. They feel they need to do something. And what they do is find the kid another school."

"Well," Cherie said lamely, "at least we can get Mark DeAvecca out of Sheldon's apartment."

"Mark DeAvecca isn't going to be back either," Melissa said. "What do you think his mother is doing up here? She *would* recognize him if she passed him on the street, and I think she may even like him; but one way or another, she's here, and he's going. And you know it."

Cherie shook her head. "It feels wrong, somehow. That he'd just go, right from the hospital, and not come back to say good-bye. That they'd all just go. As if we didn't mean anything to them."

"They don't mean anything to us, Cherie. Be sensible."

Cherie was being sensible; she just didn't think what Melissa said was true. They did mean something to her. They always did, in every dorm she'd lived in, although she needed to get away from them as much as she needed to get away from their schools when the end came.

"We don't even have a place to go next year," Cherie said. "We weren't expecting this, and we should have been. When Michael—well, when Michael. We should have started looking for a new place then. And we didn't."

"It's only March. We'll find something."

"Not as good."

"Maybe not," Melissa said, "or maybe we'll find something better. We should check out some of the places in California. The weather would be nicer. And in the meantime, we should take a vacation. It's been a long time since we had one of those."

"We should just be sure not to leave anything behind," Cherie said.

They were standing in the living room of the apartment, putting things into boxes. Or rather, Melissa was putting things into boxes. Cherie had woken up to find her with the boxes out and a checklist on a clipboard, as if they had decided on their next move, when they hadn't even talked about it. It was true, things were definitely different now that Edith was dead. Even the air was different. Up until now they had all been able to pretend that nothing really awful had happened. Michael had committed suicide. Mark was, well, Mark: a perpetual screwup and slacker, a druggie, one of those people who should never have been admitted in the first place. People thought that of him even now that they knew it wasn't true, or might not be. Once you got a reputation in a boarding school, it was nearly impossible to change it. Edith was the best teacher the school had and the most conscientious houseparent.

"Do you think it's true?" Cherie said. "What Sheldon was saying last night. Do you think that anybody who was willing to kill Edith would be willing to kill anybody?"

"I don't know," Melissa said. "What do you think?"

"I think I need some air."

2

James Hallwood knew, even while he was doing it, that he had approached his interview with Gregor Demarkian in exactly the way he shouldn't have. He had heard his own voice, and the petulance and pettiness had been unmistakable. So had the panic. It was a terrifying prospect. Here was the truth about teachers in schools like this one. They came in only three types. First and best were the natural teachers with too much respect for the traditions of Western culture to be willing to put up with public school bureaucracies that, except in the very best places, seemed to be concerned with everything and anything but academics. Next were the young ones on their way up and out. They were taking a year to teach while they made up their minds between doing doctoral work in Slavic literature or going into publishing. Finally, there were the men and women who had failed at everything else, not because they were inadequate as a matter of constitution, but because they lacked the courage or the ambition to try. That last group made up the smallest percentage of faculty at a good school, but they were very visible and very easy to spot. Sheldon LeRouve was one, scratching for his security in any way possible, angry at his colleagues and his students and the boarders in his house, angry especially at boys like Mark DeAvecca, who seemed to be so worthless and yet had no need to worry about the future. *Oh, that family money,* James thought. He hadn't had it either, and he could remember himself in college, envying the hell out of the boys who did. He didn't think he was like Sheldon, not yet. He was not angry most of the time, and he was not bitter. He could get that way. That was what his interview with Gregor Demarkian had made him understand.

Left to himself, he put in a call to David and was surprised to find him in. He realized with a pang that, in spite of all the years they had been together, he did not have David's weekday schedule imprinted on his brain. He didn't even have it memorized in outline. He thought about the night Michael Feyre had died, the way he had sat in this living room and told himself that his relationship with David was about to come to an end. The truth was, it had never really had a beginning. He had been with David as he had been with his work, here at Windsor and everyplace else he had ever been. It had seemed to him not only easier but more sensible not to allow himself to get too involved, not to allow too much to matter to him. It wasn't that he was cold. It wasn't even that he was afraid of commitment, although David would probably say he was, and had said so, more often than James liked to remember. The real issue was this: once you got involved, once you made a commitment, then all other options were closed off. You had chosen your road, and all other roads were barred to you.

When James thought of making decisions, it was closed doors he thought of, a whole corridor full of open doors crashing eternally shut. Even now, even when he knew better, even when he could hear the sound of his voice rising into panic, and see Gregor Demarkian's startled look of surprise, the idea of getting himself settled made him feel suddenly claustrophobic, irrevocably out of air. He had to force himself to dial David's number, and when David's voice came on the line he had to force himself to respond to it. For a moment he experienced a brand-new panic. David hadn't called this morning when the news had hit about the murder of Edith Braxner. Maybe James had left it too long. Maybe David had given up.

"I was wondering," James said, when David had made all the right noises about the mess at Windsor, "if you'd mind coming to stay here with me tonight."

"Stay there? At school? What's the matter, is the place about to close down so that you no longer have to worry about your reputation?"

He deserved the flippancy, James thought. He had been flippant often enough himself. "It probably will close down," he said, "but that's not why I want you here. I think it's cowardice. The place doesn't feel safe."

David stopped joking. "It isn't safe, if you ask me. You could come here to stay instead. That way neither one of us would have to worry about being poisoned at dinner."

"I don't think we do have to worry. I don't think it has anything to do with us. But I don't know if I could leave tonight. The school is falling apart. Parents are showing up to take their children home. You can hardly blame them. I've got an . . . obligation . . . not to make things worse than they are. And I feel sorry for Peter Makepeace."

"That's new," David said. "Both feeling sorry for Peter Makepeace and a sense of obligation. Are you sure you're feeling all right?"

"No, of course not. I'm feeling awful. I'm even feeling awful about poor Edith, and she and I were hardly the best of friends. It's a nasty way to go, cyanide. I looked it up."

"Come stay here," David said again.

"No," James said, "come here for the night. Maybe for the next few days. When this is over, if you're still interested, I'll move in full-time. Maybe I'll even go looking for a college job in Boston, if there's a college willing to take me after all this time in secondary schools and at my age."

"They'd take you adjunct," David said. "And you don't have to work full-time. I work full time."

James laughed. "Thank you very much, but now you're going straight off a cliff. Will you come? I don't think I can stand another day by myself in this godforsaken place."

"I'll pick you up for dinner. We'll go somewhere decent so that you don't have to risk being poisoned in the cafeteria. And yes, I will stay."

"Thank you. Bring along that material from the Matthew Shepard Scholarship Fund you wanted me to look at and I'll look at it."

"I think the world is coming to an end," David said.

No, James wanted to say, *only* my *world is coming to an end;* but that sounded silly and melodramatic even in his own head, so he let it go. "I have to get off the phone," he said. "That's Alice coming up the walk, and she doesn't look happy. This is what I really need you for, interviews with Alice. God only knows what it's about this time."

"Murders," David suggested.

James laughed. "Alice wouldn't even notice them if they didn't threaten to upset her daily routine. Specifically, her routine of sleeping with students. Never mind. I'll see you tonight."

He put the phone back in its cradle and watched Alice coming steadily down the path to Doyle House. For some reason she looked shorter than he remembered her, and he was only remembering her from the night before. Maybe she was wearing lower heels. If she was, it had to have some significance, like respect for the dead. Alice liked her heels to be as high and as spiked as possible. She talked a good game of feminism, but she preferred to see herself as a dominatrix.

James saw no reason to wait until the last minute. It wasn't as if Alice would go away or the meeting would get more pleasant the more complicated he made her approach. He left his apartment and went out to open the Doyle House front door. Alice really did look shorter than he remembered her. She also looked nervous, and James couldn't remember ever having seen her look nervous.

"Looking for me?" he asked her. The air was frigid. Keeping the door open like this made his teeth ache with the cold.

"Of course I'm looking for you," she said, brushing past him.

He closed the door and followed her down to his own apartment. She wouldn't expect the door to be locked. It wasn't. She sailed on through, leaving him to close it behind them.

"Gregor Demarkian is making the police take fingerprints," she said, as soon as he'd come into his own living room.

"Why do you think Gregor Demarkian is making them?" James asked. "There's been a murder. I believe it's customary for police to take fingerprints."

"I think he's directing the whole thing. He's giving them ideas. And, of course, he's getting the ideas from Mark. He thinks he knows Mark DeAvecca better than we do."

"Well, he does, doesn't he? He's a friend of the family."

"I don't care how close he is to the family. You never really know a person until you've lived with him, and we've lived with him. He hasn't."

"From the reports I've heard over the last few days," James said, "we haven't really been living with him either. He's not been himself."

"It's a lot of nonsense," Alice said. "It's an excuse. People don't change their personalities, even on drugs. They just become more like themselves. And caffeine is just a drug."

"I suppose arsenic is also just a drug," James said, "but its effects can be severe."

"Peter is over at the business office. The police have pulled all the house accounts, including Edith's. And the student accounts, too. Eloise in the business office says she thinks they're looking for regular payouts because that would mean somebody was being blackmailed. It's the most ridiculous thing I've ever heard of in my life. Michael didn't care about money. He had a ton of it; but even if he hadn't, he wouldn't have cared. He was used to doing without it."

James said nothing. When Alice got onto the subject of Michael, it was impossible to get a word in edgewise. He wanted a cup of coffee, but he didn't want to make it because he didn't want to offer Alice one. He didn't want to give her an excuse to stay longer than she otherwise might have.

"Besides," she was saying, "what do they think they're going to find in Edith's accounts? They were meticulous. Everybody knows that. She was legendary in the way she kept them. And those notes she used to write to people when theirs weren't perfectly done. Like it was any of her business. And do they really think Edith would be paying somebody blackmail? For what? Maybe she read Harry Potter books in secret and or went to Vin Diesel movies. And then, of course, there are the students. What they think they're going to find there is beyond me, too. I mean, of course they're going to find regular withdrawals of money. Most of them withdraw cash every Friday afternoon like clockwork. For the weekend. And God only knows, if the students were going to pay blackmail, they'd have enough money to do it. Their parents give them enough cash to found small businesses."

There was nothing for it. James had to have coffee. He started toward the kitchen and offered some to Alice. "Percolated, not instant," he promised. "And not Starbucks."

"What I really need is a shot of Scotch," Alice said. "Yes, all right, thank you. Coffee would be good. Although I don't see how anybody around here is ever going to drink coffee again with those rumors about Mark DeAvecca being poisoned by it. And Edith. For God's sake. Who would want to kill Edith? If he wasn't in the hospital, I'd have bet on Mark DeAvecca. She was going to give him a C minus in German."

"And you think he'd kill her for that?"

"It would have gotten him thrown out of school," Alice said. "You know what the policy is around here. Oh, I don't know. I just want them to get out of here. And the media. They're all over the place. We've managed to keep them off campus only by threatening a lawsuit, but that isn't going to last long. Have they taken your fingerprints yet?"

"Not yet, no," James said. "But it's early yet, if they've just started. Maybe they just haven't gotten around to me."

"I think they started with the people who were in the library last night. Did you know I was there? Not when she fell. I didn't see her fall. Afterward."

James made noncommittal noises. He knew that Alice had had a run-in with Gregor Demarkian. Everybody knew.

"If you ask me, he made the whole thing up," Alice said. "Right on the spot like that, saying it was cyanide. He couldn't possibly have known. He was just trying to make this a bigger mess than it already was and to get himself hired as a consultant so that he could snoop around here all he wanted to. I can't stand the mother either. The voice of reason on cable TV. You know what else he asked for? The lost-and-found reports."

"This was Mr. Demarkian again?" James asked.

"Of course it's Mr. Demarkian again. Oh, it's all too much. It's ridiculous. Nobody murdered Edith, and the only thing that's wrong with Mark is that he's a spoiled rich kid who just couldn't cut it. We're being ripped up and torn to shreds because Liz Toliver has no intention of letting her little darling get a rejection letter from Yale. Or wherever it is he wants to go."

"UCLA, last I heard."

"God, that figures. Not even someplace decent, like Berkeley. I can't stand it. I really can't stand it. The media isn't here, but the police are. They're all over the place, and now they've cordoned off the whole area around Maverick Pond—"

"Maverick Pond? Why? Nobody ever goes there this time of year."

"Of course I know that," Alice said. "And you know it. Every sensible person knows it. But Mark DeAvecca is saying he saw somebody there, passed out in the evergreen bushes, the night Michael Feyre died; and of course you know who he's saying it is, don't you? Me. That's who he's saying it is. As if I've ever passed out from anything in my life. As if two dozen people didn't see me that night, not including my husband. Oh, God. And of course Peter is putting up with this. He's putting up with everything. He's a complete rag where the police are concerned."

The coffee was finished. James poured two cups. He took his black, but he put not only the cups but the sugar bowl and creamer on the tray he was making ready. He brought the tray into the living room and put it down on the coffee table.

Alice was staring out the window at the quad. "I've got to go," she said. "I just thought you ought to know what was going on. Is going on. They're going to wreck this place. It's happening already. Parents have been showing up all morning. Students are leaving left and right. I don't care if Peter is fired. He's been fired before. There's life after Windsor. But I hate giving that awful little snot his victory."

Alice pulled her cape more closely around her neck and marched to the door. Her coffee was waiting on the tray. She didn't even look at it. She opened the door and went out, not bothering to say good-bye. James sat down in front of the two full cups of coffee and sighed. She hadn't even told him why she'd come to talk to him. Maybe she hadn't had a reason. Maybe he'd just been available. In any event he was now going to waste a perfectly good cup of expensive ground roast, and that summed up his relationship with Alice—and Alice's relationships with everybody—perfectly.

It gave James a great deal of satisfaction to think that if David had been here, even if they were caught in a tornado, he'd have been polite about the coffee.

3

Out in the quad Alice Makepeace found herself suddenly at a peak of anger so high and so sharp that she was stopped in her tracks. She was too angry to move, unless she could have hit somebody, and there was nobody around to hit. There were times when she understood violence. She really did. There were times when even the death penalty felt like a viable option. At the moment there was no death penalty in Massachusetts, and she belonged to an organization dedicated to keeping it out. She belonged to too many organizations. She couldn't remember what half of them did anymore.

She went around the side of Ridenour Library and stopped. The police were there, cordoning off Maverick Pond with yellow police tape, as if it were a crime scene. But it wasn't a crime scene. If it had been, somebody would have told her. There would be ambulances as well as police cars. She watched the men stringing the yellow tape on thin poles they were hammering into the ground, through the snow and ice. On television shows, they used sawhorses. She supposed they couldn't use sawhorses here. They'd skid on the ice.

She truly hated this. She hated everything about it. She hated the fact that they had taken her fingerprints, as if she were living in a police state. Maybe she was living in a police state. What else explained the fact that they could manufacture a murder case out of whole cloth, get it on the media in hours, and then treat them all like criminals?

She scanned the little crowd around the pond for any sign of Gregor Demarkian but didn't find him. The police were nothing but that man's puppets, and that man was Mark DeAvecca's puppet, and none of them were worth a tenth of what Michael Feyre might have been if he hadn't capitulated to the culture of Windsor Academy and all the places like it. There was a way of blaming it all on white male patriarchal hegemony, she just couldn't think what that way was yet.

The truth was, she couldn't think at all. She turned around and walked back through the quad. There were more police, all of a sudden. She realized they were talking to students and parents on the steps of the Houses, writing things down in notebooks. She wanted to choke. She wanted to walk over to one of them, rip his notebook out of his hand, and demand that he leave her campus. She wanted to *do* something for once, instead of waiting around for something to be done to her, the way she had been since she'd first heard Michael was dead. She knew that he had died for love of her. He had committed suicide because she was about to break off their relationship, because she had found him wanting.

She got to the door of President's House just as Sarah Lavenham and her mother were finishing their talk with the policeman outside Deverman House. Sarah had an enormous duffle bag. Her mother had a large box too full to close. Alice went up the steps to the President's House front door and let herself inside. Peter would be away. He would be away all day. The last thing she wanted to do now was to see him.

The first thing she wanted to do was to have sex, and not sex with herself either. She had always despised masturbation. Masturbation was for people who couldn't find partners, and she could always find partners. Masturbation was far too safe, even if you left the doors unlocked and risked being discovered in the act. Sex was danger before it was anything else. It was hanging off the edge of a cliff. It was risking the real, not only exposure but obliteration. Michael had been the best at that that she had ever had. He had felt more real than any other person she had ever known. When she had been afraid with him, she had known it was neither an act nor an exaggeration. She had been afraid because she had good reason to be afraid.

She went upstairs to the bedroom she shared with Peter and took off her cape. She sat down on the edge of the bed and looked at the mounds the pillows made under the bedspread. She rubbed her hands together and then ran them through her hair.

She was afraid now because she had good reason to be afraid. She was scared to death.

FIVE

1

Gregor was standing just behind Ridenour Library watching the police set up corridors and perimeters on his orders. It was going to take some time to make sure the area was securely cordoned off, mostly because he didn't really know what the area was or even what it was supposed to contain. He only knew there had to be something.

"It would make it a lot easier if we knew what we were protecting," Brian Sheehy said at one point in the proceedings. Gregor knew he wasn't really pressing. He was having the time of his life, watching the whole of the Windsor Academy campus fill up with uniformed men and seven different media vans, including one from the BBC World Service, arrayed on Main Street to film it. It was always dangerous to indulge a need for revenge, Gregor thought, but in this case it suited his purpose for Brian to do so. He wasn't about to complain.

"I don't know exactly what we're looking for," he said. "Something small, I'd guess. Something that could have been thrown or placed under those trees."

"Danny Kelly looked under those trees an hour ago," Brian pointed out. "He didn't find a thing."

"Neither did the person who went looking the night Michael Feyre died," Gregor said. "That's why Michael Feyre *did* die. If our person had found what he or she was looking for, there would have been no need to kill Michael. At least not then."

"You do understand that Michael Feyre's death was ruled a suicide," Brian said. "And I don't see how you're going to explain it as murder—yes, yes, I know, sex. But you know what I mean. Explain it so a jury would buy it and a decent defense attorney couldn't get the jury to laugh at it."

"Fortunately, I won't have to explain it that well," Gregor said. "We don't need to bring it up if we don't want to. Your prosecutor can go at this from any angle he wants to. We *will* be able to prove who poisoned Mark. And we'll have at least good evidence for who poisoned Edith Braxner. Take your pick."

"Her," Brian said.

"Her who?"

"Our prosecutor. She's a her. Siobhan Clanahan."

"Right," Gregor said. If he had belonged to one of those civil rights commissions looking into racism and favoritism in police departments, he would have started to suspect that there was a definite bias in favor of Irish Americans in Windsor's municipal government.

"How are we going to find something that the person couldn't find a week and a half ago?" Brian said. "I don't know how long you think it's been there, whatever it is—"

"Since the night Michael Feyre died," Gregor said. "Or the afternoon before. The same day. I don't think it would have been there any earlier. He was a sadist, and from all reports he didn't have much in the way of impulse control."

"Michael Feyre? No," Brian said, "he didn't. Was it Michael Mark saw?"

"No," Gregor said. "It was Michael who put what we're looking for under those evergreens. My guess is that he threw it well back, as hard as he could. Look at them. They're very low to the ground. They scrape it in a couple of places. Of course Danny didn't find anything just looking. Neither did the person who was out here looking that night."

"Did it occur to you that somebody else might have? Somebody might have seen whatever it was and picked it up before whoever it was got here."

"I don't think so. I think if that had happened, it would have been turned in to lost and found or turned over to the administration."

"So you *do* know what we're looking for," Brian said.

"No," Gregor said, "I know the kind of thing we're looking for. If this was real life, instead of a school, I'd know a lot better because then I'd have a limited number of options. I'm still flailing around where the school is concerned though. I'm never sure how they do what they do. Maybe I should have brought Mark with me."

"His mother would have killed you," Brian said. "But let's go over this one more time. Michael Feyre was blackmailing a faculty member—"

"Several, from what I can figure out," Gregor said. "James Hallwood, definitely, no matter what he says. Philip Candor, not certain but possible. Marta Coelho. I don't know about what, probably buying some pot, but there's something. Nothing else explains how incredibly jumpy she is about this whole thing. If we combed the campus and really insisted on getting information, we'd find half a dozen more."

"Right," Brian said. "We should comb the campus. That would be interesting. So one of these people—"

Out near the pond, the last of the yellow tape had gone up and the uniformed patrolmen were backing off, trying to do as little damage as possible. Gregor thought it was a bit late to be worrying about that. They'd been tramping all over everything all afternoon.

"Look," he said, "it's perfectly simple. The blackmail required evidence of some kind. I'm not sure what, but it required some form of physical evidence. Michael Feyre, in all likelihood, promised to give it back if the faculty member in question served as safety and gave him a blow job as part of an autoasphyxiation session."

"Wasn't that risky?" Brian asked. "He was blackmailing people. He must have known some of them would want to kill him."

"He was sixteen years old," Gregor said, "and sixteen year olds think they're immortal at the best of times. He was also, if the descriptions of him are accurate, and I think they are since one of them came from his own mother, a raving psychopath. Psychopaths think they're immortal, too. They think they're smarter than everybody else. They think they're braver. They think they're stronger. And most of all, they have supreme contempt for all other human beings. He may have suspected that some of his victims wanted to kill him, but I'll bet anything he didn't believe any of them would ever have the guts to actually do it."

"And you think this one did," Brian said.

"It's really very simple, if you look at it sanely," Gregor said. "Michael Feyre was a sadist. We know that, too. We know it from everything everybody has said about him, again including his mother. He had whatever it was he had, something absolutely damaging to his victim, something his victim wanted back. He put it somewhere he or she couldn't get it."

"He threw it under this stand of evergreens," Brian said.

"Apparently, yes," Gregor said, "and he told his victim that he or she could come here and get it or service him sexually so that he wouldn't talk. Or he'd come back and get it himself and turn it in. He made it damned near impossible to find, and he put a time limit on the whole enterprise. He had to have it by X hour or he'd do something about it. You've got to remember that the whole administration of this school, and a good half of the faculty, live on campus. He wouldn't have had to wait for the morning or the end of the weekend."

"All right. Then what? Our murderer comes out here and tries to find whatever it is, and Mark is up on the catwalk and sees the operation, right?" Brian said. "But Mark didn't recognize the person."

"No, he didn't," Gregor said, "but the person didn't even know he or she was being watched. The murderer tried to get under the trees and couldn't. The murderer tried for some time, which was why Mark could see the 'body,' as he puts it, lying on the ground for long."

"Motionless, he said," Brian pointed out.

"Stretching, I think," Gregor said. "And he'd moved away when the murderer got up and left. The murderer then went to Hayes House and did what Michael required to keep his mouth shut. Michael got up on that chair. The ropes were put in place on his arms, on his legs, on his neck. The murderer unzipped Michael's fly and took out his penis—and then, instead of doing the expected, the murderer kicked the chair out from under Michael's feet and let him hang. All that was needed after that was to put the penis back in the pants and zip up. Then leave."

"Everybody says Michael was a sadist, not a masochist," Brian said. "Why did he want someone to tie him up?"

"Control," Gregor said. "The idea that he was so completely in control of this other person that even hog-tied he could direct the scene and never once be disobeyed. I think Michael Feyre sincerely believed that that was what was going to happen. He wouldn't have put himself in the position he was in otherwise."

"It sounds like Alice Makepeace," Brian said, "doesn't it?"

"Yes," Gregor admitted, "it does. She's always been the one with the most to lose in all of this, and she's always been the one ruthless enough to get whatever she wanted however she wanted it. And she would have known that the suicide of a student would not close the school or even bring on much in the way of an inquiry. Nobody wants an inquiry into a student suicide. The parents don't want it; it only rakes up memories they can't handle. The school doesn't want it; it makes them look bad. The police don't want it; there isn't much of any point to it and they only end up looking like insensitive asses. You're to be commended for doing as much of an investigation as you did."

"Thanks a lot," Brian said. "Now all we have to do is start rolling some people under there and find what you think they can find, even though you can't tell them what to look for because you don't know what it is. They pay you lots of money to do this sort of thing?"

"My best guess," Gregor said, "is that it's going to be some kind of wallet."

"A wallet," Brian said.

Gregor kept his cell phone in the pocket of his sports jacket, not handy, because he never used it. Now he heard it ring, and for a moment he thought the sound belonged to something Brian Sheehy was carrying. When he realized it belonged to him, it took him long seconds first to find the phone and then to get it out where it could be useful.

He flipped it open and checked the call waiting. It was a magnificent phone, a gift from Bennis on his last birthday. It reminded him of weapons used in *Star Wars* movies, although he had to admit that he never paid much attention to *Star Wars* movies. If Tibor wanted company, Gregor went with him and half slept through a large popcorn.

There were only three people in the world who had this number: Bennis, Tibor, and Lida Arkmanian. Lida would only call if one of the other two had died. Tibor would only call in an emergency. Gregor stared down at Bennis's number showing in the identification window and said, "Excuse me. There's something I have to do."

2

Gregor had never really reconciled himself to cell phones. He knew they were convenient, and that they could be lifesavers in some circumstances. He would not like to be stranded on a deserted road with a flat tire without one, and he understood the value of them in radically traumatic events: the people who had called from the top of the Twin Towers, just before the towers themselves went down in flames, to say good-bye to the families they loved; the people who called from the edges of earthquakes and tornadoes and hurricanes; the people who called from the insides of banks during the progress of a robbery or a hostage situation. Gregor didn't think cell phones were a bad thing. He just didn't like the idea of standing out in the open where everybody and anybody could hear him, having a private conversation without even the small comfort of being able to sit down.

There was nothing he could do about that at the moment. There was no place close enough for him to retreat to. The library was several yards up the hill behind him. He didn't want to be that far from the action while the uniformed policemen moved in. He settled for backing up to just beyond the crowd of law enforcement, but not so far that he backed into the crowd of students, faculty, and onlookers who were being held back by even more uniformed police. He was surprised Windsor had this many people in its department. He wondered what crime was going unpoliced while what seemed to be the entire force was here tending to the scandal at Windsor Academy.

He turned the phone on and said, "Hello?" The wind was picking up, and although it wasn't as cold as it had been last night, it was still frigid. Gregor found himself wishing he'd worn a hat or even owned one.

"Hi," Bennis said.

"Well," Gregor said. Then he felt like an idiot. He'd known this woman for nearly a decade. He'd been living with her, officially or unofficially, for quite some time. There had to be something to say besides "well."

"I'm watching you on the news," Bennis said. "There's a camera right behind you, looks like at the top of some hill you're halfway down. They pointed you out a minute ago."

"I've moved since then," Gregor said. There were a lot of cameras behind him. He couldn't tell if one of them was aimed in his direction.

"They'll find you next time they look," Bennis said. She seemed to be breathing very heavily into the phone. "Liz called," she said finally. "She's worried about you."

"About me? Why? I haven't done much of anything here except sit around and look at papers. And talk to people. You know what that's like. Talking to people."

"I know what it's like," Bennis said, 'but I'm surprised you do. You don't talk to people much, Gregor."

"I'm using the phrase in a different sense," Gregor said. "I was talking to suspects."

"You were interrogating people, you mean."

"All right, I was interrogating them."

"You're good at interrogating people. I've seen you do it. You're not so good at talking to people."

"I'm really not good at talking to people who aren't talking to me," Gregor said. "You know, I'm not a clairvoyant. If you ask me, nobody is a clairvoyant. I can't understand what you want me to know unless you tell me first."

There was a long silence on the line. "I don't know what I want you to know. And maybe this isn't the time for it. You're on television again. They've got you from the side this time. You should button your coat."

Gregor's first impulse was to ask why she'd called if she didn't want to talk, but he wasn't entirely without the ability to understand women. He knew that she'd either go straight through the roof or descend into that icy coldness he'd had to put up with for days. He wanted neither thing to happen. He only wished that whoever was filming him would stop. There was something a little uncomfortable about the idea that Bennis could see him when he couldn't see her.

"Listen," he said, "didn't you want me to go back to work? Back on the last day you were acting like yourself—"

"I always act like myself, Gregor. I don't have anybody else to act like."

"Back then you were telling me I was driving you crazy and hurting myself by not being willing to take on a job, and here I am. I've taken on a job. I'm out. You told me I should get out. I'm not moping around."

"Aren't you?"

"Well, you know, Bennis, maybe I am, but I haven't had time to notice. There's a lot going on here. I miss you. You could have come with me. You'd have gotten a chance to see Mark again. The way this thing has worked out, you'd have gotten a chance to see Liz again, too. And Jimmy, if that's what you'd wanted."

"If Liz is there with Jimmy, it would be inevitable."

"Probably. This doesn't make any difference. I didn't do anything, for God's sake."

"You were very flippant about something I can't be flippant about."

"Then act like a sane human being and scream at me," Gregor said. "Don't just shut up for days and expect me to guess what you're angry about. I still don't know if you love the idea of marriage or hate it. And I wasn't being flippant. I was just talking."

"Being unserious, then."

"Well, I'm not likely to get serious on that subject after this reaction. I'd have had an easier time if I'd told you you were getting fat."

"You wouldn't have survived breakfast."

"Exactly," Gregor said. "You'd have lit into me and that would have been that. But this is crazy, Bennis. This really is. I've spent half my time up here worrying about it, and I don't even know what I'm worrying about. About you. I'm worrying about you. I do know that. Most of the time I'm worrying that you've just got tired of this arrangement and I hadn't noticed it."

"I don't think I can have this conversation on this phone at this time," Bennis said.

"What?"

Down near the pond, one of the uniformed officers, the youngest-looking one Gregor had seen yet, was trying to wedge his way under the evergreens. He was lying flat on his back, inching sideways very carefully, brushing the twigs and needles out of his face. Gregor didn't think he was going to make it.

"That doesn't sound good," he said to Bennis. "That doesn't sound good at all."

"No, I haven't got tired of this arrangement," Bennis said. "Does that sound better? At least, I'm not tired of being with you. How's that?"

"That's definitely better."

"It's more complicated than that."

"You know, Bennis, I never knew much about women before we got together. I met my wife, I married my wife, we got along, she died, that was it. We understood each other. But there's one thing I've learned from you. Everything is complicated. Everything. And I don't understand why it has to be."

"Nobody understands why it has to be," Bennis said. "It's one of the great mysteries of life. It just is."

"Why?" Gregor demanded. "Look, I'm standing out on this freezing hillside. I'm watching this guy, this young police officer, trying to get under a stand of evergreens that grow so low to the ground they're practically one with it, I've got two people dead and one who nearly ended up that way."

"From arsenic poisoning," Bennis put in quickly. "Liz told me."

"Good. Liz told you. Also caffeine poisoning. But the thing is, with all that, this isn't complicated. It's perfectly simple. Sex and money. That's what makes murder. Even most serial killers kill for sex. And don't give me that nonsense about how rape is an expression of power and rape-murder more so. I know. I understand that. But it's still about sex. And the rest of the time we've got money. That's it. When everything is said and done here and Brian Sheehy has his perpetrator and I come back to Cavanaugh Street, it's going to come down to sex and money. Nothing complicated. I don't understand why this has to be complicated. Do you hate the idea of me even thinking about marrying you? Fine. I'll stop thinking about it. Do you love the idea of me thinking about marrying you? Fine, too. I'll think about it. Hell, I'll go looking for a ring."

"I can't believe this," Bennis said.

"Believe what? All I said was—"

"No, Gregor, don't you get it? You didn't say. You don't ever say. You didn't say the last time either. Excuse me if I find it unpleasant to be considered a pain in the ass you have to placate by making sure I get the menu item I want."

"That didn't make any sense at all."

"It should have made sense," Bennis said. "The issue of marriage is not about what I want, or what is going to make me the least mad at you—"

"Of course it is. What else could it be about?"

"Jesus," Bennis said. "This is ridiculous. Any minute now, a white rabbit is going to show up at the door, checking his watch."

"I've read *Alice in Wonderland,* too. You don't need to patronize me. All I'm trying to do is to make you happy. And it's beyond me why that's suddenly become a capital crime."

"You're on television. You've got work to do. I'm going to get off this phone."

"I don't have anything to do but wait here until somebody gets all the way under those evergreens," Gregor said. "Don't you dare just walk out on me again, figuratively or literally. I'll break your neck."

"You've got work to do," Bennis said again, and a second later Gregor heard nothing in his ear but dead air.

Gregor was suddenly incensed, not at Bennis, not at himself, but at the idiots who had invented cell phones. They should have made them so that they gave off dial tones. They should have made them so that they gave off some kind of noise, music, even Muzak, something to buzz when the phone had been hung up in the ear of a caller who had done nothing, absolutely nothing, to deserve it.

This whole situation was beyond belief, Gregor thought. Whatever had made her call in the middle of the day like this, not when she was just hoping to catch him at a good time, but when she knew, because she was watching it on television, that he was neck deep in work? And what had she wanted when she called? What had she ever wanted? Had he ever understood that? He wasn't a complicated man. They got along. He would even have said they were in love. When you got along with a woman, when you felt close enough to her to feel you were in love, you stayed with her. You made arrangements. You made commitments. There was nothing sacred about a marriage license and a ceremony at City Hall, or even in Holy Trinity Church. It was just a formality, and one he thought no more about one way than the other. Maybe it would have been different if he was a religious man, but he wasn't, and Bennis wasn't religious either. What did she want? What was she getting at? He felt as if his entire life was about to fall apart, and he didn't have the first idea as to why.

He was belaboring the obvious for yet another time—she'd called him, not only when he was working, but when she'd known he was working; it was completely insane to have a conversation of the kind they'd just had while standing on a hillside surrounded by people half of whom were paying more attention to him than they were to anything else—when he felt a tap on his shoulder.

He turned to find Mark DeAvecca looming over him, made to seem much taller than he was by the fact that he was farther up the hillside.

"Don't kill me," Mark said. "I just couldn't stand it anymore. I mean, there I was, sitting in that stupid hospital, watching my life go by on CNN. I just couldn't take it anymore."

3

Gregor Demarkian wasn't in the mood to murder Mark DeAvecca at the moment, although he was in the mood to murder somebody and he thought he could probably be talked into taking a surrogate for Bennis if Mark wanted to push hard enough. He got it out of his mind by marveling at the impenetrability of a sixteen-year-old's brain. They really did think they were immortal, all of them. They didn't need to be psychopaths for that. He wondered where Mark had gotten the clothes he was wearing and decided that Liz must have brought them from the dorm yesterday when she'd gone to see Peter Makepeace. She obviously hadn't brought him a jacket because he wasn't wearing one. Gregor didn't think even Mark would go wandering around in chinos, turtleneck, and a cotton crewneck sweater in this weather if he'd had the option of something shiny stuffed with down. Belatedly, Gregor realized just how much Mark's clothes looked like the kind of thing Bennis would wear. Maybe it was a boarding school thing. Bennis had been to boarding school.

Mark cleared his throat. "Mr. Demarkian? I'd sort of appreciate it if you didn't tell my mother that I'd come straight here, you know, from the hospital. I mean, she's going to know I left and all, but it would probably be better if she thought I went back to the dorm."

"She's going to know you came here no matter what I say," Gregor told him patiently. "Look around."

"She's here?"

"No, Mark. How did you know to come here?"

"Oh, I was watching this story about it on CNN, there's this breaking news thing—oh. Ah. We're being filmed."

"Exactly. It's a testimony to the professional competence of Brian Sheehy's men that you managed to get all the way here without getting nailed by a reporter with a microphone. How did you get here, by the way? Everything is supposed to be blocked off."

"I came in through Hayes House. You can't really block off this campus. You'd need an army. Then I came through the library and out the faculty wing. They've got the main reading room closed, but you can get to the wing through the foyer."

Gregor turned around. "There's a guard by the wing door," he said.

Mark shrugged. "I sort of went through Marta Coelho's office and out the window."

"Sort of?"

"Well, for God's sake, Mr. Demarkian. I mean, the only reason you're here to begin with, and the police aren't just dicking around pretending like nothing's wrong, is me. Right? I was the first one to get it. And I brought you here. I'm not going to sit in a room two miles away and watch everybody else get on TV."

"I thought you didn't want to be on TV because your mother would see you."

"Nah, I don't mind being on TV. And don't tell me I should still be in the hospital. If we had an HMO like everybody else, I'd have been out yesterday. I'm fine. I feel like I've taken my life back. You have no idea what a relief it is."

"For your information," Gregor said, "Michael's mother knew there was something wrong. She talked to me, too."

"Before you got here?"

"No," Gregor said, "since."

"There," Mark said, satisfied. "What are they doing down there anyway? That guy's going to kill himself if he keeps that up."

"They're trying to get under that stand of evergreens to see if something's been left there," Gregor said. "We think—I think, might be more accurate— that the figure you thought was passed out in the snow, or dead, the night your roommate died was trying to get something your roommate had put there. Deliberately put there. Let me ask you something. Were you ever aware of Michael using the room you shared with him for, ah, assignations?"

"You mean for sex?" Mark looked amused. "Yeah, he did. Not much, you know, because he and Alice went to her place most of the time. Peter isn't much in evidence in the middle of the day. But she came up to the room some-times."

"Did you ever walk in on them?"

"No. I can hear through the door, if I put my ear against it and listen. And they'd go up there during the time when the dorms are supposed to be locked and off-limits. She could get keys. But they went up there other times, too."

"Did he ever have anybody in there besides Alice Makepeace?"

"Well," Mark said, "if you listened to Michael, he'd done every female on campus with the exception of a couple he thought were too ugly. Those, he said, he got to blow him off. It was the way he talked. You could believe it or not, depending on what you wanted. I just tried to stay out of his way. You know, that guy is going about it all wrong. He's going to end up dead and you're not going to find what you want to find. What do you want to find?"

"I'm not a hundred percent sure. A wallet, I think."

"Michael put his wallet under there? Why?"

"Not *his* wallet, no," Gregor said.

They had both turned to look at the operation at the evergreens. It was not going well. The first police officer had retired from the fray, and a new one, smaller, slighter, and more wiry, was making the attempt. Like the first man, he was starting by trying to slide in on his back. The alternative would have required him to press his face into the new snow and then down to the icy crust beneath it. He got less than half his body under the branches before he had to stop.

"That's really crazy," Mark said. "He can't do it that way. Why don't you just let me go in and get it?"

"That's all I'd need," Gregor said. "Your mother having a fit at me because you'd ended up in the hospital again, cut to ribbons by evergreen needles."

"I wouldn't be cut to ribbons," Mark said. "It's just a matter of doing it right. Come on. I'll find whatever it is. I'll do it for Alice."

"What?"

"Alice," Mark said. "She's just over there. She's inspired me. The most beautiful woman on campus."

Gregor turned to look at Alice Makepeace, standing with the crowd at the edge of the library. Her red hair gleamed in the sun. Her black cape floated in the wind. She was the most noticeable person on the scene.

He turned back and saw that Mark had already left him, skidding down the hill on what he now realized were scuffed, brown penny loafers. Snow was fly-ing everywhere. If Liz didn't kill him for letting Mark be here at all, she was go-ing to kill Mark for going out into ankle-deep snow in penny loafers and what appeared to be no socks. Gregor hurried down the hill after him. His own footwear was not exactly ideal. He consoled himself with the thought that wing tips, unlike penny loafers, had shoelaces. Why that should matter, he didn't know.

He got to the bottom of the hill just as Mark was saying, "Think of it like you were retrieving a baseball. You've got to get baseballs out of all sorts of places, right. Would you do that on your back? Would you do that humping your body up and down like you were a horny squirrel who needed glasses?"

Gregor coughed.

The wiry young police officer looked interested. "Baseballs," he said. "Yeah."

The police officer got down on the ground again, this time flat on his stomach. There was, Gregor realized, a lot of snow, much more than there seemed to be when you were standing up. Lying facedown, the police officer's face was crammed into it. When he tried to slide under the branches, it got up his nose.

"Don't push yourself," Mark said. "Pull yourself. Keep yourself flat. Hold your breath if you have to. It's only going to be for a couple of seconds."

The police officer stood up. "Jesus," he said, "you try it. I'm going to drown."

"Okay," Mark said.

Gregor should have realized what Mark was going to do. If he had, he would have stopped him. Mark was on the ground before anybody realized what was happening. Brian Sheehy saw what was going on and hurried forward. The wiry young policeman shot out a hand to stop his progress. They were all too late. Mark went flat on his face and stomach, shot out his right arm, and pulled himself under the evergreens.

"Crap," he said as he disappeared from view and then, "Got it."

A second later he had pulled himself out again, this time by sticking out his left arm and pulling the other way. When he got to his knees, he was holding the wallet between his teeth, and the entire front of his sweater was coated with snow. In a minute, Gregor knew, the snow would melt and he'd be soaking wet.

"Take it," Mark said, handing it to Gregor. "If it's not what you want, I'll have to go in again. Because you can't see anything under there, not the way you have to be lying to fit. That's not Michael's wallet by the way. I've seen his wallet a million times. It doesn't look anything like that."

Gregor hadn't expected it to be Michael Feyre's wallet. He hadn't expected it to have anything in the way of money or credit cards in it either. He took it from Mark and bent it back and forth in his hands. It was stiff with plastic cards, but none of them were in the cardholders.

Mark looked, curious. "Where are they? I could feel them, but they're not there."

Gregor felt along the inside edges at the crease between the cardholder pocket and the fold for paper money. He found the slit in the lining without too much trouble. He stuck his fingers in and came out with a thick stack of Windsor Academy student ID cards. There were ten of them, all of boys.

"Holy crap," Mark said. "That's my lost card. That's *Michael's* card."

"I expected that would be here," Gregor said. "Michael lost his card. Then he figured out who had it." He shuffled through the cards quickly, and toward the middle he found the anomaly, the one he had been looking for. This was not a photo ID, and it was not a Windsor Academy card. It was a VISA debit card issued by something called the First National City Bank of Sheboygan, Wisconsin.

"What's that?" It was Brian Sheehy, moving in from the hill. A lot of people were moving in, including Danny Kelly and several uniformed police officers. "That's a bank card. Who's M. C. Medwar? Do we have an M. C. Medwar in this case?"

"It all depends on how you look at it," Gregor said. Then he handed the wallet, and its contents, to Brian Sheehy. "There it is, everything Michael Feyre needed to hang somebody with and what got him hanged himself. I knew there was only one person who could possibly have done all this. I just couldn't figure out why."

SIX

1

Oddly, **Peter Makepeace was** calmer than he had ever been before in his life. He was calmer than he had been on the day he had interviewed for this job, in spite of the fact that he had known, at that interview, that there was virtually no chance that he would be turned away. It seemed to him now that he had spent his entire life afraid. As a boy, he had been afraid that he would not measure up to his father's idea of what Makepeace boys were supposed to be. He would not be athletic enough, or socially graceful enough, or intellectually easeful enough. It was ease, not achievement, that mattered in the Makepeace boys when it came to education. It was not acceptable to fail, but it was also not acceptable to swot. Peter had had disturbing tendencies toward swotting that he had only put down with great difficulty. If he had been born into another kind of family, or aspired to another kind of life, he would have done graduate work in philosophy and written a book on aesthetics. He had tried to do just that a few years ago when being who and what he was had suddenly seemed not nearly enough, but it was too late. Whatever spark he might have had for it when he was first in college was gone now. He had been unable to think of anything to say that wasn't a cliché.

He had no idea why he was thinking about aesthetics now, but he was, and at the back of it was the greatest revelation he had ever had about himself as a human being. He was a coward. There was no other word for it. He had not only lived on fear, he had let it rule him, even when the smallest effort at thought would have revealed his fears to be mostly fantasies. Maybe the truth was that he had loved fear, but that didn't feel quite right. It was more a lack of imagination. He had never been able to picture himself as other than what he was. When he had tried, he had felt as if he were sinking into an abyss. His father would have had no respect for him if he had become the greatest professor of philosophy in the Western world and written the greatest work of modern philosophy. In the end he would have had no respect for himself if he had done those things either. The problem was he had no respect for himself for having not done them or for having done what he had actually done.

My self-esteem is a cesspit, he thought, and almost laughed. He remembered, at the last minute, that he was still standing outside. He had only thought of going back to President's House and making the calls he needed to make. He didn't want Gregor Demarkian or that repulsive police chief to start staring at him as if he were a lunatic or, worse yet, think that he had murdered Edith Braxton and tried to poison Mark DeAvecca. They thought Alice had done both, Peter knew that. If he were completely honest with himself, he thought so, too. Alice was a profoundly foolish woman, foolish to the point of being dangerous, but she was not a coward.

He turned carefully away from the scene where Mark was standing in his cotton crewneck sweater—that kid was a mess; he couldn't even remember to wear a coat in subzero temperatures—and began to make his way back up the hill to the library and then from the library to the quad. There were phone calls he needed to make, people he had to talk to, arrangements he had to finalize. He saw Alice on the other side of the hill, but he didn't go to her. She didn't need him. She never needed him. He didn't want her. It was all going to be bad enough without hearing in her his father's voice.

After he had been afraid of disappointing his father, he had been afraid of disappointing his "friends." He understood now that these people were not friends as the word was ordinarily defined. They were not people he was particularly close to or for whom he felt a particular responsibility. Rather, they were men and women he had grown up with, in that peculiar world where nobody was really rich but private schools and subscriptions to the symphony were assumed as a matter of course. He tried to think of himself outside of that world and couldn't. It had its own rules and its own language, as any world did, and he knew neither the rules nor the language for any other.

He got all the way across the quad without being stopped. He had expected somebody, parents arriving to take their children if no one else, to insist that he explain it all on the spot. He was grateful that it didn't happen. He got to President's House and climbed the front steps. He went into the foyer and down the hall to the study. He had other pictures of Alice, ones he hadn't burned. He didn't go looking for them.

He thought, instead, of a man who had taught at Windsor one of the first years he was here. His name had been Steve something. The silly custom of using only first names often meant that he couldn't remember anyone's last name. It didn't matter. Steve was just about to defend his dissertation at MIT in something called "behavioral psychology," and the school had hired him to teach one half-year course in psychology and three sections of intro biology. If they hadn't been in a bind, with their regular biology teacher out sick with uterine cancer on no notice at all, they would never have hired him. Steve most definitely did not fit the Windsor ethos. In fact, Peter thought now, Mark DeAvecca reminded him a little of Steve—or at least Mark did when he wasn't being odd on whatever it was he was being stoned out on. The two of them had the same odd attitude to all things intellectual, and the same air of being absolutely at home with Shakespeare as well as Homer Simpson.

It was the at-homeness that Peter was thinking about now. He was at home in his own world among his own people, but outside of that he was uncomfortable everywhere. Steve had been comfortable no matter where he was, and in spite of the fact that he didn't fit and that he must have known that people disapproved of him, he didn't seem to care. There were teachers here who made it a policy to show enthusiasm for the things "the kids" really liked, as a way of staying relevant. They pretended to love *Spiderman* and *Triple X* and the music of Jack Off Jill. The operative word was "pretended." It was a conscious decision, and it was made on the assumption that these same kids would one day abandon their enthusiasm for all that and choose to like jazz and Robert Altman instead.

Steve had not needed to pretend, not in either direction. In spite of the fact that he was a "science person," he had a knowledge of English literature that was both wide and deep. He had read Jane Austen and Henry James with insight and understanding. He had also read Stephen King and Isaac Asimov. He made none of the kinds of distinctions Peter was used to seeing academics make when they dealt with popular culture. He didn't pick out one small esoteric corner of science fiction or horror, one little group of authors most people had never heard of, to heap with praise and compare to Dante. He enjoyed both Stanislaw Lem and space operas.

In fact, Peter thought, "enjoyment" was the word for Steve. Steve enjoyed himself. He enjoyed his research. He enjoyed his teaching. He enjoyed reading and music and politics and debating. There must have been some things that left him cold, but Peter couldn't remember ever having found any.

I do not enjoy myself, Peter thought, and that was true. He had never in his life enjoyed himself in the way Steve did every day. Steve had successfully defended his dissertation and gone off to the University of California at Santa Barbara to work with a woman named Leda Cosmides, who was the most important researcher in his field. Peter was sure he was enjoying himself there, too. California was the place where everybody was supposed to enjoy himself. Steve enjoyed Big Macs and Whoppers, chain-restaurant tacos, and the best food in Boston when it was provided by the Board of Trustees. He enjoyed PBS documentaries on the glories of Rome and the continuing advantages of South Park, Colorado. He enjoyed "Song of Joy" and "Sugar Sugar."

"He makes no distinctions," Alice had said, with distaste, at the time—and at the time he had agreed with her and shared that distaste. When he wasn't sharing the distaste, he was feeling either annoyed or frightened. He was frightened of Steve because Steve was so damned anarchic. He was annoyed with Steve because Steve threatened to undo all the work they did at Windsor to turn their children into serious, successful adults.

Fear, Peter thought again. He picked up the phone and felt the weight of it in his hand. It was an old-fashioned sort of phone. It was heavy. He wished he could get Steve back, right now, just to talk to him. He wished he remembered some of the things Steve had been so enthusiastic about, the authors, the television shows, the music. He thought about going out to exit 30 on I-95 and getting himself a Big Mac, but he couldn't really see himself eating it. He'd never developed the taste for that kind of thing. He'd trained himself too well to think of that kind of thing as anything but a walking heart attack.

Fear, he thought again. He just wanted to break free, one time, and not be running on fear. Fear of the past. Fear of the present. Fear of the future. Fear of living, because the longer you lived the more chances you had to screw up.

He put the phone down, picked up the receiver, and punched in the number for Jason Barclay's Manhattan office. Jason Barclay was the president of the Windsor Academy Board of Trustees. Peter was sure he was expecting this call. Somebody would have been keeping him informed about the progress of the police investigation. He would have heard about the police tape going up around Maverick Pond, even if he hadn't seen it for himself on CNN.

The phone was picked up on the other end by Adele, Jason's secretary. Peter told her who he was and waited. He did not have to wait long.

"Well," Jason said, when he came on the line, "what's going on?"

"The best information is that they're going to make an arrest sometime this afternoon," Peter said.

"Arrest of who?" Jason asked.

Peter corrected the pronoun in his head. Then he wondered why the women who graduated from "good schools" had no trouble remembering the grammar they were taught as students, but the men always did.

"I don't know who the chief suspect is at the moment," Peter said. "It's not the kind of thing they're telling me."

"You should have made it your business to find out."

"I have made it my business to find out," Peter said, "but as far as I can tell, Demarkian isn't telling anybody—not even the police."

"We have somebody in the Windsor Police Service, don't we?"

"In the mayor's office," Peter said. "And in the prosecutor's office. It works, most of the time."

"I hope it's going to work this time," Jason said. "We've got to do something. It's all over the national news."

"I don't think there's much you can do with a murder investigation. And this *is* a murder investigation now that Edith is dead. You might as well be prepared for it. It may turn out that Michael Feyre was murdered, too."

"I'm more interested in that other one, the kid who didn't die. The one whose mother is a newspaper reporter or whatever she is."

"She's a columnist. I think you're very intelligent. That's the one I'd worry about, too."

"And?"

"And we have absolutely no control over her whatsoever and probably can't get it. I think we're going to have to face the fact that we lost the ability to control this mess days ago, and we're not going to get it back. Parents have been arriving all day taking their children out of school. I think they'll go on arriving for some time now."

"Taking their children out permanently?"

"I don't know. You'd have to talk to the bursar, or the dean of academic affairs, or whoever they're talking to. They're not talking to me."

"Are they talking to Alice?"

"I doubt it. She isn't the kind of woman people confide in."

There was a silence on the other end of the line. Peter could imagine what was going on in Jason's head. Jason had had an affair with Alice himself that first year they were at Windsor before he'd been elevated to the chairmanship of the board. That was back before Alice had settled on her modus operandi, and her conviction that only working-class boys could give her real orgasms.

"Peter?"

"I'm here."

"Say something. You're close to this situation. I'm not. Tell me what you're thinking about. Give me a clue."

"I was thinking about orgasms."

"What?"

"Orgasms," Peter repeated. "Orgasms are supposed to be great releases. You're supposed to lose all sense of yourself, to get lost in the moment. I don't think I've ever had one, although I've ejaculated often enough."

"I think you're losing your grip."

"Maybe. I think I'll quit this job now before you get around to firing me next week. You will get around to firing me. And I find, thinking about this, that I don't really care one way or the other what happens to Windsor Academy. I just know I don't want to be the one to deal with it."

"Well," Jason said, "the board will of course consider the submission of your resignation—"

"No, Jason, I'm not submitting my resignation. I'm quitting. Right here. Right now. As of this moment. I'm done. Get somebody else to deal with this mess. I won't."

"You can't do that," Jason said automatically. "You've got a contract. You're required to give us notice. If you walk out, we could sue you."

"Go right ahead. I don't own much. Most of what we have is Alice's, and most of it's untouchable."

"You'll never work in another school."

"No," Peter said, "I won't. Thank God."

"This is completely and utterly irresponsible."

"Of course it is," Peter said, "and I've been responsible all my life. And now I've stopped. I really have stopped, Jason. I don't want to do this anymore. I don't want to do anything anymore."

"But you can't—" Jason said.

Peter hung up the phone in his ear.

He had had no idea that he was going to do what he had just done, but he was very happy he had done it. It was the right note, the note he had been looking for all day. He went out of the study into the living room. He wondered where Alice was, and what she was doing. He wondered if it would matter to her one way or the other if she came in and found him dead on the floor. The furniture all belonged to the school. A headmaster was no different than any other faculty member in a boarding school. His life belonged to the school, twenty-four seven. He owned nothing but what he wore. His housing, his furniture, even his food were all provided.

He went to the living room fireplace and looked at the rifles there. They were perfectly useful rifles as far as he knew. They had not been disabled in any way, although they contained no ammunition. There was something so alluringly English about guns over a fireplace; even a school as "progressive" as Windsor had not been able to resist using them. He could go into Boston and buy ammunition. He didn't think he would.

The sensible thing would be to hang himself, as Michael Feyre was supposed to have done, to put a rope from the utility room over the sprinkler system pipes and stand on a chair and then kick the chair out from under him. He looked at the sprinkler pipes. They looked fragile. They probably weren't. He went out into the hall again and then to the back where the kitchen was. The utility room was just through the kitchen near the back door. He went in and stood next to the washing machine and looked at the coil of rope where it sat on the shelf above the freezer and had sat the whole time he had been at Windsor. He tried to imagine it as a snake, the way horror novelists were supposed to like to do. He had never read a horror novel either. There were so many things he had never done. There were so many things he would never do. It wasn't true that where there was life there was hope. Some people left some things far too late.

All of a sudden a song popped into his head, a song from his early adolescence, that had been big on the radio when he was a teenager and had stuck with him in spite of the fact that he'd thought at the time that the music was stupid and the lyrics were stupider. "Sixteen Tons," that was what it was called, all about selling your soul to the company store, sung by somebody called Tennessee Ernie Ford. There was a lot of bass, and not much melody. The whole thing was brain-dead and repetitive. He couldn't get it out of his head.

He'd sold his soul to the company store, all right. He was going to go on selling it, too, because he knew now that he did not have the courage even to commit suicide. He would not load one of the guns in the living room. He would not throw this coil of rope over the sprinkler system pipes. He would not down an entire prescription bottle of whatever Alice might have in the medicine cabinet upstairs. He had used up what little store of courage he'd had when he'd quit his job, and now he regretted even that.

He sat down on the utility room floor abruptly, slamming his coccyx against the floor tiles with such force that he was sure he'd broken it. There was pain, but it felt very far away. Mostly there was nothing, this room, this floor, the sight of his long-fingered hands on his knees, nothing and nobody, nowhere. It didn't matter. He would not kill himself. He would not leave this world he was used to. He might leave Alice, if she didn't leave him, but he would trade her in for another woman of the same type, if perhaps with more sexual discretion. He had nowhere to go. What was worse, he had nothing he really wanted. He couldn't abscond to the Bahamas or take up the bongo drums and become a Beatnik or take to drink and end up on Skid Row. Sartre had had it right. There was no exit, and hell was other people.

That's trite, he thought.

Then he put his head down on his knees and began to cry.

2

For Philip Candor life had become both simple and purposeful. As soon as Gregor Demarkian had left his apartment, Philip had gone into action. He had given his situation a great deal of thought. He had seen too many people who had gone "underground" only to be discovered in middle age and dragged back to face the spotlight. In his case he was branded with an identity he had never chosen for himself or wanted to choose for himself. When all that happened in Idaho he had been not much more than a child, and he had not been on some crusade to rob banks for the revolution or blow up town houses for world peace or destroy federal office buildings to strike a blow against One World Government. He'd been doing nothing but protecting himself and his family from armed men who were determined to kill them, and who had proved that determination a hundred times by firing shots right past their gate and into their house. It was true that you didn't really have a right to self-defense against government officers who had come to arrest you, but they hadn't come to arrest him, and he hadn't fully understood what they were doing at the gate or why they had a right to be there. He had had no source of information about the outside world except his father—and, let's admit it, his father was a raving nut. Philip thought he had known that even then, or at least suspected it.

The problem was that Philip didn't want to turn himself in, didn't want to risk the chance that he would not get a new trial after all, didn't want to spend even a single day more than he already had in federal prison. They were supposed to be cushy berths, federal prisons, but Philip knew better. They were brutal places, and the fact that you didn't have to worry so much about getting porked up the ass by a man convicted of beating his baby to death did not make them easier to endure. Prison was the death of civilization. It was the place where you ceased to be a human being. It was the place where he himself had been frozen in time, so that it wasn't until he'd walked out the door and gone on his own that he'd begun to change in the ways he had needed to change in order to grow up. He was not sorry that he had killed the two officers he had killed. He had only returned fire when fired upon. He was sorry that he had had to leave his brothers with his mother and the same vicious isolation he had experienced himself. He had a terrible feeling he knew what they would be like now if he could ever risk the chance of seeing them.

Fortunately, he was prepared for this, and he knew enough about the game to know what he must and must not do. He took his wallet out and left it on the coffee table in the living room, taking only the bills in the fold. He left everything else: ID card, driver's license, credit cards, health insurance card, library card. He got an American Airlines flight bag out of his closet and looked under the stiff plastic shape board in the bottom. He had another wallet with another driver's license in it, in the name of Joseph Baldwin, from the state of Colorado. There was also a bank debit card and a small key to a safety deposit box in a bank in Chicago. The safety deposit box held the rest of his identity cards, but no other bank debit cards. It was too hard to service two of those at once. He would have to go to Chicago first and get a safety net and set up yet another bank account. He could never be too careful.

He had ditched his clothes in the bedroom, then thought better of it and deposited them carefully in the hamper. He had changed his shoes and packed his favorite pair of sneakers and a good dress pair. He had filled the airline bag with all the underwear he could cram into it and a few things he might need to change. It was better to carry as little as possible. What you carried weighed you down. He dressed in chinos and a sweatshirt. He found the contact lenses that changed his blue eyes to a deep brown and popped them in. He found the dye comb and ran it through his hair. Joseph Baldwin was supposed to be a blond. He couldn't really get that good an effect with a dye comb, but he could at least make his hair nothing like it was now.

He had stepped away from the mirror and looked himself over. The idea was not to completely transform his appearance. It was to look uninteresting so that nobody paid attention to anything you did. People could only see what they looked at.

Then he had gone back out into the living room and gotten the gun from the drawer in which he'd put it. He was not a naturally violent man. He was not a revolutionary. He wasn't even a fugitive, at least not in his own mind. He was somebody named Philip Candor, not somebody named Leland Beech. He was a teacher of mathematics with a good degree from a Little Three college, not a back country yahoo surviving on roots, berries, populism, and conspiracy theories.

Joseph Baldwin, he reminded himself now.

The other car was parked in a garage in Boston, the space paid for by the month on Joseph Baldwin's account. He stopped in during the summers to take it out, a man who lived in Colorado and came to Boston to see his parents during the vacations when he didn't have to teach school. The men who worked in the garage were mostly transients. They saw hundreds of people a day, dozens who had long-term parking deals. They wouldn't remember him from one day to the next, if any of them bothered to look at him at all. He went up to the top floor, where the long-terms were kept, and got into a silver gray Volkswagen Golf. The trick was never to buy a memorable car or one in a memorable color. Philip Candor's car back at Windsor, however, *was* memorable. It was a bright yellow Jeep Wrangler, as noticeable on Main Street as a circus elephant would have been, if Windsor had allowed circuses. It didn't. It considered circuses to be hotbeds of animal abuse.

He eased the car out of its space and down the ramps. He turned on the news and listened for any sound of his name. There was none. There was a lot on the investigation at Windsor Academy, but either the feds were slow on the uptake—not an unusual occurrence in his experience—or Demarkian hadn't called them yet. Since he couldn't believe the second, he had to assume the first. That gave him a little time. If he was careful, if he never drove any faster than the speed limit, if he did not do what they would expect him to do, he ought to be out of their line of sight long before they realized he was gone.

He was going to miss it though. He knew that. He liked the life he had built for himself. He liked teaching, and he liked mathematics. He had quite a bit of money put aside, but not enough so that he would never have to work again. Teachers didn't make that kind of cash, and although his stabs at the stock market had been lucrative, he was nobody's Warren Buffett. He would have to find something to do, and inevitably it would be less pleasant work than what he had become used to.

He could always fake credentials, but he knew he wouldn't. That was far too risky, and it was far too easy to get caught. Besides, he could never fake credentials as good as the ones he had earned honestly, and he was very proud of those.

He was just making his way onto I-95 north when it hit him: he was his father's son after all. He might not restrict his reading to the Bible and *The Turner Diaries*. He might not live out in the middle of nowhere convinced that the mailman was an agent of the One World Government bent on destroying him by any means necessary. He was still living a life of subterfuge and deception. If his father could see him now, he'd be proud as hell of him. He'd managed to trick them at their own game. He wasn't so much as a blip on their radar.

Of course his father couldn't see him now. His father was dead, shot in the back by a federal agent wielding a rifle he only half understood how to use. His brothers were living God only knew where, doing God only knew what, except that Philip didn't believe in God and had never understood how anybody could. He had left all that behind in Idaho, too.

He wondered if it mattered that his paranoia was justified, while his father's had not been, and then he saw the entrance to the interstate and slowed down to make his way onto the ramp.

Paranoia was paranoia. It didn't matter if it was justified or not. You had to go where it took you.

3

Back on the hill, Mark DeAvecca had finally gotten cold. He let Gregor and the police chief mess around with the wallet he had found for them and whatever else it was they were looking for under those evergreens and retreated to the library, where there was a possibility that he might get warm. He was, he'd realized, actually himself again. His head was not fuzzed. He didn't feel anxious and panicked. He could think and think clearly. What he was thinking was that it was time for him to get out of this place once and for all. His mother had a point. There was something wrong here, or at least something wrong for him. He had heard the talk today about how the school was about to close. Parents were showing up at the gates ready to take the boarding students home, and the day students weren't here at all, since they were still on the hiatus that had been declared when Michael died. It didn't matter. He didn't want to be here anymore. Even if it meant having to repeat the tenth grade—well, okay, that rankled. That made him completely nuts—but even so, it was time to get out of here and do something sane. Maybe he could convince his mother that, given the ordeal he had been put through, he deserved to do something more interesting between now and the end of the school year besides vegetating in Connecticut while Geoff finished third grade.

321

He had just settled himself on the deep ledge of the window in the air lock just inside the doors to the faculty wing of the library and begun contemplating the arguments he could use to convince his mother that he'd be just fine taking a practical filmmaking course nights at NYU and living on his own at Jimmy's place in the city, when the door from the inside of the wing slammed open and Alice Makepeace came in. For a moment he was simply surprised to see her. He had seen her going through in the other direction just a little while ago, and he had assumed that she was on her way back to President's House. Now she was here again, and he almost said, "I'm beginning to think you're following me around."

He stopped himself just in time. The woman had no sense of humor. She'd think he meant it seriously. And although he might not be attracted to her in the way she wanted him to be, and he was sure she wanted him to be, he couldn't ignore the force of her personality. He sank back a little onto the window ledge. She looked him up and down as if he were some kind of garbage she'd found, inexplicably, on her bedroom floor.

"Jesus Christ," she said, "I can't get away from any of you."

"I was sitting here when you came in," Mark said.

"I just had to duck out the back door of my own house to avoid my own husband," she said. "It's intolerable what's going on here. It's entirely your fault."

Mark thought of that evening in the cafeteria, the one that had ended with his nearly dying. He could still feel the pain in his stomach and the even worse pain in his esophagus and chest as everything came up in racking spasms. Coffee, ice cream, chicken soup from Gregor Demarkian's room service order: it had all come flying out of him. He might not remember it hitting the ceiling of Sheldon's apartment's bathroom, but he did remember what it felt like. He remembered being scared to death.

Suddenly, he was as angry at this woman as he had been at God when his father died, and that was in the days when he had believed, with perfect trust, that God not only could do everything but would do everything, if you asked Him. He didn't know where he'd gotten that idea. His parents were not religious. He did know that it was lodged in his head as firmly as the knowledge that his name was Mark, and that when his father had died in spite of his prayers it had become dislodged and what had followed it was fury so cold and all-encompassing that he had come very close to killing the funeral director who had been responsible for cremating his father's body.

His anger at Alice was like that, but this time he didn't even want to stop it coming out.

"I thought they would have arrested you by now," he said. "I'm surprised you haven't taken off in a Ford Bronco."

"Don't be an ass."

"You gave me the coffee," Mark said, "twice. I was going to get it for myself, and you wouldn't let me. You went and got it by yourself. There was enough sugar in it to give me diabetes."

"You asked for enough sugar in it to give you diabetes."

"You did something to make Michael commit suicide," Mark said. "You did it because he was going to screw you over, and you tried to kill me because you knew I knew it. He'd been talking about it for two weeks. He said you were old and you disgusted him. He said you fucked like an animal, and it was gross in a hag like you. He said you'd never dare do anything about it because he could screw you over for real if you tried."

"Don't be ridiculous," Alice said. "You don't know what you're talking about."

"I do know what I'm talking about, and when I get finished telling them, they'll have everything they need."

Alice looked him up and down like garbage yet again. Mark thought she had the most amazing ability to make people feel like garbage.

"Have you decided yet why I should kill an old fool like Edith Braxner?"

"Because she knew, too," Mark said quickly. "Or she knew that you'd tried to poison me. She knew too much and you killed her."

Alice smiled slightly, and when she did Mark realized that he hadn't gotten through to her before. She was a magnificent woman, but her magnificence resided in her egotism, and it was only by overcoming that that he could have had some kind of victory over her. He had no idea what victory he wanted. He only knew that he hadn't made a dent.

She gave him one last sweeping look of contempt and then headed back outside to the hill, her long curtain of red hair swaying like a perfect swathe of scarlet silk in the wind let in by the opening of the door.

If he ever married, Mark thought, he would marry somebody not beautiful but kind.

SEVEN

1

It had come to the part in every case that Gregor hated most: the part where there was nothing left to do but wait. Waiting left him with much too much time to think, and his thinking went off on tangents: Bennis, Mark, terrorism, Windsor, the fact that he had once again solved, not the case he had been hired to solve, but a different and connected one that nobody would ever be prosecuted for. It seemed to him to be a deep truth about himself that he could never look any problem directly in the face. He was carrying a Windsor municipal check for one dollar in his pocket, handed to him on the assumption that he would aid Brian Sheehy and his force in the investigation into the death of Edith Braxner. So far all he'd done that was directly connected to Edith Braxner was to let the forensics people know they were looking for something portable Edith might have eaten or drunk while she was in the library. Little or nothing had come out of that so far. Edith had been carrying a box of vanilla Myntz in her bag, but there was no sign that any of them had been tainted, and Gregor didn't see how they could have been. Myntz were hard little things. There was a possibility that you could take one and paint it with liquid cyanide, but Gregor's hunch was that that would have taken much too much time and been too finicky an attention to detail than this murderer was able to provide. If Edith was in the habit of sucking on Myntz throughout the day, there was no way the murderer could be sure she wouldn't pop the tainted one into her mouth then and there, voiding the advantage that would come if she died of the poison elsewhere, with the murderer not in evidence. If she wasn't in the habit, it might be days before she ate the tainted mint, or she might give it to somebody else. In either case she would have gone on being the threat she always was.

"We can only speculate about why it was suddenly necessary to kill her when it hadn't been before," Gregor told Brian Sheehy as they walked back up the hill toward the quad. The police tape was still up and would be now for at least a day. Brian Sheehy wasn't going to take the chance that there was something else lying around that might connect the murderer to the crime. "I can't see that she could have known anything new about what was going on. Nothing's happened here in the days since Michael Feyre died. Everything's been on hold. Maybe she just realized the importance of something she had considered trivial before. Or maybe not. Maybe she was harping on some detail that she thought was unimportant, but that was instead very important, and our murderer didn't want her around talking when at any moment the things she said could make people think about all the wrong things."

"It would be good if we had all that nailed down for the prosecutor," Brian said. "He doesn't like fuzzy thinking much. Juries hate it."

"Juries are supposed to," Gregor said. "But this isn't as fuzzy as it seems. Edith stuck her nose into everybody else's accounts. She scolded people for handing in sloppy ones. That means she was at least looking at them. From the way people talk, she was looking at all of them. Wouldn't you say that?"

"We'll get Danny to ask the women in the financial office."

"Maybe she had friends there," Gregor said, "or maybe those things are left lying around where anybody could look at them, but nobody but Edith did. She's dead, though, because of the fact that she did. And because of the fact that she complained to people about them, therefore letting them know that she did. Somehow I doubt that she realized what was actually going on. If she had, I think she would have gone either to Peter Makepeace or to the police."

"How do you know that she didn't go to Peter Makepeace?" Brian said.

"Because he hasn't said anything yet to cover his ass on the issue," Gregor said. "I don't mean I'd expect him to get all giggly and be unable to stop talking about it, but I think he would have said something, something out of the way and in passing, that would at least have lessened the chances that we'd take Edith's habit of snooping all that seriously. And he didn't. He never said a thing. Whether he was protecting himself or the institution, if Edith had come to him with a story about how the accounts were being tampered with, he'd have said something to try to distance himself from it and to exonerate the school."

"He could have done it himself then," Brian said. "That's an idea I like. Arrest the headmaster of Windsor Academy for bank fraud, grand theft, and murder."

"At the moment you can't arrest anybody," Gregor said. "Not for anything. And although I can promise you that you'll have the evidence to arrest somebody for bank fraud and grand theft, I can't promise that you're going to be able to arrest anybody for murder. I miss the FBI sometimes. In spite of all the nonsense you hear on television, what we did in the Bureau was mostly deal with idiots. You see all this stuff about careful investigators tracking clever killers. Clever my foot. These idiots would bash some old woman's head in and walk around for three days carrying her pocketbook in broad daylight. They'd walk into a convenience store in Kansas, blow everybody away with a shotgun, take the twelve dollars in the cash register, and then hijack the store truck that was painted lime green with a big logo on it and use that to try to make it over the border to Nebraska. It was mind-numbing. That's why I could never make myself watch that movie *Dumb and Dumber*. Stupidity isn't funny; stupidity is lethal."

"Well, it's like that on the municipal level, too," Brian said. "But it's a good thing, if you know what I mean. If criminals were too intelligent, we probably wouldn't catch them."

"Maybe we don't," Gregor said. "Maybe there are crimes happening day and night that we know nothing about because the perpetrators are too intelligent to let us know they've happened and too intelligent to let us catch them."

"Do you think that's true?"

"No," Gregor said. "I'm not saying there are no intelligent criminals. There must be. But by and large, it's like Isaac Asimov said, 'Violence is the last resort of the incompetent.'"

"I like that," Brian said. "Guy who wrote science fiction. I remember him. Is it really going to be grand theft? Because it sounds nuts to me, picking up the nickels and dimes from kids' allowances."

Gregor gave Brian a look. "Do you have kids? Teenagers?"

"They're grown," Brian said. "Out of college and on their own. Why?"

"Well, Mark told me, the day I arrived here, that the school recommended that parents give students two hundred dollars a week in allowance, but his mother gave him two fifty because she was convinced that if she didn't he was going to spend so much on books he wouldn't have anything left to eat."

"Two hundred dollars a week?"

"That's what he said. We could check it out. My guess is that most of the kids in a place like this get more. I'd say many get more than Mark."

"But two hundred dollars a week," Brian said. "That's almost as much as you'd make on the minimum wage, before taxes."

"You knew they were rich. What did you expect?"

"I don't know," Brian said. "Fifty a week? Seventy-five? Sanity?"

"These are people who spend thirty thousand dollars a year to send their kids to high school," Gregor said, "and they probably feel guilty about the boarding part of it. I know Liz Toliver does, and it wasn't even her idea for Mark to go away to school."

"Jeez," Brian said. "When I was a kid, okay, not really a kid, you know, in high school, there was the thing with Jackie Kennedy. All the stories in the papers. And I remember it said that at this boarding school she went to, the girls were only allowed to have five dollars a week. That was a rule. So they didn't get too stuck up about being rich, and the really rich ones couldn't make the poorer ones feel bad."

"John F. Kennedy died almost forty years ago," Gregor said. "His children grew up. He'd be a grandfather if he were alive today. A lot has happened in the meantime."

"Inflation hasn't gotten that bad," Brian said.

"No, it hasn't," Gregor said, "but attitudes have changed. People throw money around more now than they used to. If you've got it, flaunt it."

"I thought that was the sixties."

"It's a part of the sixties that hasn't gone away," Gregor said. "But seriously, think about it. There are, what, about three hundred and fifty students in this school? Some of them will be on scholarship—"

"They must be miserable if all their classmates have two hundred dollars a week."

"Yes. Well. Some of them will be on scholarship, but most of them won't be. Let's say that two hundred students have allowances of two hundred dollars a week or more. If you skimmed off ten dollars a week from every account, that would be two thousand dollars a week, week after week, throughout the school year."

"The school year is nine months, which is about thirty-six weeks," Brian said. "That would be, let's see, seventy-two thousand a year—"

"And not just this year," Gregor said. "I think we'll find, when we look into it, that this has been going on for close to a decade. Students come and go, after all. And if your perpetrator was careful, he'd come and go, too. He wouldn't always do the same thing at the same time in the same way. He or she, I should say. The British police give their murderer a name when they start their investigations, or they do if you can believe P. D. James. She's the only detective novelist I read anymore. Maybe because it's the British police forces she's dealing with, and I don't know enough about those to know when she's wrong. With the American mysteries, I'm always fighting with the writer about procedure."

"So this has been going on for years," Brian said. "We could pull the records and demonstrate that?"

"I don't know," Gregor said. "It won't look like anything different than ordinary student withdrawals. Our perpetrator must be intelligent enough to make the filching look like ordinary transactions. If not, he or she would have been caught years ago. I wouldn't bet on the records by themselves; I'd bet on Mark DeAvecca."

Brian raised his eyebrows. "What, Mark DeAvecca has some secret knowledge about the theft as well as about the death of Michael Feyre? I mean, okay, Gregor. He's a bright kid when nobody's poisoning him. I had him wrong. I apologize. But you're turning him into a regular James Bond."

"I'll bet he'd like that," Gregor said. "But no, it's not that he's a James Bond. It's not what he knows about the perpetrator or about the death of Michael Feyre. It's what he knows about himself."

"And that's supposed to mean what?"

"I've been thinking about it. The symptoms increased in severity after Mark came back to school after Christmas vacation, but they existed before then. They were just milder. Both Liz and Jimmy have said that Mark was being very peculiar when he came home for Christmas break. Now, that could just be the caffeine. He was drinking so much it could account for a whole lot of peculiarity. I wish they had videotapes of the way he was when he came home. Because the possibility exists that he was being poisoned long before Christmas, going back well into the fall."

"But look at him now," Brian protested. "He's been away from the poison for a day and a half, and he's a completely different person. Shouldn't that have happened over Christmas break? If he was being poisoned up here, and he went home, then after a couple of days he should have started to feel much better."

"Maybe he was still being poisoned when he went home."

"His mother was poisoning him, too? What?"

Gregor brushed this away. "Edith Braxner is dead. She's dead because she ingested cyanide. Cyanide works very quickly, within seconds, within minutes at the most. That means she had to have ingested the cyanide in the catwalk nook only moments before we found her. With me so far?"

"Of course."

"She was up on that catwalk alone. I know that because I was standing in the main reading room right near the circular staircase that is the only way on or off it. How did she get the cyanide?"

"Marta Coelho was right there," Brian said. "She could have given it to her."

"Oh, I agree," Gregor said. "Marta Coelho definitely could have given it to Edith, but even if she did, she must have given it in some form that would delay the ingestion. The perpetrator did not want to be around when Edith died. So Edith must have been given something, brownies or doughnuts or candy or something, to eat *later*. Right?"

"We've been over this before," Brian said.

"Apply it to Mark," Gregor said. "Think about him taking something home over the vacation, a gift somebody gave him, cookies laced with arsenic. Something."

"It would have been risky as hell," Brian said. "He could have had a pig out and gotten himself killed. He could have given the damned things to somebody else and killed them."

"Maybe there was something Mark and only Mark would eat, and that he'd only eat one of a day. Can't you think of something like that?"

"No," Brian said.

"I can," Gregor said. "Prescription multivitamins."

"What? Who gets prescription multivitamins?"

"Lots of people do," Gregor said, "especially rich and relatively rich people who fret about their health and their children's health. And no, don't ask. Mark was taking prescription multivitamins. In capsules. He took his last one on the day I showed up here. He took it with water in my room at the inn."

"Jesus Christ," Brian said. "This person has to be crazy. Either that or a megalomaniac. Why the hell would he—he or she, whatever—why would he bother to do that?"

"Because there'd been a mistake."

"What kind of a mistake?"

"That's what I meant when I said look to Mark," Gregor said. "I think that sometime in the fall the perpetrator made the wrong withdrawal at the wrong time. Something happened. Mark was away for the weekend, maybe, or in the infirmary, or otherwise tied up so that he *could not* have made the withdrawal in question. And that's the nightmare in this kind of scheme. That one day you'll make a withdrawal, a relatively sizable withdrawal, under circumstances in which the victim not only knows but can prove that he didn't make it himself. I say sizable because a ten-dollar mistake might be shrugged off as some kind of minor anomaly. Take fifty dollars, though, or a hundred, and once the mistake is discovered people will start to ask questions. I think that's the kind of mistake that was in fact made. And when Mark began to question what was going on with his account, the perpetrator needed to take his mind off it. So Mark got fed either the arsenic itself, or something else likely to make him immediately and violently ill, and by the time he made it back to the dorm from the infirmary, the perpetrator had already tampered with the multivitamins. It wouldn't have been hard. In fact it would have been easier and easier as time went on, because the more arsenic Mark took, the more dysfunctional he would have become. In no time at all it would have been a case of nobody believing him if he did say something about the missing money."

"And it got worse after Christmas because arsenic builds up in the system," Brian said.

"That and the perpetrator decided to screw Mark up totally by playing around with the caffeine. Don't forget there were caffeine tablets in his body as well as arsenic the night he collapsed."

"That was because the perp was trying to kill him."

"At first it was because the perpetrator was trying to make sure Mark didn't know that Michael Feyre was engaged in this particular bit of blackmail. And that would have been very hard to keep secret when Michael was Mark's roommate, and Michael was a hinter. Definitely a hinter. Let me ask you something. Did your people ask around about where on this campus somebody could find poison, specifically arsenic and cyanide?"

"Of course."

"And what did they find out?"

"Both of them, up straight, so to speak, in the science materials closet. A couple of different insecticide powders with arsenic in them in the groundskeeper's shed."

"Exactly," Gregor said. Then he looked up toward the library's wing-side door and watched Alice Makepeace sailing out of it, her long, red hair bouncing and whipping in the wind. "She's a remarkable woman, isn't she? Never mind the downside. She really is a remarkable woman. One of those people who command attention. I don't envy her. It's like a drug. And drugs are kinder."

A moment later it was Mark DeAvecca coming out of the door, his shoulders hunched, looking cold even though he'd just been inside. He saw Gregor and Brian Sheehy and came over to them.

"Hi," he said. "I need my jacket. It's really awful. I'm serious. I should have remembered. And it's not like I'm forgetting things anymore."

"I want to ask you something," Gregor said. "Sometime this fall, did you get sick? Very sick? As sick as you'd ever been before?"

"Yeah, September thirtieth. At least that was the day I went to the infirmary. I think it was Monday. I got sick on the weekend, but the infirmary isn't open on weekends. I was throwing up all over the place."

"Did you end up in the infirmary?" Gregor asked.

"For the day," Mark said. "Not even overnight. They don't like to keep you in the infirmary in this place. I don't think it's anything sinister though. That happens in a lot in schools at the beginning of the year. Everybody brings their bugs that they're immune to already and gives them to those who aren't."

"What about before that weekend?" Gregor said. "Did you go home for a weekend before then? Or did you go away?"

"No, I couldn't have. You're not allowed to leave campus for the first month. You're supposed to be getting acclimated."

"You didn't go anywhere at all?"

"Well, I went into Boston with some people. For the day, you know. We saw some movies and had lunch."

"Aha," Gregor said. "And when you got back and looked at your student account, it was short more than it should have been."

Mark looked surprised. "Yeah, it was. A hundred dollars. I looked in the book and it said I'd withdrawn it at ten o'clock, but I hadn't. I'd been in Boston at the time. I hadn't taken any money out for that trip because Mom had been up a few days before and she'd taken me out to lunch, and when she does that she always ends up slipping me more cash than I know what to do with. I'd forgotten all about that."

"Exactly," Gregor said.

Brian Sheehy cleared his throat. "I thought you wanted to go over to Hayes and look at the death scene," he said. "I don't know what you think you're going to find, but if you want to do it, we probably ought to do it now. This place looks like it's about to become a ghost town."

They all looked out over the campus, at the Student Center in front of them to their left, at the beginnings of the quad to their right. The campus was not deserted. It was full of students and their parents. They were all leaving.

2

Hayes House was full, too. The last time Gregor had been there, he had been aware of the sound of students moving just out of sight on the upper floors and in the common rooms. This time, he could see them everywhere. The front door was propped open with a clay pot filled with dirt, making it easier for students to come and go with boxes in their hands. A middle-aged woman in a long, formal coat and good gray flannel dress pants was standing near the front staircase directing a tall young man who looked buried beneath suitcases. How much stuff could these kids cram into their rooms? Gregor decided not to ask. The man he remembered as Sheldon had come out onto the front porch, livid.

"It's freezing in here, don't they understand that?" he demanded. "We have to keep this door closed. This is intolerable."

"The door *will* remain open," the woman in the gray flannel pants said, "until Max has his room cleared of his things. I have no intention of being held up. And if you try to stop me, I'll sue you. You personally. Don't think I won't do it."

Sheldon shrank a little and retreated inside, muttering to himself. If he had noticed Mark, or Gregor Demarkian, or Brian Sheehy, he gave no indication of it.

"We can start with Sheldon," Gregor said. "What's his last name anyway?"

"LeRouve," Mark said. "Do you mind if I just stay out of sight? He's only going to yell at me again. I can't take it. I'm recuperating."

"Relax," Gregor said. "I just want to check one thing."

They went through past the milling students and knocked on Sheldon Le-Rouve's door. He opened up, looked at the three of them, and practically spat.

"I've said as much as I'm going to to any policeman. I'm not saying any more. If you want to talk to me, talk to my lawyer."

"I don't think that's really necessary," Gregor said. "I just want to know one thing. On the night that Michael Feyre died, did you go to the upper floors of this house at any time?"

"I don't have to answer your questions," Sheldon said. "Get out of here."

"Then I will assume that you did go to the upper floors during the evening," Gregor said.

Sheldon reared back. "Don't be ridiculous. I don't go upstairs. I don't even do bed checks anymore. What do you take me for? It's enough that I'm stuck with these idiots day after day, I don't have to go climbing two flights of stairs five times a night to check on what kind of stupidity they're up to next. Especially that one," he cocked his head toward Mark. "That one is a real mess. A bigger one than his roommate was."

"Then you weren't upstairs that night?"

"No."

"And you would say that it is so seldom your custom to go upstairs that if you had gone, somebody would have noticed it as odd?"

"How the hell would I know what somebody would notice as odd?" Sheldon said. "They're all so drugged out most of the time, they'd probably think pink elephants were perfectly normal."

"But it would have been odd," Gregor insisted.

Sheldon looked them all over again and slammed the door in their faces.

"Well," Brian said, "that was helpful."

"It was helpful," Gregor said, "but I needed to be sure. It's the kind of man he is, though, don't you think? Everything, no matter what, would be too much trouble. Even the smallest obligation will be chucked onto somebody else if at all possible. I take it he's got seniority as a houseparent."

"Seniority?" Mark said.

"That he's been here longer than Cherie Wardrop."

"Oh, yeah," Mark said, "a lot longer. He's sort of like the school Grinch. I don't know why they don't fire him. They're so big on the ethos of the school. Maybe he's got money though. They'll put up with a lot of things in this place if you've got money."

"Let's go see the upstairs," Gregor said.

A few moments later, Gregor was almost sorry he'd insisted. There were not only two flights of stairs, but two long and steep flights of stairs. He was breathless by the time they reached the second floor and only too happy to have a chance to stop and look around. The hallway and landing were narrow. The stairs climbed along one wall. There were at least a dozen doors, most of them now open, with students packing inside them.

"Hey, Mark," people called.

Mark called "Hey" back. Gregor was happy that he didn't seem inclined to stop and give his dorm mates a play-by-play of his last few days.

They went up the next flight, which was thankfully the final one. It was the same scene here as it had been below, with the exception of the door just opposite the top of the stairs, which was not only closed, but sealed by yellow police tape.

"That was your room?" Gregor asked.

"Yes," Mark said.

"We can go in it if you want," Brian said. "I've told the Detective Division that you might want to break the seal."

"It isn't necessary," Gregor said. "It's the way the door is situated that I wanted to see. Mark, tell me something. When students are in their rooms, do they usually leave their doors open or closed?"

"Open," Mark said, "unless they're sleeping. Or, you know."

"No," Gregor said. "What?"

Brian cleared his throat again. "Unless they're engaged in self-abuse," he said helpfully.

"Michael used to keep the door closed most of the time," Mark said, "when I wasn't there. When I was, you know, I'd get to feeling hemmed in. But he didn't talk to people around here if he could help it."

"But the other doors would have been open, is that right?" Gregor said. "And would people have been home?"

"It was a Friday night," Mark said, "so most of them wouldn't have been. But some of them might have been. Kim Jun, for one. He's from Korea. He studies more than most people breathe."

"Good," Gregor said. "Exactly what I needed to hear. Timing is everything."

"What's that supposed to mean?" Brian said.

"Just what I said. Timing is everything. Let's go downstairs. There's one last thing to do. And then I'm going somewhere and getting something serious to eat. I've spent this whole trip living on crackers, soup, and a vegetarian omelet."

"It's not a bad omelet," Brian said.

Gregor ignored him, and they all trooped downstairs again. The trip down was a lot easier than the trip up, although it, too, required them to dodge students with boxes. The whole place was humming like bees on the wires in summer; and in spite of what was happening and why, everybody seemed to be almost unnaturally cheerful. He would not want to listen in to teenagers of his acquaintance if he ever came to a sticky end himself. He wouldn't want to hear some nice young person he'd known for years saying, "He was *decapitated?* Cool!"

They got to the ground floor and Gregor led them toward the back door again and the narrow corridors leading to the faculty apartments. He was still having a hard time keeping straight in his mind what part of the House was the front and what was the back. Mark said hello to seven or eight more people and stopped to talk to two, but he didn't linger. Gregor thought Mark must actually be interested in what the grown-ups were going to do. If somebody had tried to kill him, Gregor thought, he'd be interested, but he no longer understood much about people Mark's age. Except for not wanting to miss out on the action, Mark seemed to be taking the whole thing as a matter of course.

They got to Cherie and Melissa's apartment and knocked. They didn't have to wait long before the door was open and Cherie poked her head out.

"Oh, Mr. Demarkian," she said, "I thought it was one of the parents. I should leave the door open, I know I should. They do need to talk to me some of the time, or to talk to a houseparent at any rate, and Sheldon is, well, he's busy—"

"He's a son of a bitch," Melissa called from inside the apartment.

Cherie flushed. "Sorry. She's right, of course."

"Do you mind if we come in?" Gregor asked.

Cherie backed up and let them come. The apartment was stripped bare and full of boxes. Even the curtains had been taken down. Gregor was sure that the school provided the furniture for these apartments. He would have expected the school to provide the curtains as well. Maybe he was wrong, or maybe the school had but Cherie and Melissa hadn't liked them.

They all trooped into the living room, and Melissa looked up from the box she was taping. "Take a good long look," she said. "You're seeing history in the making. Windsor's first lesbian couple houseparents, symbol of all things progressive at Windsor Academy, packing up and getting out. Not that that has anything to do with our being lesbians, of course, but if the school magazine wrote it up, that's the way they'd put it. We're this year's poster children for the virtue of tolerance."

"Well, you might be," Gregor said, "but I'd be very surprised to find that you were actually lesbians. I suppose it's possible, but from what I've seen it's very unlikely. It was a good cover, though, given that this place is what it is."

"What is this?" Melissa asked. "A new version of 'don't tell me you're gay, you just need a good fuck'?"

Cherie winced at the language. "Melissa."

"Do you mind if I sit down?" Gregor said. He didn't wait for an answer. He took off his coat, laid it over the back of the couch, and sat. Melissa was suddenly very wary. Cherie looked as helpful and clueless as always. Gregor sat.

"You know," he said, "as soon as I knew that Mark had been poisoned with arsenic, I knew that there were only two people who could have possibly given it to him—three, if we count Melissa. But it had to be either Sheldon LeRouve, or you, Cherie. You were the only people who were with him in the right time period."

"There were students here at the time," Melissa said. "Don't forget that."

"Oh, I'm not forgetting it. But Mark didn't go upstairs that night. He wasn't sleeping in his dorm room. He was bunking in with Sheldon LeRouve. Any student who was going to poison him, not only with the arsenic but with the caffeine tablets, had to manage to do it in full view of the common rooms and in a very short time. But when Mark came home, he came to this apartment because Cherie invited him here."

"I did invite him here," Cherie said. "I felt sorry for him. Sheldon was being a bastard as usual, and Mark looked so sick."

"He should have looked sick," Gregor said. "He'd just come from my room at the Windsor Inn, where he'd taken his multivitamin right in front of me, and the multivitamin was full of arsenic."

"What?" Mark said.

"I've already explained all that to Brian here once today, so I won't do it again now," Gregor said. "But Mark came here, and you invited him in, and you gave him a cup of coffee and a packaged ice cream sundae."

"He asked for the coffee," Cherie said, "and he said he was hungry. He'd missed dinner. It was the only thing I had."

"The extra arsenic was in the coffee," Gregor said. "The pieces of caffeine tablets were in the sundae. That means you'd been planning this for a while, at least for the day. Why? Because I was here?"

"You're being ridiculous," Melissa said.

"Unfortunately, I'm not being ridiculous at all," Gregor told her. "It's a matter of the timing. Nobody else could have poisoned Mark that night, and nobody else could have killed Michael Feyre."

"Michael committed suicide."

"Michael was murdered, and you murdered him because he had proof of the scam you'd been pulling; and once people started looking into that scam, they'd realize Windsor wasn't the only place you'd pulled it. Find a school. Become a houseparent. Pull—something. Not always the same something you pulled here, but in every school there will be a way to make money if you know how to do it, and you did it. We'll get Brian to pull the records on the last few schools you've been at. Now that he knows what to look for, it won't be hard to find. Up until Windsor, you were always very careful. And my guess is that you always left quickly, long before anybody would get suspicious. It's too bad you didn't do that here."

"You don't know what you're talking about," Melissa said. "And you can't prove any of it. You're just speculating."

"I know that Michael Feyre did not have sex with men and that any other woman would have been both suspect and noticeable if she appeared on the third floor of this house," Gregor said. "I know that nobody else could have tampered with Mark's vitamins consistently, and nobody else had access to cyanide—"

"I thought you said arsenic," Cherie said.

"Arsenic, too. Arsenic for Mark. Cyanide for Edith Braxner because you wanted that to be quick. I don't know what you put that in, but the police will find out. They always do. Edith Braxner snooped into people's accounts. My guess is that she knew something was wrong with yours, but I think she still thought it was mostly sloppiness. Given the police presence, though, and me here, you couldn't risk it, so you didn't."

"This is ridiculous," Melissa said. "We don't have to listen to this."

"You killed Michael because he got hold of your wallet with the student IDs inside. That's how you were stealing what you were stealing here. You'd get the IDs and the students would think they'd lost them. You'd put in for new IDs that were supposed to be changed in some way in case the old ones had been stolen, but if we check we'll find that they weren't changed at all. You just didn't bother to ask for the change in the first place. So you had the IDs, and you could use the accounts. As I said we found them, ten of them together, all boys, and I'd venture to say all residents of this house. We found something else, too."

"What?" Cherie said. "A smoking gun."

"In a way," Gregor said gently. "We found a bank card from the First National City Bank of Sheboygan, Wisconsin, in the name of M. C. Medwar. Melissa Medford. Cherie Wardrop. It's really just that simple. All we have to do is talk to the tellers, go to the bank, and look at the records. It won't be hard to trace the account to the two of you. And then there's that timing I talked about. Nobody else could possibly have killed Michael Feyre, and nobody else could possibly have poisoned Mark DeAvecca, and that means nobody else could or would have wanted to kill Edith Braxner. A prosecutor will be able to stack this evidence up in court and hang you both."

"They don't have the death penalty in Massachusetts," Cherie said absently, but she had sat down abruptly on the floor and she was in tears.

PART FOUR

Violence is the last resort of the incompetent.
—ISAAC ASIMOV

1

Bennis Hannaford was not on Cavanaugh Street when Gregor Demarkian got home. He climbed the stairs past old George Tekemanian's first-floor apartment and Tibor in Bennis's second-floor apartment and walked through his own front door, hoping to find her sitting in front of the computer she had installed in the living room, but she was nowhere to be found. It was a cold first Friday in March, and he thought that the least he should have been able to expect was that she would sit still to fight. That, he had finally realized, was what had so disturbed him about the last week. It wasn't that Bennis was mad at him. Bennis got mad at him. There were times when he thought she practically made a hobby of it. The real shock was that Bennis didn't want to talk, not even to yell at him. It wasn't like her. What was worse, it was ominous as hell. A nontalking Bennis was a violation of the natural law, like a river that flowed upstream.

He got out of his traveling things and left his clothes on the floor of the bedroom when he took them off—if she was anywhere in the vicinity, *that* would get her yelling at him—and took a shower. When he got out of the shower, he looked around again, but she was still gone. He changed into "casual clothes," which these days meant he wore a sweater instead of a jacket but still wore a tie. He stared at the clothes on the floor and then picked them up. It wasn't only Bennis who yelled at him when he did that. His wife had yelled at him, too. He'd come to think of it as the definitive mark of having a woman in his life: as long as she was with him, clothes could be in closets, or in hampers, or even over the backs of chairs, but they couldn't be on the floor. He was just about to go back out into the living room when he saw the white envelope lying on his pillow, his own first name written across the front of it in Bennis's strong, sloping hand.

His first instinct was not to open it. If she had left him—but why would she leave him? What was all this about?—there was some advantage in not reading her letter. When she got back in touch with him again, he could say that he'd never found it. She would have to get back in touch with him again because her clothes were still here. He'd seen them in the closet. He got up and went through the drawers. Yes, most of them were still here. Even her underwear was still there. He sat down on the edge of the bed, on *her* side of the bed, and opened the envelope. It was one of her Main Line envelopes, the thick, cream stationery she had monogrammed every year at some place in the city of Philadelphia.

"Gregor," the letter said. He tried not to wonder what it meant that it didn't say "dear." He couldn't even remember if she ever started letters with "dear." They didn't write each other many letters.

> I don't want you to think I've run out on you. I haven't. I've just taken off for a week to think. I haven't been thinking much since we first met. I saw you, and Cavanaugh Street, as a chance at salvation, a road out of the emotional insanity of my family, a safe place. There's nothing wrong with safe places. We all need them, and I need this one, still. But it seems to me that that really isn't enough in a situation like ours. It never occurred to me, before these last few months, that you might see me as something else than a woman you loved, or that the love you say you feel for me might be something other than what I feel for you. I'm all grown up, Gregor. I need a safe place, I even need protection, but it is the protection of strength and not the shelter you give to a wounded child. I'm not even wounded anymore. I need to be to you what I would have been if you had never seen me as a waif you had to rescue, and I don't know if that's possible. I hope it is. I hope you'll take the time I'm gone to figure it all out. Figure out what it is you want from me, and who it is you think I am. Maybe we'll get lucky, and your idea of me and my idea of me will match. If not, there's nothing lost, no matter how much it feels there is. I haven't left an address or a phone number. I don't want to talk for a while. I'll see you on the twenty-first of March, unless you want to run out on me and buy yourself tickets to Pago Pago so I won't find you waiting when I get home. I love you. Bennis.

Gregor put the letter down on the bed and stared at it. The woman was insane. He'd never in his life seen her as a waif, and he'd certainly never considered the possibility that he had to rescue her. She could walk through a snake pit and come out the other side without a mark on her. Had she really spent all her time on Cavanaugh Street feeling like a needy child being taken care of by the grown-ups? He looked at the letter again. That wasn't what she had said. What she had said was that something he'd done recently had made her think that that was the way *he* saw *her*. This was rapidly turning into one of those things women found desperately important but men couldn't figure out at all. Men couldn't even figure out what the topic was.

He stuffed the letter into the pocket of his pants and went into the living room. He picked up the phone and called downstairs to see if Tibor was in his second-floor apartment. There was no answer. He checked the clock and realized it was almost five. Tibor was probably at the Ararat, not to eat—he ate late, most of the time—but to hang out with everybody and talk. He wondered if they knew Bennis was gone. Then he stopped himself. This was Cavanaugh Street. *Of course* they knew that Bennis was gone.

He got his coat back on and went out onto the landing, careful to lock the door behind him. People in this building were so complacent about the safety of Cavanaugh Street, they forgot there was a relatively unsafe city all around it and didn't bother to lock up. He practically ran down the stairs to the ground floor, if you could call slipping on the stair edges running. He went out onto Cavanaugh Street and turned toward the Ararat. It was getting dark, but not as dark as it had been at this time of night just a few days ago. Gregor wondered if that was the result of the year marching on, or of the fact that he was now farther south. He decided he was going insane. His thoughts were no longer connecting to reality. He passed the church, still under reconstruction. It looked no more finished than it had been when he left.

He turned into the Ararat and saw Tibor sitting at a big, round table in the middle of the room with old George Tekemanian, Howard Kashinian, and Grace Feinman. Grace lived on the fourth floor of his building and played the harpsichord. He hadn't even realized he wasn't hearing it. He had no idea if he loved Bennis the way Bennis wanted him to love her—*What the hell was that supposed to mean anyway? Why did women say things like that? Why wasn't love just love, for God's sake?*—but he did know that he cared for her enough so that he hadn't even noticed that the nonstop harpsichord music that had become the background to his life was not in fact in attendance. The Ararat was nearly empty. This was a good thing because Gregor had no intention of talking to Tibor in front of half the neighborhood.

He made his way over to Tibor's table, grabbed him by the shoulder, and said, "Excuse me" to Grace, Howard, and old George. He pulled Tibor over to a table along the wall and checked the window seat table to see who was there: Lida Arkmanian, Sheila Kashinian, Hannah Krekorian, and one of the Ohanian women, probably plotting another fund-raising project for the new church. He turned his mind away from the question of whether he would be asked to dress up like the Easter Bunny this time in order to collect a few thousand dollars to buy pew cushions, took the letter out of his pocket, and handed it over to Tibor.

"Look at that," he said. "Tell me what that means."

Tibor opened the letter, read it through—it was at least short; given the fact that Bennis's novels ran to eight hundred pages or more, that was unexpected—and put it down on the table.

"It means," he said authoritatively, "that she wants you to ask her to marry you."

This was not what Gregor had expected to hear. "She does? Why?"

"Because it is getting to the stage where she feels she needs to be married?" Tibor ventured. "I'm not a mind reader, Krekor. I can only tell you what I think."

"But if that's what she wants, why doesn't she say so?"

"Because she doesn't want to say so. She wants *you* to think of it."

"But I *did* think of it," Gregor said, "and she stopped talking to me. For a week. I thought she hated the idea. And then, and then, Tibor, she called me while I was in Massachusetts, got me on the cell phone while I was standing in the wind on a hillside in subzero weather, and hung up on me. Hung up on me. This is insane."

"It is possible she does not actually want to get married," Tibor said. "It is possible that she needs only to be sure that *you* want to get married."

"If you keep that up, I'm going to take to drink."

"I'm just trying to cover all the mounds," Tibor said. He shook his head. "Bases. All the bases. I've been listening to Tommy again. Krekor, really, it is all right. Tell me about your case in Massachusetts. I've been listening to the news, but they never tell me very much. Bennis will be back next week. You can think about it then."

"Do you know where she's gone?"

"No. And I am not lying, Krekor. I am no use keeping a secret. I don't know where she's gone. Donna might know."

"I'll go talk to Donna."

"She and Russ have taken Tommy to see a musical and then to dinner. You must calm down, Krekor. It is all right. It is only that Bennis did not realize before that she loved you, and now she does. She doesn't know what to do with it."

"She's been telling me she loves me for quite some time."

"Yes, Krekor, I am sure; but that is being in love, that is not loving. You should know that yourself. Tell me about the case. It will take your mind off it."

Gregor doubted if anything would take his mind off it. He had a sneaking suspicion that that was the point of the letter—although, he had to admit, he'd have been no calmer or less obsessive if Bennis had taken off without leaving a letter. Linda Melajian came over with the menus and two glasses of water. She put the water on the table and said, "You two need these, or do you just want to tell me what you'll have?"

"Yaprak sarma," Tibor said.

"A steak the size of Kansas," Gregor said, "and french fries."

"Yaprak sarma and oil and vinegar on the salad," Linda said, "and something the man could have picked up in any white bread restaurant in central Philadelphia and blue cheese on the salad. Glass of wine for the father. You want me to bring you a beer and a shot just to let you finish off this little fit of yours?"

"I'll have a glass of red," Gregor said. "I'm not in the mood for this; I'm really not."

"The first thing everybody on this street is going to do when Bennis gets back," Linda said, "is tell her all about this steak."

She walked off. She hadn't bothered to write down a thing on her pad.

"I'm living in one of the largest cities on the planet," Gregor said, "and I might as well be living in a village in the old country. They know my blood type around here."

"And usually you like it," Tibor said. "Pay attention to me, Krekor. Tell me about your case. It won't do you any good to dwell on it. It will only make you crazy."

He would dwell on it as soon as he got back to the apartment and found himself on his own. Gregor knew he would. It was the kind of thing he not only dwelt on, but that he was meant to dwell on. There had to be some sort of middle ground here. Women should be expected to meet you halfway. They never did. Why was that? Why did they get away with it? Why couldn't you just tell them to make sense and have them do it?

The salads came. His had enough blue cheese dressing on it to reconstitute France on the North American continent. He was suddenly very happy that nobody on Cavanaugh Street had gone in for renaming things Freedom Fries.

"Krekor?" Tibor said.

Gregor shrugged. "There isn't much to tell," he said. "It looked complex on the surface, but it wasn't. These two women, Cherie Wardrop and Melissa Medford, had been ripping off schools for years. Cherie would get a job at some expensive private school as a biology teacher and take a place as a houseparent, which wasn't difficult because most people would rather not be houseparents.

You can't blame them. They want to live on their own without having to be at work twenty-four seven. Anyway, they'd do that. Melissa would take an apartment in the nearest town. They'd look around and figure out the best way to skim the system, and then they'd do it: house accounts, student drawing accounts, all kinds of things. It only required patience and ingenuity, and they had both. Brian Sheehy, the police chief in Windsor, was just calling around to the other places they'd worked when I left. He'd found at least three other scams that the schools hadn't even caught. They never stayed very long in one place just in case. And they had a bank account in the name of M. C. Medwar—that was supposed to be clever, a combination of the two names—to stuff the money in that wasn't their own accounts, which were clean."

"This was it? There was no complicated motivational background, a bad childhood, a hidden rape?" Tibor said. "It doesn't feel right somehow. It doesn't feel like an American crime."

"I know what you mean." Gregor was finished with his salad. He pushed the bowl away. "At Windsor they were ripping off the student drawing accounts. Parents deposited money in school accounts, which students were allowed to draw from; but as a safety precaution they had to sign off on the transaction with their houseparent before they took the cash. Then they used their student ID as a debit card. The IDs had those magnetic strips on the back."

"Ah, yes, I see," Tibor said.

"Well," Gregor said, "Cherie and Melissa stole the IDs, which wasn't hard to do. Kids leave their wallets all over the place; they leave the IDs in backpacks and wherever. They'd pick them up. The student concerned would report an ID missing. They'd put in for a new one for the student, and when they did they were supposed—well, Cherie was supposed to; she was the responsible faculty member—they were supposed to change the PIN number. And sometimes they did, but the thing is, also as a safety precaution, the PIN had to be on file and guess who kept the files?"

"Oh," Tibor said, "that was very stupid."

"The school seemed to think that since the student IDs could only access the drawing accounts, it was more important for the school and houseparents to be able to get into the accounts than it was to make sure they couldn't be stolen from. Anyway, there they were, it was a perfect setup, and they were able to skim more than two thousand dollars a week."

"A week? I think students have much more money now than when I was one," Tibor said.

"I'm sure they do," Gregor said. "But they'd stayed at Windsor a lot longer than they had anywhere else because they were making a lot more money and it was a lot easier. Then, when Mark and Michael Feyre started school this fall, things started to fall apart. First they made a mistake with Mark and made a withdrawal at a time he knew he couldn't have made it himself. It didn't matter that they'd forged his signature on the account book. He knew where he had been at the time he was supposed to have been signing it, several miles away in Boston. So the first thing they had to do was to neutralize him so that he couldn't pursue it, and Cherie took care of that by making him sick with arsenic. Then, while he was in the infirmary, she went up to his room and tampered with his multivitamin capsules by putting a very small amount of arsenic into each one. That kept him sick, and it kept him screwed up, and they figured that if that went on long enough, he'd flunk out or be asked to leave. Which is probably what would have happened if it hadn't been for Michael Feyre."

"Ah," Tibor said. "The boy whose mother won the lottery. That was on CNN."

"Yes, the boy whose mother won the lottery," Gregor said. "Unfortunately, he was an out-and-out psychopath. He was a bully and worse. And everybody knew it. At some point he found out what Cherie and Melissa were doing, and he got hold, not only of a whole bunch of stolen student IDs that were all of students in Hayes House, but of the bank card for the secret account as well. He stole it and he told Cherie Wardrop that if she wanted it back she had to go get it for herself. He threw it under a stand of evergreens out near a pond at the back end of the Windsor campus. She went out there to try to get it back, and Mark saw her from a window in the library, lying flat on her stomach and trying to push herself under the branches. He thought she was a student or somebody from town passed out. It was Friday. He figured somebody had been drinking. By the time he got out there, Cherie was gone, and he started to think he was hallucinating. Except something about the scene bothered the hell out of him and went on bothering him.

"In the meantime Cherie had gone back to Hayes House and gone up to see Michael Feyre. According to her, he told her that since she was too stupid to find the cards for herself, he'd give them to her, but only if she 'serviced' him. What he wanted was to have her tie him up and put a noose around his neck, to, uh—"

"Autoasphyxiation erotica," Tibor said. "I am not a child, Krekor. I read the papers. They tie themselves so that they are almost strangling and that gives them a bigger orgasm. Or they think so. I have never tried it. I think it's very stupid. Every year there's another case at UPenn or Penn State, and the silly boy ends up dead."

"Yes, well, Michael Feyre had no intention of ending up dead. He always made sure to have women there for safeties. And there were always women. He was good at sexual blackmail, our Michael. Cherie said he warned her that if she tried anything funny, the cards were where somebody would be able to find them; and she wouldn't know where to get them on her own. But she didn't believe him. She thought he either had the cards on his person somewhere, or in the room, or that they were right there under the evergreens where he said he'd put them. So as soon as she got the scene all set, instead of unzipping his fly and giving him the blow job she was supposed to give him, she kicked the chair out from under him and let him hang. Then she searched the room, and when she couldn't find anything, she decided the cards were under the evergreens, and there wasn't anything she had to worry about. She went back downstairs to her apartment. Mark came home and found Michael hanging and dead. End of problem."

"But not end of problem," Tibor said, "or you wouldn't be telling me this."

"Right," Gregor said. "Mark was still disturbed about the death of his roommate, and he was disturbed about what he'd seen out the library window, and he called me. But he didn't think Michael had been murdered. He thought Michael had killed himself over Alice Makepeace."

"Alice Makepeace?"

"The headmaster's wife."

Tibor brightened. "The one with the red hair who was on the news this morning? She's a compelling woman, Krekor. Very odd when she talks, but very compelling. This Michael Feyre had an unrequited love for her, and Mark thought he had killed himself for love of her?"

"Not unrequited, no," Gregor said. "Alice Makepeace made a habit of sleeping with students. Michael was the flavor of the month, and everybody knew it. And Alice is Alice. She *is* a very compelling person, the person everybody pays attention to. So everybody, Mark included, thought that whatever had happened to Michael Feyre had happened because of Alice Makepeace, which suited Cherie and Melissa just fine. Then, Mark asked me up to school, and Cherie and Melissa knew that I was going to hear about the 'hallucination,' the person under the evergreens near the pond, and they decided they just couldn't risk him talking to me. So when he got back to the dorm on the night I arrived, Cherie invited him in for coffee, spiked the coffee with a lot more arsenic than he could handle, and gave him a prepackaged ice cream sundae with chocolate chips in it, which she'd doctored beforehand with chunks of caffeine tablets. That way, when Mark died throwing up all over creation, the hospital would find the chunks and assume caffeine poisoning. They wouldn't need to look any further. It was sheer accident and Mark's good luck that he started throwing up so soon he got most of it out of his system, and I showed up on the scene and made sure he got to the hospital on time. You wouldn't believe how hard Cherie tried not to call nine-one-one. She told me she had to get permission from President's House. She dithered. I thought she was a damned fool. She was just trying to make sure she got the job done, which she didn't. There was so much luck in this, it makes me sick to think about it."

"There was also another murder, yes? Edith. I have never known anyone named Edith. I have always thought it was a beautiful name."

"Yes, well," Gregor said, "Edith. The official explanation is that Edith knew there was something wrong with the Hayes House accounts, and that was why Cherie had to kill her. And I think that's mostly true. She was notorious on campus for checking the accounts. Her own accounts were pristine. She wrote scolding little notes to people on the mess theirs were in. She undoubtedly noticed quite a lot. She seems to have been a noticing kind of woman. But I'll bet anything that that wasn't all of it. When she died, she was up on that catwalk in the library where Mark had looked out and seen Cherie trying to get those cards. I wonder if she'd seen the same thing on the same night from another angle."

"How will you find out?"

"I won't find out," Gregor said. "Some things will have to remain mysterious. There's never a murder investigation where you know everything you wish you knew. I'll be happy to find out what Cherie put the cyanide in, what Edith ingested up there on the catwalk that caused her to die. Cherie's kept her mouth shut on that one, and I don't blame her. Edith's the death she's most likely to get sent away for good for, if they can convict her for it. She must have been in a hurry, though. Cyanide is a lot quicker than arsenic and a lot surer, too."

Linda Melajian came over and put their big entrée plates down in front of them. Then she picked up the salad plates in a stack. "Look at that," she told Gregor. "Mom really went to town on the french fries. She says she doesn't want Bennis to think you didn't get enough cholesterol while she was away. Are you going to have desert? I want to reserve enough hot fudge if you are, since you seem to be intent on killing yourself tonight."

349

"I never eat hot fudge," Gregor said.

"I do," Tibor said. "You could reserve enough for me."

"Some people just don't know what's good for them," Linda Melajian said, walking off with the salad plates.

Gregor looked down at his steak and then across at Tibor's yaprak sarma and decided he'd made the right choice. He needed red meat, and close to raw, and lots of it. Linda came back with their glasses of wine, and he drank half of his in a single gulp.

"Right," she said. "I'll get you another one."

Then she was gone again.

Gregor looked around the Ararat. It was filled with people he knew, most of them people he had known almost all his life. He could remember Lida and Sheila and Hannah as girls, walking home from school in wool jumpers with white blouses underneath them, wearing those thick-soled, black tie-up shoes that were supposed to be good for your feet. Bennis hadn't even been born then; and when she was born, she wouldn't have worn those shoes. While he was plugging away in graduate school, she had been wearing crinolines and white gloves and learning to be polite at dancing class. Did that matter? He didn't know that it did. He wished he understood what made up identity and how much of it had to do with nothing but sheer idiosyncratic perversity.

"Women," he told Fr. Tibor Kasparian, "are nuts."

2

Three days later, out in the wilds of Litchfield County, Connecticut, Mark DeAvecca was bored. Everybody always said that they wished school was over, but he'd been around long enough to know that when school was over there was never anything to do. What was worse, he was feeling really good, and really restless, and yet his mother and his doctor both wanted him to "rest." He had been resting for about a week, and he was in the mood where he understood why some people felt the need to do physical damage to furniture. His mother had gone into the city. His brother, Geoff, was asleep, spending his long spring vacation from Rumsey by staying up as late as he could get away with and then crashing for most of the day. Jimmy was in the big loft over the family room, banging away on the piano, composing something.

Mark left the house without telling anybody, half walked and half jogged the three and a half miles into the Depot, and bought a *New York Times*. Alice Makepeace's picture was on the front page in a story telling how she'd left her husband in the row over "the events at Windsor Academy." There was more coverage of the case on the inside pages, and Mark found himself thinking that it figured. Alice being Alice, even the *New York Times* thought she was more newsworthy than the discovery of what Edith Braxner had eaten that was full of cyanide, or the fact that Windsor Academy would be closed for the rest of this academic year but would open in the fall. Mark wondered who they would get to be headmaster. He thought if they had any sense, they would get one without a wife.

He jogged most of the way back home and came in to hear that there didn't seem to be any piano pounding coming from the loft. He threw his jacket over a hook in the mudroom, went through the family room to the circular stairs, and ran up.

"Hey," he said.

Jimmy was sitting at the piano, making furious notes on a sheet of lined music paper. Mark leaned against the nearest couch.

"Hey," Jimmy said, looking up, "don't you ever sit all the way down? You make me tired just looking at you."

"I went into the Depot and bought the *Times*," Mark said. "Don't tell Mom. She'll have a cow. They found out what Dr. Braxner ate."

"What did she eat? Who's Dr. Braxner?"

"The one who died at school, you know, while you were there. Didn't you pay any attention at all?"

"Mostly I was paying attention to your mother, who wasn't exactly in a good mood, and to you. Who'd almost died. I remember that part."

"Yeah, well, they killed Dr. Braxner later when I was in the hospital. I was thinking, you know, that if this had been an Agatha Christie book, I'd have been the murderer. That would have been cool."

"Somehow I can't see you as a murderer."

"I can't either," Mark said, "but I'm not in a novel. Anyway, they put the cyanide in a chocolate-covered cherry. That's what the *Times* said, anyway. Dr. Braxner liked candy. She couldn't have known that Cherie was stealing from the school if she took it though. The *Times* said somebody saw Cherie give it to her in the cafeteria at dinner that night. One of the kitchen staff, not somebody I know. I bet they can't prove it though. I mean, they can show she had the cyanide, right, but how can they be sure it was in the chocolate-covered cherry? How do they do those things?"

"Don't ask me," Jimmy said, "ask Mr. Demarkian the next time you talk to him. Is it all that important?"

"I'd like to see them both go to jail," Mark said, "preferably forever. I mean, I'm not for the death penalty, but I'd just as soon not have them wandering around loose where they can feed me more cyanide, if you know what I mean."

"Absolutely. Listen. I want to talk to you about something."

"Shoot."

Jimmy put the music paper away and turned so that he was sitting on the piano bench with his back to the piano now. Before Jimmy had married Mark's mother, this loft had been used as a haphazard storage space. Mark thought he liked it much better as a music room. Maybe he could talk Jimmy into driving him into the mall in Danbury for the afternoon. Jimmy didn't like to go to malls. Enough people still thought of him as a celebrity so that he couldn't really do that without getting mobbed. Mark just thought he was going to go crazy if he didn't get to do something interesting soon.

"It's about next year," Jimmy said, "about you and school—among other things."

"I thought that was all set," Mark said. "Mom is paranoid and doesn't want me living away from home next year. She's already talked to Canterbury. I don't mind the idea of going to Canterbury. It's a good school. And I've got friends from Rumsey there."

"I know, but something has come up. Actually it came up before all that stuff with you and school exploded, but then your mother and I didn't have time to talk it out because we wanted to get up to see you. We've talked about it a little since, and we thought—I thought, really—that we'd leave it up to you. Because I'm ambivalent. So you can decide. The future of the family is on you."

"Excuse me while I go back to bed and sleep for a month," Mark said. "I turned sixteen two months ago. I don't want the future of the family to be on me."

"Hear me out," Jimmy said. "I've had an offer, like I said, from the London symphony. To spend a year there as composer in residence. If I took it, we'd take you and Geoff and move to London for a while. Not just a single year, you know, because we wouldn't want to have you jumping around to different schools. We'd stay at least three years so that you could finish high school. We'd put you and Geoff both in the American School. We'd buy a house—"

"Wait," Mark said. "London? Are you serious? For three years? Doesn't Mom hate this? I mean, she's got stuff to do here. She's got teaching. She's got television."

"She's willing to give up the teaching," Jimmy said. "According to her, it's started to depress her. She'd keep the office here and still do CNN on and off, four or five times a year. She's talking to the BBC about some kind of arrangement over there. And I told her I'd buy her a house in South Kensington near the Natural History Museum. I don't know why, but it seems she's always wanted a house near the Natural History Museum. There's a big one up for sale, six stories or something. I offered to buy her something in St. James Place, but she's adamant about the Natural History Museum."

"We used to go there practically every weekend before my dad got sick," Mark said. "She's right. I'd rather be in South Ken than St. James Place. Or Grosvenor Square, which is the other biggy where Americans buy expensive houses in London. Three years? In London? Seriously?"

"I take it you're in favor," Jimmy said.

"Hell, yes, I'm in favor. I'm surprised you got her to agree to the American School. She didn't used to like it. She kept saying that if we were going to be in school in England we should go to English schools."

"Apparently, it's too late now. You were supposed to start in sixth grade. Although how you can start high school in sixth grade is beyond me."

"It's a different system," Mark said. "Think of the Harry Potter books. They start at Hogwarts in what we'd call sixth grade. They're eleven. You're sure she doesn't mind this? She isn't going to get over there and resent the fact that she's had to jerk around her career?"

"Does your mother look like somebody who would offer to do something if she thought she'd resent it later?"

"I don't know," Mark said. "Nothing like this has ever come up before. You're really serious here. Mom actually wouldn't mind this?"

"I think she's actually gung ho in favor of it, to tell you the truth," Jimmy said. "She lives out here because of you two, but I don't think she's a country girl at heart."

"Well, damn," Mark said. "Yes. If I get to decide, definitely yes. Is Geoff okay with it?"

"We haven't told him yet."

"Don't worry about it. I'll work on him. And it'll help that we go to the same school, even if we are in different divisions. Will the American School take me? My grades are sort of sucky this year, what with everything and—"

"They'll take you," Jimmy said. "Your mother's already asked. I don't think they're going to get overly worried that you've got a B minus average this year instead of an A minus one, assuming they're going to ask for a transcript at all, since that school of yours seems to be imploding. Your mother says she hated that place from the start. Why didn't you?"

"I have to hate every place that she hates?"

"No," Jimmy said, "but I met some of those people. You should have known better."

"They weren't the same people I met," Mark said. "They weren't on the admissions committee or anything. Never mind. London. For three years. I wonder if I could take A levels even if I am in the American School. I'll bet they get people who want to do that. Maybe I could go to Oxford. Wouldn't that be a gas?"

"I thought you wanted to go to UCLA and study film."

"There's always grad school," Mark said. "Listen, I'm going to go make something to eat, okay? I'm starving to death. I actually jogged into the Depot. You want me to make you something?"

"No, thanks. I'm at that age where if I eat it, I wear it."

"Right." Mark had no idea what Jimmy was talking about, but it didn't matter. He was very, very happy, and he went down to the kitchen thinking he'd actually take some trouble this time and cook the frozen pizza in the oven instead of doing Pizza Rolls in the microwave. Geoff wasn't going to be happy at first, but he'd be able to change that. He knew he would. He wondered if Christina still lived where she was living the last time he was in London. He remembered her from Westfields Primary School, and she'd been cute then; but when he'd seen her last year, well—that had really turned out okay. Better than okay.

In the kitchen he threw the newspaper on the counter and went looking for frozen food. Alice Makepeace's face stared up at him from a smudged photograph in those odd colors the *Times* used when it was trying very hard not to be black-and-white.

Something about the light, or the angle at which he was standing, made the picture seem to shimmer and change.

All of a sudden, Alice Makepeace looked like a gargoyle.

12   05